SAS

STORIES OF HEROES III

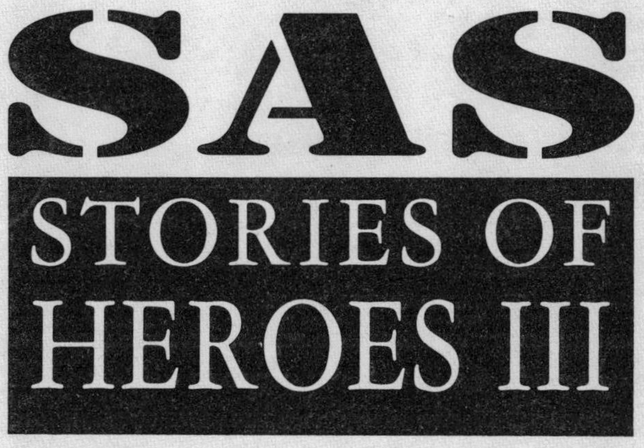

SHAUN CLAR

BLITZ EDITIONS

This edition published in 1995

Published by Blitz Editions
an imprint of Bookmart Limited
Registered Number 2372865
Trading as Bookmart Limited
Desford Road, Enderby
Leicester, LE9 5AD

ISBN 1 85605301 6

Typeset by Hewer Text Composition Services, Edinburgh
Printed in Great Britain by Cox and Wyman Limited, Reading

SOLDIER G: SAS

THE DESERT RAIDERS

Shaun Clarke

Prelude

'It's one helluva sight to behold,' Lieutenant Derek 'Dirk' Greaves said, shading his eyes with his hand. 'Very impressive indeed.'

The camp was located just outside Mersa Brega, in Libya's vast Cyrenaica Desert. It was a sprawling collection of tents, lean-tos, makeshift huts and caravans overflowing with the men of the 7th Armoured Division and Selby Force, 4th Indian Division, 6th Australian Division, Royal Electrical and Mechanical Engineers (REME), Royal Army Medical Corps (RAMC), sappers, a Cypriot labour battalion and the hundreds of ragged Italian 10th Army soldiers packed into POW cages near the southern perimeter. Though holding a vast array of artillery and tanks, the camp was also protected by British infantry divisions spread out in a defensive line consisting of a series of 'boxes' – slit trenches for the infantry, gun pits for the artillery –

surrounded by barbed wire and minefields, though these were far away, well spread out, and out of sight.

The camp itself, Greaves noticed, was ringed with the 25-pounders of the Royal Horse Artillery, an equal number of British six-pounders, Bofors anti-aircraft guns, stone sangars manned by teams equipped with Bren guns and 0.5-inch Browning machine-guns, and even some captured Italian 75mm and 79mm guns to be manned by infantrymen, signallers, orderlies and cooks if battle commenced. It also contained what appeared to be hundreds of armoured vehicles. All dispersed evenly behind the line, these included the M3 Stuart light tanks of the 8th King's Royal Irish Hussars, the Grant tanks of the Royal Gloucester Hussars, the Matildas of the 7th Royal Tank Regiment, the Bren carriers of the 9th Rifle Brigade, and Marmon Herrington armoured cars.

Beyond the perimeter, on all sides, Greaves saw nothing but the 'blue' – the soldiers' term for the desert – stretching away to the dust-wreathed horizon under a brilliant azure sky. By night the desert was freezing cold, but during the day the heat was fierce, shimmering up off the desert floor, hurting the eyes, making the sweat flow and leading to short tempers and fist fights. Tempers were also sparked off by the constant dust, blowing every second of every day and night, covering everything, filling the throat and nostrils, getting into food and drink and even sleeping bags, and which swirled in moaning clouds and drifted over the plains of rocky ground, soft sand and gravel. The dust also charged the metal parts of vehicles with electricity, shorting out the engines, often stopping the vehicles altogether and giving the men electric shocks.

Even worse were the flies, thousands of them, all enormous, attacking eyes and ears, dropping into the tea and bully beef, the tinned 'M and V' (meat and vegetables), into the herrings and tomatoes and dehydrated potatoes, buzzing noisily, frantically, all day long, and making a visit to the 'thunderbox' to answer the call of nature a veritable endurance test.

As for the freezing nights, though there was some respite from the flies, an alternative torment came in the shape of lice, bugs and cockroaches and, if a soldier became too careless, poisonous scorpions. All of these drove the men crazy and led to frayed tempers.

Last but by no means least of their torments was a constant and hellish thirst. The water, which had to be transported laboriously from Cairo or Alexandria, was warm, salty, distilled sea water that just about kept them alive while failing dismally to assuage the unrelenting dryness of their throats. Foul to drink on its own, it was more satisfactory in a brew-up, though even then its high salt content curdled the tinned milk and filled the mugs with soft, disgusting curds. The tea was more refreshing than the water, but even that failed to quench their thirst.

In combination with the heat, dust, and insects, the thirst may have contributed to some of the men's crazier antics. Having just completed their spectacular rout of the Italian 10th Army, the Tommies were flush with victory and displayed it in the way they dressed. A company commander of the Argyll and Sutherland Highlanders wore an Italian brigadier's uniform with sea boots; British troops of the 2nd Armoured Division boasted Australian slouch hats, a *bersagliere's* plumed hat, or the regalia of Blackshirt colonels; soldiers of the 9th Australian Division bore captured Italian pistols, with binoculars slung rakishly around their necks, as well as wearing the ceremonial gold-braided tunics of Italian officers instead of their own plain army jackets. In general the men preferred Italian uniforms, usually obtained by bartering with the POWs, to their own.

This sartorial excess, Lieutenant Greaves had

noticed, was complemented by a great deal of high spirits, including the indiscriminate firing of enemy rifles and pistols, exploding Thermos bombs, a lot of showing off in captured enemy vehicles, collecting wild dogs as vicious pets, bartering with Italian prisoners, betting on organized scorpion fights, hunting gazelles and other desert animals. There was a surprising indifference on the part of most officers to such undisciplined, and often dangerous, activities.

Lieutenant Greaves, formerly with the Scots Guards, now 8 Commando, was there for only two days as an observation officer from the Middle East Headquarters (MEHQ) in Cairo and due to fly back the following day from Tobruk. Though he understood the men's high spirits, he did not approve of their behaviour. The scorpion fights, in particular, were a particularly vicious form of blood sport in which someone would dig out a circular shallow in the sand, pour petrol around the edge, set fire to it, then place two scorpions inside the ring of fire. The heat of the flames would drive the scorpions wild and they would viciously fight one another – so much so that often one of them would inadvertently sting itself fatally with its own tail. Another sport, equally unsavoury, was hunting desert gazelles, which the men would pursue in trucks, firing at the unfortunate creatures with their rifles. While the deaths of the animals had the undeniable merit of supplementing the men's rations, Greaves viewed it as yet another barbaric activity spawned by a combination of victorious excitement, post-victory boredom, and a general lack of discipline.

Since the start of the British offensive in December, these men, including the 4th Indian Division, had resolutely pushed back the Italian forces in Egypt, stopping their advance at Sidi Barrani, taking Sollum, capturing Bardia with 40,000 Italian prisoners, and then Tobruk, and finally, after two months of relentless fighting, cutting off the main body of the Italian Army at Beda Fomm, with approximately 130,000 enemy troops captured. Now, in the closing days of March 1941, aware that advance elements of General Irwin Rommel's Afrika Korps, including the 15th and 21st Panzer Divisions, had recently arrived in Tripoli and, supported by the Italian mechanized Ariete Division, were advancing across Cyrenaica, the men, still torn between high spirits and boredom, were in no mood for the necessary discipline of camp life.

Greaves would put this into his report when he returned to MEHQ, where the staff officers, known contemptuously as the 'gabardine swine' because their uniforms were made of that material and the Tommies thought they had an easy life, were anxiously biting their nails over the arrival in Tripoli of Rommel and his Afrika Korps.

Greaves could understand the Tommies' contempt for the staff officers back in Cairo. Life there was certainly much easier and, in some cases, even luxurious. And yet, while he was supposed to be going back on an RAF Hudson transport the following day, he realized he would prefer to stay in the desert. A man who thought of himself first and foremost as a soldier, not as an officer, he was experiencing the frustration of the born soldier with no war to fight.

Even as he stood there beside one of the Bofors anti-aircraft-gun sangars, contemplating the vast, seemingly empty plains of the desert in the dimming afternoon light, he saw a long, thin cloud building up where the blue sky met the earth on the eastern horizon.

'Looks like a sandstorm coming,' he said to Major Gervase Reynolds, 3rd Hussars, one of the Regiments of the 7th Armoured Division.

'I hope not,' Reynolds replied, tugging distractedly at his handlebar moustache. 'Bloody dreadful things. Make you feel you're being buried alive and bugger up everything. Absolutely the worst thing about this damned place, which has many bad things.'

'It certainly looks like a sandstorm,' Greaves said as he squinted into the heat haze, surveying the distant horizon beyond El Agheila. The cloud was taking shape as an elongated band of darkness that spread higher and ever wider as it advanced across the flat, sun-scorched plain.

'No wind,' Major Reynolds observed. 'Not the slightest breeze, Captain.'

Greaves sucked his forefinger and held it up. 'Damn it, you're right,' he said. 'No wind at all.' Continuing to stare across the dazzling plain, he saw the cloud growing and still advancing at what he estimated was about thirty miles an hour. Then a series of black dots appeared in the sky above the horizon, distorted in the heat haze, but growing fatter by the second, racing forward above the duststorm until, in under half a minute, they took shape as winged birds.

Greaves realized they were not birds when he heard a familiar, distant rumbling sound.

'JERRY!' someone suddenly bawled behind him.

As the distant rumbling grew louder, the silhouetted birds became a squadron of German Ju-87 Stuka dive-bombers, all heading straight for the camp.

'Damn it!' Reynolds exclaimed. 'He's right! We'd better take cover.'

Even as Greaves recognized the enemy aircraft and, like Reynolds, hurled himself down behind the stone wall of a 25-pounder emplacement, the air-raid sirens wailed and the men in the laagers roared instructions at one another, frantically preparing their Bofors anti-aircraft guns. Jeeps and Bren-gun carriers roared into life and raced this way and that, churning up clouds of sand, as some of the men, arriving late, raced after them to jump aboard or get hauled up by their mates. The many troops in the tents poured out to grab weapons and helmets, then rushed to find cover in the defensive trenches around the perimeter. Others burst out of the latrines, some still pulling up their trousers.

Greaves and Reynolds hurled themselves down behind the nearest sangar wall as the first of the Stukas reached the camp, primitive, ungainly and with swastikas clearly marked on their fins, and peeled off to begin their dive-bombing.

The Bofors gun in the sangar exploded into action with a deafening roar, jolting dramatically as it belched fire and smoke, forcing Greaves to cover his ears with his hands as sand and gravel whipped up by the backblast swept hissing across him. The other anti-aircraft guns began roaring at the same time from all around the perimeter as the Stukas, which had been growling softly in an almost slumberous manner, screeched loudly, making their first attacks, their machine-guns firing as they descended. The bombs exploded nearby with a catastrophic roar and Greaves felt the earth shake beneath him as some Stukas screeched directly overhead before climbing above the pall of smoke. A lot of Tommies opened up with their .303 rifles and Mark 6 Webley pistols, adding their staccato snapping to the general bedlam.

'Fat lot of good that'll do!' Greaves shouted to Reynolds, who was crouched beside him, removing his hands from his ears and shaking his head to remove the dust from his ears.

Reynolds glanced at the men firing rifles and pistols, then tweaked his walrus moustache and grinned. 'It'll do the men good. Make them feel less helpless. That's a good sign, old boy.'

The Stukas were slow in flight but extremely fast when diving, the pilots fearlessly holding their course, ignoring exploding flak and streamers, and not levelling out until they were practically scraping the ground, when they would release their bombs, wobbling visibly as the load was dropped. Then they would straighten up and ascend steeply, back through the black clouds of flak and criss-crossing tracers, gaining velocity even as the bombs were exploding around the British positions.

'Courageous buggers!' Major Reynolds bawled. 'Got to hand it to them, old boy. The Jerry pilots are admirable. I . . .'

He was cut short by a series of explosions that tore up the ground nearby, creating a mushroom of swirling soil, gravel and debris, including large rocks and sandbags from the wall of a nearby sangar. The screaming of an injured Tommy daggered through the general clamour but was swiftly blotted out by the even louder bellowing of the British six-pounders, Bren guns and 0.5-inch Browning machine-guns, and the captured Italian 75mm and 79mm guns. The gun positions were hurriedly being manned by infantrymen, signallers, orderlies and cooks, most of whom were stripped to the waist, gleaming with sweat, and were gradually being covered in a film of dust and sand as swirling smoke obscured them.

'The tanks!' Reynolds bawled, rising himself to his knees and jabbing his finger to the front.

Sitting up, Lieutenant Greaves saw the Mark III and Mark IV tanks of the Afrika Korps Panzer divisions emerging from a billowing cloud of dust, spread out over half a mile, followed by motorized infantry and six-wheeled armoured cars.

'God, there's a lot of them!' Greaves exclaimed.

'Too many,' Reynolds sighed. 'They must have broken through our defensive boxes, forming a wall between them and us, which means the boxes won't be able to help us now.' He turned away from Greaves and bawled for the nearest radio operator to come and join him. When a sand-smeared 4th Armoured Division corporal with a No 11 wireless set had crawled up to Reynolds, the latter grabbed the wireless mouthpiece, contacted the tank commander of the Royal Gloucester Hussars and told him to move out. Still holding the wireless mouthpiece, but with the switch turned off, he looked back to the front. 'Let us pray,' he whispered.

As falling shells exploded between the German tanks, the enemy's 55mm and 77mm guns opened fire, creating a curtain of smoke and fire. With the British guns responding in kind, the noise was truly hellish and made marginally worse when the Grants moved out between the gun pits and sangars, to engage the Germans on the open ground beyond the perimeter.

The Panzers emerged from their own smoke with pennants fluttering from wireless aerials and their treads churning up sand, gravel and billowing clouds of dust. Assuming hull-down positions, they blasted the Grants, which were advancing with their 37mm and 75mm main guns firing at once, creating another nightmarish curtain of fire-streaked, streaming smoke.

The battle was awesome, like the clash of dinosaurs, the tanks obscured in the swirling smoke and boiling sand resembling hunchbacked, fire-spitting beasts. But it was a battle in which the odds were distinctly against the British, who were greatly outnumbered and lacked the practised skills of the Germans. The advancing Grants were soon stopped in a gigantic convulsion of erupting soil, swirling smoke and raining gravel, many of them exploding internally, others losing their treads, the rest peppered by 55mm and 77mm fire, which also cut down the men trying to escape.

'Oh, my God,' Greaves said to Reynolds. 'It's a slaughter.'

Major Reynolds responded by switching on the wireless mouthpiece and ordering the Bren carriers to move out. As the Grants were exploding, bursting into flames, shuddering and belching oily black smoke, with the survivors clambering down from the turrets, some on fire and screaming dementedly, the Bren carriers moved out to give them cover. While the Bren guns roared, spraying the German tanks and the infantry moving up behind them, the

Tommies firing their .303s and M1 Thompson submachine-guns on the move from the open-topped armoured vehicles. Unfortunately, they too were slaughtered by the Panzers' guns, many falling right out of the carriers and slamming into the sand.

The British gun batteries then unleashed a heavy concentration that made the German Mark IIIs and Mark IVs withdraw slightly. But they did so only long enough to let their infantry move against the flank exposed by the advance of the British Bren carriers. Reynolds immediately called up the Northumberland Fusiliers, who soon arrived with their heavy guns and temporarily plugged the gap, allowing the survivors of the Bren carriers to make their way back inside the perimeter as darkness fell.

'Incoming message for you, Major,' the radio operator said. Reynolds listened to the earpiece, then handed it back to the corporal and turned to Greaves. 'We're pulling out, Lieutenant. Back to Tobruk. Let's get up and go.'

With the German tanks temporarily withdrawn, they were able to evacuate the camp under cover of darkness. Soon the tanks, Bren carriers, armoured cars, Bedford trucks, jeeps and marching men formed a vast column on the road leading back through the desert to the harbour town of Tobruk.

Unfortunately, with too many units on the move at the same time, there was an almost palpable sense of panic, with many men abandoning the all too frequently stalled trucks and running to get on others without bothering to check what was wrong with theirs. Other vehicles were abandoned when they ran short of petrol – even though there were many three-ton trucks loaded with petrol passing by on either side. This, too, was a sign of growing panic.

Eventually, however, without being fired on by the German big guns or dive-bombed by the Stukas, the men found themselves inside the perimeter of Tobruk, mingling with the Aussies, who directed them to numerous positions along the wired perimeter, between gun pits and slit trenches. The tanks and trucks were lined up behind the wire to afford further protection.

'You've got to hold that position at all costs,' Major Art Wheeler, 6th Australian Division, said to Reynolds. 'That's the order I've just received from the gabardine swine. Fat lot those bastards know!'

Spitting in the sand, Wheeler stomped off to supervise the activities of his men. Greaves and Reynolds did the same with their own men before taking cover behind their jeep. They had barely done so when German infantry broke through the wire a mere hundred yards away and surged forward through the moonlit darkness.

'JERRY!' someone yelled again.

A British lieutenant with a corporal and five troopers rushed out to meet the Germans, charging against heavy machine-gun fire. Two of the troopers went down, convulsing as the bullets struck them, but the others managed to reach the first of the advancing Germans, killing some with their bayonets before succumbing themselves to bayonet and bullet. The rest of the Germans then rushed through the gap, ghostlike in the smoke-filled darkness, followed by the tanks, which headed straight for the British gun positions, located three miles inside the perimeter.

About forty tanks managed to get through before the Tommies could bring up enough men to engage the enemy infantry and gunners who were trying to bring their guns through the gap. The Tommies shot up their crews before they could get into action and the Aussies, fierce fighters as always, did the same along the barbed-wire perimeter.

One German was trapped on the wire, bent belly-down over it, screaming in agony. 'Put that bastard out of his misery!' one of the Aussies shouted and another, not hesitating, rammed his bayonet down through the soldier's spine, slamming him deeper into the barbed wire so that he kicked convulsively before he was silenced for all time. The Aussie withdrew his bayonet with a jerk, then dropped to his knees, raised his rifle to his shoulder and started firing again at the advancing Germans, ignoring the bloody, twisted corpse on the wire beside him.

'Those Aussies are impressive,' Greaves said. 'I'm glad they're on our side.'

'Damn right,' Reynolds replied.

After the tanks went through, the gap was closed and no German guns or infantry got past the Tommies or Aussies.

'Let's get back to the defensive line,' Reynolds said. 'Leave the men to mop up here.'

While the medics raced out to the closed gap to tend to the dead and wounded, Greaves followed the major to his jeep, climbed in beside him, and was driven away from the perimeter, following the three-mile route taken by the Panzers. As the tanks could only travel at thirty miles per hour, the jeep soon caught up with them and Reynolds raced boldly between them, determined to reach the British defensive line before the Germans. He had just driven up over the crest of a low hill, giving a clear view of the British six- and 26-pounders, when the tanks behind him opened fire and one of the first shells came whining down to explode with a mighty roar.

Greaves heard the roar of the explosion, felt the blast hammering at him, then was picked up and spun in the air, before falling through a great silence. He smashed into the ground, bounced up and rolled over it, then blacked out.

Regaining consciousness, he found himself on a stretcher, being carried back through more explosions, geysering soil, sand and gravel, to where the big guns were belching fire and smoke. Laid down on the ground beside Reynolds, who was on a stretcher and covered in blood, Greaves, whose lower half was numb, was forced to watch the ongoing battle without being able to take part in it.

While he had been unconscious the Panzers had continued their advance, firing their 55mm and 75mm guns, with the tracers illuminating the darkness like neon lights. When the tanks were about 700 yards from the British gun positions, the gunners fired on them with their 25-pounders and anti-tank guns, about 100 rounds per gun, which temporarily stopped them again. Then the British tanks moved out to engage them and, with luck, push them back a second time.

Two of the heavy enemy tanks tried to get around

the British flank. One was hit by a 25-pounder shell and exploded, breaking down as it tried to struggle back. The other fired and hit the British 25-pounder and its crew, causing dreadful carnage before making its escape with the other tanks.

After knocking out seven of the Panzers with their 25-pounders, the gunners eventually turned them back for good. Escaping through the gap they had created when they broke into the perimeter, the German tanks left pursued by a hail of shells and bullets from the Tommies who had taken command of the gap.

A sudden, startling silence reigned until, as if only slowly realizing that they had won, the gun crews clapped and cheered.

Still stretched out on his stretcher and not able to move, Greaves felt a spasm of panic, then groping carefully, discovered that he had broken his left leg and badly bruised the other, but was otherwise not seriously hurt or permanently injured. Glancing sideways at Reynolds, he saw that although covered in blood, he seemed fairly perky.

'Are you OK?' he asked.

'Lots of blood from shrapnel wounds in the thigh,' Reynolds replied with a cheerful grin. 'Looks much worse than it is, old chap.'

'Well, we certainly appear to have given Jerry a

good hiding,' Greaves said, wanting to sound as cheerful as Reynolds looked.

'We did,' the major replied, 'but I wouldn't call it a victory. Tobruk is now surrounded by the Germans and in a state of siege. This could last for months.'

Greaves tried to sit up but passed out from the pain. He dreamt that he was relaxing on the deck of a ship with a cool breeze blowing across the open deck and cooling the sweat on his fevered brow.

Regaining consciousness a few hours later, he found himself lying on a stretcher on the open deck of a British destroyer heading from Tobruk to Alexandria. Glancing sideways, he saw Reynolds, now swathed in clean bandages and still relatively lively.

'Rommel,' Major Reynolds murmured as if continuing a conversation with himself. 'He's a formidable enemy.'

'We can beat him,' Greaves said quietly.

1

'I agree,' 24-year-old Lieutenant David Stirling said, packing his rucksack on his cluttered bed in the Scottish Military Hospital in Alexandria. 'Rommel's a brilliant general, a man to respect, but he *can* be beaten.'

'And doubtless you know how to do it,' Lieutenant Greaves replied sardonically, knowing that Stirling was a man who loved soldiering and was full of ideas. Born in Scotland of aristocratic lineage – his father was General Archibald Stirling of Keir – young Stirling was a bit of an adventurer, passionately fond of hunting, shooting and mountaineering, as well as being devoted to the Army.

'Of course,' Stirling replied with enthusiasm. 'I've been studying the subject for weeks. Saved me from going mad in this bloody place and kept the marbles . . .' He pointed to his head with his index finger. '. . . well polished. Know what I mean, Dirk?'

'Yes,' Greaves said, also packing his rucksack, for he, too, was finally leaving the hospital. 'If a man spends too much time in bed, his brain tends to rot.'

'Too right.'

Having been in hospital for over six weeks, Greaves understood the dangers of chronic boredom. He had managed to get through his own first few weeks by dwelling on how he came to be there, although it was rather like reliving a bad dream.

After being knocked unconscious by the explosion, he had regained his senses as he was carried on a stretcher through a series of explosions to the Regimental Aid Post a few hundred yards away. Placed on the ground in a large tent between men worse off than himself, including those classified as Dead On Arrival, he had to wait his turn while the harassed doctors and medics assessed the injuries of those being brought in, carried out emergency surgery, including amputations, and passed the casualties along the line.

Reaching Greaves and Reynolds, they found that the former had broken his left leg and the latter had suffered serious perforations of the stomach from shell fragments. Greaves's leg was put in a temporary splint, Reynolds's stomach was temporarily bandaged, then both were placed with other wounded men in an ambulance and driven to the Main Dressing Station in a white-painted stone building in an area being torn apart by the shells of enemy tanks and dive-bombing Stukas.

Lying on a real bed in a large, barn-like room converted into a makeshift hospital ward, receiving warm smiles from the RAMC nurses, Greaves nevertheless could not shut out what was going on around him: essential first-aid and medical treatment, including blood transfusions, the removal of shell splinters from bloody limbs, and even more complicated amputations and other operations. It was a grim sight, made worse by the moaning and screaming of men in terrible pain.

Greaves's broken leg was reset and encased in a proper plaster, then, even as Reynolds was being wheeled into the surgery for an operation, Greaves was picked off his bed, placed on a stretcher and carried out of the building, into another ambulance. He was then driven to the harbour of Tobruk where, under cover of darkness, he was casevacked – casualty evacuated – in a small boat to one of the four destroyers anchored in the harbour. Those swift vessels, he knew, were the lifeline to Tobruk, running the gauntlet of Stukas under cover of darkness to bring food, ammunition, letters, and reinforcements to the besieged harbour town, as well as shipping out the casualties.

While crates of supplies were being lowered on slings down one side of the destroyer, Greaves and the other wounded men were hoisted up the other and carried down on their stretchers to the sick bay located deep in the crowded, noisy hold. There they had remained until the ship reached Alexandria, when they were transferred from the ship to the present hospital. After a minor operation to fix his broken leg, Greaves had been transferred to the recuperation ward where he had been given a bed right beside his fellow lieutenant, David Stirling, who was recovering from a bad parachute drop.

The hospital was pleasant enough, surrounded by green lawns bordered by fig and palm trees where the men could breathe the fresh air while gazing at the white walls and bougainvillaea of Alexandria, as well as the blue Mediterranean stretching out beyond a harbour filled with Allied destroyers. Yet a hospital it remained, with all the boredom that entailed, and Greaves and Stirling had passed the time by swapping stories about their experiences, the former in Tobruk, the latter along the Cyrenaican coast, and speculating on the outcome of the war and how best it might be won.

Stirling was a man who liked conversation and was brimful of energy. Greaves liked him a lot.

'The problem with Rommel,' Stirling said, taking up a favourite theme, 'is not that he's invincible, but that we're going about him the wrong way.'

'Meaning?'

'Well, for instance, take those raids we made with Laycock along the coast of Cyrenaica. Bloody disasters, practically all of them! Why?'

Greaves thought he knew the answer. He and the energetic former Scots Guards officer had been members of 8 Commando, posted to General Wavell's Middle Eastern Army with other commandos on attachment to 'Layforce', the special unit formed by Colonel Robert Laycock to mount raids against the Axis forces in Rhodes, Crete, Syria, around Tobruk, and all along the coast of Cyrenaica. However, after a series of disasters which were blamed on a chronic shortage of manpower and equipment, Layforce was disbanded and the men and ships used for other, presumably more fruitful, missions.

'Bad weather,' Greaves began, echoing his own thoughts. 'Shortage of manpower and . . .'

'No! That's damned nonsense cooked up by MEHQ to save face. The raids were disasters because we took too many men, inserted by orthodox means – in other words, by sea – and so couldn't keep ourselves hidden; usually being observed well in advance of the raids by Axis reconnaissance planes. The Krauts or Eyeties on the ground were therefore waiting for us to arrive, all set to cut us to pieces and send what was left of us packing. The very idea of using up to 2000 men for raiding parties landing by boat is ridiculous. Impossible to keep such an op secret. Just begging for trouble.'

'We're back to your idea of hitting the enemy with small groups of men rather than whole regiments.' Greaves said, completing his packing, tightening the ropes of his rucksack, and glancing along the ward, his eyes settling on a pretty RAMC nurse, Frances Beamish, whom he hoped to get to know better once he was on convalescent leave in Cairo. 'It's become an obsession.'

Stirling laughed. 'What's a man without an obsession? How do you think I ended up in this hospital? By trying to prove a point! You don't use large groups of men, which are bound to attract attention. You use small groups of no more than four or five and insert them as invisibly as possible. If you land them well away from the target area, letting them hike the rest of the way, they can *really* take the enemy by surprise. That's the point I was trying to prove – and that's how I ended up in this damned hospital, wrapped up like an Egyptian mummy, as stiff as a board.'

Greaves had heard the story before. Learning that another former Layforce officer, Captain 'Jock' Lewes, Welsh Guards, had acquired fifty static-line parachutes offloaded in Alexandria, Egypt, for shipment to India, Stirling had charmed the taciturn but adventurous Welshman into joining him in experimental jumps with the chutes. Unfortunately, he and Lewes made two of the first jumps from a Valentia, an aircraft quite unsuitable for this purpose. To make matters worse, both men lacked the experience required for the task. After tying his static line to the legs of a passenger seat, because the Valentia did not have the proper overhead suspension for the static lines, Stirling jumped out the wrong way, snagged and tore his chute on the tailplane, dropped like a stone and practically crashed to the ground. He was lucky to be alive. In the event, he had been knocked unconscious by the fall and came to in the Scottish Military Hospital, badly bruised and with two damaged legs. Now, after weeks of treatment and exercise, he was, like Greaves, about to leave for a period of convalescence.

'Look,' he said, lifting a clipboard off his still

opened rucksack and waving it dramatically in the air, 'I even wrote some notes on the subject. Want to hear them?'

'I'm all ears.'

Stirling grinned. 'The Germans and Italians,' he read, 'are vulnerable to attacks on their transports, vehicle parks and aerodromes along the coast. However, plans to land the 200 men of a commando for such raids against a single target inevitably destroy the element of surprise when their ship has to be escorted along the coast – a high risk in itself for the Navy.'

'I agree with that,' Greaves interjected, recalling many of his own doomed ventures with 8 Commando along the coast around Tobruk, when the boats had been attacked by Stukas or Italian fighters.

Stirling nodded, then continued reading. 'On the other hand, landing five-man teams with the element of surprise could destroy about fifty aircraft on an airfield which a commando would have to fight like blazes to reach. Such a team could be inserted by parachute, submarine or even a disguised fishing boat. They would then approach the enemy by crossing the Great Sand Sea, south of the Jalo and Siwa oases, which Jerry doesn't have under surveillance. By making the approach from that unwatched flank, moving overland under cover of darkness, the element of surprise would be total.'

'Makes sense to me,' Greaves said, 'except for one problem. The Great Sand Sea presents enormous difficulties of navigation and survival. I don't think we could cross it.'

Grinning like a schoolboy, Stirling held his forefinger up in the air, calling for silence. 'Ah, yes!' he exclaimed. 'But that problem's already solved. I've been hearing stories about a little-known unit called the Long Range Desert Group, composed mostly of old hands from Major Ralph Bagnold's desert expeditions of the 1920s and 30s. It's now being used as a reconnaissance and intelligence-gathering unit that operates in the desert with the aid of ten open-topped Chevrolet lorries. Those men know the desert like the back of their hands and could be used as a taxi service for us. We parachute in, make our raid against the enemy, then rendezvous with the LRDG at a preselected RV and get driven back to base by them. I think it would work.'

'Sounds fair enough,' Greaves said. 'The only problem remaining is to keep your newly formed group under your own command. I think it should be separate from the main body of the Army and devise its own methods of training.'

'I don't think the top brass would wear that,' Stirling said, placing the clipboard on top of the other gear in his rucksack and tightening the rope to close it up.

'Well,' Greaves said, smiling automatically when he saw Nurse Beamish coming along the ward towards him, 'tell them you want the raiding force to come under the Commander-in-Chief Middle East. In real terms that doesn't mean a damned thing – the raiding party would soon get conveniently lost in that command and you'd have virtual autonomy over your own men.' He grinned at Stirling. 'Naturally that presents you with another problem: how on earth do you persuade them to let you do it?'

'Oh, I think I can manage,' Stirling replied deadpan. 'I've already written a detailed memorandum on the subject for the attention of the Commander-in-Chief Middle East Forces. Once he's read it, I'm sure he'll agree.'

While recognizing Stirling's boldness, Greaves was struck by his naïvety. 'Are you joking?'

'No,' Stirling replied. 'Why would I joke about it?'

'If you submit that memo through normal channels, it will almost certainly get buried by a staff officer and never be seen again.'

'Which is why I'm going to deliver it personally,' Stirling said with a big, cocky grin.

Greaves was opening his mouth to reply when Nurse Beamish, petite, with black hair and green eyes, stopped between him and Stirling, smiling warmly at each in turn but giving most of her attention to Greaves, who had flirted relentlessly with her during his stay here.

'So you two are ready to leave,' she said.

'Yes, dear,' answered Stirling.

'Corporal,' Nurse Beamish corrected him.

'Yes, dear Corporal,' Stirling replied.

'Where do you plan to stay in Cairo?' Nurse Beamish asked of Greaves.

'Shepheard's Hotel.'

'Oh, very nice!' the nurse said, raising her eyebrows. 'My own leave starts on Friday, but I'm restricted to a miserable leave camp. Perhaps I'll give you a call.'

'That would be delightful,' Greaves said. 'I look forward to it.'

Nurse Beamish smiled, nodded at Stirling, then turned away and walked off, her body very pleasantly emphasized by her tight-fitting uniform.

'I think you've made it there, old son,' Stirling said. 'That woman is keen.'

'I hope so,' Greaves said softly, and then, after

a pause: 'You're not *really* going to try delivering that memo personally to the C-in-C, are you?'

'Who dares wins,' Stirling said.

Lieutenant Greaves picked up both rucksacks from the beds, waved goodbye to the other patients, then followed Stirling. In an instant the Scotsman was on his crutches and out of the hospital to catch a taxi to the station for the train to Cairo.

2

While Stirling went off to the British Embassy to collect the key to his brother's rented flat in Cairo's Garden City quarter, where he would be staying, Greaves booked into the opulent Shepheard's Hotel, which was off-limits to other ranks and used mainly as a place where officers could meet their lady friends. Once booked in, Greaves shucked off his desert clothes, drank whisky while soaking in a hot bath, then shaved and put on his dress uniform. In fact, though Stirling did not know it, Greaves had a date that same evening with Nurse Beamish and would, when the time came, be wearing an immaculately tailored bush jacket and slacks. He was wearing his dress uniform for the sole purpose of escorting the cheeky Stirling to MEHQ in his bold attempt to take his memorandum personally to the Commander-in-Chief. While Greaves was of the opinion that Stirling did not stand a chance, he could not resist the opportunity of going along with him to see what transpired.

Dressed, Greaves drank another whisky by the window while looking out on the great sprawl of Cairo, with its bustling pavements, open-fronted cafés, shops, bazaars and its white walls strewn with red peppers and purple bougainvillaea, covered in green vines and shaded by palm trees. Here many of the women still wore black robes and kept most of their face covered; the men dressed in jellabas and sandals. Around tables in the cafés, some of which were directly below, the men drank coffee, smoked hashish pipes, played backgammon and talked noisily all day, ignoring the soldiers swarming up and down the pavements, hotly pursued by filthy, screaming bootblacks. It was a dreadfully noisy city, with radios blaring out shrill music and high-pitched singing, trams clattering to and fro, horse-drawn gharries clattering over loose stones, water gurgling from pipes and splashing onto the streets, and cars, including many military vehicles, roaring and honking in a never-ending traffic jam. It was also, as Greaves knew, a smelly city, but the closed window spared him that.

When he heard a knocking on the door, which was unlocked, he turned away from the window and told the visitor to enter. Stirling entered on crutches, his head almost scraping the top of the door frame. After kicking the door closed behind him, he crossed the room and sat on the edge of the bed, leaning the crutches against the bed beside him.

'I'll be glad to get rid of these things,' he said. 'What's that you're drinking?'

'Whisky.'

'Just the ticket,' Stirling said. While Greaves was pouring him a drink, Stirling glanced around the room. 'A nice hotel,' he said without irony.

'I think so,' Greaves replied.

'I notice it's conveniently located almost directly opposite Sharia il Berka,' Stirling continued, referring to the Berka quarter's notorious street of brothels.

'Quite so,' Greaves replied solemnly. 'That's where the other ranks are commonly to be found with a much lower class of lady than you'll find in this building.'

'Such as Nurse Beamish.'

Greaves grinned. 'Let us pray.' He handed Stirling the glass of whisky.

'Are you ready to leave?' Stirling asked.

'Yes.'

'Good. Let's go.' Stirling polished off the whisky in one gulp, handed the glass back to Greaves, picked up his crutches and awkwardly balanced himself between them.

'How much longer will you need those things?' Greaves asked.

'I can actually walk without them,' Stirling replied, 'but for short distances only. Then my legs start hurting. However, I should be finished with them in a week or so. Well, let's get at it.'

They left the room, took the lift down, crossed the lobby and went out of the hotel. Immediately, on the pavement outside, they were assailed by the bedlam of Cairo: blaring music, clattering backgammon pieces, the babble of conversation; the clanging and rattling of trams with conductors blowing their horns; and the roaring and honking of cars and military vehicles of all kinds, including the troop trucks of the Allied forces. To this deafening cacophony was added the growling and occasional screeching of the many aircraft flying overhead. They were also assailed by the city's many pungent aromas: sweat and piss, tobacco and hashish, petrol and the smoke from charcoal braziers and exhausts; roasting kebabs, *kuftas* and ears of corn; rich spices and flowers.

'The Land of the Four S's,' Greaves said, waving his hand to indicate the busy road and pavements, which were packed with Arabs in jellabas, women in black robes and veils, grimy, school-aged boot-blacks, and the troops of many nations, most of them swarming through the city in search of a good time. 'Sun, sand, sin and syphilis.'

'You can think about those while you take your pleasure,' Stirling replied. 'For now, let's stick to business.' He turned to the jellaba-clad hotel doorman and spoke one word to him: 'Taxi.'

'Yes, sir!' the doorman said in English, flashing his teeth and waving his hand frantically even before reaching the edge of the pavement.

Less than a minute later, Greaves and Stirling were sitting in the back of a sweltering taxi, heading for Middle East Headquarters.

As Greaves soon found out, even on crutches Stirling was both agile and adroit. When the taxi dropped them off at the main gates of MEHQ, he attempted to bluff his way in by pretending he had forgotten his papers and hoping that the sight of his crutches would dispel any doubts the guard might be harbouring. The ruse did not work, and although perfectly polite and sympathetic, the guard was adamant that Stirling could not enter without proper papers.

Unfazed, Stirling thanked the guard, turned away, manœuvred himself on his crutches to one end of the long double gates, then glanced up and down the road, ostensibly looking for another taxi. But, as his nod indicated to Greaves, he had noticed that there was a gap between the end of the guardhouse and the beginning of the barbed-wire fence, and clearly he intended slipping through it when the guard was not looking.

His chance came within minutes, when the guard was leaning down, his back turned to Stirling and Greaves, to check the papers of some officers in a staff car. As soon as the guard turned away, leaning down towards the side window of the car, Stirling dropped his crutches, waved to Greaves, then led him through the gap.

'Act naturally,' he said to Greaves while gritting his teeth against the pain of his unsupported legs and trying to walk as normally as possible. 'Behave as if you belong here.'

Feeling an odd excitement, like a naughty schoolboy, Greaves followed Stirling across the field to the main building of MEHQ. Just as Stirling reached it, one of the guards called out to him – either he had recognized him or seen his crutches in the road – ordering him to return to the main gate. With surprising alacrity, considering the state of his legs, Stirling ignored the guard and hurried up the steps to enter the main building, with an excited and amused Greaves right behind him.

Once inside, Stirling marched resolutely, if at times unsteadily, along the first corridor he saw, searching for the office of the C-in-C. Before he found it, however, he heard the guard behind him, asking in a loud voice if anyone had seen two 8 Commando officers enter the building.

Immediately, Stirling opened the first door he saw, which was marked 'Adjutant-General'. He came face to face with a startled Army major, who demanded to know what the hell he was doing bursting in unannounced. As Stirling was trying to explain who he was and what he wanted, the major, who turned out to be one of his old instructors from Pirbright, where Stirling had done his basic training, recognized him and became even angrier.

'Still acting the bloody fool, are you?' he climaxed after a lengthy tirade about Stirling's unorthodox behaviour, past and present. 'Well, not in this office, you don't. Get out of here instantly!'

Greaves backed out first, followed by Stirling, who was, to his amazement, grinning broadly.

'Worst instructor I ever had,' he said coolly. 'Come on, Dirk, let's keep searching.'

'I think we might be pushing our luck,' Greaves warned him.

'Tosh!' Stirling barked.

Wincing occasionally from the pain in his unsupported legs, he led Greaves further along the corridor, brushing past many senior staff officers, looking for the office of the C-in-C.

'That guard's bound to be trying to find us,' Greaves said, 'so if we don't come across the office of the C-in-C soon, he'll be on our backs.'

Stirling stopped at a door marked 'DCGS'. 'Beggars can't be choosers, Dirk. Let's try our luck in here.' Boldly, he pushed the door open and stepped inside.

Greaves followed him in and closed the door behind him. Though bold in war, Greaves now suffered a racing heart at the thought of facing the Deputy Chief of General Staff without an appointment, let alone a pass into the building. His heart thumped even more when he saw the DCGS, General Neil Ritchie, looking up in surprise from his cluttered desk.

'Who . . .?'

'Lieutenant Stirling, Scots Guards, sir,' Stirling interrupted breathlessly. 'And Lieutenant Greaves, also Scots Guards. Both with 8 Commando and formerly part of Layforce.'

Before the general could respond or get over his surprise, Stirling apologized for bursting into the office, explained that there had been no time to arrange it and said that he had come on a matter of particular urgency.

'It had better be,' General Ritchie replied darkly. Then, distracted by Stirling's ungainly stance, he asked, 'Why are you standing in such an odd way, Lieutenant?'

'Spot of bother with the legs, sir. Parachute drop. Just got out of the Scottish Military Hospital and had to leave my crutches at the gate when we sneaked into the camp.'

'You came here on crutches?' General Ritchie gazed at Stirling in disbelief, then smiled a little and leaned back in his chair. 'You have five minutes, Lieutenant. Take that chair and rest your legs. Then you'd better start talking.'

Relieved, Stirling withdrew his memorandum from the inside pocket of his tunic, handed it to Greaves, then gratefully sank into the soft chair facing the desk while Greaves handed the memo to the DCGS. Ritchie read it carefully, taking rather longer than five minutes, then spread it carefully on the desk and looked up again.

'Interesting.'

'Thank you, sir.'

'It could work, but I'm not at all sure that the C-in-C would welcome such an unorthodox approach. A sniff of guerrilla operations there, Stirling, and General Wavell doesn't approve of that business.'

'That may be true, sir, but rumour has it that he's under considerable pressure from Churchill to stop the relentless advance of Rommel.'

'Those rumours are based on fact. Nevertheless, he may not thank me for this kind of proposal. A lot of risk involved, yes?'

'It's a safe bet for you, sir,' Stirling said cleverly. 'If things go wrong, the casualties will be few in number. If successful, they could change the course of the war in the desert and bring credit to all of us.'

Ritchie thought about it, then nodded in agreement. 'All right, Lieutenant, I'll bring the subject up with the C-in-C. If he's interested I'll show him your memorandum. You should hear from me within a matter of days. In the meantime, no more nonsense from you – such as this break-in. I'll get a sentry to escort both you men out. Next time get a pass.'

'Yes, sir!' Stirling and Greaves said at once, with big, dopey grins.

The general picked up his phone and called for

a guard. Five minutes later a triumphant Stirling and Greaves were being escorted out of MEHQ. As they passed through the main gates, the guard who had pursued them stepped out, grinning broadly, to hand Stirling his crutches.

'Well done, sir,' the guard said with a grin.

Stirling smiled back at him, put the crutches under his armpits, and waited patiently beside Greaves while the latter hailed a passing taxi.

'Now we can only wait,' Stirling said, 'so let's have a good time.'

Three days later, when Greaves and Stirling were beginning to feel more exhausted from having a good time than they ever had on an operation, Stirling received a call from the DCGS's office, inviting him back to see General Ritchie.

While Stirling was at that meeting, Greaves enjoyed a long lunch with his attractive nurse, Frances, whom he had been wining, dining and bedding for the past two days and nights in his hotel. In fact, she had just left his room when Stirling turned up, flushed with excitement.

'The meeting wasn't just with General Ritchie,' he told Greaves. 'The C-in-C, General Auchinleck, was also there. So was the Chief of the General Staff.'

Greaves gave a low whistle of appreciation. 'So, what transpired?'

'Permission granted,' Stirling said, 'on the following conditions. 'I've just been promoted to captain. Five officers and sixty other ranks will be recruited. For the time being, we'll recruit only from former Layforce men. We'll train the men ourselves and prepare them for raids against five airfields Jerry is using as bases for his latest Me 109F fighters. Auchinleck felt that five-man teams are too awkward, so teams of four instead of five will be the operational basis of the raiding parties. Our parent body will be a non-existent Special Air Service Brigade, or L Detachment . . .'

'Why "L"?' Greaves interrupted.

Stirling's grin was mischievous. 'L for Learner. Anyway, that's what we're calling it: L Detachment, SAS Brigade. To Axis agents and others it should suggest that there are more than sixty-six parachutists in Egypt. Meanwhile, we can get on with the real business. Now let's go and find some men.'

Jubilant, they embarked on a search of Cairo to find the men who would be the bedrock of L Detachment.

The first officer, Lieutenant William 'Bill' Bollington, they found immediately, in the bar of

Shepheard's Hotel, where Bollington was staying. A Gordon Highlander whose father and grandfather had been senior NCOs, he was instantly excited by the idea of a new raiding team and agreed to join them.

'I strongly recommend Sergeant Ralph Lorrimer,' he told them. 'Dorset Regiment, but now with the LRDG. Apart from being a hell of an NCO in his own right, and an expert on the desert, he'd probably be your ticket to the LRDG. He's also, incidentally, unbeatable with the Browning 12-gauge autoloader. A good man in a tight spot.'

'Where will we find him?'

Lieutenant Bollington grinned and pointed down through his room window, in the direction of the Sharia il Berka. 'Down there. He practically lives in Tiger Lil's place. I think he keeps a room there.'

'Very good,' Stirling said. He and Greaves left the hotel and walked across to the notorious street of brothels. Tiger Lil's was a gloomy, echoing barn of a place where the men queued up at the doors of the rooms, often peeping through keyholes to see how the first man was getting on and shouting words of encouragement: 'Come on! Get on with it! We're all waiting out here!' Tiger Lil, the immense, good-natured madam, who was sitting behind the cash desk by the front door, told them the number of Lorrimer's room. As they climbed the stairs, they came across many young girls, no more than eight or nine, who were running in and out of the rooms with towels, cleaning rags and bottles of Condy's disinfectant.

When Stirling and Greaves reached the room which was, according to Tiger Lil, rented permanently by Lorrimer, Greaves hammered on the door with his fist and a gravelly male voice bid him enter. Doing so, he and Stirling found Sergeant Lorrimer, wearing his shirt and trousers, though bare-footed, stretched out on his bed, propped up slightly with pillows, reading the latest edition of *The Strand*.

Surprised to see two officers in his room, he slid his feet down to the floor and sat on the edge of his bed. He was of medium height, but broad-chested and muscular, with a handsome, world-weary face and a fearless, blue-eyed gaze.

'Yes, sirs?' he asked, clearly puzzled by their presence in his room.

Stirling introduced himself and Greaves, then explained why they had come. As soon as he had finished, Lorrimer agreed to join up.

'Can you get us the cooperation of the LRDG?' Stirling asked.

'Yes, I think so.'

'Excellent. Please get in touch with them immediately, then contact me here.' He scribbled his brother's private phone number on a piece of paper and gave it to Lorrimer. 'That's where I'm staying while I'm in Cairo. Get in touch when you've fixed up a meeting with the LRDG. If it can't be arranged immediately, fix it up for later.' He was leaving the room with Greaves when the latter, unable to contain his curiosity, turned back and asked Lorrimer: 'Do you rent this room on a full-time basis, Sergeant?'

Lorrimer nodded. 'Only during my leave periods,' he said. 'I'm a married man with three kids and a healthy sexual appetite. This room's cheaper than anything else I could hire and the girls are conveniently located. What more could a man want?'

'You're a man of initiative,' Greaves replied. 'I think we made the right choice. See you soon, Sergeant.'

Their next stop was the MP barracks at Bab el Hadid, where one of Greaves's favourite men, Captain Patrick 'Paddy' Callaghan, No 3 Commando, was languishing in one of the cells, pending a court martial for knocking out his commanding officer. Formerly an Irish rugby international and accomplished boxer, Callaghan was normally an amiable, courteous man, but unfortunately he had a violent temper. Indeed, before actually striking his commanding officer, Callaghan had run him out of the officers' mess at the point of a bayonet. He was, nevertheless, an exceptional soldier who had already been mentioned in dispatches for his bravery in action.

When Stirling and Greaves proposed that he avoid his pending court martial by joining their new unit, he said, 'Why not? I'm going out of my mind with boredom here. Count me in, gentlemen.'

The rest of the main group had to be searched out across the length and breadth of Cairo, in nightclubs such as Groppi's, the Blue Nile and the Sweet Melody Cabaret where soldiers, sailors and airmen, drunk on the deadly Zebeeb, groped the 'cherry brandy bints'; in the Union Jack pension with its egg 'n' chips and Greek proprietor; in the numerous bars and brothels of the Berka; in the healthier Springbok Recreational Club at Helwan; in the surprisingly sedate Cairo Club, which was a services club reserved for sergeants and warrant officers; and in the Anglo-Egyptian Union, an officers' club located outside the city.

From these and other places Stirling and Greaves, sometimes together, other times separately, trawled the rest of the men they personally knew, respected and wanted. These included Captain 'Jock' Lewes, Welsh Guards, former Layforce member, and the man who had made the first experimental static-line parachute jumps with Stirling. A superbly fit ex-Oxford rowing blue with a low boredom threshold, Lewes had already proven himself to be a superb exponent of night-time raids behind enemy lines in the Tobruk area. He also had a talent for devising training programmes and techniques, which Stirling intended putting to good use.

Finally, Stirling called for general volunteers, inviting them to a meeting in a tent in Geneifa, outside Cairo. Among those who came forward were Sergeants Bob Tappman, Pat Riley and Ernie Bond; Corporals Jim Almonds, 'Benny' Bennett, Jack 'Taff' Clayton and Reg Seekings; and Privates Neil Moffatt, Frank 'Frankie' Turner and Jimmy 'Jimbo' Ashman.

A few days later these men and more were gathered together at the chosen base camp at Kabrit, in the Suez Canal zone, to begin their special, brutal training.

They were called the 'Originals'.

3

Located by the Great Bitter Lake, about 95 miles east of Cairo, and south of Aden, Kabrit was a desolate piece of flatland, fully exposed to the scorching sun, plagued by swarms of fat, black flies, and consisting of no more than three mouldering tents for the men, a command tent with a rickety card-table and stool, and one badly battered three-ton lorry.

'Bloody hell!' Corporal Jack 'Taff' Clayton said as soon as he had jumped down off the back of the three-tonner and was standing in a cloud of dust with the others. 'There's nothing here, lads!'

'Not a damned thing,' Private Frank 'Frankie' Turner agreed, swatting the buzzing flies from his sweating face. 'No more than a piss-hole.'

The men were already wearing clothing more suitable to the desert: khaki shirt and shorts, regular Army boots with rolled-down socks, and a soft peaked cap instead of a helmet. Each man also had a Sykes-Fairburn commando knife and Browning 9mm handgun strapped to his waist.

'Damned flies!' Private Neil Moffatt complained.

'Bloody hot!' Corporal Jimmy 'Jimbo' Ashman exclaimed.

'All right, you men!' Sergeant Lorrimer bawled, his legs like tree-trunks in his floppy shorts, his hands on his broad hips. 'Stop moaning and groaning. Go and put your kit in those tents, then come back out here.'

'Yes, Sarge!' they all chimed.

Picking their kit off the desert floor, they crossed to the three tents and wandered around them in disbelief.

'These tents are in tatters,' Neil observed mournfully, wiping the sweat from his face and neck with a piece of cloth that could have come from one of the tattered tents.

'They're also too small,' Frankie Turner put in. 'Might as well sleep out in the open for all the good these'll do us.'

'More holes than a fancy Eyetie cheese,' Jimbo said, spitting on the ground between his feet. 'And how the hell we're all supposed to squeeze in there, I can't imagine. I think this calls for a talk with our soft-voiced friend, Sergeant Lorrimer.'

'Right,' Taff said. 'Let's pitch our gear temporarily in a tent, then we'll go and sort this out.' He ducked low to enter one of the tents and was immediately followed in by some of the others. The tents had been raised over the desert floor; there were no beds or groundsheets. 'Fucking beautiful!' Taff exclaimed. 'We're supposed to lie on the bloody sand and get eaten alive. Not me, mate.' Dropping his kit on the ground, he ducked low again and left the tent. The others did the same and gathered outside, where Lorrimer had indicated.

Lorrimer was over by the three-tonner, deep in conversation with Captains Stirling and Callaghan and Lieutenant Greaves. While the men waited for him to come over they had a 'smoko', which helped to keep the flies at bay.

'I can tell we're all going to be driven mad here,' Jimbo said, 'by these bloody flies and mosquitoes.'

'Creepy-crawlies as well,' Frankie said darkly.

'Snakes, scorpions, spiders, ticks, midges,' Neil said mournfully. 'You name it, we've got it here all right. We'll be eaten alive.'

'Dust,' Taff said, flicking ash from his cigarette and watching it fall to the desert floor, on all its hidden horrors. 'Sandstorms . . . Burning hot days, freezing nights . . . I feel ill already.'

'What are those two bastards talking about?' Frankie asked, gazing at Lorrimer and Stirling.

'We're about to find out,' Jimbo said, 'and I'm not sure I want to know.'

Eventually Stirling climbed up onto the back of the three-tonner and Lorrimer bawled that the men were to gather around. This they all did, most still smoking and puffing clouds of smoke.

'Sorry, lads, about the state of this place,' Stirling said, waving his right hand to indicate the tents behind the men, 'but I'm sure we can do something to improve on it.'

'With what?' Jimbo called out.

'Shut your mouth, soldier, and let the boss speak!' Lorrimer bawled.

'Boss?' Taff whispered to Frankie. 'Did he use the word 'boss'?'

'SILENCE!' Lorrimer roared.

'I appreciate your frustration, lads,' Stirling continued, 'but all is not lost. Indeed, I'm led to believe that there's a splendid Allied camp about fifteen miles south of here, where the New Zealanders, in particular, live rather well.'

'Is that some kind of message?' Neil asked.

Stirling's manner was deadpan. 'Without being too specific, let me merely remind you that your first priority is to complete the construction of this base camp by whatever means are at your disposal. I'll be returning to Cairo immediately to collect more vehicles from the Royal Corps of Transport and weapons from the armoury at Geneifa. When I get back here I expect to find things greatly improved. How you do it is not my concern; nor will I be here to witness it. I can only add the information that the Kiwis will be away from their base on manœuvres most of tonight and their tents will therefore be empty. That's all. Class dismissed.'

Taking the hint, a dozen of the men drove in the battered three-tonner that same evening to the large, fenced compound fifteen miles away, stretched out across a dusty plain above the Mediterranean and being used by British, Australian and Indian troops, as well as the Kiwis.

Deciding that the only thing to do was bluff it, Jimbo drove boldly through the main gate as if they belonged there. 'New Zealand Division!' Taff yelled as the lorry passed the bored Indian guard. Receiving no more than a nod of permission from the guard, Jimbo continued driving, passing row upon row of tents, tanks, other armoured vehicles and the many trucks of first the British, then the Indian lines, until arriving at the New Zealand area. There he switched off the headlights and the rest of the men piled out, letting their eyes adjust to the darkness, then using torches to locate what they needed in the tents temporarily vacated by the Kiwis.

It took them quite a while, but it was well worth the effort, for they managed to pile the three-tonner high with lamps, tables, chairs, steel lockers, wash-basins, mirrors, cooking utensils, proper camp beds, mattresses, sheets, towels, portable showers and latrines, tents large and small, camouflage netting, and even crates of beer and spirits.

'Come on, lads!' Taff whispered when they had been busily thieving for an hour. 'Let's take this lot back to base. Then we'll return for some more.'

'You've got a fucking nerve,' Jimbo said, grinning.

'Piece of piss,' Taff replied.

They made three runs in all, boldly driving in and out of the camp, waving cheerily at the Indian guard and passing the British and Indian lines as if they belonged there. Eventually, even the daring Taff checked his watch, noted that it was almost dawn, and became a bit nervous.

'Let's pack it in and get out of here,' he told them. 'It'll soon be first light and the Kiwis will probably return then. We can't afford to get caught now.'

'Right,' Frankie agreed. 'Let's get going.'

They were hurrying out of the last, largest tent,

obviously used as a mess tent, when the musically inclined Jimbo stopped, stared lovingly at a dust-covered item in one corner, near a long trestle table, and said, 'Oh, God, look at that beauty!'

'What?' Neil asked, perplexed.

'I want her. I *need* her!'

The rest stared at Jimbo as if he was mad. 'Are you kidding?' Frankie asked eventually. 'That's a bloody *piano!*'

Jimbo ran his fingers lovingly over the keyboard without making any sound. 'A real darlin', lads. Going to waste here. It could cheer things up a bit in our mess – *when* we get a mess going. What about it?'

'Jesus, Jimbo!'

'We could have a regular Saturday night. Make the beer slip down even smoother. Come on, lads, let's grab it.'

'Oh, for fuck's sake,' Taff said, exasperated and amused at the same time. 'Just grab the bloody thing and let's go. Move it, lads! *Now!*'

The piano was humped onto the lorry, easily placed there because this last load was light, then the dozen men climbed up to seat themselves around it. Jimbo then drove boldly back through the camp and waved as usual to the Indian guard at the main gate. The latter, seeing the piano, looked suspicious for the first time, but Jimbo was off and gone in a cloud of dust before he could be stopped.

Once back at Kabrit, where the sun was shedding dawn light over the Great Bitter Lake, painting it crimson, the men unloaded their last haul, had a brew-up and cold breakfast to get them through to lunchtime. They then enthusiastically raised the brand-new tents they had stolen, camouflaged them with the netting, filled them with beds, steel lockers, tables and chairs, hung mirrors from the uprights, filled the lockers with their belongings, and placed family photos on their tables and cupboards.

When their sleeping arrangements had been sorted out, they raised the biggest tent, to be used as the mess tent, helped the cook set up his kitchen, carried in the long trestle tables and chairs, stacked the crates of beer and spirits beside a refrigerator run off a portable electric generator, and finally wheeled the piano in.

Jimbo stood back to admire it. 'Looks beautiful, don't it?'

'A real treat,' Frankie told him. 'What about a tune?'

'You mean now?'

'Why not? Having just nicked it, we'd like

to know if you can actually play the fucking thing.'

'I can play,' Jimbo said.

When he had expertly given them a Vera Lynn medley, his fingers light on the keys, they all gathered outside to help two former REME men raise the portable showers and thunderboxes. Jimbo had an experimental shit and pronounced the latrines operational. For the rest of the hour leading up to lunchtime, there was a general rush to make use of them.

Later that day Stirling returned from Cairo in a jeep, leading a convoy of other jeeps and lorries for the use of L Detachment. When the vehicles had been parked, the Royal Corps of Transport drivers climbed into a Bedford and were driven back to their own base at Geneifa. Stirling then told his SAS troopers to unload the assortment of large and small weapons he had brought in one of the lorries. These included the brand-new Sten gun, Vickers and Browning heavy machine-guns, the M1 Thompson sub-machine-gun, and the obligatory Bren light machine-gun. These were stacked up in one of the smaller tents, to be used as an armoury under the charge of Corporal Jim Almonds.

By nightfall, when the burning heat was being replaced by freezing cold, the desolate 'piss-hole' of Kabrit was a well-equipped operational base and Jimbo was playing the piano in the noisy mess tent.

4

Their training began at first light the next day with a more intensive weapons course than any of them had ever undergone before. Assuming that their greatest need would be for a barrage of fire at relatively close range to cover a hasty retreat after acts of sabotage, Sergeant Lorrimer gave only cursory attention to the standard bolt-action rifles and instead concentrated on the new 9mm Sten sub-machine-gun. This was only 762mm long, weighed a mere 3.70kg, was cheap and crude in construction, with a simple metal stock and short barrel, yet could fire 550 rounds per minute from 32-round box magazines and had an effective range of 45 yards.

To cover the same needs, great attention was also given to the M1 Thompson sub-machine-gun, better known as the 'tommy-gun' and immortalized by the Hollywood gangster movies of the 1930s and early 40s. A heavier, more accurate and powerful weapon, the tommy-gun had a solid wooden stock and grip, a longer barrel, and could fire 11.43 rounds at the rate of 700 per minute from 30-round box magazines, with an effective range of 60 yards.

Everyone was also retrained in the use of the 0.5-inch Browning heavy machine-gun, which could fire 400–500 rounds per minute from a belt feed, and was effective up to 1600 yards; the beloved Bren gun, the finest light machine-gun in existence, which could fire 520 rounds per minute from 30-round box magazines and was effective up to 650 yards; and finally the lethal Vickers 'K' .303-inch machine-gun, actually an aircraft weapon, which fired 500 rounds per minute from 100-round magazines filled with a mixture of tracer, armour-piercing incendiary and ball bullets.

This stage of the training was undertaken on a primitive firing range that was really no more than a flat stretch of desert, baked by a fierce sun, often covered in wind-blown dust, forever filled with buzzing flies and whining mosquitoes, and with crudely painted targets raised on wooden stakes at the far end, overlooking the glittering Great Bitter Lake. The firing range was also used for training in the use of 500g and 1kg hand-grenades, including the pineapple-shaped '36' grenade and captured German 'potato mashers', which had a screw-on canister at one end, a screw cap at the other and a wooden handle.

'These Kraut grenades are better than ours,' Frankie observed, 'because this nice long wooden handle makes them easier to throw.'

In fact, most of the men, once over their initial nervousness, enjoyed throwing all kind of grenades and watching the great mushrooms of sand, soil and gravel boiling up from the desert floor with a deafening roar. It made them feel powerful.

'I can't imagine any fucker surviving *that*,' Jimbo said with satisfaction after a particularly good throw that had blown away a whole strip of the escarpment on which they were training.

'They *do* survive, Private,' Lorrimer corrected him. 'You'd be amazed at what those Krauts can survive, so don't get too cocky. You throw a grenade, think it's blown the target to hell, so stand up feeling good . . . and you get your balls shot off by the Jerries you thought you'd killed. Take nothing for granted, lad.'

'Thanks for the encouragement, Sarge. I feel really good now.'

'NEXT!' Lorrimer bawled.

Training in demolition, which also took place on

the firing range, was given by Sergeant Derek Leak, former Royal Engineer sapper and ammunition technician with the Royal Army Ordnance Corps. A watchful, humourless man who had been burnt and scarred by the many accidents of his profession, he demanded their full attention when he taught them about low explosives, such as gunpowder, and high explosives, such as RDX or PETN, requiring initiators or time fuses and firing caps. Lessons were given not only in the handling of such explosives, but in precisely how they should be placed in a variety of circumstances, such as the blowing up of aircraft, bridges, roads or buildings, as well as the setting of booby-traps.

'I hate this shit,' Jimbo complained to his mates as he nervously connected a time fuse to a non-electric firing cap. 'It gives me the willies.'

'Yeah,' Frankie said sardonically, 'we can see that by the shaking of your hands.'

'This stuff is dangerous, lads,' Jimbo reminded them, trying to steady his hands. 'One mistake and it'll blow you to hell and back.'

'It isn't that bad,' Taff said, not handling it himself and therefore able to be more objective. 'It isn't really as dangerous as people think . . . *if* you handle it properly.'

'Is that so?' Neil asked morosely. 'Have you

noticed Leak's face? He's got more scars than fucking Frankenstein – and they all came from accidental explosions.'

'And *he's* a former sapper,' Jimbo said. 'An explosives specialist! So don't tell *me* it's safe.'

'For fuck's sake, Jimbo,' Taff exclaimed, suddenly nervous, 'keep those bleedin' hands steady! You almost dropped that bloody stuff then.'

Jimbo managed to insert the fuse into the firing cap, then sat back and smirked. 'Piece of piss,' he said. 'I believe you're the next to try this, Taff. I just hope *you've* got steady hands.'

As the training continued, with radio, first aid, nocturnal navigation, and enemy vehicle and aircraft recognition added to the growing list of skills to be learned by the men, it became apparent to them all that they were in a combat unit like no other, with no distinction in rank and everyone, including the officers, compelled to meet the same exacting standards.

The informality went beyond that. The word 'boss', first used, perhaps accidentally, by Sergeant Lorrimer, gradually replaced 'sir' and so-called 'Chinese parliaments', in which decisions were agreed between officers and other ranks after informal discussion, became commonplace. This in turn increased the mutual trust between the men and greatly enhanced the feasibility of the four-man patrol. Also, as each of the four men had a specialist skill – driver/mechanic, navigator, explosives and first aid – but all had been cross-trained to do the other men's jobs if required, this made them uniquely interdependent.

Their psychological bonding was made even solider by the harsh fact that anyone who failed at any point in the training, or who dropped out from fear, exhaustion, thirst or other causes, was RTU'd – Returned to Unit – without mercy. As the numbers were whittled down, those remaining were forming the kernel of an exceptional band of widely talented, closely knit and proud fighting men.

'We're the fucking *crème de la crème*,' Jimbo said. 'That's why we're still here, lads.'

The taciturn but brilliantly inventive Captain 'Jock' Lewes, who was constantly devising ways of testing the men to their limits, increased the chances of being RTU'd himself by introducing desert marches by day and by night. Not a man to demand of others what he could not do himself, Lewes turned himself into a guinea-pig by making the first marches entirely alone and gradually increasing the distance he had to hike, the length of time he had to go without water in the desert, and the weight he had to carry in his bergen backpack. Finally, he set himself precise navigation tests that had to be completed within a certain time.

'He's a fucking genius, that Lewes, I'm telling you,' Jimbo informed his mates. 'Remember that day he took me out on my own, just the two of us? He said we were gonna hike to an RV twenty miles away and that he'd know when we'd done exactly that. The desert's so empty – no landmarks to navigate by – I couldn't figure out how he would manage it. Then I noticed he was carrying lots of small stones in the pocket of his trousers and kept transferring them, one at a time, from that pocket to the other. When I asked what the fuck he was doing, he said he'd just devised this new way of navigating and measuring distance. What he did was count his paces. After each hundred steps, he'd transfer one of the stones to the other pocket. The average pace, he said, was thirty inches, so each stone represented approximately eighty-three yards. That way he could easily calculate just how far he had marched. Pretty damned clever, eh?'

'Too right!' Frankie said.

The men admired Jock Lewes not only for his many inventions and innovations, but because he never asked them to do anything particularly demanding or dangerous without first doing it himself. Indeed, regarding the murderous hikes into the desert, only when he had personally ascertained that they could actually be accomplished did he introduce them as part of a specific, extremely demanding selection course. These included nights sleeping in laying-up positions, or LUPs, scraped out of the freezing desert floor; signals training, covering Morse code, special codes and call-sign signals, all undertaken in the field; the operation of radios, recognition of radio 'black spots', and the setting up of standard and makeshift antennas; the weapons maintenance in the windswept, freezing desert darkness; the procedure for calling in artillery fire and air strikes; and general desert survival, both by day and by night. Those who failed to meet the rigorous standards set by Lewes were brutally RTU'd. But in view of the fact that Lewes did all those things himself, the men understood why.

'If he can do it,' Taff said, 'then we should be able to do it as well. If we can't, we don't deserve to be here. Lewes has set us the highest of standards.'

While Captain Stirling was forced to spend an increasing amount of time by himself, either developing the strategies to be used for forthcoming operations or commuting between Kabrit and Cairo to keep MEHQ informed of their progress,

Lieutenant Greaves and Captain Callaghan between them supervised the general training and ensured that the administrative side of the camp ran smoothly. They also, however, took part in the many arduous physical tests devised by Lewes and thus forged a close bond with the other ranks. This bond was further strengthened by the officers' willingness to forget their rank and meet the men on a level they understood.

For instance, one day, after Lieutenant Greaves had checked the men's water canteens to ensure that they had not drunk more water than permitted during their latest hike, a particularly troublesome trooper complained that the *officers'* canteens were never checked. Greaves instantly handed the man his own canteen and invited him to 'finish it off'. When the man opened the canteen, he found it completely full – because Greaves had deliberately made the whole hike without drinking a drop. This revelation, while shaming that one trooper into enduring his thirst, impressed all the other men.

Again, when the men were resting on a sun-scorched escarpment after another murderous march, Captain Callaghan, who had a short temper and took no nonsense from anyone, got fed up with a trooper complaining that they needed a rest. He grabbed the man by the shoulders, picked him bodily off the ground, and held him over the edge of the cliff, threatening to drop him into the sea if he did not shut his trap. The terrified man shut up and the other men, rather than resenting Callaghan, respected his flamboyant way of dealing with the situation.

When Captain Stirling heard stories like this, he felt even more guilty.

'I hate being away so often,' he explained to Greaves and Callaghan, 'but I simply have to keep pushing at MEHQ. Those sods don't approve of us – they think we're a bunch of cowboys – and a lot of them are actively working against us in the hope that we'll fail. I'd rather be here, working with you and the other men, but it just isn't possible. Please bear in mind, though, that if you think I need to set an example by taking part in a particular exercise, you have only to say so.'

'That's understood, boss,' Greaves said.

'I think the men understand the situation,' Callaghan added. 'As long as we officers do what *they* do, they'll be all right about it.'

Greaves grinned at that. 'And we do it, David, believe me. We have the bruises to prove it.'

Stirling nodded, relieved. 'I'll be with you when the raids commence,' he said. 'Of that you can rest assured.'

During one of Stirling's many trips to Cairo, Sergeant Lorrimer, as requested, fixed up a meeting between him and Lieutenants Beevor and Parkinson of the LRDG. The first meeting took place in the desert near Tobruk, where the LRDG was acting as a reconnaissance and intelligence-gathering unit under the very noses of the Germans. The two widely experienced lieutenants, both old hands from Bagnold's desert expeditions of the 1930s and now just back from another dangerous R and I mission around besieged Tobruk, were instinctively sceptical about the raiding-party concept of the immaculate, urbane Captain Stirling, but they agreed to read the report he had put together and give their response. The second meeting took place over glasses of whisky in the Anglo-Egyptian Union, the officers' club located just outside Cairo, where the same two LRDG officers admitted to being impressed with the report and agreed to act as a 'taxi' service to L Detachment when the first raids were mounted. The four men then shook hands and went their separate ways: Beevor and Parkinson back into the desert around Tobruk; a delighted Stirling and Lorrimer back to the sun-scorched camp at Kabrit, now more determined than ever to ensure that L Detachment became a viable entity.

Parachute training began a few weeks later with the building of a steel framework some 35 feet high, from which the men could be dropped to learn the skills of landing. While reasonably effective in teaching the men how to land properly, the static frames could not be used to simulate the vertical and lateral movement of a proper parachute drop. Stirling therefore contacted the only parachute school then extant, Ringway in England, and begged for assistance. Largely ignored, he asked the inventive Jock Lewes to devise their own methods of training.

After personally experimenting with various ways of rolling as his feet impacted with the ground, Lewes decided that the best way to simulate the two-directional movements of a proper parachute jump was to have the men leap from the back of moving Bedfords onto the hard desert floor, then roll in the direction of the lorry, which would simulate the wind movement of a real drop. At first the Bedfords travelled at a relatively safe 15mph, but as the men became more efficient, Lewes gradually doubled the speed, which made the jumps a lot more dangerous and eventually led to many accidents, including severe sprains and fractured bones.

'That Lewes is barmy,' Taff said. 'I respect him, but he's crazy. Those jumps from the Bedfords are more dangerous than real ones could possibly be. We've lost a lot of good men through them and those of us still here are black and blue. That crazy bastard will kill us all.'

'He's making the jumps as well,' Neil reminded him.

'Just shows he's mad,' Taff replied.

Nevertheless, the brutal jumps from speeding lorries continued until it was time for the remaining men to make their first jumps from an aeroplane. MEHQ had finally made a Bombay bomber available on a daily basis for this purpose; however, as Ringway was still being uncooperative, the Detachment had to rely on guesswork and self-tuition. Luckily, unlike the Valentia which had almost killed Stirling, the Bombay had a proper overhead suspension for the static line of the chutes, allowing for the use of a snap-link.

Feeling that it was necessary for him to make a showing at this point, Stirling made the first two jumps with the men. These were successful and the men were euphoric. But during the next jumps, when Stirling remained on the ground to visually check the air and landing patterns, the snap-links attaching the static lines of the first two parachutists to the overhead suspension cable twisted, the rings slipped free, the parachute canopies remained in their packs, and the men plunged screaming to their deaths.

Shocked, Stirling cancelled the rest of that day's jumps and gave the men the day off. Nevertheless, the jumps were ruthlessly resumed the following morning, with Stirling setting a good example by being the first out of the aircraft. This time the snap-links were carefully checked and there were no further casualties. Within a matter of weeks the remaining men were expert, confident paratroopers.

One major problem remained. As the main purpose of the planned raids was to destroy enemy aircraft and other vehicles on the ground, as well as fuel and ammunition dumps, the men, if using orthodox explosives, would need to hump murderously heavy loads to their chosen targets, then set them off almost instantly and make a quick getaway. Given the state of contemporary explosives, neither of these ideas was feasible: most explosives were too heavy to carry over such distances and the usual constituents – gelignite, thermite and ammonal – took too long to be ignited or exploded.

What Lewes wanted was something smaller and lighter, and therefore easier to carry. What he also wanted was a combination of the explosive and the incendiary that could be set off almost instantly. When told by a disdainful Royal Army Ordnance Corps expert that this was impossible, he studied the subject during his three busy months in Kabrit, eventually producing a blend of plastic explosive (PE) and thermite kneaded together with a lubricant into a bomb the size of a tennis ball. This explosive-inflammable mix gave a charge of about 400g.

'On the boss of a propeller,' Lewes explained to Stirling, Greaves and Callaghan, 'it will not only damage the prop itself but also set alight any petrol or other fuel within range of the blast. In other words, it's perfect for destroying grounded aircraft and other vehicles – and certainly for fuel and ammunition dumps. It's also exceptionally small and light, and so easy to carry. Last but not least, with the explosive fused in its own right and the incendiary device timed to ignite just *after* the explosion, you won't find anything quicker or more devastating.'

'I'm not sure what all that means,' Stirling said with a broad smile, 'but I'm sure it will work.'

It did. Tested in the presence of Royal Army Ordnance Corps representatives, the device was highly successful and immediately named the 'Lewes bomb'.

'Thank you kindly,' Captain Stirling said to the RAOC representatives, speaking on behalf of the man he now considered to be a modest genius. 'It's the least you can do.'

Vengeance being sweet, it was now time for L Detachment to stop practising and see some action. Stirling was well aware of the fact that the only kind of man who could pass the tests set by Lewes was the kind of man who could not easily endure boredom. This belief was confirmed when Greaves and Callaghan informed him that the men were becoming frustrated with their endless retraining in the furnace of Kabrit and wanted to put their learning to good use. As it happened, their enthusiasm coincided with General Auchinleck's first major offensive to relieve Tobruk and push Rommel's seemingly invincible Afrika Korps out of Cyrenaica.

'To aid this push,' Stirling explained to the whole detachment at a briefing convened in the mess tent, 'we will raid five forward airfields spread around Gazala and Timini. This will involve five separate raiding parties of twelve men, travelling in five aircraft and being dropped at five specific locations, well away from the targets. The drop will take place on the night of 16 November. You will march throughout the night to lying-up positions in view of the targets. From your LUPs you will observe the targets and assess their individual situations. Infiltration of the airfields, the placing of bombs and detonation will take place in the early hours of the morning. The fuses will be coordinated, as far as possible, to detonate under cover of darkness. The groups will then make a forced march before first light, back to a preselected RV to join up with the LRDG, who will return them to base. Exfiltration will be by LRDG lorry to Siwa Oasis, then back to here. Average distance from airfield to RV will be forty miles. The commanders of the five groups will be myself with Sergeant Lorrimer as second-in-command; Captain Callaghan; Lieutenant Greaves; Lieutenant Bollington; and Captain Lewes. Are there any questions?'

'Yes, boss,' Sergeant Lorrimer said after a long silence. 'When do we leave?'

'This afternoon,' answered Captain Stirling.

5

The five raiding parties boarded five Bombays late that afternoon with a certain amount of trepidation, since reports of likely ground winds of thirty knots – almost twice the hazard level – had led Stirling to call a last-minute Chinese parliament, asking if the men were willing to carry on despite the dangerous weather, which could scatter them widely over the desert. The men were unanimous that they should go anyway, particularly as the last three raids planned by Layforce had been cancelled earlier that year, leaving most of them extremely frustrated.

'Then let's do it, lads,' Stirling said.

With packed bergens strapped under their Irvin X-Type parachute packs, and burdened down with a wide variety of weapons, they were heavily laden. The weapons included 9mm Sten sub-machine-guns, M1 Thompson sub-machine-guns, or tommy-guns, and Bren light machine-guns. Their criss-crossed webbing was festooned with 30 and 32-round box magazines, hand-grenades, water bottles, survival kits and, of course, the brand-new Lewes bombs. Strapped to the belt around their waists were the ubiquitous 9mm Browning High Power handgun, Sykes-Fairburn commando knife, bayonet, compass and binoculars. The bergens were crammed with other items, including food, and weighed nearly 90lb on their own.

When Stirling's Bombay took off, at 1930 hours, the roar of its twin engines made conversation impossible among the twelve men sitting on the fuselage floor above the bomb racks. The lack of room was made even worse than usual by the enormous long-range fuel tank taking up the middle of the plane, down much of its length.

'Are we expecting flak on this flight?' Jimbo asked nervously.

'Yes,' Frankie replied. 'And I know just what you're thinking. If any hits that fucking fuel tank we can call it a day.'

'Too bloody right,' Jimbo said.

Though the Bombay had taken off in a clear, windless night, the weather soon deteriorated, and as they neared the target area the engines laboured more strenuously through dark storm clouds and the vibrations became worse. Shortly after they had flown into those boiling clouds, the clap of thunder was heard above the labouring engines and fingers of lightning illuminated the sky.

Even as the aircraft began to buck and shudder wildly from the storm, the sound of anti-aircraft guns was added to the bedlam and tracers began flickering past the windows, as if competing with the lightning to light up the dark sky with jagged phosphorescent lines.

'Shit!' Neil exclaimed. 'If we don't get it from the weather, we'll cop it from the flak. Let's get the fuck out of here.'

While the aircraft bucked and rolled crazily, Stirling made his way along the hold and disappeared into the captain's cabin at the front. Eventually returning to the men, some of whom were now feeling airsick, he said, 'I feel obliged to tell you that the captain's having trouble estimating the force and direction of the wind, which means he's having difficulty navigating. He dropped a sea marker flare which showed that we're off course, so he's going to attempt to use the coastline's configuration as a navigational aid. This will, of course, expose us to more anti-aircraft fire, so be prepared for the worst.'

'Fucking great!' Jimbo muttered.

The worsening vibrations of the struggling Bombay almost numbed the paratroopers' senses as they methodically checked their gear for the last time. Five minutes later, however, when the aircraft was flying through an inferno of thunder, lightning, tracers and exploding flak, it was hit by something, rocked violently, then shuddered and started descending in what was clearly not a controlled manner.

Though it was impossible to stand upright without support, Stirling again made his way along to the pilot's cabin and returned to inform his men that the aircraft had been hit by flak, but had not been badly damaged and was continuing on to the DZ, the drop zone. Lieutenant Bollington's Bombay, however, had taken a worse hit and its entire instrument panel had been shattered. It was now leaking petrol from a damaged wing tank and losing power, so the pilot planned to head back to base.

'*If* he makes it,' Neil whispered mournfully, then looked a bit alarmed as the Bombay abruptly banked steeply.

'Don't worry,' the RAF dispatcher informed the paratroopers. 'We've just banked into our inland turn. You have six minutes to zero hour. On your feet, boys and girls.'

When the men had done as they were told, the dispatcher, an RAF sergeant who would supervise the jump, checked their static lines. Designed to jerk open the chutes as each man fell clear of the aircraft, they were fixed to 'strong points' in the fuselage. A man's life could depend on them, but in this obsolete aircraft the fixings looked suspiciously flimsy. If these twisted free, the canopies would not open and the men would plunge to their deaths. However, a sharp tug on each line by the dispatcher satisfied him that the new clips would hold firm. He then moved to the door and nodded to the aircraftman to open it. When the latter did so, cold air rushed in with a startling roar.

With their senses abruptly revived by the shock of the cold, rushing air, the paratroopers lined up to make the jump. Supply packs of weapons and explosives tied to parachutes were stacked up in the rear of the fuselage, behind the lines of men, waiting to be pitched out by the airmen when the last of the paratroopers had gone; other boxes with parachutes were clipped to the bomb racks, also ready for dropping. Unable to be heard above the roar of wind and engines, the dispatcher mouthed the words 'Get ready' and pointed to the lamp above his head.

The sounds of anti-aircraft fire and exploding

flak heard a few minutes earlier as the plane had banked into its inland turn had set the men's adrenalin racing. Now, though nerves were steadier, their knowledge that the pilot was having difficulty finding the DZ, increased their fear of the unknown.

When Stirling's gaze turned towards the small lamp mounted by the doorway, his eleven companions did the same. Men eased their shoulders more comfortably into their harnesses, fidgeted with their weapons, checked their equipment yet again, and forgot the discomforts of the two and a half hours already spent in the plane. At once nervous and relieved, they now just wanted to jump, to get it over and done with.

The red light came on. Two minutes to go.

Stirling, leading the drop, was first in line, at the door, waiting for the green light. When it flashed on, the dispatcher slapped his shoulder and he threw himself out. The second man, Lorrimer, moved up to take Stirling's place and waited for a similar slap. He saw his predecessor's line snake out and jar taut for a split second, before it trailed slackly from the door. Lorrimer heard a bawled 'Go!' before he felt the signal, then he he was out in the black void, the wind of the slipstream slapping at him, its noise deafening, as he held himself upright, heels together, waiting for the slipstream to release him and let him drop vertically, which it did within seconds. A sudden jerk and the roaring wind ceased, then Lorrimer dropped down through darkness and silence, looking for the ground. Where the hell was it?

By now Stirling should have felt, or at least seen, the ground, yet the blackness seemed bottomless as he continued drifting down. Suddenly, however, as he gripped the rigging lines, preparing to swing himself clear of anything harmful, he was smashed against a rocky stretch of desert. Hitting the ground with a jolt, he rolled over and was dragged away by the fierce wind, but he managed to roll again, this time onto his stomach, meanwhile wrestling to control the rigging lines, collapsing the canopy. Breathless and battered, with darting pains shooting through him, he was snatched away again by another strong gust of wind, then bumped, cut and bruised as he was dragged at great speed over sharp rocks and abrasive gravel. Somehow he managed to punch the release box and unravel his harness. Then he passed out.

Regaining consciousness, Stirling found himself lying on his belly. Rolling onto his back, he saw patches of stars between drifting storm clouds and, below them, the pale white flowers of other parachutes descending too far away.

'Damn!' Stirling whispered.

Attempting to stand, he was almost knocked off balance by the wind. Stinging granules of rock, the so-called 'sand' of the desert, stung his face, made breathing difficult and finally forced him to turn downwind, into the desert.

The gale had blown for several hours and put the other paratroopers well beyond their intended DZ, but Stirling did not know that just yet. He expected to find the rest of his party downwind. But when he reached what should have been the DZ, not one man was in sight.

Stirling was all on his own, lost in the desert, in the middle of the raging sandstorm that had reduced visibility to almost zero.

After fighting to get his breath back, gritting his teeth against the pain of his many cuts and bruises, and checking that his bergen straps and webbing were in one piece, Stirling switched on his torch and headed resolutely into the dark, storm-lashed desert.

Fighting against the raging storm and almost blind in the darkness, Stirling marched in the direction of where he thought he had seen the other paratroopers. Though shouting his name constantly, his words were lost in the wind, so he shone his torch left and right as a beacon, hoping someone would see it. Eventually, after what seemed like an eternity, he saw the light of another torch veering from side to side, then another, and at last heard voices calling out to him. He soon came face to face with Ashman and Turner, both smeared with a film of sand and dust, leaning into the howling wind.

'Have you seen anyone else?' Stirling bawled.

Private Ashman nodded and pointed west. 'Yes!' he bawled back. 'Over there! About half a mile away.'

'Let's go and find them!' Stirling bawled.

Heading in that direction, the three men managed to link up with two others in the group, Lorrimer and Moffatt, then the search for the others continued, with all the men yelling out their names and waving their torches. In this manner it took nearly two hours for ten of the original group to link up. The eleventh man, Corporal Tanner, was missing and a further two hours of searching failed to find him.

'He was probably dragged out into the desert,' Stirling ventured with a sinking heart. 'Almost certainly that's what happened, likewise to the ten packages of weapons that were dropped.'

'There's two of them over there,' Frankie Turner said, pointing east. 'In the bed of a wadi. I didn't see any more.'

'Let's go and fetch them,' a dispirited Stirling said.

One of the parachuted crates contained Lewes bombs without fuses. There were also a few rations, but only enough for one day, and twelve water bottles, containing in all just over two gallons of drinking water.

'Fat lot of good this will do us,' Lorrimer said as they squatted on the cold wadi bed, protected from the howling wind but still covered in swirling sand, nibbling at some of the rations and quenching their thirst with the water. 'No weapons apart from our pistols. No explosives. Nothing. We can't do a damned thing, boss.'

'We can at least have a look at the enemy installations,' Stirling said stubbornly, refusing to go back empty-handed.

'I'm willing,' Lorrimer said, understanding Stirling's frustration, 'but I don't think we should put the men through that after this bloody disaster.'

'But you'll come with me?'

'Yes, boss.'

Stirling checked his watch by the light of his

torch. 'Three hours to daylight,' he said. 'That should give us enough time.'

'Just about,' Lorrimer agreed.

Stirling called Sergeant Bob Tappman over to tell him what they had planned. 'Our objective,' he said, 'is the German airfield near Gazala in Cyrenaica – one of the five we were to raid in this area. It should have been only a few hours' march from here, so although we can no longer raid it Sergeant Lorrimer and I are going to have a look at it while you take the remaining men direct to the rendezvous with the LRDG lorries. If we're at the correct DZ, the RV should be less than 30 miles away.'

'*If* we're at the correct DZ,' Tappman said bitterly.

Stirling shrugged. 'What is there to lose?'

Tappman returned to the men crouched on the dark floor of the wadi, grateful for its protection from the freezing, howling wind. When he had conveyed the news to them, they climbed wearily, dispiritedly to their feet, fell into single file and clambered up out of the wadi one by one, gradually disappearing into the stormy night. When they had all gone, Stirling and Lorrimer likewise climbed out and headed in what they assumed was the direction of Gazala.

They marched through the cold and dark until the grey light of dawn broke, when they laid up for a short break and a few nibbles of their remaining food. They then continued the march, taking their bearings from the Trig El Abd, a track line in the desert, previously used by the camel trains of the slave trade, then by either Axis or Allied vehicles, depending on who was holding the area.

After a hike of about ten miles, with the weather changing again and returning to a fierce, dry heat that lasted until last light, they reached a featureless desert plateau that led to an escarpment: a line of cliffs from which they could see the Mediterranean beyond the coast road. The road itself was the military supply route (MSR) for German and Italian forces loosely holding a line from the sea at Sollum, on the Egyptian border, 120 miles to the east of Gazala, well beyond the Allied enclave at Tobruk. Seeing the MSR, and the constant flow of Axis traffic heading along it in both directions, they realized that they had been dropped well south of their intended DZ, only ten miles or so from the coast.

'There's no airfield here,' Lorrimer said, lying flat on his belly beside Stirling on the escarpment and studying the MSR through his binoculars. 'We're miles away, boss.'

'Then let's not waste our journey,' Stirling replied stubbornly. 'We'll stay here for a bit and gather as much info as we can on the troop movements along that route. That at least will be something.'

'Yes, boss,' Lorrimer sighed wearily.

Unfortunately they were foiled in even that simple plan. They laid up all night and recced the MSR the following morning, but late that afternoon black clouds formed in the sky and they knew that another storm was coming. Hoping to find shelter, they advanced the last four miles to the edge of the escarpment, where they took shelter in a dried-up wadi bed, which they planned to use as their observation post (OP).

This was a mistake. When the clouds broke in a deluge of rain, they were caught unawares in the last thing that newcomers to the desert expect to encounter – a 'flash flood.' As the rain poured down with the force of a tropical storm, hitting the sand like bullets and making it spit and splash as mud, the bed of the wadi gradually filled up with water, becoming first a stream, then a fast-flowing river. This forced the pair to clamber up out of the wadi, where they were exposed to the full force of the storm, lashed by a freezing wind and now drenched completely by the torrential, incredibly noisy rain. Even as they lay there, hardly believing what they were experiencing, the river in the wadi became a raging torrent that swept baked sand and gravel along with it as it took the line of least resistance and roared along between the high banks of the wadi.

To make matters worse, the storm and flash floods – the latter were deluging other wadis – had blotted out the landscape and made surveillance of the MSR impossible. It was now clear to Stirling that their presence here could serve no valid purpose.

'There's no alternative but to head for the RV,' he said, sounding bitterly disappointed, even though the storm was starting to abate. 'And I think we should start straight away, before another storm comes.'

'No argument,' Lorrimer said.

The RV, they knew, lay 40 miles inland, back along the Trig El Abd. Luckily, as the rain was still falling, they were able to fill up their water bottles before leaving. When they did eventually set off, the rain was still falling, they were thoroughly soaked, and Stirling's beloved, carefully packed cigarettes had virtually disintegrated in his sodden kit.

'I can't bear to be without a smoke,' he said. 'That's worse than anything else.'

Lorrimer laughed at that.

Again they marched throughout the night. In the early hours of the morning, about three hours before first light, Lorrimer realized that he could barely put his weight on his swollen ankle, twisted during his parachute landing but passing virtually unnoticed in the tension generated by their many arduous, dangerous activities since the drop. Now it hurt like hell. Nevertheless, he followed Stirling steadily in the direction which the latter had judged would bring them to the RV where, it was hoped, the LRDG's A patrol would be shining a Tilley lamp from a small hill as a welcoming beacon.

By 0700 the next morning, they had been over 36 hours in the desert. When the rain stopped, about dawn, they slumped in the shade of a hillock and slept the sleep of the dead for four hours. Their wet clothes had dried on them before they moved off again in the midday haze. By then the heat was fierce, scorching their skin, blistering their lips and filling them with an unceasing thirst that compelled them to finish off the water they had gathered from the rainfall on the escarpment the previous day.

Late that afternoon, just as they were both starting to feel that they might go mad from thirst, the weather turned yet again, becoming much cooler and, more importantly, bringing back the rain and enabling them to fill their bottles. Replenished and cooled down after their long, thirsty journey through the fierce heat, they continued the arduous march across the scorched, barren waste.

They were some 12 miles from the RV when Stirling spotted movement far to the south. Through his binoculars he made out nine figures heading for the Trig El Abd.

'Nine men,' he said to Lorrimer, 'heading westward. It can only be Sergeant Tappman and the others. Let's hope they make it the rest of the way without being caught.'

'Let's hope *we* do,' Lorrimer said sardonically, still limping badly when he walked, but marching on anyway.

Stirling and Lorrimer marched throughout a third night, stopping only to watch a sudden, fierce sandstorm blowing up in the distance, where they had seen the other nine men.

'Poor bastards,' Sergeant Lorrimer murmured.

When the sandstorm had abated, they marched on again, finally lying up in the early hours of the morning, dropping off almost immediately and once more sleeping like dead men.

On waking just before first light, they saw what they thought was a star very low in the sky. But when they continued their march and drew closer to the glowing object, they realized that it was A Patrol's lamp shining in the south, no more than two or three miles away.

They had made it back.

An exhausted Stirling and a badly limping Lorrimer found the LRDG lorries hidden under camouflage nets in a small ravine. There they were welcomed with hot tea laced with whisky, which perked them up temporarily. They were further buoyed up to find Lieutenant Greaves and Captain Lewes already at the RV with eight of their ten men. They, too, had had a disastrous drop and been up to the coast to fix their position before marching to this RV. Likewise Paddy Callaghan, who had come in just before Stirling and Lorrimer, having waited nearby to be sure that he had correctly identified the position of the patrol.

But Stirling's brief euphoria was dashed when Callaghan told him what had happened to his group.

'By the time we reached our DZ, much later than your lot, we found ourselves parachuting down through winds blowing at 90 mph. You can imagine! A lot of the men were injured as they landed, others were lost, and the rest of us, having no choice, marched on into the desert as planned, though with most of our weapons and supplies missing. The storm didn't let up. More men were lost. Another had a fatal heart attack. After that I accepted that our situation was hopeless and led the remaining men towards the coast. When I reached there, I used the configuration of the coastline to navigate my way back to the RV. No enemy airfields were sighted, let alone sabotaged, and I lost eighty per cent of my men. A complete disaster, I fear.'

'Has anything else been heard of the Bombay that was damaged and tried to limp back to base?'

'Lieutenant Bollington's plane?' Callaghan looked none too happy. 'According to Captain Owen, commander of this LRDG group, Bollington was captured with his men. The damaged Bombay made a forced landing west of Tobruk. The crew made emergency repairs and took off again, but they were forced to crash-land for a second time after being attacked by an Me 109F. That's when they were captured – all twelve of them, plus the air crew.'

'Damn!' Stirling growled.

He was further deflated when he found Privates Ashman, Turner and Moffatt huddled together against the wheels of a lorry, covered with sand and gravel, red-eyed, clearly exhausted, and comforting themselves with tea and whisky.

'You men look like you've had a rough time,' Stirling said. 'What happened out there?'

Turner and Moffatt glanced at Jimbo, who then spoke up for all of them. 'When we left the DZ we soon learnt that we'd been dropped far off the mark.'

'Yes,' Stirling interjected impatiently, 'I found that out as well.'

'So,' Jimbo continued, ignoring the interruption, 'we couldn't find our bearings and got even more lost. To make matters worse, we then ran into winds of over 90 mph . . .'

'You as well!' Stirling murmured bitterly.

'. . . and a lot of us then lost one another and were widely scattered. We three' – Jimbo nodded, indicating Turner and Moffatt – 'found ourselves still with Sergeant Tappman, who managed to lead us out of the storm. We were looking for the Trig El Abd, but just before last light we turned in the wrong direction and instead ran into a Kraut patrol. There was a brief fire-fight – we only had our Browning handguns – and Sergeant Tappman deliberately exposed himself to the Krauts, distracting them, while we made our escape along a wadi bed. We saw him being captured and taken away. Eventually, we made our way back to the Trig El Abd, which eventually led us back here. A good bloke, that Tappman.'

When the figures were calculated the results were truly shocking. Totting up those captured, missing or presumed dead, it became clear to Stirling that of the original sixty-two men, only twenty-two had made it back.

Dispirited and badly shaken, though not yet defeated, Stirling and the remainder of his men were driven back to the base at Kabrit by the LRDG.

6

The LRDG took Captain Stirling and his twenty-one men to Siwa Oasis, nearly 200 miles to the south-west and across the frontier, at the crossroads of the old caravan routes. With its salt-water lake, fierce dry heat, and swarms of black flies, Siwa was noted for its ability to tax a man's strength and destroy his will to work. For this very reason Stirling had no desire to leave his men there very long.

All the same, it was a beautiful place. Seven miles long and two miles wide, it was abundant with water and palm trees. Beyond the palm groves, to the south, rolled the great white dunes, running north to south in the Great Sand Sea. An area approximately the same size as Ireland, it could only be crossed 130 miles south of Siwa by a route that passed the artesian well at Ain Dalla, the last watering-hole in over 300 miles en route for Kufra.

To the north-west of Siwa lay the Quattra Depression, running further northward to stop only 50 yards from the sea near El Alamein. Unfortunately, its floor was so far below sea level that it was impassable to ordinary vehicles.

A month after arriving at Siwa, bored and frustrated, Stirling managed to arrange a meeting with Brigadier D.W. Reid, in the Jalo Oasis garrison, nearly 250 miles away. There, in the brigadier's tent, Stirling got down to business.

'Kufra is the key settlement to the control of the inner desert,' he promptly informed Reid. 'Over 1000 miles from the coast and stretching for some 1300 miles from the Nile westward – an area about the size of the Indian subcontinent.'

'True,' Reid said, topping up his tea with whisky and looking up to see if Stirling wanted the same. When Stirling nodded, the brigadier also laced his tea with whisky, then sat back on his dusty wooden chair. 'Unfortunately, it's haunted by the ghibli . . .'

'Pardon?'

'A hot wind laden with dust, rather than sand,' Reid explained. 'In fact, true sandstorms are rare in these parts, though duststorms, as you well know, occur frequently and can be devastating. The ghibli is even worse. Also, the great variation in temperature inland – fifty degrees by noon, frost in the morning – can lead ill-equipped or irresolute men to die from exposure. In short, the Great Sand Sea was well named when the Arabs dubbed it the Devil's Country. It's a murderous terrain for all but them.'

'Yet some SAS men,' Stirling said, not missing his opportunity, 'crossed that desert without boots, water or even rations, in their determination to survive. That's why, despite the failure of our first raid, we have to try it again.'

Brigadier Reid smiled, admiring Stirling's tenacity, the more so because it was a virtue he possessed himself. Indeed, even as Stirling was being brought into Siwa by the LRDG, Reid had been leading his 'Oasis' force with great skill and tenacity to take Aujila and then capture the 600 Italians of the Jalo garrison, despite a dreadful pounding from Axis aircraft. His tenacity, and that of his men, had finally won the day.

Now, here in Jalo, the former trading centre of the Majabra Arabs, he was deciding whether or not he should help Stirling in his bid to return to the desert for another series of raids in which LRDG patrols would also be used. Their FOB, or forward operating base, had been set up around the few sand-blown huts and Italian buildings which were all that remained of this once prosperous settlement. But it was ideal for L Detachment's purpose: raids which would destroy German aircraft at Agedabia and elsewhere on the coastline of the Gulf of Sirte.

'I still have my doubts about whether you should try this again,' Reid said, easing his massive frame into his chair and puffing out his bright red cheeks to blow a stream of blue smoke from his cigar. 'Nor am I alone in this. MEHQ also has doubts. There's even been talk of pulling you out of the field altogether. Sorry to be so blunt, dear boy, but those are the facts.'

Recalling his sodden cigarettes on the escarpment over the MSR that ran from Sollum to Gazala, Stirling was smoking with relish now while his brain worked overtime. He had always known that there were those among the gabardine swine who wanted to have L Detachment 22 SAS disbanded altogether, so he was hardly shocked to hear the brigadier confirm it. Nevertheless, he had to make his move now, before the voices of his enemies gained sway. Luckily, he had an ace up his sleeve: his old supporter, General Ritchie, the former Deputy Chief of General Staff, Cairo, who had since been placed in command of the Eighth Army.

'I don't mind your bluntness, Denys, and I accept what you're saying, but not *everyone* at MEHQ is against me. In fact, General Ritchie still had great faith in the enterprise – even more so, given the tenacity displayed by my men in that desert after the first raid, irrespective of the failure of the raid itself. I'm sure he'll support us.'

Reid smiled again and revealed his pleasant surprise. 'I knew that all along, David. In fact, I spoke to Ritchie about it. Ritchie in turn spoke to the C-in-C. Auchinleck's not only prepared to let you continue your raids, but is giving you a free hand to plan the details.'

At this news Stirling felt a great surge of joy well up inside him. In truth, he had been suffering a deepening sense of failure and despair since the disaster in the Gazala area and wished to repair the damage as soon as possible. The damage was not only to the reputation of the new-born L Detachment, but to the morale of the individual men. Many of them had been deeply shocked by the loss of friends during the disastrous parachute drop and afterwards. Others had taken the failure personally and were blaming themselves for it. Those negative feelings had not been eased by their month in Siwa Oasis, where they had little to do but endlessly retrain to keep an edge to their skills. Apart from the retraining, which bored most of them anyway, they had too much time to brood on the widely discussed failure of the first raids and its effect on the reputation of L Detachment. This doubtless explained why tempers were short and fisticuffs not infrequent during the evenings. Already many had asked to be sent back to Kabrit, which was at least nearer to Cairo, but so far Stirling had refused. He had his reasons.

'That's wonderful news,' he said to Brigadier Reid, puffing streams of cigarette smoke between each precisely placed word. 'I'm really thrilled, Denys.'

'Naturally,' Reid replied, 'since all of your few remaining trained men will be needed in the field, I'll be happy to help you overcome your supply problems until you decide on a parent organization for L Detachment.'

'I've already decided,' Stirling said. 'I want it to be the LRDG.'

Reid nodded, puffed another cloud of cigar smoke, then flicked the ash into his ashtray with a surprisingly elegant movement of his large hand. 'A good choice. L Detachment and the LRDG are natural allies, involved in similar business and operating virtually the same way. You can learn a lot from the LRDG.'

'I've always been happy to take their advice.'

'That's why you work well together.'

The field telephone on the brigadier's desk – actually a trestle table – gave a loud, jangling ring. The brigadier picked the phone up, listened briefly, then put it down and smiled at Stirling.

'Major Steele has arrived,' he said, rising as someone entered the tent behind Stirling. Standing up and turning around, Stirling found himself face to face with Major Don Steele of the LRDG. The two men shook hands.

'Delighted to meet you at last, old chap,' Steele said, taking the chair beside Stirling, facing Reid. 'I've heard a lot about that last op and was very impressed.'

'The last op was a failure,' Stirling said, 'that brought me a lot of flak.'

Steele grinned. 'I'm sure it did. There are, however, lessons to be learnt from failure. Though the raids were not successful, your men performed magnificently. Their hikes across an average of 50 miles of desert to the RV have already become almost legendary. Never mind the sceptics of MEHQ. L Detachment has nothing to be ashamed of and a lot to be proud of.'

'It's a relief to hear that,' Stirling said, meaning

it, liking Steele immensely. 'The failure hit the men hard.'

'You won't fail this time.'

'Now that the backslapping is finished,' Reid said tartly, 'can we get down to business?'

Steele grinned again. 'Yes, sir.'

Reid stood and went to the covered blackboard raised up behind his desk. After picking up a pointer, he removed the canvas sheet covering the blackboard, to reveal a large map of the Cyrenaica Desert.

'While your good friend General Ritchie has recently been reinforced,' he said, 'the Axis forces are short of men and supplies – mainly because the Allies now control the Mediterranean. This is a situation which Ritchie wants to exploit. He intends reaching Derna by 19 December and, with forward elements of the 22nd Guards Brigade, be 10 miles east of Benghazi by the 23rd.'

'Ambitious,' Stirling said. 'What's our role?'

Reid tapped the word 'Agedabia' with his pointer. It was on the coast, approximately 120 miles north of Jalo Oasis and 75 miles south of Benghazi. 'My Flying Squadron is under orders to link up with Brigadier Marriott's force in this area and be in position by 22 December, in support of the Allied advance on Benghazi. My problem in doing this is the threat from the German aircraft at . . .' He tapped the names off, one by one, with his pointer. '. . . Agedabia, Sirte and Agheila. Your job is to remove that threat before we move out.'

Stirling nodded, then stood up. He went to the map and studied it carefully.

'My suggestion,' Steele said carefully behind him, 'is that you take as few men as possible – though enough to do the job – and, instead of parachuting in, let us take you on LRDG vehicles to within striking distance of Sirte.'

'Why Sirte?' Stirling asked, still studying the map covering the blackboard.

'It's considered to be the most important,' Reid replied.

Stirling nodded again, inhaled on his cigarette, studied the map with his cheeks puffed out, then blew out a cloud of smoke and turned back to face the other two officers.

'Right,' he said firmly, having decided. 'I'll move out with Paddy Callaghan and ten men on 10 December, targeting Sirte. Captain Lewes will be assigned to Agheila, moving out on the 9th. Both groups will attack on the night of the 14th. Finally, Lieutenant Greaves will target Agedabia, in support of your move . . .' Stirling nodded, indicating Reid. '. . . Greaves will move out on the 18th to make his attack on the 21st. By the time you advance, Denys, the airfields should all be out of action.'

'Let's hope so,' Reid said.

'This time I have no doubts,' Stirling told him. 'My men are ready, willing and able. They'll do a good job.'

'With good support from us,' Steele said. 'Of that you can rest assured.'

'More mutual backslapping,' Reid said sardonically, relighting his cigar and belching out more smoke. 'May I remind you, gentlemen, that actions speak louder than words.'

'You'll get all the action you want,' Steele said with a wide, boyish grin. 'Of *that* you can rest assured!'

'We're gonna hang out our washing on the Siegfried Line,' Stirling said, quoting the lyrics of the morale-boosting song. 'And it will all start right here in North Africa.'

The three men chuckled at that, then Stirling left his fellow officers in the tent and marched enthusiastically across the sun-scorched oasis, with its cool water and palm trees, to raise the spirits of his men with what he regarded as exceptionally good news.

He was not surprised, when he told them what was going to happen, that the men cheered and applauded for several minutes.

7

'So those are the targets,' Stirling said, completing his summary of the forthcoming operations at a briefing in a large tent pitched in the shade of a grove of palm trees, close to the glittering water of the Jalo Oasis. The men had arrived there the day before, after a long, hot drive in lorries over the Great Sand Sea from Siwa Oasis. 'This time, however, instead of parachuting in from Bombays, we'll be driven in by the LRDG.'

A disgruntled murmuring made Stirling glance uneasily at Major Steele, who was sitting in a chair beside him, behind the long trestle table, directly facing Captain Lewes, Captain Callaghan, and Lieutenant Greaves. All three officers were sitting in the front row of hard chairs with the rest of L Detachment seated behind them and Sergeant Lorrimer, his thick arms crossed on his broad chest, standing at the back of the tent, keeping a beady eye on his increasingly frustrated, contentious men.

'Before any of you start complaining,' Stirling said, waving them into attentive silence, 'please let it be noted that the LRDG, apart from their exemplary reconnaissance and intelligence-gathering work, have actually paved the way for the kind of raids we're planning to launch. Indeed, only last week . . . Well, I'll let Major Steele tell the story.'

Looking surprisingly nervous, the normally polished Major Steele pushed his chair back, stood up and cleared his throat.

'In late November,' he said, 'the Eighth Army was embroiled in a battle with Axis forces between Sollum and Tobruk. Two LRDG patrols, G1 and G2, were ordered to intercept transport on the road running 70 miles north from Agedabia to the main Axis base at Benghazi.'

'Big deal!' Frankie Turner whispered contemptuously to his good friend Jimbo Ashman, though not loud enough for Steele to hear.

'The patrols were attacked from the air when nearing the coast,' the major continued, 'but the commander of G1, Captain Tony Hay, led his patrol in an attack at dusk on the 28th against a roadside eating house located about 30 miles south of Benghazi. His eight vehicles, having driven several miles down the main road under heavy air attack, turned into the parking area and fired armour-piercing and incendiary bullets from their machine-guns. While they were doing so, a man on each lorry lobbed grenades at some thirty Axis vehicles. The patrol then escaped in the gathering darkness.'

Always willing to listen to a tale of derring-do, the SAS men, though in a contentious mood, gave Steele breathing space. He used it to cough into his fist, clearing a throat made dry by self-consciousness, then gamely continued.

'The men of G1 weren't followed, but after lying up next day in the desert, they returned to the road at dusk to shoot up a fuel tanker, killing its driver and passenger, forcing it off the road. The rest of the Axis drivers then fled back in the directions they had come from while the LRDG vehicles drove back into the safety of the desert – again unmolested.'

Taff Clayton yawned melodramatically, pretending to hide it with his hand, only removing his hand from his face to ask: 'So? Did they make it back?'

'Yes,' Steele answered, suddenly showing a little mettle, or perhaps anger, in his formerly shaky voice. 'After spending the rest of that night in the desert, they spent a further day near the road, but were recalled and reached Siwa on 3 December.'

When Stirling saw the blank faces of his men, most of whom thought of themselves as a cut above the average, including the LRDG, he straightened his shoulders, which made him look even taller, and said forcefully: 'The point we wish to make is that that LRDG raid, and others just like it, forced the enemy to withdraw troops from the main battle area to protect his lines of communication – a ploy we are now going to exploit to the full with the invaluable help of the LRDG, who have, incidentally, thankfully already paved the way for us.'

Stirling nodded appreciatively in the direction of Steele while some of the more dissenting SAS men rolled their eyeballs or shook their heads from side to side in disbelief.

'Any questions so far?' Sergeant Lorrimer bawled.

'No, Sarge!' some of the men shouted back.

'Then stop all that whispering and fidgeting and listen to your CO!'

'Yes, Sarge!' they shouted back in unison.

'All right, men, all right,' Stirling said with a grin, raising his big hands to silence them. 'Fun time is over.' When they had settled down, he continued: 'Now that the proper briefing is over, we'd like you to take the opportunity to ask Major Steele anything you want to know about the LRDG. Only sensible questions, please!' He cast his gaze left and right, along the rows of seated men, then to the back of the tent where Lorrimer had put his hand in the air to set the ball rolling. 'Yes, Sergeant?'

'What does the LRDG consist of, precisely? I think we're all a bit vague about that,' Lorrimer asked, looking round for confirmation.

'At present we consist of ten patrols,' Major Steele informed him. 'Each of those has the use of modified four-wheel-drive Ford F60 cars and 30 cwt Chevrolet lorries with a single tank range of 1100 miles. We have a survey section, where we make up our own maps. We have our own artillery section with a 4.5-inch howitzer, an 88mm 25-pounder, and a light tank, each mounted on a ten-tonner. We have an air section with two American WACO light aircraft purchased by the War Office. Last but not least, we have a heavy section of three-ton supply lorries, and a Light Aid Detachment for vehicle maintenance. In short, we're a self-sustaining outfit and we're well equipped.'

'Above or below?' Jimbo whispered to Frankie, who had to stifle his coarse laughter.

'What was that?' Steele asked sternly.

'Nothing, boss! Please continue.'

'Thank you, soldier, I will.' Steele stared steadily

at Jimbo for a moment, then shook his head in disgust and continued.

'The first LRDG patrol, formed by Major, now Colonel, Bagnold, had two officers and thirty other ranks with eleven vehicles, each carrying a single machine-gun, supplemented by an early Bofors – a 37mm used as an anti-tank gun – and four Boyes anti-tank rifles. Those and subsequent patrols, including G1 and G2 from the Guards Brigade, spent last summer patrolling from this oasis and Kufra, and their experiences led to a number of fundamental developments in our techniques and roles. Our job was traffic surveillance on the Axis coast a good distance away from the main battle area. We also dropped and picked up agents for the Secret Service, recced terrain which the enemy might have to cross, and occasionally raided enemy transport convoys. Our new role is to be a taxi service for you lot.'

This encouraged cheers and jeers from the men, which Sergeant Lorrimer subdued by bawling: 'Shut your mouths you lot and only speak when you've an intelligent question to ask!' The laughter tailed off into helpless chuckling, then even that died away as they felt Lorrimer breathing down their necks.

'So what were these changes in technique then?' Jimbo asked to fill the ensuing silence.

'They were related mainly to the size of patrols,' Steele replied. 'By that September we'd split the patrols into fifteen or eighteen-man teams led by an officer, with five vehicles. Our methods of crossing soft sand and navigating thousands of miles in featureless desert had improved, but they were still based on relatively simple ideas pioneered by Major Bagnold in Africa in the 1930s.'

'Which were?' Frankie Turner asked.

'Bagnold developed the steel channel strips laid for vehicles to cross soft sand. In fact, he first did this in the Sinai Desert in 1926, where he used corrugated iron. By the early 1940s all vehicles carried such channels in the desert.'

'Anything else?' Taff Clayton asked, practically yawning.

'Yes. As you probably know . . .'

'Probably!' Neil Moffatt called out from the back.

'. . . it's difficult to set up a prismatic compass in a motorized vehicle as you invariably get magnetic interference from tool-boxes and other movable metal parts.'

'I was right,' Moffatt crowed. 'We all know that!'

'Are you being funny, soldier?' Lorrimer bellowed.

'No, Sarge!' Moffatt replied.

'Then shut up and listen!'

Ignoring both of them, Steele continued: 'To use a prismatic compass in a motorized vehicle, the navigator has to get out and walk far enough away to be clear of the car's magnetic field. Even then, the compass can be an inaccurate guide – sometimes up to 400 yards out on a 20-mile march.

'Doesn't sound much to me,' Taff Clayton said.

'It's equivalent to four and a half miles adrift after a 400-mile drive. I'd say that's a lot.'

'So what did old Bagnold do?' Jimbo asked, blowing a cloud of smoke from his Woodbine.

'Major Bagnold had his navigators use a sun compass with its horizontal disc marked off in degrees and a central needle casting a shadow – rather like a sundial. The graduated disc was mounted in the car, to be rotated as the sun moved across the sky; the needle's shadow then fell to indicate the bearing on which the car was travelling. By reading the milometer, the navigator could work out his position along this bearing.'

'You've got to hand it to the LRDG,' Frankie said. 'They sure as hell know their science!'

'But even this method wasn't infallible,' Steele

continued, refusing to be drawn into this unusual detachment's verbal sparring which, so he had been informed by Stirling, was encouraged to bond the other ranks to the officers. Steele had his doubts, but was wisely keeping them to himself. 'So each night,' he continued, 'the navigator would take star bearings to fix the car's position.'

'How?' Sergeant Lorrimer asked in a perfectly normal tone of voice.

'By calculating the longitude and latitude with the aid of a theodolite and astro-navigation tables.'

'Very bright!' Jimbo said.

'Brighter than you are, soldier,' Major Steele came straight back, getting into the swing of things. 'Any more questions?'

'How do the different patrols keep in touch?'

'A sensible question from Sergeant Lorrimer,' Steele teased, then turned serious again. 'Each patrol has a radio truck with a No 11 set, which has a range of about 20 miles, and a separate set to pick up the BBC's time signals.'

'Here's an intelligent question from the other ranks,' Jimbo said. 'What about communications in general from deep in the desert?'

Steele nodded, smiling. 'It's not bad. The radio operators are able to pick up Morse from a background slush of atmospherics when working at ranges beyond the normal operational limits of the No 11 set. Their radio links from patrols to the LRDG's forward base and from the base to MEHQ in Cairo, and to the Eighth Army, are more tenuous. These operate on ground aerials at frequencies which mean that sometimes a patrol can't contact base until it's about 300 miles along its route. Our radio procedures, however, follow French civilian routines. Invariably, this makes those listening in think they're hearing a commercial station in Turkey communicating with ships in the Levant. Certainly it appears to have deceived the German radio-interception services. Because of this, our operators are able to transmit for relatively long periods at night, over great distances, without being identified or interfered with.'

'Water?' someone asked sensibly.

'I thought you heroes only drank beer,' Steele responded.

'We drink piss if we have to,' Jimbo said, 'but not if water's available.'

Steele laughed, glancing at the grinning Stirling, then answered the question. 'A gallon per man per day for all purposes, including the topping up of the individual's vehicle. No shaving permitted.'

This last encouraged an outburst of cheering and clapping. When Steele had managed to coax the men back into silence, he said: 'Once the briefing's over, I'll be taking you out and introducing you to the men designated as your "taxi drivers". Treat them with respect. Like yourselves, the LRDG has suffered a number of losses recently. In January, a soldier formerly of the Egyptian Survey Department, and one of our most valuable men, was captured along with seven of his patrol. Y Patrol lost all its officers and G Patrol lost five trucks. In short, they've been through some hard times and don't need too much ragging from you lot.'

'I would appreciate it, men,' Stirling interjected, 'if you would take those particular remarks seriously. I want no nonsense between L Detachment and the LRDG. Those men deserve your respect.'

When Steele glanced at him, he smiled and nodded, indicating that his colleague should continue.

'My men are more than mere taxi drivers,' Steele said. 'In fact, their job is to teach you everything they know about the desert – and since they're mostly old hands who've been in the desert for years, both here and in Africa, they certainly know as much as anyone about the place – perhaps even as much as the Arabs. They've learnt to live hard, carrying the minimum amount of food and water, and to read the tracks of other men, vehicles and camels in what you might think is smooth sand. They can teach you all this and more.'

Sobered by these remarks, the men remained silent until Taff Clayton put his hand up and, at a nod from Steele, asked: 'What do the various initials of the LRDG patrols stand for?'

'When Bagnold was recruiting for the LRDG he first took on a large contingent of New Zealanders, followed by Rhodesians, then a bunch from the Guards Brigade, and, finally, from all over the place. He therefore divided them into lettered patrols: S Patrol for Southern Rhodesians, G Patrol for Guards, Y Patrol for Yeomanry, and so on. It's as simple as that.'

He glanced briefly at each of the men in turn, then asked, 'Any more questions?' Seeing only a sea of shaking heads, he checked his watch, then looked up again and said, 'Right. Go and have a brew-up and be back here in exactly twenty minutes. By that time the vehicles will be here and you can commence your basic desert training.' However, just before they were dismissed, Taff Clayton put up his hand again.

'Yes?' Steele asked.

'According to what you're telling us,' Clayton said, 'we seem to have an awful lot to learn. How much time do we have?'

'Three days,' Steele answered. 'That just about gives you time for your brew-up, so you better go and get it.'

Taken aback by the tightness of the schedule, the men hurriedly filed out of the tent. When they had gone, the remaining officers – Steele, Stirling, Lewes, Callaghan and Greaves – gazed at one another in an uneasy silence that was finally broken by Steele.

'Do you really think they can do it in three days?' he asked, looking concerned.

'They had better,' Captain Stirling replied curtly. 'If they don't, we go anyway.'

He stood up and walked out.

8

What the men did not realize when they returned from their brew-up and smoko was that their three-day programme of training was going to take place in the desert, by day and by night, beginning the minute they climbed into the LRDG vehicles. These they found waiting for them in the scorching heat of noon when they returned from the relative shelter of the large mess tent. The vehicles were modified Chevrolet four-wheel-drive lorries armed with a Boyes anti-tank rifle fixed to the rear and a pintle-mounted Browning M1919 machine-gun operated by the steel-helmeted front passenger. They were covered in dust, badly battered and, in some cases, peppered with bullet holes.

'Now you know what we're in for,' Jimbo confided to his mates. 'A bleedin' suicide mission!'

After being assigned their vehicles, the men were rekitted with clothes favoured by the LRDG for use in the desert: shirt, shorts, Arab headgear and special sandals. The headgear consisted of a black woollen *agal*, a small hat, and a *shemagh*, a shawl with tie thongs, which went around the head, flapped in the wind, kept the face cool, and also protected the nose and mouth in a sandstorm. Normal Army boots were useless because they filled up with sand, so they were replaced with a special kind of sandal, the Indian North-West Frontier *chappli*, originally chosen by Bagnold and obtained from the Palestine Police stores. Worn with rolled-down socks, the *chappli* was particularly tough and had a hole in the toe, enabling the wearer to kick out any sand that got in without having to stop when on the march. Also supplied were funnel-shaped leather gauntlets, which stopped sweat from running down the arms and onto the weapons.

Once dressed properly, they were then able to fix to their belts the obligatory holstered 9mm Browning High Power handgun and Fairburn-Sykes commando knife. They were then loaded up with a selection of larger weapons, including the Lee-Enfield .303-inch bolt-action rifle, the 9mm Sten sub-machine-gun, the heavier M1 Thompson sub-machine-gun, and two machine-guns: the Bren light machine-gun and the Browning 0.5-inch.

'What the fuck do we need all these for?' Jimbo asked, 'if we're only learning about desert survival?'

'You'll find out,' Corporal Mick 'Monkey' Madson of the LRDG told him. 'Now get back to the transport.'

After being led back to the modified Chevrolet lorries, the men were broken up into small groups of two or three and each group assigned to a vehicle. When they had placed their weapons on the back seats, piled up around the fixed tripod-mounted Boyes anti-tank rifles, they were given a thorough briefing on the unusual vehicles. These, apart from their bristling weapons, were also fitted with reinforced sand tyres, special filters, larger fans and radiators, wireless sets, sun compasses, sextants, sand shovels, jerrycans, water condensers, woven sand mats and steel sand channels, the latter two to be used when the vehicle became trapped in deep sand.

Once a cursory summary of the vehicle's armaments had been dispensed – 'cursory' because Monkey knew that these men were familiar with such weapons – they were given a quick lesson in the use of the sun compass fixed to the vehicle's bonnet and familiarized with the workings of the sextant. They were then shown how to improvise a simple compass by stretching a string from the bonnet up to a row of nails on top of the cabin – in the case of a Bedford QL four-wheel-drive lorry – or, in the case of the Chevrolets, to another string with hooks stretched taut between the side supports of what had been the windscreen.

'Every hour,' Monkey informed them, tugging lightly at the fixed line of cord, 'you switch the string one notch along.' He removed the knotted end of cord from one of the nails hooked, in this case, to the cord strung between the windscreen uprights, and looped it over the hook beside it. 'The driver simply follows the line of the shadow created by the string and that keeps him in the right direction.'

The men were then shown how water could be conserved from the radiator. In this instance, when the water boiled, it was not lost through the overflow pipe, which had deliberately been blocked off to prevent this from happening. Instead, the steam from the boiling water was blown off into a can that was bolted to the running board and half filled with water. When the engine cooled, the trapped steam would condense and the topped-up water would be sucked back into the radiator.

'If it works properly, without leaking,' Monkey told them, 'you can go the whole life of the truck without ever putting water in after the initial top-up.'

'Pure bleedin' genius,' Taff, a car enthusiast, said in genuine admiration.

'Right, men,' Monkey said, grinning from ear to ear with pleasure at Taff's remark. 'Into your vehicles and let's go.'

The men all piled into their respective Chevrolets and were driven out of the palm-fringed oasis into the vast, barren wastes of the desert. Immediately assailed by the ferocious heat, they were grateful for the wind created by the vehicles' forward movement, even though this also created huge clouds of sand that threatened to choke them. Covering their faces with their *shemaghs*, they could keep the sand out of their mouths and nostrils, but that in turn made breathing difficult. Within minutes they were all sweating profusely and covered in a fine film of sand that stuck like slime to their sweat. Within half an hour most of them felt that they were in hell and some of them were already feeling nauseous.

After only an hour's drive, Sergeant William 'Wild Bill' Monnery ordered all vehicles to stop and the drivers got out to check the tyres, let some air out lest they burst from heat, and make sure that there was no sand in the carburettors. They also checked the petrol, oil and water, adjusted the compasses, and checked all weapons for sand blockage.

The SAS passengers were obliged to do the same and most of them, to their dismay, found that their weapons already had sand in them and had to be cleaned. When it became clear that most of them were unable to clean their weapons properly because of the sand still blowing, the LRDG corporals showed them how to do it blind. A towel was thrown over the weapon resting on the man's lap and the separate components were cleaned and reassembled beneath it. This process, which was frustrating and caused a lot of angry swearing, was repeated time and again until the SAS troopers got it right. And as they were soon to learn, with increasing despair, this tedious procedure was carried out every hour on the dot, greatly lengthening the time of the journey and causing a great deal of exhausting work.

Eventually, when the noon sun was almost directly overhead and the heat was truly ferocious, they stopped in the middle of what seemed like a boundless, barren wasteland, where they were told they would be making camp for the night. Shelters were raised by tying the top ends of waterproof ponchos to the protuberances of the vehicles and the bottom ends to small stakes in the ground. In some cases, where the men did not like the smell of petrol, they made similar shelters by using three-foot-long sticks as uprights instead of a vehicle's protuberances. In both cases, however, a groundsheet was spread out on the desert floor beneath the triangular poncho tent.

Exhausted already, covered in a fine layer of sweaty sand and burnt by the sun, the men crawled into their shelters with a great deal of relief, hoping to enjoy the shade as they ate a light lunch of sandwiches, known as 'wads', with hot tea and a cigarette.

Their pleasure was short-lived, as they were allowed only a thirty-minute break before being called back out into the blazing heat and informed by Wild Bill Monnery, with his grimly smiling fellow sergeant Lorrimer by his side, that they had to hump their heavy bergens onto their backs, pick up two small weapons – a rifle and a sub-machine-gun – and follow the two of them into the desert to learn navigation.

'So why do we need the bergens and weapons?' Neil Moffatt asked resentfully.

'Because we're simulating a real hike across the desert and that's what you'll be carrying.'

It was murder. They hiked for four hours and

only stopped, about every hour, to learn one of the various methods of desert navigation. After being trained in the proper use of a compass and sextant, they were shown how to make an improvised compass by stroking a sewing needle in one direction against a piece of silk and suspending it in a loop of thread so that it pointed north; by laying the needle on a piece of paper or bark and floating it on water in a cup or mess tin; or by stropping a razor blade against the palm of the hand and, as with the sewing needle, suspending it from a piece of thread to let it point north.

By last light they had learnt that although in the featureless desert maps were fairly useless, they could get a sense of direction from a combination of marked oases and drawn contour lines. Whereas the marked oases gave a specific indication of direction, the contour lines showed changes in height which represented wadis, escarpments, particular areas known for their sand dunes, and the difference between convex and concave slopes, the latter being impossible to climb and so best avoided. They also learnt how to find local magnetic variations, when not recorded on a map, by pointing their compass at the North Star and noting the difference between the pointer and the indicated north. Lastly, while the sun was still up, they were shown how to ascertain direction by planting a three-foot upright in the desert floor, marking the tip of its shadow with a pebble or stick, marking the tip of the moving shadow fifteen minutes later, and joining the two with a line which would run from east to west, thus revealing north and south as well. This was known as the 'shadow stick method'.

Once darkness fell, bringing the blessing of cool air, they were made to march even deeper into the desert. There they were taught to navigate by the timing of the rise and fall of the moon, or by the position of certain stars or constellations.

'So,' Wild Bill asked at the end of the final lesson, when the SAS men were unmistakably exhausted, 'did you understand all that?' Eager to return to base and get some sleep, the troopers either said 'Yes!' or nodded affirmatively. 'Good,' Wild Bill said, climbing up into his Chevrolet, just as the other LRDG men, along with that other experienced desert hand, Sergeant Lorrimer, were doing the same. 'If that's the case, let's see you prove it by making your own way back to the camp. Goodbye and good luck!'

Temporarily shocked speechless, the SAS troopers just stood there as the LRDG trucks roared off, churning up great clouds of sand, and eventually disappeared into the darkness, letting the eerie silence of the desert settle around the men.

'Jesus!' Frankie said, almost whispering, glancing about him at the vast, moonlit wilderness. 'This is pretty scary.'

'I'm not scared, I'm exhausted,' Neil said. 'I don't think I can walk a step.'

Taff studied the stars, recalled what he had been taught, then pointed towards the invisible horizon with his index finger. 'That way, lads. Let's go.'

They began the long hike back to the camp.

Surprisingly, they all made it back. Some had fallen behind, others had broken away from the main group and become temporarily lost, but all of them made it back somehow, albeit in the early hours of the morning and in a state of utter exhaustion.

Falling straight onto the groundsheets under their poncho covers, they attempted to sleep, but found it almost impossible. Some were too exhausted to sleep, others dozed fitfully, and all were tormented by a combination of the freezing cold and the usual swarms of fat black flies, mosquitoes and midges, which buzzed and whined constantly in their ears, seemingly oblivious to the cold. Curses exploded up and down the separate tents as the men tossed and turned and, in some instances, gave up altogether, lighting cigarettes and talking instead.

'Cor blimey,' Jimbo said to Frankie, lying next to him, 'I don't mind being in the Army, doing my bit, but this place is bloody ridiculous. For the first time since I've been away, I've been thinking of home.'

'Wapping, wasn't it?' Frankie asked.

'S'right. Good old Wapping. I was there when it took the brunt of the Blitz, but I didn't mind that. When the air-raid sirens wailed, we didn't go to the bomb shelters; we just locked the doors of the pub and sat out the bombing. Buildings ablaze all around us and the ARP and Fire Brigade at work, but we knocked back the mild and bitter and sang our songs until it was all over. They're a good lot in Wapping.'

'What about the missus?'

'What about her?'

'She all right?'

'Not bad, I suppose. I mean, I could've done worse. She kept the house clean and looked after the kids. A decent girl, really. But I joined up before the war started, so I didn't see her that much.'

'That's why you're still married.'

They both chuckled at that, inhaled and blew clouds of smoke. Allied aircraft were passing overhead, very high in the sky. When they were gone, there was silence.

'You were born in London?' Frankie asked.

'Course. Right there in Wapping. Lived there all me life, worked me old man's fruit cart, first Brewer Street, then Covent Garden, but eventually joined the TA, then went into the Army. Smart, see? I knew there was a war on the way and that if I joined up, instead of being conscripted, I'd have certain advantages. That's why I'm now a corporal and you're a private, you poor bleedin' conscript. I joined up the day England beat the Aussies at the Oval and Len Hutton had an innings of 364. I'll never forget that.'

Frankie grinned and had another drag on his cigarette. 'Don't like cricket m'self,' he said. 'I like a bit of football. I follow Arsenal 'cause that's near where I live. They have some good matches there.'

'Bleedin' Paddy Town over there. That's Finsbury Park, ain't it? All them bloody Paddies livin' off the bleedin' dole. Should send 'em back on the boat.'

'Good place, Finsbury Park. Lively. Know what I mean? The Paddies enjoy a good time in the pub, plenty of chat, and are a generous lot. There's lots of Paddies in my street and they're a good bunch. My Mum and Dad swear by them.'

'You live with your Mum and Dad?'

'Never left home,' Frankie said. 'We have a nice three-storey house in Stroud Green Road. The tube's only five minutes' walk and the buses go right past us.' Frankie's father was a train driver on the London and North-Eastern Line, between London and Newcastle, while his mother looked after the house and enjoyed her neighbours' company. 'Now there's air-raid shelters up the side streets and black-out curtains all over the show. My girlfriend's keen on black-out curtains. It makes her feel safe.'

'You mean . . .?'

'You've got it. We know we're not being watched when we do it.'

In fact, like most of his mates Frankie lied about his girlfriend Pam and only did 'it' with her in his dreams. Of course he had groped her a lot, sucked her tits, but that was about as far as he had got in the eighteen months that he had known her. She was a respectable girl from Crouch End, up the hill, which put her a cut above him – or so she thought. She wanted respect, so she had told him, and that could only mean marriage. Frankie, who had a good life at home, and was spoilt by both of his parents and two doting older sisters, had his doubts about leaving home for marriage. A man could make a mistake that way.

'Funny, ain't it?' he said.

'What?'

'The way we think about London,' Frankie went on, 'about it being divided up into areas with different classes of people, that's the way people think of the whole country. Divided between north and south, I mean. You take Neil there, and Taff Clayton – they think they're real folk up in the north while we're artificial.

'Taff Clayton's a Welshman.'

'But he thinks the same way. The Welsh and the Scots, they think just like the northerners. They think they're better – more real and genuine – than we are in the south. It's a queer thing, ain't it?'

'I wouldn't give the time of day to the north of England,' Jimbo replied. 'Nor to Scotland or Wales. A right worthless shower they are.'

'Neil and Taff are all right,' Frankie said, suddenly feeling sentimental and generous towards his mates.

'They're a pair of piss-heads,' Jimbo replied. 'They don't know the real world.'

Frankie sighed. 'Yeah, I suppose you're right.'

Jimbo mumbled something else and then started snoring. Frankie swatted the flies away and lit up another Senior Service. He could not sleep to save his life; he was just too tired.

The men were up at first light the second day, some having slept only a couple of hours, some none at all, to swallow a quick breakfast of wads and hot tea, desperately trying to protect both from the swarms of bloated black flies and mosquitoes that had driven most of them mad throughout the night.

After breakfast and a clean-up, with their mess kit put away, they had their final shit in that place and then poured petrol over the temporary latrines, lit it and burned everything. It seemed an odd thing to do in the middle of the desert, but no one thought to question it – or indeed had time to do so – as they were then obliged to hurriedly dismantle their shelters, roll and pack their groundsheets and ponchos, remove all signs of the camp, and load their gear in preparation for another drive into the desert.

Before setting off, however, they gathered around their LRDG instructors, in the already fierce heat of the morning, to receive lessons in how to maximize the use of their precious water. The first method was to clean their teeth, spit the tiny amount of water in their mouth out into a container, use that to shave with, then put it into the radiator of their vehicle. Monkey Madson then showed them how to make an improvised filtering system out of stacked four-gallon petrol cans, using a layer of sand and small stones in the top can, pouring the dirty water onto it, and letting it drip through to the lower can, when it could be recycled.

'You can also use one of these instead of the layer of sand and stones,' Monkey said, removing the filter from a captured Italian gas mask and placing it over the opening in the top can. 'So, when you've picked up your meagre water-bottle ration, you clean your teeth, swill your gob out with the water, then spit the water into the filter to run back into the can.'

'I feel ill already!' Neil said.

'Then,' Monkey continued enthusiastically, 'when you've got half a can of water, you wash your face in it and pour it back into the top can to be filtered and used again. You can even wash your socks in it, then, as before, pour the dirty water back into the can to be filtered and . . .'

'Fucking great,' Jimbo said. 'You clean your teeth with it, wash yourself with it, wash your socks and shitty underpants in it . . . and drink it as well. I don't think I'm hearing right.'

'You heard right,' Monkey told him. 'It's a

continuous recycling process and you better get used to it. Mind you, most of us don't drink the water as such; we have it as a brew-up. That way you can swallow it.'

To the amusement of the others, Taff rammed his fingers down his throat and pretended to choke and die.

'We're moving out!' Wild Bill Monnery bawled, interrupting Taff's act. 'Get to your vehicles!'

This time, when they were driven out into the fierce heat of the wilderness, they were taught to drive the Chevrolets across smooth, hard ground, up and down deep wadis and steep sand dunes, and across a rocky terrain that alternated dangerously with patches of soft sand and gravel – and to fire the weapons fixed to the vehicles while doing so.

When going through soft sand, the vehicles often became bogged down and had to be dug out; the men learnt the hard way just what the sand mats and channels fixed to the vehicles were for. Invariably, the nose of the car would be tipped right forward, the axle buried deep in the sand. Getting it out was dreadfully hard work that would have been impossible without the sand mats and channels. The former were woven mats; the latter were heavy metal channels five feet long that had originally been used in World War One as the roofing for dugouts.

First, the men had to unload all their gear from the vehicle to make it lighter. After laboriously digging and scraping the sand away from the wheels of the trapped vehicle, they pushed the sand mats under the front wheels and the steel sand channels under the rear wheels. When these were firmly in place between the wheels and the soft sand, the vehicle, with its engine running in low gear, could then be pushed forward onto a succession of other sand mats and channels until it was back on harder ground.

It was a sweaty, back-breaking, exhausting business that had to be done at least every couple of hours.

'I'll never joke about the LRDG again,' Jimbo said breathlessly to Frankie, after both of them had helped rescue their Chevrolet. 'These blokes earn their pennies!'

After a full day of this kind of activity in the relentless heat of the barren plains, the men were about ready to collapse when ordered to stop and make up a camp for their second night in the desert. However, once they had put up their poncho shelters, where they had hoped to relax while waiting for the cook to prepare the evening meal, they were dragged out by Wild Bill to be instructed in the art of desert cooking.

This lesson was given by Corporal Tod 'The Toad' Harrington, a great beast of a man who drove them crazy with hunger when, instead of cooking for them, he arrived in their midst with a portable soldering kit and took two hours showing them how to make their own cooker out of a large biscuit tin and a small cheese tin. After cutting the latter in two, he poured sand and petrol into one half, to be used as fuel. He then cut holes in two sides of the biscuit tin, put a funnel through the middle, welding it to the sides of the holes, then surrounded it with a water jacket that contained a gallon of water and could be brought to the boil in three minutes when placed over the burning petrol in the cheese tin.

'Any questions?' he asked the men sitting around him in the sand, most of them nearly demented with exhaustion and hunger.

'Yeah,' Jimbo said. 'When do we eat?'

Grinning maliciously, the Toad picked up the hard biscuits he had removed from the biscuit tin before turning it into a cooker, placed them on a large stone, then proceeded to pulverize them with the handle of his handgun. When they were completely crushed, he scraped the crumbs into the unused other half of the cheese tin, added condensed milk, jam, sugar and hot water from the modified biscuit tin, then stuck a spoon in it and handed it to Jimbo.

'*Voilà*!' the Toad exclaimed in a tone that suggested whisky had ruined his vocal cords.

Jimbo looked down in disgust at the steaming mess in the cheese tin. 'What the fuck is it?'

'Porridge!' the Toad explained proudly.

'Vomit, vomit!' Taff gurgled, again sticking his fingers down his throat.

Nevertheless, they were fed that night, not with the Toad's porridge, but with his bully beef, tinned M and V, dehydrated potatoes, herrings in tomato and some noodles obviously rifled from the Italians.

'It's an international cuisine,' the Toad explained, 'so I want no complaints.'

'We're too busy gagging to complain,' Frankie replied, 'so you've no need to worry about that.'

Attempting to sleep out in the open that night, on the cold groundsheets under their poncho tents, but otherwise exposed to the freezing cold and the relentless flies, mosquitoes and midges, which appeared able to defy the cold, Taff and Neil tossed and turned, moaned and groaned, then gave up and lit cigarettes – Taff a Woodbine, Neil a Players – and tried to pass the time with conversation.

'Amazing, isn't it?' Neil said, his words following a cloud of smoke out of his trembling lips. 'Here we are, two working-class lads who otherwise probably would never have left their home towns, in the middle of the bleeding North African desert, looking up at the stars.'

'Very poetic,' Taff said. 'I've got a lump in my throat already.'

'No, seriously, I mean it. I mean, here we are, just two common lads, and now we're members of the toughest regiment in the British Army, fighting in a desert in North Africa. It really makes you think, doesn't it?'

'How the bleedin' 'ell did *you* get in the Army?' Taff asked him, not being in the mood for philosophy.

'I was a weekend soldier,' Neil replied solemnly. 'Territorial Army. I volunteered in my local drill hall, in Blackburn. On 11 April 1939 – the day Glasgow banned darts in pubs as too dangerous. That's how I'll always remember it. I mean, what kind of people would stoop to that? Bleeding mad, those Scots are.'

Taff recalled the first air-raid shelters, the evacuation of the children from the cities, the eerie silence when the kids had left; then the beginning of the war, the first air-raids, the pounding ack-ack guns and exploding flak, the German bombers and Spitfires, the blazing, crumbling buildings of bombed cities. He thought of all that and wondered how on earth Neil could only remember the day he had volunteered to fight as the day darts were banned from Glaswegian pubs. You wouldn't credit it, would you?

'Aye, right,' he said, getting back to mad Scots. 'We should send them all to Blackburn, where they'd seem perfectly sane.'

'Ha, ha,' Neil said. 'How did *you* get in the Army? Volunteered as well, did you?'

'Are you bloody mad? You think I've got a hole in *my* head? I'd rather be down in the coal mines of Aberfan – that's where I lived and worked, mate – than takin' a lot of bloody shite from English Army thickheads. I didn't *volunteer*, mate. I was bloody conscripted. I tried sayin' I was doin' a job that was in the national interest, but the bastards replied that bein' single I could serve better elsewhere. They then put me on the bus with all the others and drove me away from the village. Booted me into boot camp, then into the Welsh Guards. So, here I am, mate.'

'Not only in L Detachment, SAS, but now a

corporal to boot. If you hate the Army so much, how did you manage that?'

Taff puffed a cloud of smoke while tapping his temple with his forefinger and giving Neil the wink. 'No screws lost here, mate. I made the best of a bad thing. I was good at soldiering, see? I mean, the mines toughened me up. So when I saw that I was good, I thought what the hell, and decided to milk it for all it was worth by tryin' to get a quick promotion. Worked my fanny off, ended up in Tripoli, and was shipped on leave to Alexandria just before Jerry surrounded Tobruk. Then, while still on leave, I read Captain Stirling's memo about that meeting in Geneifa and thought there might be something in it for me. When I heard him talkin' I figured he might be a man goin' places, so I decided to volunteer to go with him. Now, here I am, in the middle of the North African desert, gazing up at the stars. I feel a right bleedin' Charlie!'

He stubbed his cigarette out, lit another, and blew a couple of smoke rings. One of them ringed the pale moon and then dissolved into it.

'You're not a Charlie,' Neil told him. 'You're a good soldier, Taff'. I mean, you come from Wales and the Welsh are like northerners: they're real folk, they endure, they have qualities you don't find in the south. Know what I mean, Taff?'

'The bloody English!' Taff exclaimed. 'I mean those bastards from the south. I don't mean the northerners like you – they're a good-hearted lot – but them Londoners and the like, they all have airs and graces, even if they come from the working class.'

'Jimbo's all right.'

'I'll give you that. He's not bad. But that Frankie from Finsbury Park, he thinks he's cock o' the walk.'

'It's being born in the south, being a Londoner, that makes him that way. He can't help it.'

'They'd blunt his tongue in Aberfan,' Taff replied, 'if he wagged it as much as he does with us. Still, he's all right, I reckon.'

'A good soldier,' Neil said.

'That's why he's here,' Taff said. 'As Jimbo said, L Detachment is the cream de la cream and that makes us somethin' special, see?'

Receiving no response, he glanced to the side and saw the cigarette fall from Neil's fingers and drop into the drifting sand. It smouldered there for a minute, the smoke curling upwards, spiralling in front of Neil's closed eyes before vaporizing. By the time it had gone out, Neil had started snoring.

'Silly sod!' Taff whispered, then he too closed his weary eyes and was soon fast asleep.

The third day was taken up with desert survival, including tactics for avoiding dehydration, sunstroke and sunburn; locating and using artesian wells; hunting desert gazelles for food; the correct disposal of garbage and human waste; desert camouflage and the digging of shallow 'scrapes' and other lying-up positions; treatment of the bites of poisonous spiders, scorpions and snakes, or illness caused by lice, mites, flies and mosquitoes; using condoms to keep dust out of weapons; constructing a desert still to produce drinkable water from urine; and avoiding drowning when caught in a wadi during a flash flood.

'Drowning in the desert!' Frankie laughed. 'You wouldn't credit it, would you?'

Though close to serious exhaustion, he was actually in a good mood because he and the others had just about survived the long day and were scheduled to return to Jalo Oasis that evening, when they could have a decent meal in the mess tent, get drunk in their own tents, and have a desperately needed sleep on a real camp-bed.

For that very reason he almost went into a state

of shock when told by Wild Bill – while Sergeant Lorrimer smiled sadistically right there beside him – that they would indeed be returning that evening – but they had to do it on foot, navigating in the darkness by themselves.

'That should get you back to the oasis by first light,' Wild Bill said. 'Always assuming, of course, that you don't get lost.'

Frankie was not the only soldier who almost gave up there and then, but in the event neither he nor any of the other SAS troopers did. Encouraged by those temporarily less exhausted, they began the long march. They managed to keep going and even repaid a debt by encouraging those who had encouraged them and who, suddenly exhausted, were themselves about to give up. All in all, then, they learned to lean on one another until, just before first light, they all finally made it back. They were a sorry sight to behold, but their pride was obvious.

Impressed, Sergeant Lorrimer let them all have a fry-up washed down with cold beer, followed by a shower and a sleep that lasted till noon.

When they were up dressed, they were called to Stirling's tent, where they were told by the tall, aristocratic captain that the rest of the day was free, but that the following morning they would begin their preparations for the raids against the German airfields.

'Ready, willing and able,' Jimbo said.

He spoke for every one of them.

9

Pleased with the report from Sergeant Monnery on the successful training of the SAS troopers in the desert, Captain Stirling left the Jalo Oasis after dawn on Sunday 8 December, a couple of days earlier than originally planned, to raid the airfield at Sirte.

'I'm anxious to get on with it,' he explained to Brigadier Reid, 'because we could be recalled to Cairo any time. There are still too many officers on the GHQ staff who prefer more orthodox methods of warfare and resent what we're doing out here. They tend to think that L Detachment – and the LRDG as well – are using the guerrilla-warfare tactics of which they so strongly disapprove. In fact, when last I was in Cairo one of those bloody fools told me that this was an ungentlemanly way to fight – one not suited to the forces of the British Empire. That particular officer may be a pompous idiot, but he has many friends.'

'I agree,' Reid said as they shared a cup of tea in his big tent near one of the palm-fringed pools of the oasis. Through the open flaps, between the tent and the pool, the trucks of the first patrol, camouflaged pink and green to blend in with the desert, were gathered together, surrounded by the LRDG and SAS men preparing to leave. 'You'd better get out of here before they stop you – and nothing's lost if you're early. Gives you time for a little mistake or two. Time to change your plans if necessary. Are all the patrols leaving today?'

'No. I want to make the maximum use of surprise, so Captain Lewes will be attacking Agheila airfield the same night as the other patrols hit Sirte.'

'That's only half the distance that you have to travel.'

'Exactly. So although we're attacking the same night, Lewes won't be setting out with S Patrol until two days after I leave.'

'Who's taking you, David?'

'S1 Patrol.

'Commanded by Captain Gus Halliman – a good man.'

'Indeed.' Stirling glanced back over his shoulder

and saw that the last of the men had taken his place in his Chevrolet. 'They're all set to leave,' Stirling said. 'I'd best be going.' He stood up and offered his hand to the brigadier. The two men shook hands.

'Good luck and God speed,' Reid said warmly.

'Thank you, sir,' Stirling replied, then left the tent, climbed into his designated Chevrolet lorry, and nodded to Captain Halliman, indicating that they could now start the journey. Halliman nodded back, then raised and lowered his right hand. The lorries all roared into life simultaneously, then moved out of the oasis, churning up billowing clouds of sand in their wake. They soon reached the vast open plains of the desert where, with the force of a hammer, the sun's blazing heat hit them.

Halliman, a big-boned, fair-haired Englishman, led his mainly Rhodesian drivers with the confidence of a man who knew the desert well. In fact, he had served in the Royal Tank Corps before joining the LRDG, but his experience with the latter was considerable and now he was one of their best men. He rode in the leading truck with his navigator, Mike Sadler, another Rhodesian.

Stirling and Captain 'Paddy' Callaghan were in the second truck with their nine SAS troopers perched all around them where they could get a footing on the piles of gear. Indeed, each of the seven trucks was close to being overloaded with petrol, water-cans, blankets, camouflage nets, weapons, ammunition, and the seventeen other men of the LRDG. However, the LRDG put great faith in the reinforced springs of their vehicles and so drove on into the dazzling light of the desert with calm confidence.

'I hope these Rhodesian bastards know where they're going,' Jimbo said, not as confident as the drivers appeared to be. 'I don't want to be lost in this bleedin' desert.'

'I think we're in safe hands,' Frankie told him. 'They seem pretty capable.'

'I'll believe it when I see it, my old mate. For now, I'm keeping a tight arse.'

'I'll stop holding my nose then.'

The LRDG men worked to a routine that was automatically followed by the SAS troopers. As the day warmed up, they shed the sheepskin jackets that kept out the chill of the early hours. By 1000 hours the sun was well up in the sky, at over 20 degrees, throwing a sharp shadow from the needle of the sun compass so bright that it started to hurt the men's eyes. An hour later the blasts of warm air on the ridge tops had forced the gunners perched high on each lorry to discard most of their clothes. By noon, with the sun almost directly above them and the desert plain had taken on a stark, white lunar quality, the vehicles were halted in the shadow of a steep wadi side where they would not be seen by overflying enemy aircraft.

'Thank Christ for that,' Jimbo said as Mike Sadler took a fix on the sun through the smoked glass of his theodolite, the radio operator contacted base for any fresh orders, and the rest of the men lay under the shade of a tarpaulin stretched between two trucks. 'You could have fried a bloody egg on my head, it was getting so hot.'

'I feel like gagging in this heat,' Frankie replied, 'it dries my throat out so.'

'Hey, Taff!' Jimbo called out to the Welshman, who was sitting in the shade of his own truck, smoking. 'Is that dark stain around your crutch sweat or have you just been tugging it off again?'

Taff stared steadily, sardonically, at Jimbo, then thoughtfully blew a couple of smoke rings and watched them dissolving. 'At least I've got something to tug,' he said. 'I have my doubts about you, lad.'

Jimbo grinned. He always enjoyed a good comeback. 'I'm told the Welsh are very good at singing when they reach the crescendo.'

'We always climax well,' Taff responded, 'and leave the audience gasping.'

'With horror, no doubt.'

'On your feet!' Sergeant Lorrimer roared. 'Move it! Let's go!'

'He can sing even better than you,' Jimbo said to Taff, as they climbed to their feet with the others.

'Right,' Taff said. 'A heavenly choir. It reverberates endlessly. Well, here we go again.'

By early afternoon they had left Jalo well behind them and were heading for El Agheila, across the perfectly smooth, hard sand of a vast landscape, with the sheer cliffs of the upland plateaux visible beyond the heat haze in the north and alluvial sand dunes, awesomely beautiful, rising and falling to the west. For most of the afternoon the heat was truly appalling, felt particularly on the head even through the black woollen *agal* and *shemagh*, but it cooled to more bearable levels in the late afternoon, when Halliman started looking out for a place to laager before last light. By the time he had found a suitable spot, again in a shaded wadi, the patrol had travelled over 90 miles from Jalo. Luckily, the day had been without incident other than the usual punctures, trucks bogged down in soft sand and the minor repairs required after motoring over grit, sand and rock. They had not seen any sign of the enemy; nor had they caught a glimpse of a single Arab.

'This place is as empty as the far side of the moon,' Callaghan said to Stirling. 'We're the only ones here.'

'I wouldn't bet on that,' Halliman said, climbing down from the lorry. 'Don't relax for a second.'

When the vehicles laagered, they parked across the wind. Each driver then pinned the folded tarpaulin by two wheels on the lee side, with the upper half forming a windbreak and the lower a groundsheet. Before resting, however, the LRDG drivers had to check their day's petrol consumption and make the usual maintenance checks, including water, oil, tyres and the possible clogging of the carburettor with sand. While the drivers were doing this, the SAS were checking and cleaning their weapons with equal thoroughness, even though they had already tried to protect them from the sand by wrapping them, to the accompaniment of many ribald remarks and howls of laughter, in stretched condoms.

Meanwhile, the cooks had a fire going (which almost certainly would be mistaken for an Arab camp fire by Axis aircraft flying overhead) and water on the boil for a brew of tea. When this was ready, the men drank it gratefully, smoked a lot of cigarettes, washed themselves as best they could, trying to get rid of the blend of sweat and sand, and then tucked in enthusiastically to the 'international cuisine' dreamt up by the immense Corporal Harrington. It was some kind of bully-beef curry and it wasn't half bad.

Afterwards the men stretched out under the trucks and tried to sleep as best they could, given that the night was bitterly cold and that the buzzing flies and whining mosquitoes were oblivious to it. You could hardly call it a restful night.

The following morning Captain Stirling received a signal from Jalo stating that the main battle was static, with Rommel at Gazala and the Eighth Army reorganizing for a further advance. Now even more confident that they were doing the right thing, he passed the news on to Halliman, who, over the next two days, moved the patrol steadily north-westwards towards Sirte.

Just before the midday halt on the third day, approximately 65 miles south of Sirte, an Italian Gibli fighter plane, lightly armed but highly manœuvrable, appeared seemingly out of nowhere, its wings glinting like silver in the clear blue sky.

It banked to begin its attack descent.

'Damn!' Stirling exclaimed. 'That blighter could radio our position back to his HQ.'

'He could also blow us to Kingdom Come,' Halliman replied, glancing back at the rest of his column, which was crossing a rocky stretch of desert at a mere 6 mph with no shelter in sight. 'That's all *I* need to know.' He turned to his black-bearded Rhodesian gunner and snapped, 'Open fire!'

The Boyes anti-tank rifle roared into life, firing a hail of bullets and tracer at the Gibli as it barrelled down out of the azure sky, its own machine-guns hammering as it dived and making the sand spit in long, jagged lines that snaked towards the slow-moving vehicles. The other LRDG gunners also opened fire, but failed to hit the plane as it dropped its two bombs. It levelled out, roared very low overhead and ascended again, just as the bombs exploded with a deafening roar.

Sand and soil erupted in mushrooming smoke to the east of the column, showering the men as it rained back down again. The Italian plane flew off and disappeared into the heat haze as the exploded sand and soil settled, some of it still smouldering, and the black smoke trailed away, revealing two enormous charred holes in the desert plain's bleached white surface, mere yards from the trucks, which continued to move forward, untouched.

'Close one,' Stirling said.

'We didn't hit that bastard,' Halliman reminded the others, 'and he's flown back to his base. Before very long, his friends will come back to look for us. We'd better go into hiding.' He turned around in the lorry and raised his right hand, indicating 'Stop'. Then, when the other drivers had come to a halt, he swung the same hand out from the hip and back in again, indicating 'Follow me'. He then told his Rhodesian driver to backtrack to where he had seen a patch of scrub that could be the basis for a camouflaged position. When they arrived there and Halliman could survey the area properly, he realized that there was not enough scrub to camouflage the vehicles but just enough, in combination with the camouflage nets, to give decent cover.

Turning to Wild Bill Monnery, he said: 'Sergeant, tell the men to form a laager inside this area of scrub and then fling their cam nets over the vehicles and move well clear of them. Also, get some of the men to hike out to where we were and erase all signs of our tracks from our main route to here. There's no point in trying to fight off an air attack, as any machine-gun fire will only draw attention to the vehicles hidden under the netting. So tell the men to simply lie low until the enemy planes have come and gone. Then we'll move on.'

When Monnery conveyed Halliman's orders to the men, they did as they were told, the drivers forming a tight laager close to the scrub, other men covering the trucks with camouflage nets, and some of them hiking back out to where they had been attacked, to erase the tracks of the trucks by brushing the sand over them as they made their way back to the laager.

With their woven shreds of desert-coloured hessian, the nets blended perfectly with the surrounding shrub, making the lorries practically invisible from the air. The vehicles' tracks, though trailing back across the desert where the column had come from, stopped dead where the column had been attacked. From the air it would now be difficult to know where the column had gone.

Still in their parked vehicles, almost suffocating under the heavy camouflage nets, the men waited for the Italian aircraft to arrive. No one spoke. The tension was contagious. Eventually, after what seemed like hours, but was in fact forty minutes, three Italian bombers flew overhead, searching for the tracks of the vehicles. They found only the tracks well away from the patch of scrub and turned back to strafe that area and also drop a number of small bombs. The explosions, when they came, were both noisy and spectacular, great mushrooms of sand, soil and smoke, but they destroyed nothing more than the desert's formerly unblemished surface.

'My compliments,' Stirling whispered to Halliman. 'That was a good idea.'

Halliman just grinned.

Once the clouds of sand and dust had settled, the Italian aircraft departed and the men picked themselves up and went back to their vehicles. No one was hurt and no damage had been done – not even a tyre punctured – so the men settled down to a lunch of wads and tinned fruit. The latter, in particular, drove the flies and mosquitoes into a frenzy of buzzing and whining.

'We'll move off again at 1400 hours,' Halliman told Stirling and Paddy Callaghan as they had their meagre lunch in the shade of the former's Chevrolet. 'We intend dropping you and your men off at a point about three miles from Sirte and approximately the same distance from the coast road – far closer to Axis traffic than we'd normally take vehicles when on reconnaissance. We should be there by midnight.'

'You've done a damned good job so far,' Paddy Callaghan said. 'Very impressive. I must say.'

'What we do, we do well,' Halliman replied. 'I think that's something you understand.'

'Absolutely!' Stirling affirmed.

Halliman grinned. 'I knew you'd say that. Now it's time to move on.'

The following five hours were uneventful, other than for the expected difficulties, all of which, combined, doubled the time the same journey would have taken on a decent road and trebled the workload of the already exhausted men.

To add to their frustration, a second Italian fighter plane spotted them just before last light, when they only had 40 miles to go. It swept down unexpectedly, making a dreadful din, to rake the convoy with its machine-guns, then drop its two little bombs. As before, the explosions were catastrophic but well off the mark, creating a spectacle of mushrooming sand, dust and smoke, but doing no damage to the column. Having run out of ammunition, the pilot eventually flew away.

'Charming people, the Italians,' Stirling said, 'but obviously as blind as bats.'

'That's why you're charmed by them,' Callaghan told him. 'You think the Eyeties are harmless.'

The column pressed on, now closed up in convoy

formation, no longer spread out as a precaution against an air attack.

'No point,' Halliman explained. 'We're practically there.'

They covered the last 20 miles without using their headlights, which made for a bumpy, dangerous ride. Eventually, as most of them suspected would happen, a bad combination of unseen pothole and soft sand led to another vehicle, the last in the convoy, being bogged down only 1600 yards from the DZ selected by Halliman.

It was clear that it would take a long time to dig out the lorry.

'Damn!' Stirling exploded as a bunch of his men hurried to rescue the bogged-down vehicle with sand mats and steel channels. 'This could cause complications.'

'Damned right, it could,' Callaghan replied. 'It could take hours to dig out the bloody thing.'

'And the pilot of that last Gibli,' Halliman added, 'is bound to alert his fellow Eyeties to our presence here. A change of plan is called for.'

Standing upright in the rear of the Chevrolet, glancing at the darkening desert plain all around him, clearly boiling up with frustration, Stirling lit a consoling cigarette, blew a cloud of smoke, then nodded, as if at a ghost, and finally spoke.

'Right!' He turned to Callaghan. 'If we fail to hit Sirte, we'll attack at least one other airfield and the way to do that is to break up. There's a new airfield at Tamit, about 30 miles west of here, and I want you, Paddy, to take eight men and hit it.'

'Right, boss.'

'Meanwhile, Sergeant Lorrimer and I will take a patrol on foot to raid Sirte.'

'Sounds good to me, boss.'

Stirling checked his watch, then looked up again. 'We'll both plan to set off our charges at 2300 hours tomorrow night. When that's done, Sergeant Lorrimer and I will rendezvous with Captain Halliman back here. The other six lorries – three for each party – will pick up the rest of the raiders in the early hours of the next morning, Friday, and travel independently to the desert RV.' He turned to Halliman. 'Is this feasible?'

Halliman shrugged. 'Who dares wins,' he said.

10

Before the two groups could separate, Corporal Mike Sadler, the LRDG navigator who had been checking their position with a combination of map reading and eyeball recce, returned to Halliman's truck to say that they were far closer to the coast road than he had expected.

'It's lucky we didn't go a further 1600 yards to the north,' he said, 'because there the road bends southwards in a way that isn't shown on this bloody map.'

'What does that mean?' Stirling asked.

'It means we're practically on the perimeter of the Sirte airfield,' Halliman said. 'Practically in the lap of the Germans. It means they could be all around us already and we'd better be careful.'

Even as he was speaking, he thought he heard a distant sound, so he used a hand signal – still just about visible in the evening's dying light – to tell the other drivers to switch off their engines. When they did so, the distant sounds became clearer. First they heard barely distinguishable voices, then the growling of a road-patrol vehicle gathering speed as it moved off.

'That confirms it,' Halliman said. 'Those Gibli pilots have reported our presence in the area and Jerry's now on the alert for a raid against the traffic going along that sea road.'

'It's a Jerry MSR,' Sergeant Lorrimer reminded them, 'so they're bound to be doubly concerned.'

'Then we'd better get started,' Stirling said. 'Get this over and done with before they launch a full-scale search.' He turned to Lorrimer. 'I don't want any tell-tale footprints showing that we separated from the main patrol and headed for Sirte, so let's get ready to jump off a good distance from here, where Jerry's not likely to look for us. Let's get on the running board.'

'Right, boss.' Even as Sadler turned on the ignition and moved off, Lorrimer was clambering over the side to stand on the narrow running board and cling to the door. Because he was carrying a bag of Lewes bombs and fuses, as well as his heavy rucksack, this was more precarious for him than it was for Stirling. As the Chevrolet picked up speed, followed by the others, Stirling did the same at the other side of the vehicle, hanging on precariously and being dragged down by his rucksack while also being whipped by the snapping slipstream.

When the lorry was a good half mile from where the patrol had stopped, still travelling at a mere 15 mph and heading west for the new airfield at Tamit, Stirling shouted, 'Now!' He then threw his carefully wrapped Sten gun to the ground and jumped off the running board.

His parachute training stood him in good stead. Deliberately bending his legs when his feet touched the ground, he let his body relax, tried not to resist the impact, and rolled over a few times, choking in the dust created by his fall, but otherwise unharmed. When he picked himself up, resting there on his knees, he saw Lorrimer doing the same a few yards away. As the sergeant clambered to his feet, brushing the dust off his clothing, he was wearing a big, cheesy grin.

'I'm getting too old for this,' he said, 'but that made me feel like a schoolboy.'

'Me, too,' Stirling said. Looking west, he saw the last of the trucks of S1 patrol, already obscured by dust boiling up in their wake, then eventually disappearing into the darkness.

'Best of luck,' he murmured, then he and Lorrimer looked around for their weapons and the bag of

Lewes bombs. After finding them, they removed the padded wrapping from the weapons and cleaned them thoroughly. This done, Lorrimer picked up the bag of Lewes bombs and fuses, then nodded at Stirling. 'Let's go,' said the latter.

They hiked side by side through the growing darkness, being careful to stay low and listening intently for the sounds of German patrols. The desert plain was hard, a pale white in the moonlit darkness, its flat surface running out to an escarpment overlooking the Mediterranean. It was covered with a fine film of dust, stirred by the wind blowing in from the sea and constantly drifting.

Suddenly, coming up over a low ridge, they saw a group of Italian soldiers marching along in file formation on routine patrol. Throwing themselves to the ground, they waited for the patrol to pass, a mere 15 yards away. Climbing to their feet again, the two SAS men hurried off in the opposite direction, heading away from the escarpment overlooking the sea, down the northern slope, towards the Sirte airfield.

Being much closer to the airfield than they had expected, practically on its perimeter, they soon found themselves making their way between its outer buildings which, to their surprise, were neither fenced in nor guarded. Once past the buildings, they came to the dispersal area, again without hindrance, where they saw a row of unguarded Axis aircraft.

'Italian Capronis,' Lorrimer whispered.

'Very nice, too,' Stirling said. 'Just waiting for a necklace of Lewes bombs and a baptism of fire and smoke.'

'They're certainly tempting,' Lorrimer whispered. 'Why not do it right now?'

'Because by blowing them up now we'd alert them to what we're up to and jeopardize S1's chance of success at Tamit.'

'So what do we do in the meantime?'

'We recce the airfield and plan tomorrow's raid, then we get the hell out of here and find a safe hide.'

'Sounds fair enough to me, boss.'

After counting the aircraft – there were thirty in all – they moved on, circling the airfield and taking note of anything that might help them when they returned as raiders. They saw the odd German guard here and there, wandering lazily to and fro, rifles slung across their shoulders, but they all seemed half asleep and the recce was completed without problems.

Until, on the way back out of the airfield, Stirling

stumbled over the body of an Italian sentry sleeping on the ground.

The man jerked upright automatically, throwing off his blanket. Seeing Stirling and Lorrimer, he yelled a warning, alerting the whole garrison, then reached frantically for his rifle. Stirling kicked the weapon out of the Italian's reach, then he and Lorrimer ran like the wind back the way they had come.

The snap of a firing semi-automatic rifle behind them was followed by the sound of bullets whipping past their heads as the guard they had awakened fired after them. To avoid the rifle fire, they made a sharp left, rolled down a dip in the upward slope, then climbed back to their feet and ran on towards the escarpment. The sentry behind them stopped firing – probably to run back towards the airfield to tell his friends which way the Englishmen had gone.

As Stirling and Lorrimer were hurrying up the slope north of the airfield, sirens started to wail and the guns of the garrison, large and small, began firing out to sea. This noisy barrage soon developed into a full-blown shadow fire-fight as the men in the garrison tried to prevent an imagined assault from the sea or, even worse in their view, from enemy troops advancing inland. The tracers from their anti-aircraft guns looped in beautiful, phosphorescent-purple lines towards the sea, criss-crossing in the dark sky, exploding in black clouds of flak above the water just beyond the escarpment. To the initial clamour of the big guns was added the savage roar of numerous machine-guns and, in one instance of obvious panic, the distant thud of a firing mortar whose shell exploded with a mighty eruption of earth and smoke further down the slope.

Once on the hillside, Stirling and Lorrimer turned east and zigzagged along the edge of the escarpment, under an umbrella of tracer and exploding flak, until they were well away from where the guard would have reckoned them to be. Eventually, feeling safer, they crawled into a patch of bushes, carefully covered themselves with foliage, and watched the rest of the spectacular, colourful fire-fight directed at a non-existent invasion force.

'We really stirred up a hornet's nest there,' Lorrimer said with a grin.

'Yes,' Stirling replied. 'They can't work out if we're attacking by air, sea or land, but they certainly think we've arrived.'

'Do you think they'll come out to find us?'

'No. I think they'll dig in, reinforce their defensive positions and wait for the assault they imagine is about to commence. We're probably fairly safe here.'

'But we're stuck here until tomorrow night.'

'I could do with a good sleep,' Stirling said, 'and that's what I'm going to have.'

He turned on his side, tugged the foliage closer over him, used his rucksack as a pillow and went to sleep quickly. Sighing, thinking he could not possibly sleep in such circumstances, Lorrimer nevertheless did the same, though with his body bent up in a foetal position, wrapped around the bag of Lewes bombs and fuses.

In fact, he too fell asleep within minutes of the end of the firing from the airfield, which left a vast silence only broken by the distant murmur of the sea. The sergeant slept like a log.

When he awoke, just after dawn, Lorrimer found Stirling already awake and scanning the surrounding area with his binoculars. Now, in the early morning light, they found themselves with a good view of the beach dunes to the north, the white houses of Sirte to the west, and, most importantly, their targets at the bottom of the escarpment.

After studying the airfield with some care, Stirling lowered the binoculars and turned to Lorrimer. 'Well,' he said, 'I don't think we can approach the airfield the same way tonight. Every gun in the garrison is probably aimed in that direction. Instead, I suggest we approach by their eastern flank, directly down this hill, sneaking in from the side. Agreed?'

'Agreed.'

Stirling smiled. 'You still look tired, Sergeant.'

'We only slept a couple of hours.'

'That's true enough. My own eyes feel as heavy as lead, so I think I'll rest them again. I strongly recommend you do the same. You'll wake refreshed.'

'I couldn't possibly wake feeling worse, so I'll take your advice.'

Having selected the route by which they would get to the thirty aircraft that night, both men stretched out once more and went back to sleep.

11

They were awoken by the sound of voices and looked up at the same time, seeing only the dazzling azure sky and realizing, from the height of the sun, as well as the appalling heat, that it was still only noon. Not saying a word and trying to move as little as possible, they turned their heads in the direction of the voices and saw two Arab girls, both wearing black veils, stooped over as they toiled with mattocks on one of the few cultivated patches of fertile earth in the surrounding desert.

Stirling and Lorrimer glanced at one another, but again said nothing, fearful that the two girls would hear them. Again studying the girls, they saw that they were intent on their work and had no idea of the presence of two men hiding under the hedges behind them. Unfortunately, there was nothing that Stirling and Lorrimer could do other than wait until the girls had finished their work and left. That could be a long wait.

In fact, it was three hours, during which time Stirling and Lorrimer were forced to lie motionless in their hide, making not a sound, trying not to sneeze, unable even to flex their cramped muscles or relieve their straining bowels. Eventually, however, in the late afternoon, the girls finished work and departed.

'Thank Christ for that,' Stirling said, stretching his long body, flexing his muscles and taking deep breaths to encourage a general relaxation. 'I thought they would never leave.'

'They may have left too late,' Lorrimer replied, pointing at the sky.

Glancing over his shoulder and instantly despairing, Stirling saw that the Italian Capronis were taking off from the airfield and heading inland. They were lifting off two or three at a time and soon an awful lot of them were airborne.

'Oh, damn!' he exclaimed softly. 'I don't believe it!'

'They must be flying to the front,' Lorrimer said, 'to make night attacks against our transports. There go our targets.'

This much was true. As Stirling and Lorrimer looked on in horrified fascination, all the aircraft they had come so far to destroy took off and disappeared beyond the horizon. So agitated was Stirling that he counted them off as they left – 'Fifteen . . . seventeen . . . twenty . . . twenty-three . . .' – mouthing the words silently, in despair, until he had counted a total of thirty and then there were no more.

Every single Caproni spotted on the runway had flown away, leaving nothing to attack. They had gone there for nothing.

Stirling's silent gestures spoke eloquently of his despair. He simply dropped his forehead onto his crooked arm and let it rest there for some time as he took deep, even breaths, trying to soothe his racing heart and subdue his frustration. He remained like that for a long time, as if frozen by dejection, then eventually raised his head again and glanced at the sky, then all around him and finally at Lorrimer.

'I'm think I'm going crazy,' he said. 'I simply cannot accept this.'

'You were always crazy, boss,' Lorrimer replied, 'but you'll just have to accept it. Our targets have gone.'

Lying belly-down, Stirling rested one elbow on the ground, cupped his chin in his hand and gazed first out to sea, then west to the blood-red sun just above the desert's horizon. He stayed in that position for some time, as inscrutable as the Sphinx, then finally sighed, raised himself to his knees and spread his hands as if releasing a trapped bird.

'No use crying over spilt milk,' he said. 'Let's just pray that the others do better than we did. As for us, we might as well go back to the RV and wait for Captain Halliman to pick us up. Not much else to do, is there?'

'Not really,' Lorrimer said, though not without noting the acute disappointment in Stirling's voice. 'It's the luck of the draw, boss.'

After slinging their rucksacks onto their backs, and with Lorrimer again carrying the bag of Lewes bombs and fuses, they headed back to the road in the fading light. Feeling the weight of Stirling's despondency as they made the short hike, Lorrimer was relieved when they reached the road in darkness, just before midnight, and saw flashes and the glow of fires in the far distance, illuminating the western horizon.

'That's Captain Callaghan's group,' he told Stirling, filling up with excitement. 'Tamit's on fire!'

'They've succeeded,' Stirling replied, looking as if he wanted to sprout wings and fly. 'Those flashes are bombs going off. It wasn't *all* wasted, Sergeant!'

Impulsively, they hugged one another, then, getting their senses back, hurried to hide by the side of the road before any Axis traffic came along and saw them.

'Damn it,' Stirling said, 'I can hardly contain myself. We can't just sit here and watch those bombs going off on Tamit airfield. We've got to do *something*.'

Lorrimer glanced up and down the dark road, looking for oncoming Axis traffic. When he saw that nothing was coming, he patted the heavy bag at his feet.

'I have a couple of small land-mines here,' he said, 'so let's plant the buggers.'

'Better than carrying them back,' Stirling responded. 'Yes, damn it, let's do it!'

While Stirling kept watch, Lorrimer unpacked the three small land-mines he had been carrying with the Lewes bombs. After scooping out enough earth to bury them slightly and cover them up again, he spaced them out at equal distances across the road. No traffic came along as he was doing this and soon he was back beside Stirling, hiding in a dip between the road and the desert.

'If Halliman comes along first,' Stirling said, 'let's make sure *he* doesn't drive over the mines.'

'He'll come in off the desert,' Lorrimer said,

'coming right up behind us. We've no need for concern there.'

With nothing else to do but wait, they took the cold food from their rucksacks and ate it while watching the silvery light of the distant explosions in Tamit, which made them feel better. They had finished the food and were just opening their water bottles when an Italian Army oil lorry came along the road from the direction of Sirte, almost certainly heading for the airfield.

Stirling and Lorrimer dropped low, forgetting their thirst, and watched keenly as the huge tanker trundled along the road and ran straight on to the buried land-mines.

The mines went off simultaneously under the front of the vehicle, blowing the surface of the road apart and lifting the driver's cabin right off the ground on a fountain of shattered tarmac with soil and sand spewing up around it. Even as the cabin was rising up and toppling over, the back of the tanker kept moving forward, propelled by its own momentum, and bounced up off the cabin to form a screeching tangle of steel over the confusion of soil and smoke. Then the cabin turned over, smashing sideways onto the road, and the tanker, crashing down onto the cabin, was caught in the heat and force of the exploding land-mines and exploded with even more force, spewing the vivid-yellow fire of blazing oil into the smoke-blackened sky.

The noise was unbelievable, almost palpable in its force, making Stirling and Lorrimer cover their ears, even as the awesome heat from the burning oil swept over them in what seemed like a series of separate, accelerating, scorching blasts. The ground shook beneath them when the tanker crashed back down, bounced once or twice, belching out even more burning oil, then finally settled at the far side of the road in a pool of fire that filled the sky above with billowing black smoke.

In the flames, in that circle of dazzling yellow fire, the steel frame of the tanker, already scorched black, was melting like tar and dripping onto the melting tarmac of the road. The men in the driver's cabin, killed instantly by the blast, were turned into dripping fat and charred, crumbling bone that would, when the flames had died down, be no more than dust.

'Christ!' Lorrimer exclaimed softly. 'I wasn't expecting . . .'

Stirling cut him short by placing his hand on his wrist and gently shaking it. 'A lot of Axis planes will now go short of petrol,' he said. 'We've just done our bit, Sergeant.'

Nevertheless, the fiercely burning vehicle was

bound to draw the attention of the Axis forces in the airfield, so Stirling and Lorrimer were greatly relieved when, at the agreed time, almost to the minute, at 0015 hours, Captain Halliman returned in his LRDG truck to pick them up and drive them back to the desert RV. He glanced at the blazing oil tanker and said, 'What the . . .?'

'Let's go,' Stirling said.

Halliman's driver took them 90 miles across the desert, stopping only to repair the odd puncture, and had them back at the RV by eight the next morning.

'How did it go with Callaghan?' was the first question asked by Stirling when he entered the radio room in Jalo base camp.

12

Captain Callaghan's group had spent an uneventful Thursday before being dropped by the LRDG within striking distance of the Tamit airfield. When the trucks had moved off again, Callaghan glanced around him and saw that he was in the middle of a flat desert plain with no cover whatsoever, other than starlit darkness. The airfield, however, was only a few miles due west and could be seen in the distance, its hangars visible as rectangular blocks darker than the night and framed by the stars. An MSR ran straight through the desert directly to the airfield.

'We're completely exposed out here,' Callaghan told his second-in-command, Jim 'Jimbo' Ashman, 'so let's get there as quickly as humanly possible. Single file. Let's hike it.'

Jimbo raised his right hand with the palm open, to indicate 'Single file', and the men obeyed his silent command, moving out behind him and Callaghan one by one, until they had formed a long, irregular line with Jimbo out front as lead scout, Frankie Turner coming up the rear as Tail-end Charlie, and the rest of the men covering firing arcs to the left and right.

Callaghan, close behind Jimbo, was carrying the bag filled with Lewes bombs and fuses, as well as a Thompson M1928 sub-machine-gun with a 50-round drum magazine. The rest of the men were armed with tommy-guns, Sten guns and Lee-Enfield .303-inch bolt-action rifles. Everyone in the group was also carrying a Browning 9mm High Power handgun holstered at the waist, but otherwise they were travelling light, with no cumbersome rucksacks, or even water bottles, to slow them down. The only sound as they hiked across the flat plain was the clanking of weapons.

Little could be seen in the dark other than the outlying hangars and other buildings of the airfield, which loomed larger and became more detailed as the patrol advanced on them. Surprisingly, there was no fencing around the airstrip and no sentries had so far been seen. Out to the side of the buildings the aircraft were lined up along the runway, a mixture of German Ju-87 Stuka dive-bombers and Italian Capronis, none of them guarded.

They must be pretty sure of themselves, Callaghan thought. Too damned confident for their own good.

About 20 yards from the wooden buildings, he raised his right hand to halt the men, then leaned forward on his left leg and waved the hand in towards his outstretched right leg, signalling that the men behind him should lie belly-down on the ground. When they had done so, Callaghan studied the buildings and noted that a faint line of light was escaping from below the door of one of the wooden huts. Even at this distance, he thought he could hear the murmur of conversation.

Climbing to his feet, he ran forward at the crouch and dropped down again beside Jimbo, who was lying on the ground with his Sten gun aimed at the building.

'You stay here with the men,' Callaghan whispered, 'while I advance and check that building. I think there are soldiers inside.'

'I think you're right,' Jimbo said.

'Take this bag of Lewes bombs. At my signal, or at the first sign of trouble, head straight for those aircraft and destroy them.'

'With you all the way, boss.'

After leaving the bag with Jimbo, Callaghan jumped up and advanced at the crouch until his shadow was touching the line of light beaming out under the door of the long wooden building. The windows were covered in black-out curtains. Stopping at the edge of the line of light, Callaghan heard laughter and a babble of talk from inside. This convinced him that the building was either a mess or the aircrew's briefing hut.

Callaghan, who had been bored for a long time, felt an edge of excitement.

What the hell, he thought. If we try bombing the planes someone's bound to hear us, so I might as well do as much damage here as I possibly can.

He glanced back over his shoulder and saw his men still on the ground. Turning back to the front, he took a deep breath, then kicked the door open and rushed inside.

The light briefly dazzled him. All conversation was stilled. The Germans were gathered around a long table, drinking beer, smoking cigarettes and playing cards or reading. They stared at him, startled, not quite realizing who he was, and were still trying to come to terms with his presence when he opened fire with his tommy-gun.

The noise was shocking in that small space, and made worse by the additional screaming of the men as they died in the hail of bullets, falling out of their chairs or over the table, knocking over bottles and mugs, smashing plates, making ashtrays flip and spin in the air, scattering clouds of grey ash. Others kicked their chairs back and dived to the floor, scrambling under the table, some of them bravely grabbing for their weapons even as the bullets were stitching them.

Callaghan fired in a wide arc, turning from left to right, the roaring weapon jolting his whole body as he backed towards the door. More men shuddered and died. The wounded screamed in pain. Bullets ricocheted off the walls to make a harsh drumming sound that seemed worse when some light-bulbs exploded, plunging the room into semi-darkness.

One of the Germans rolled over, raising his Luger pistol and taking aim, but Callaghan put a short burst into him, shot out the remaining light-bulbs, then backed out through the door as the survivors scrambled frantically in the darkness. As Callaghan stepped outside, some of the Germans in the hut fired their weapons and he heard the bullets whistling past him.

Turning around to face the night, he saw his own men racing across the dark field to get at the Axis aircraft. He raced after them, bullets still hissing by, and only turned around to give the men covering fire when he reached the edge of the airfield. He cut down some of the Germans running out of the building, but others were bunched up behind the windows and firing from there.

'Bugger this for a joke!' Callaghan muttered, determined to blow up some planes himself. 'You men!' he called out to the SAS troopers racing past him. 'I want four of you to stay here and keep those bastards over there occupied. Pour a fusillade of fire through those windows and keep them pinned down.'

'Yes, boss,' Corporal Peterson said, waving three of the troopers over to him. 'Spread out and give covering fire,' he told them. 'Pour it in through those windows.'

The corporal and three privates were already firing a combination of Lee-Enfield .303s and tommy-guns from the kneeling position when Callaghan raced after the other men. He finally caught up with Jimbo, who was kneeling beside a Junkers, distributing Lewes bombs and fuses to the troopers. Some of the men were already racing between the aircraft and lobbing the small bombs up onto their wings as if on a cricket pitch.

'Give me a couple of those,' Callaghan said. 'I've waited a long time for this.'

'Haven't we all?' Jimbo replied, handing Callaghan three of the conveniently small, light bombs. 'The fuses are set for thirty minutes, so don't hang around, boss.'

'I won't,' Callaghan said. Glancing back over his shoulder, he saw that Peterson and his three troopers were still pumping bullets into the hut. Running towards the nearest untouched Italian Caproni to place his first Lewes bomb, Callaghan noticed that when the other men had planted their supply of bombs, they were going back to swell the ranks of Peterson's group and add to the covering fire.

'Good men,' Callaghan whispered as he lobbed his first Lewes bomb up onto the wing of the Caproni. When he saw it nestling safely, he ran on to the next plane, another Caproni, and did the same, hardly aware that German bullets were zipping by dangerously close to his head. After placing his third bomb, he raced back to Jimbo, who was sitting upright over the collapsed canvas bag, opening and closing both hands to show that they were empty.

Glancing behind him, Callaghan saw that there were no more troopers in the vicinity of the aircraft – they had all joined Peterson to pour fire into the hut – so he knew that they had all disposed of their bombs.

'How many bombs were in the bag?' he asked Jimbo.

'Twenty-three,' came the reply.

'Damn!' Callaghan growled in frustration. 'There must be at least thirty planes here. What a bloody waste!'

'Twenty-three planes knocked out isn't bad,' Jimbo said. 'Assuming, of course, that the bombs go off. I think we'd better pull out now.'

Callaghan checked his watch. 'Five minutes to zero,' he said. 'Yes, Jimbo, let's go.'

Though pleased that twenty-three bombs had been planted, Callaghan still could not bear the thought of not doing more damage. Thus, as he was beating a retreat with the other men, still aiming a fusillade of fire at the barracks to keep the Germans pinned down as long as possible, he could not control himself when he saw the glow of instrument lights in the cockpit of a Caproni that obviously had just been worked on.

'Damn it!' Callaghan exclaimed, staring hungrily at the glowing aircraft. 'If I can't bomb another of those bastards, I'll take it out with my bare hands.'

'No, boss!' Jimbo bawled over the sound of his own roaring tommy-gun as the Germans poured out of the distant barracks. 'Those planes are about to blow up!'

Ignoring him, Callaghan raced across the airstrip

to the glowing Caproni, even as the German troops were also heading in that direction.

Some of the Germans stopped to take aim and fire at Callaghan, but as they did so, the first Lewes bomb exploded, blowing the wing off a Junkers, setting fire to its fuselage, then igniting its oil and making it erupt with a mighty roar, spewing jagged yellow flames and billowing black smoke.

Callaghan was climbing onto the wing of the Caproni, to get at the cockpit, when another Lewes bomb exploded, setting fire to a second Junkers, followed almost instantly by a third explosion, which blew a hole in the side of a Caproni. The heat of the fires beat back the advancing Germans, then obscured them in oily smoke, enabling Callaghan to reach the cockpit of the Caproni, where, in a fit of mute fury, he ripped the instrument panel out with his bare hands. Other Lewes bombs were exploding in quick succession, destroying more planes and filling the night with fire and smoke, as Callaghan threw the instrument panel to the ground, then followed it down. He glanced around him with pleasure as more aircraft exploded, then followed Jimbo and the others, now using the pall of smoke to give them cover as they raced away from the airfield.

Knowing that there was no time to lose, after reaching the head of the column Callaghan set a punishing pace for the march back to the desert RV. Rising to the challenge, and with little more to carry than their personal weapons and ammunition, the men kept up the pace and had soon left the airfield far behind. When they glanced back over their shoulders they could only make it out by the crimson glowing in the sky caused by the fires, and by the spasmodic, fan-shaped, silvery light of further explosions.

Reaching the general area of the RV, where they had expected to find the lorries, the men were briefly but dangerously confused by lights which at first they thought were being waved by the LRDG. In fact, they were torches being flashed by the Germans and Italians who had come in pursuit of them, losing them in the darkness and now circling blindly around them, unaware of their presence.

Callaghan used a hand signal to order his men the lie belly-down on the desert floor, where they stayed, making no sound, until the lights from the Axis vehicles had moved off to the west. When they had disappeared completely, heading away from the SAS men, Callaghan let the latter stand up again and use the whistling signals they had devised for attracting the LRDG in the desert's darkness.

Eventually, while Callaghan was carefully following his compass course, he heard the first whistled replies. Heading in that direction, he eventually saw the dark outline of the LRDG lorries, none of which had its headlights on. Drawing closer, he saw some of the men waving.

'A sight for sore eyes,' he said.

'Too right,' Jimbo agreed.

'I'm dying for a bloody drink,' Frankie informed them, 'so let's waste no more time, lads.'

As the SAS troopers hurried across the starlit plain, the LRDG soldiers stepped out to greet them like long-lost brothers; a lot of backs were slapped, hands shaken and congratulations offered.

'Twenty-three hits? Bloody terrific. Here, have a drink, mate!'

Desperately thirsty, Frankie was one of the first to be handed a water bottle by one of the Rhodesian drivers. He swallowed a huge mouthful before realizing, as his throat burned and he almost choked, that the water bottle contained rum. Recovering, and ignoring the laughing Rhodesians, he drank even more, then passed the bottle to his good friend Jimbo.

'When you get right down to it,' he said, 'there's nothing like water – pure, clean water.'

After drinking deeply from the same bottle, Jimbo felt obliged to agree.

'Great water!' he said.

Both of them slept like the dead throughout the long, rough journey back across the desert to the Jalo Oasis, where they were awakened by welcoming bursts of gunfire and cheers from most of their mates.

Even as Callaghan was marching to Stirling's tent to submit his report, Lewes and the men of S2 Patrol were on the road to El Agheila.

13

Because El Agheila was only half the distance from Jalo Oasis that Stirling had had to travel, Captain 'Jock' Lewes did not set out with S2 Patrol until two days after him. He was, in fact, just beginning his journey as Stirling and Callaghan were being brought back from Sirte and Tamit by the LRDG.

Lewes led his convoy of trucks out of Jalo with a great deal of pleasure, delighted to be back in action at last. Ever since serving in Layforce's No 8 Commando in Syria, he had gained a taste for adventure and was more easily bored than he had ever been. A low boredom threshold had always been one of his problems, but now his tolerance for inactivity was non-existent. Though superficially quiet and thoughtful, Lewes was a man of restless energy and vivid imagination who had to be kept engaged all the time.

While the early training of L Detachment in

Kabrit had kept him busy and satisfied – perfecting parachute landings, studying the art of desert survival, even inventing the bomb named after him – there could be no denying that since arriving at the Jalo base, where Stirling had been forced to wait for the right time to launch the raids, Lewes had almost gone mad with boredom. He had, of course, filled the time with more desert training and weapons practice, but those could not compensate for the real thing and his patience had worn thin.

Now, as he was driven out of Jalo Oasis by his LRDG driver, Thomas 'Tom Boy' Cook, he felt almost joyous.

This was regardless of the fact that the burly NCO in the rear seat, LRDG Sergeant Brendan McGee, did not approve of Lewes's insistence that they travel in this wonderful old Lancia staff car instead of an LRDG Chevrolet lorry.

'The Lancia's a fancy car all right,' McGee had sternly informed him, 'but it's not one to get you through the desert. Take a Chevrolet, sir.'

'I don't want a lorry, Sergeant. I want a bit of fun in my life and this car's just the ticket.'

'You're the boss, but don't ask me to approve. Be it on your own head.'

'Oh, stop being so po-faced, Sergeant McGee.

The Lancia will be perfectly fine, and that's what I'm travelling in.'

Lewes was wrong. The Lancia was, at least initially, a disaster. Everything was fine and dandy as they raced across the perfectly smooth, hard sand of the vast desert plain, but as soon as they reached an area of soft sand and gravel, the Lancia began bogging down and had to be dug out.

Though clearly infuriated, as his purple face showed, Sergeant McGee said nothing, other than to snap orders at his men as they slaved and sweated at this murderous task. Lewes, highly embarrassed, avoided his sergeant's steely gaze and concentrated on his map-reading. But when, a couple of hours later, they had to pass through an area of rippling sand dunes and the car bogged down three times over a distance of ten miles, Sergeant McGee's steely gaze had turned white-hot and was burning through the back of Lewes's neck.

'Don't say, "I told you so",' Lewes finally said to break the chilling silence.

'No, sir,' McGee replied. 'I won't say I told you so.'

'I was wrong, Sergeant. My fault. I apologize. I should have bowed to superior experience and not let my schoolboy's love of sporty-looking cars blind me to reason.'

McGee sighed, smiled a little, and stroked the bonnet of the Lancia as it was pushed by some troopers off the last of the sand mats and steel channels, back onto hard ground. 'I must admit, it's a beauty,' he confessed. 'It's just in the wrong place.'

Relieved, Lewes ordered the resting men back into their vehicles, then the convoy took off again, heading across a mercifully flat, hard plain, into the deepening crimson light of dusk. By last light they were well on the road to El Agheila – at least halfway, according to Lewes's calculations – so they made camp for the night, first erecting triangular poncho shelters between the vehicles and the ground, then lighting fires to cook up hot food.

'What about Axis aircraft?' Lewes asked McGee, who was now more friendly towards him. 'Won't they see our fires?'

'They'll see them all right,' McGee replied, automatically looking up at the vast, magnificent, star-filled sky, 'but being out here, they'll assume we're a bunch of Arab nomads. No need for concern there.'

Apart from the usual whining mosquitoes, fat flies and innumerable creepy-crawlies, the night passed uneventfully. By first light the men were all up to have a quick breakfast, clear away all signs of the camp, and hit the road while the heat was still bearable.

The first couple of hours were painless, with the forward momentum of the vehicles creating a cooling wind. Also the men's mouths and nostrils were protected from the billowing sand by the fluttering *shemaghs* wrapped around their faces, leaving only their eyes exposed. By eleven, however, the sun was high in the sky and not even the beating, snapping wind could counter the fierce, draining heat.

Just after noon, when the column had managed to advance half the remaining distance to El Agheila without a vehicle bogging down – not even the Lancia – a great dark wall formed on the horizon directly in front of them. McGee, still sitting in the rear of the Lancia, leaned forward to tap Tom Boy on the shoulder and tell him to stop. As the driver was braking carefully to avoid becoming bogged down, McGee stood up in the back and signalled with his right hand for the rest of the column to stop too.

'What is it?' Lewes asked.

'See that big dark wall on the horizon?' McGee asked by way of reply.

'Yes.'

'Now listen. What do you hear?'

Listening, Lewes heard what sounded like a train emerging from a tunnel and approaching rapidly.

'Sandstorm!' McGee bawled. 'Everybody take cover!'

The more experienced LRDG men were out of their vehicles so fast that they took the SAS men by surprise. Certainly McGee was out of the Lancia, huddled on the ground beside it and unrolling his poncho even as Lewes was still putting his feet down. Glancing back over his shoulder, Lewes saw that great wall of darkness growing larger as it advanced, blotting out the whole horizon, making the desert floor shake dramatically, and now sounding even more like an approaching train. The sun was gradually obscured by great spirals of sand and eventually disappeared altogether, leaving darkness almost as deep as night.

The oxygen seemed to go out of the air and the flies were swarming and buzzing like crazy things. Lewes could hardly breathe. 'Get down here!' McGee shouted, waving him down as sand suddenly swirled howling around the captain.

When Lewes dropped down beside McGee, the burly sergeant threw his poncho over both of them and told him to hold his corner down tightly. Lewes did so just as the sandstorm, travelling at nearly 50mph, swept over the Lancia with a mighty roar, tearing and punching at the poncho, making the car rock dangerously, sucking all the air out of the enclosed space beneath the poncho, and blowing the sand in through every opening, no matter how slight.

Lewes's throat went dry and he had great difficulty in breathing. The roaring wind was deafening and filled his ears with stabbing pains. For a moment he felt that he was going to be picked up bodily and carried off by the storm. In the event, he escaped this fate.

The sandstorm took only minutes to pass on, but it seemed more like hours. Eventually, however, the noise and the wind abated, the sand settled down and the suffocating heat was replaced with breathable air. When McGee tugged the poncho away to let Lewes look out again, he saw the sandstorm racing towards the southern horizon, now very far away, growing smaller as it rapidly receded. The sun was reappearing in the sky as the swirling sand settled down.

'Christ!' Lewes said softly.

'Your first one?'

'Yes.'

McGee grinned. 'The first one always comes as a shock. *Now* look at your Lancia!'

Completely buried, the car resembled a small sand dune. This time, however, most of the Chevrolets had suffered exactly the same fate.

'Oh, God!' Lewes groaned in exasperation. 'We're going to have to dig this lot out.'

' 'Fraid so.'

After dusting themselves down, the troopers and LRDG men set above scraping the sand off the trucks with their bare hands. They had to do this before they could even get at the spades and shovels, buried with the rest of their kit. Once they had regained those, they were able to remove the sand more quickly, though it still took some time and, in the ferocious heat of noon, made them all sweat like pigs. Two of them were rendered nauseous by the heat and threw up in the sand. The digging took nearly two hours and was punctuated by a series of five-minute breaks to avoid further such problems. Even then, when the vehicles were cleared, they had to be pushed out with the aid of sand mats and steel channels. By the time they were ready to set off again, most of the men were exhausted.

'Do you think they'll be fit enough for the raid tonight?' McGee asked Lewes, obviously referring only to his SAS troopers, not to the more experienced LRDG.

'Yes,' Lewes replied without hesitation. 'They'll get their strength back just sitting in the lorries for the rest of the journey. We're nearly there, Sergeant, so with luck we should get there without any more problems.'

Luck was with them at last. The rest of the journey passed without incident and by last light they were on the outskirts of El Agheila, with the Gulf of Sirte visible in the distance, beyond the sandy cliffs of the coastline. Their luck then took a turn for the worse once more when, approaching the unguarded airfield under cover of darkness, they found no planes on the runway.

'Damn!' Lewes exclaimed softly, lying belly-down on the summit of a low ridge and studying the airfield through his binoculars. 'There's not a damned thing down there. Just a few huts and a couple of Kraut and Eyetie soldiers. That isn't an airfield – it's just a bloody staging post for planes passing through.'

'I fear so,' McGee replied, also studying the empty runway through binoculars. 'It's been rumoured that the Axis air forces have begun dispersing their planes to fields where they can be properly guarded. I think that's happened here – and if that's the case, the planes won't be coming back. As you say, this is probably now just a staging post for aircraft that have to land temporarily, probably for refuelling. Apart from that, it's inoperative. You can tell that by the lack of facilities and the small number of guards. It's been a wild-goose chase, Captain.'

Lewes rolled onto his back, placed the binoculars on his belly, and gazed up at the stars. 'Buggered if I'll have this,' he said, suddenly sitting upright and hanging the binoculars around his neck. 'I'm not going to waste *my* bag of bombs. I want to see them put to good use.'

McGee sat up beside him. 'What does that mean, Captain?'

'According to our intelligence reports, there's a building not far from here, in Mersa Brega, where the German top brass regularly conduct intelligence meetings. I'm going to find that building, Sergeant, and blow it to hell.'

'That's taking a mighty big chance, Captain.'

'That's what life's all about. Are you with me?'

McGee shrugged. 'Why not?'

The men, many of whom were as disappointed as Lewes, were ordered back into the vehicles and followed the Lancia away from the airfield, heading back for what was marked on the map as an Axis MSR. When they reached the road, which was certainly wide enough for heavy-duty military traffic and raised a few feet above the desert floor, they parked a good way from it, hidden in the darkness at the bottom of the sloping ground. While waiting, the men ate their wads and drank hot tea from vacuum flasks. When a sizeable German convoy rolled past on the road above, they hurriedly packed away their remaining wads and the vacuum flasks, started up the engines and followed the Lancia up onto the road.

With a daring that took even Sergeant McGee's breath away, Lewes urged Tom Boy to drive faster until he had caught up with the tail of the German column, where he insisted that he remain for as long as possible. In fact, they stuck to the tail of the column, with their own column of LRDG lorries strung out behind them, until the convoy reached Mersa Brega.

If any of the men in the German column looked back, they must have assumed, in the darkness, that the Lancia and the lorries behind it were their own.

'I've got to hand it to you, Captain,' Sergeant McGee said, his eyes never moving from the back of the German lorry directly ahead. 'Apart from your unfortunate choice of cars, you're a cool-headed officer.'

'I try to be,' Lewes replied.

Eventually the German convoy reached a fenced

compound, beyond which was a single large brick building and a vehicle park. The first vehicles in the column slowed down, stopped, then started moving into the compound one by one, passing heavily armed guards.

'This must be the place we want,' Lewes said. 'It wouldn't be so well guarded otherwise.'

'Are we going in?' McGee asked in disbelief.

'We can try. We won't be noticed until we reach the guardhouse. The second we get there, we open fire with our small arms, picking off the sentries, then race into the compound with the rest behind us. We can shoot up the building as we approach it and then bomb it to hell.'

'Christ!' McGee said, though he grinned with pleasurable anticipation and unslung his tommy-gun from his shoulder. 'Did you get all that, Tom Boy?' he asked the driver.

'Yes, sir!' Corporal Cook replied. 'The minute we get to the guardhouse, I put my foot down.'

'Make sure you do, Tom Boy.'

In fact, the Italian sentry at the guardhouse recognized the British markings on the Lancia just before it reached the open gates. He bellowed a warning and lowered his rifle as the siren on the guardhouse started to wail. Tom Boy instantly put his foot down and roared towards the gate, hard on the tail of the German lorry that had just passed through.

Meanwhile Lewes unholstered his Browning High Power handgun and put two bullets into the sentry. The impact threw the Italian backwards into the wall. As the Lancia swept past the guardhouse, Lewes emptied the handgun into it, in the hope of cutting down the other sentry.

Glancing back over his shoulder, he saw the other LRDG lorries racing between the open gates, one after the other, with some of the men also firing at the guardhouse with their semi-automatic weapons, causing showers of wood splinters to fly off it and almost certainly killing anyone still inside.

Tom Boy braked sharply, going into a skid, when he saw that the German lorries up ahead had stopped and were disgorging their heavily armed soldiers. As the Lancia skidded to a halt, the LRDG lorries coming up behind spread out around it and also slid to a standstill, allowing the SAS troopers to pour out, already firing their small arms at the advancing Axis soldiers.

'Damn!' Lewes rasped, hauling the bag of bombs onto his lap and looking ahead at the Axis soldiers fanning out across the compound and blocking the way to the brick building. 'We'll never get past them.' He glanced sideways at the parking area, which was filled with dusty troop lorries and gleaming staff cars. Bullets zipped past his head in both directions, being fired simultaneously by his SAS troopers and that formidable mixture of Germans and Italians. 'So!' he said. 'If we can't blow up the building, we'll destroy as many vehicles as possible. Come on, Sergeant, let's go.'

He jumped out of the Lancia, still holding the bag of bombs. McGee did the same, then hurried around the back of the car to join Lewes, who was rummaging about in the bag, taking out as many of the small bombs as he could carry. He then handed the heavy bag to McGee. 'Distribute these to some of the other men and tell the remainder to keep those soldiers away from us.' He had to shout above the general bedlam, to which was suddenly added the sharp roar of Tom Boy's Sten gun, which the driver was firing from the front seat of the Lancia.

Glancing at the Axis troops, Lewes saw some of them dropping, but the others were still returning the SAS fire while gradually spreading out across the compound.

'We're going to have to be quick,' McGee said.

'Then get going, Sergeant!'

While the SAS troopers kept the Axis soldiers busy, Lewes ran towards the parking area. By the time he reached it, McGee had distributed the Lewes bombs and the troops armed with them were running forward to join Lewes. They spread out, planting bombs on lorries and staff cars alike, and managed to complete the job before the enemy troops could head in their direction.

As each man planted the last of his bombs, he ran back to rejoin his own lorry and add his firing to the increasingly ferocious barrage aimed at the enemy.

One SAS trooper fell, then another, and a third. The Axis troops were falling at a greater rate, but that was not encouraging. Leaving their dead where they were lying, the SAS men backed towards their own lorries, firing as they retreated, and scrambled up into them. The last men were still hauling themselves up, or being hauled up, as the lorries turned around on screeching tyres and raced out of the compound.

The time fuses on the Lewes bombs had been set for the minimum delay of ten minutes. As the last of the LRDG trucks roared out of the compound, Lewes glanced sideways from the Lancia, out on lead, and saw the Axis troops hurrying towards the parking area to remove the bombs.

Lewes crossed his fingers.

The first lorry to explode did so with a thunderous noise just as the enemy troops were approaching. It went up in smoke and flames, blowing apart, spewing metal, forcing the Axis troops to throw themselves to the ground or beat a hasty retreat. The lorry was followed by a staff car, then another lorry, then another, until the area had become a spectacular inferno of vivid-yellow flames, black, boiling smoke, melting rubber and flying, spinning, red-hot metal.

The Axis troops could do nothing but watch the continuing destruction – so shocked that they made no attempt to pursue the men who had caused it.

As he raced away in his Lancia, Lewes looked back with pride, counting ten, twenty, then thirty Axis vehicles either destroyed completely or seriously damaged.

'That makes up for a lot,' McGee said.

Lewes heard cheering from the SAS troopers in the trucks behind him. He uncrossed his fingers and stuck his thumb up in the air as the lorries headed back to Jalo Oasis, over 120 miles away, beyond the moonlit horizon.

14

Lieutenant Greaves was scheduled to raid Agedabia airfield just before the Oasis Force's advance, due to start on Tuesday 20 December. Brigadier Reid and his staff had worked out that by Wednesday the Force would be nearing the area of regular Axis air patrols. Therefore anything Greaves could do to hamper these, particularly by destroying enemy aircraft, would be of invaluable help to the campaign.

'We can't make that advance if the number of Axis planes aren't greatly reduced,' he said. 'That's the job of L Detachment, Lieutenant, and failure isn't acceptable.'

Greaves left Jalo Oasis with only two of his own men, Corporal'Taff' Clayton and Private Neil Moffatt, a few hours before Stirling returned. The group, driven by an LRDG private, Bob Purbridge, had a reasonably uneventful journey to Agedabia, with only a couple of punctures to contend with; and each mile that took them closer to their target was also, Greaves suddenly realized, taking him back to where he had been before meeting Stirling: in that great Allied camp located just outside Mersa Brega in the vast desert of Cyrenaica.

That had only been seven months ago, but it seemed more like seven years. Three days after Greaves had been casevacked from Tobruk, Rommel's Panzer divisions had cut off the port. Seventeen days after that, while Greaves was recovering from surgery in the Scottish Military Hospital in Alexandria, German troops had occupied Halfaya Pass and the British had been forced to retire across the border into Egypt. A month later, when the British attempted to take the Pass back with Operation Brevity, they were defeated again.

By the middle of June, when Greaves was still recuperating in hospital in Alexandria, the British attempted to relieve Tobruk with Operation Battleaxe, but were quickly forced back to the starting line. In July, a few days after Captain Stirling was moved into the bed beside Greaves, General Claude Auchinleck replaced General Wavell as Commander-in-Chief in the Middle East. Then in November, when Captain Stirling, admirably energetic even when on crutches, was telling Greaves about his idea for small raiding parties, another major British offensive intended to defeat the Axis forces in Cyrenaica and free Tobruk, began with a series of confused battles around Sidi Rezech, but ended with more gains for the Germans.

Now, in late November, the major battle for control of the Western Desert had begun and Stirling's dream of small raiding parties had become, at least in principle, a reality. Whether or not the raids would be successful was another matter entirely.

They'd better be successful, Greaves thought grimly as his Chevrolet raced across the vast, featureless plain, taking him closer to Agedabia, only 40 miles from Mersa Brega, where the retreat had begun. If they don't, he thought, the fate of L Detachment will be sealed and Stirling's dream will be smashed. The SAS will be no more.

Shocked by that idea, Greaves straightened in his seat and glanced at the setting sun, going down like pouring lava and spreading its crimson fire across the horizon, bringing darkness to Tunis and Tripoli and the Gulf of Sirte, to the unforgettable blue of the Mediterranean and the desert's dazzling whiteness. The other raiding parties, he knew, had already done what they could do in that same protective darkness – at Tamit, at Sirte, and at Agheila – but whether or not it had been worth it he had yet to find out.

Had they succeeded or failed? Had they lived or died? Would he ever see Stirling, Callaghan, Lewes or any of the others again? Indeed, would he himself return from this mission? That, too, he would soon find out.

'There's the sea, Lieutenant,' Private Purbridge said. 'That must be Agedabia.'

'It is,' Greaves replied.

He glanced all around him at the vast, darkening desert, seeing, due east, nothing but mile upon featureless mile but for the black lines of distant dunes; and, due north and north-west as far as Tripoli, the glitter of sea sinking into sunset. It was difficult to accept that this vast, barren wasteland joining Tripolitania to Cyrenaica was filled with the tanks, lorries, armoured cars and seasoned troops of the legendary General Rommel's Panzer divisions. In the silence of the desert's failing light there was no sign of war.

Nevertheless, Greaves reflected, they are all around us, so we must be careful from now on.

'The airfield's just over that ridge, due north-west,' he told Purbridge. Drop us off near the top of the ridge, where we should still be out of sight.'

'Will do, Lieutenant.'

Five minutes later the lorry was bouncing over a mixture of soft sand and gravel as it made its way up the gentle slope of the low-lying ridge. Just before it reached the top – where it would have been silhouetted against the skyline – Private Purbridge braked to a halt.

'Home and dry,' he said.

Greaves and the other two clambered out, carrying their small arms. Taff then picked up the bag of Lewes bombs and slung it over his shoulder. Greaves walked the few steps to the edge of the ridge, peered down through the darkness, then returned to the lorry.

'It's too dark to see much from here, so we'll have to start hiking willy-nilly.' He checked his watch, then spoke to Purbridge. 'Without knowing just how far away the airfield is, or how well it's guarded, I've no way of knowing how long this is going to take or when we'll get back. My suggestion, therefore, is that you wait here until first light. If we're not back by then, assume we've been captured or shot and drive yourself back to Jalo. If, on the other hand, you hear sounds of activity – gunfire, sirens or, hopefully, our exploding Lewes bombs – you can assume we're in the thick of things and will be attempting to make our way back. In that case, keep your eyes peeled for us and prepare to get going. Understood?'

'Yes, sir.'

Greaves turned to Taff Clayton and Neil Moffatt. 'Right, lads, let's get going.'

With that, he led them over the low ridge and down the dark, gentle slope at the other side, marching towards the airfield. It was not an easy march. In fact, the area surrounding the airfield was patrolled constantly by German troops, both on foot and in lorries, so the SAS men had repeatedly to drop to the ground, faces pressed to the soft sand, and wait for the patrols or trucks to pass, silently praying that they would not be seen. Naturally, this made their advance on the airfield slow and nerve-racking. Eventually, however, they reached the perimeter and found it not only securely fenced, but patrolled by the crack troops of the Panzer Grenadier Regiments of the 90th Light Division.

'This is not going to be easy,' Greaves whispered as he knelt behind a sandy ridge, beside Taff and Neil, a good half mile from the wire. 'We have to get across that flat stretch without being seen, then somehow get through the wire. Not easy at all.'

'What *I'd* like to know,' Taff said, 'is . . .' He coughed into his fist. 'Is it actually possible?'

Surprisingly, it was the solemn, almost anonymous Neil who gave them the impetus. 'Of course it's possible. We just advance an inch at a time, belly-down on the ground, stopping every time we spot a guard or when those searchlights come in our direction. It might take us a little bit of time, but in the end we'll get there.'

'You think so?' Taff asked doubtfully while scanning that distant wire.

'Yes,' Neil replied firmly, yet glancing at Lieutenant Greaves for support.

'I agree,' Greaves told him. 'Besides, what else can we do? We can't turn back now.'

'Just watch me,' Taff said. 'I'll be out of here like a bat out of hell.'

'I'm not dragging this bag of bombs anywhere,' Neil solemnly informed him, 'except through that wire.'

'Well, Corporal?' Greaves asked, giving Taff the choice.

Taff sighed. 'Oh, what the hell? Yes, sir, let's do it.'

'Good man,' Greaves said. He glanced at the heavy bag of bombs. 'You won't be able to drag that with you, so let's divide them up between us right now. How many are there?'

'Thirty-five,' Taff said.

'*What?*'

'Thirty-five.'

Greaves sighed. 'Right, Corporal, that's eleven to you, eleven to Neil and thirteen to me. But how the hell do we carry them?'

'There are smaller bags inside this one,' Taff said. 'We take one bag apiece.'

'Excellent. Quick, man!'

Taff opened the big bag, pulled out three smaller bags, divided the small Lewes bombs into three piles, with two extra for Greaves, then put them into the separate bags and gave the heaviest to Greaves. Each man then slung his own bag onto his back and tied it to his shoulders with its fixed cords. They were now all set to leave.

'Right,' Greaves said. 'Let's go.'

They moved out immediately, first running at the crouch but soon forced to drop to the ground and crawl forward, first on hands and knees, then belly-down. This was both tedious and arduous, every yard a struggle. Thirty minutes after starting they were already feeling the strain and realized that they had advanced only a little. Slithering like snakes down a sand-and-gravel slope to the bed of a dried-up wadi, they took a short break, tried to ease their aching muscles, then began the crawl up the other side. Reaching the top and peering over the rim, they saw that the area between there and the perimeter was literally swarming with German troops.

'Jesus!' Taff whispered.

'I don't care how long it takes,' Greaves said, also whispering, 'but we're going to go through that damned wire. Any arguments, gentlemen?'

Taff and Neil did not argue.

It took four hours, for they advanced an inch at a time. The guards marched to and fro, and the searchlights swept the terrain, as the three SAS men snaked forward on their bellies, stopped, started again and repeated this pattern endlessly, feeling like worms in the earth, but obliged to continue, working their way unseen to the wire.

First one hour, then two, and still with half the journey to go. At one point a truck raced past them so close it spewed sand over them; at another they had to lie as still as corpses for an hour with Germans and Italians congregating yards away. The Axis troops lit cigarettes, conversed in their separate languages, shared a flask of water or wine, then finally wandered off in opposite directions, letting the SAS men advance again – a very slow advance, the so-called 'leopard crawl', painstaking and stealthy.

The third hour ran interminably into the fourth

and they had finally made it. They were right at the fence.

Greaves checked his watch and saw that it was nearly midnight, which just made him feel more tired.

Checking left and right, he saw that the nearest guarded entanglements were quite a long way off and that the searchlights were hitting the ground well away from the fence. Relieved, he rose to his knees and removed a small pair of wire-cutters from his webbed belt.

'Have you got the same?' he asked Taff and Neil.

'Yes,' they replied simultaneously.

'Good. Get to it, lads.'

Between them they managed to cut through the wire in no time, taking care that it did not shake too much, lest it attract the attention of the guards at the entanglements on both sides. When the wires had been parted, they left the cutters on the ground – they were now an unnecessary burden – and made their way quietly through the opening, heading straight for the airfield.

Probably because the wired perimeter was so heavily guarded, there were no guards on the airfield itself, nor on the parked aircraft, which were mostly CR42s, an Italian biplane fighter-bomber.

'A gift from God!' Greaves whispered, smiling delightedly at Taff and Neil. 'When you've planted all your bombs – or if Jerry sees any of us before we've done so – head straight back to the opening and try to make your way back to the lorry. Good luck, lads. *Go!*'

They all scattered in different directions, heading out in triangular formation to work their way down the three rows of planes. They went from one plane to the next over the next forty-five minutes, placing their thirty-five bombs one by one, each man waving to the others each time he planted one, before moving on to the next plane. No one came near them. Nor did they see any Axis sentries. The job took all that time, but it was easy to do, and when they had disposed of all their bombs, they met under the wing of one of the last two planes, the three of them as happy as Larry.

'We're short of two bombs,' Neil said.

'Damn!' Greaves exclaimed.

'If these thirty-five bombs go off,' Taff said, still grinning, 'I won't complain about the two short.'

'Those fuses are set for sixty minutes,' Neil reminded them, 'so we'd better get going.'

'Shit, yes!' Taff said.

In fact, the bombs began exploding before they cleared the airfield, five minutes earlier than anticipated. Most went off at the same time, some only slightly later, and the combined effect was spectacular, creating a stunning display of searing white flames and billowing smoke, accompanied by a cacophony of explosions composed of the actual bombs and the igniting petrol tanks of the planes. Within seconds the whole airfield resembled a modern version of hell, with flames eating into flames, smoke spiralling and billowing upwards to form immense, oily black clouds, and burning rubber, melting perspex and red-hot metal spewing skywards and raining back down.

Luckily, by then the three SAS men had already made it to the barbed wire, gone through the opening, and were running at the crouch back into the darkness unseen by the Germans, most of whom were racing the other way, towards the unexpected hell of the airfield.

This time, since they did not have to crawl on their bellies, Greaves and his two companions covered the same distance in an easy thirty minutes instead of an arduous four hours. When they got back to the ridge, Purbridge was waiting for them, the engine of the Chevrolet already turning over.

When they were safely in their seats, he took off – in the words of Taff – like a bat out of hell.

15

With all the raiding parties back in Jalo Oasis, Captain Stirling called a meeting between his officers to discuss their various adventures and decide what changes to their techniques had to be made in the light of their experience. Gathered around the long trestle table in Stirling's large tent, the officers smoked like chimneys, drank a lot of whisky or beer, swapped jokes and informal conversation, then eventually got down to serious business.

'So what was this problem you had coming back, Dirk?' Captain Stirling asked Lieutenant Greaves.

'Once we'd completed the raid,' Greaves told him, 'we laid up most of that night, then started across the desert the next day. Everything went smoothly – not a German in sight – until, still deep in enemy territory, we were mistaken for an Axis patrol by two of our own Blenheims.'

'Damn!' Stirling exploded.

'They attacked us with their guns,' Greaves continued, recalling it vividly, with anger, 'and though I and my two men managed to get out of the lorry in time, one of the Blenheims stitched it with bullets and killed the LRDG driver, Private Purbridge, before we could exchange recognition signals.

'Bloody rotten luck!' Lewes exclaimed softly.

'Those RAF prats!' Callaghan added with some venom.

Greaves just shrugged his shoulders. 'When the pilots finally recognized us and flew back where they had come from, we buried Purbridge in the desert. Private Moffatt of L Detachment then took over the driving.'

'You navigated yourself?' Lewes asked him.

'Yes.'

Callaghan gave a low whistle of admiration, then glanced at Lewes. 'Your training wasn't in vain, then,' he said.

'So what happened next?' Stirling asked impatiently.

'Unfortunately,' Greaves continued, 'one of the Blenheims had shot up the petrol tank and though we managed to patch it up temporarily, it was losing fuel at an increasing rate and the engine was gradually packing up. As luck would have it, later that day we reached Wadi Faregh, where Brigadier Reid's Force was passing through to their night laager some 25 miles from the airfield. They fixed us up with another lorry and driver, so finally we made it back here.'

'An absolutely tragic end to a successful raid,' Stirling said. 'My condolences, Dirk.' He was, however, keen to hear some good news. 'So how, precisely, did the raid go?'

'Perfect,' Greaves said with some pride. 'The place was heavily guarded and we had difficulty getting in – at least it took a long time – but we didn't have a single encounter with the enemy while planting our bombs.'

'The bombs all went off?' Lewes asked anxiously.

Greaves smiled at him. 'Perfectly, Jock. A little earlier than planned, but that may have turned out to be a blessing. Certainly Jerry had no time either to remove them or come looking for us. We practically *walked* away from that airfield as the planes were all blowing up.'

'*All* of them?' Stirling asked.

'We were two bombs short,' Greaves said, 'which made me a little angry. But, as Corporal Clayton pointed out, thirty-five hits out of thirty-seven is no cause for complaint.'

Stirling nodded. 'Quite right.'

Lewes wasn't so happy. 'I'll have to check the fuses,' he said of his own invention, the Lewes bombs. 'Yours weren't the only ones to go off early.'

'Right,' Callaghan said. 'Ours were set for thirty minutes, but they went off in twenty, nearly accounting for us with the aircraft.'

'We didn't even get the chance to try ours,' Stirling confessed bitterly.

'Oh, why?'

'Damned aircraft at Sirte took off before we could launch the raid. All thirty of them. Leaving us with all those unused bombs. So,' he said, changing the subject, 'what *was* the success rate?'

'We got twenty-three planes out of thirty,' Callaghan said, 'and only failed to get the rest because we ran short of bombs.'

'We didn't get any aircraft at all,' Lewes confessed, 'but we destroyed or seriously damaged thirty Axis vehicles.'

'We got thirty-five out of thirty-seven,' Greaves said, 'and like Captain Callaghan's group, we only failed to hit the others because we ran short of bombs.'

'Bloody stupid!' Stirling said angrily. 'Another

example of lack of proper planning and intelligence.' He drummed his fingers on the table, looking distracted, then had a slug of whisky and perked up. 'Nevertheless, looking on the bright side, in a single week we destroyed a total of fifty-eight enemy aircraft, thirty enemy vehicles, and one enemy oil-tanker. We also caused a lot of disturbance and kept their troops distracted. Not bad at all, gentlemen!'

Stirling topped up his glass, passed the bottle around the table, then held his glass out in a toast. 'To the first successes of L Detachment, SAS,' he said. When the officers had toasted their own success, they drank more whisky, lit up more cigarettes, filled the tent with smoke, and returned to the more serious business of the rights and wrongs of the raids.

'Any complaints about the LRDG?' Stirling asked.

'None,' Callaghan said.

'They were perfect,' Lewes added.

'No one could have done it better,' Greaves insisted. 'They were bloody marvellous.'

'I concur,' Stirling said. 'The failures are all down to us, so we have to address that fact.'

He glanced outside the tent where the other ranks were either bathing in the pools of the oasis or relaxing under the palm trees, drinking and smoking as well, but also reading or writing letters home. The sun was blazing out of a sheer blue sky, making the vast, flat desert look almost white.

'In future,' he said, turning back to the officers smoking and drinking around the table, 'we have to try to avoid the kind of disaster that befell us at Sirte. In order to do this, we have to ensure that we have good intelligence beforehand.'

'Hear, hear,' Callaghan said.

'Here are just a few of the things that went wrong,' Stirling continued, counting them off on the fingers of his right hand. 'Some of our targets flew away before we could get at them. We had no idea if the airfields we targeted were guarded or not. Captain Lewes turned up at an airfield that was, in fact, merely a staging post containing no aircraft. We should have known these facts in advance.'

'Right,' Lewes said.

'Another damaging delay was caused by the simple fact that two Arab girls decided to tend their garden. This also could have been avoided with prior intelligence. In short, we should have known about that garden.' Stirling glanced at each of the men in turn, letting them know he was serious. 'And there were, alas, other silly mistakes.'

The officers glanced uneasily at one another

when Stirling deliberately paused for dramatic effect.

'Captain Callaghan, for instance, made the mistake of firing at the enemy before his men had planted their bombs, thus alerting the garrison to what his group was doing.'

'Sorry about that,' Callaghan said. 'I just got carried away.'

'Please don't let it happen again, Paddy.'

'I won't, boss, I promise.'

'Captain Lewes ignored the advice of his experienced LRDG sergeant and took a vehicle unsuited to the terrain.'

'Guilty,' Lewes said. 'I stand corrected.'

'He also engaged the enemy before planting his bombs, thus running the risk of alerting them to what was happening. In his case, the circumstances were mitigating, but again, if we'd had proper intelligence, he wouldn't have turned up at an empty airstrip and had to go elsewhere.'

This time Lewes made no comment.

'Regarding the timing of the raids, in future we'll also have to make allowance for the unexpected, such as the sandstorm that delayed Captain Lewes's patrol.'

'A terrible experience,' Lewes said, 'albeit a brief one.'

'As for myself,' Stirling continued, 'I must confess that I was careless enough to trip over an Italian sentry who then alerted the whole damned garrison. Had that not happened, we might have attacked the airfield earlier and the planes would not have flown away before we could get to them. I believe this happened because I was too tired – but I shouldn't have been. I should have laid up the night before the raid to ensure that I was fully alert. I, too, stand corrected.'

His fellow officers smiled at that.

'So,' Stirling summarized, 'in future, whenever possible, a number of guidelines will be followed. No raids will be mounted until the targets have been fully recced and accurate intelligence is received. No recces will be made without a day's lying-up before the raid. The raiders will not engage in gun battles *before* they've planted their bombs. The fuses of the bombs will be double-checked for precise timings. The number of targets must be accurately ascertained and no patrol will have a shortage of bombs. All future schedules will incorporate allowances for unexpected desert phenomena, such as sandstorms and the bogging down of vehicles. Last but not least, with regard to being shot at by our own bloody aircraft, the pros and cons of disguised vehicles will have to be looked into before we make any further raids. I think those are the lessons we've learnt, gentlemen. Are there any questions?'

'Yes,' Callaghan said, bored already and eager to get back to work. 'When and where are the next raids?'

'As it's clear that the success of the raids depends on surprise, we'll strike next where the enemy will least expect us.'

'Where's that?' Lieutenant Greaves asked.

'Exactly where we raided before,' Stirling, in better mood, replied with a wicked schoolboy's grin. 'At Sirte and Tamit – but approaching by a different, more westerly route.'

'When?' Captain Callaghan asked impatiently.

'A couple of weeks from now,' Stirling told him. 'To be precise, Christmas Eve.'

'My Christmas present!' Lewes said.

16

By the time Stirling's raiders moved out again the situation in the Western Desert of Cyrenaica had again changed dramatically. The 5th South African Brigade had been annihilated by the Afrika Korps south-east of Sidi Rezegh; fierce fighting then took place between the Axis forces and the New Zealand Division; General Ritchie's Eighth Army sustained heavy casualties, but still managed to weaken the Afrika Korps, causing Rommel to withdraw his forces from the Crusader battle rather than let them be destroyed; and finally, on 10 December, Tobruk as relieved and the Afrika Korps began its retreat, first to Gazala, then as far south as El Agheila. Stirling's raiders, therefore, in leaving the Jalo Oasis on Christmas Eve, even as units of the Eighth Army were advancing on Benghazi, found themselves travelling towards the southern flank of the retreating Axis forces, under skies filled with

Axis and Allied aircraft, all flying to and from the battle zone.

'To get to our targets,' Stirling said to Captain Halliman, 'we're going to find ourselves practically in the lap of the Axis forces now dug in around Agheila. This could be rather tricky.'

'Damned right,' Sergeant Lorrimer said from the rear seat, where he was sitting as Stirling's second-in-command.

Even as they were speaking, the faint throb of engines made them squint up at the sky where they saw a fleet of Handley-Page Halifax four-engine bombers heading north to pound Rommel's forces.

'Good lads,' Stirling murmured.

As before, he was travelling with S1 patrol, commanded by LRDG Captain Gus Halliman. This time, however, instead of targeting only Sirte, the plan was for Stirling's raiding party to be dropped off within hiking distance of Sirte while another, led by Captain Callaghan, would make a return journey to Tamit for a second attack based on the wisdom of hindsight. When the two raids were completed, both teams would meet up with the LRDG lorries at a desert RV due south of the targets.

Meanwhile, a third raiding party led by Captain Lewes, with Lieutenant Greaves as second-in-command, was being transported by the LRDG

T2 Patrol, mostly composed of New Zealanders, to Nofilia, over 120 miles east of Sirte, where they would launch a simultaneous raid.

The first day's journey across the vast, flat plain passed uneventfully and with even less punctures than before, because the LRDG, after their previous experiences, were now using specially reinforced tyres. As usual, the men were all wearing *shemaghs* to protect their faces, not only from the fierce heat, but also from the billowing clouds of sand churned up by the lorries' wheels. These, however, did little to alleviate the sweat that soaked through their clothing. Nevertheless, as they gazed across the vast expanse of the desert, seeing the cliffs of the upland plateaux beyond the heat haze in the north and the golden sand dunes framed by azure sky in the west, few of them were immune to the desert's lunar beauty and most realized they would never forget it.

This time they passed a few Arabs on their camels, desert traders carrying their wares to other Arab camps irrespective of the aircraft overhead or the tanks and armoured cars massed to the south. Seen in the distance, with their loose robes fluttering, wobbling precariously on their camels, distorted by the heat haze shimmering up from the desert floor, the Arabs looked archaic, ever unreal.

'You wouldn't bleedin' credit it, would you?' Jimbo said to his mate, Frankie, sitting beside him in the rear of one of the Chevrolets as it carried them across the burning sands. 'Those bleeders haven't changed in a million years and aren't likely to. Here we are with our tanks and armoured cars and aircraft, fighting with 25-pounder guns and semi-automatic rifles, and those bastards are still crossing the desert on camels with nothing but swords on their hips. Fucking unbelievable!'

'Right,' Frankie replied, yearning desperately for a fag but not able to light one because of the wind beating at his face. 'One minute you're looking at the blackened wreck of a Daimler armoured car or Sherman tank, all rag and bone inside; the next you see an A-rab on a flea-ridden camel and you think you're hallucinating from the heat.'

'Or a mirage,' Jimbo said.

'I see *them* all the time, mate. Great pools of water, naked women, pints of bitter, plates of roast beef and Yorkshire pudding. I see 'em and smell 'em night and day. That's what this place does to you.'

'Know just what you mean,' Jimbo said.

That night, when the trucks were laagered, the men erected their standard triangular poncho tents between the vehicles and the ground, put up (and rushed to use) the thunderboxes, then lit a few camp-fires and used petrol-can cookers to make their own fry-ups of bacon rashers, tinned tomatoes and bread, the eggs being too fragile to carry.

Alas, when these more pleasurable activities had been exhausted, they were compelled to undertake the more tedious, yet vitally necessary, chores. For the men of L Detachment, SAS, it meant removing their bolt-action rifles, semi-automatic weapons and machine-guns from their wrappings of stretched condoms, cleaning them yet again, no matter how minute the traces of sand found in them, and then wrapping them up again for another day's travel across the desert.

'That's the first time I've ever used a contraceptive,' Neil confessed. Then, realizing what he had said, he blushed a deep crimson.

'Ho, ho!' Frankie roared.

'The secret's out!' Taff added.

'Virgin, are you?' Jimbo asked him with a sly grin. 'So no use for a rubber?'

'Course not!' Neil insisted, blushing an even deeper crimson. 'I just don't use a johnny, that's all. It deadens the sensation, my girl says.'

'Mmmm,' Jimbo responded, grinning slyly at Frankie. 'Deadens the sensation, does it? What do you do, then? Pull out before you come?'

'Hey, come on, Jimbo!' Neil protested, pretending to be involved with his kit, this giving him an excuse to keep his head down and hide his reddening cheeks. 'You don't ask a bloke that kind of thing!'

'Yes, you do. I've asked Frankie here. We're mates and that's what mates talk about. Isn't that right, Frankie?'

'It is,' Frankie replied, pleased to be discussing Neil's virginity instead of his own. 'Mates shouldn't have secrets from one another, after all. What are friends for, if not for sharing their little secrets?'

'Right,' Taff said emphatically. 'So come on, Neil, let us have the filthy facts. If you don't use a johnny, how do keep your little bit of fluff from getting a bun in the oven?'

'Show some respect, Taff!'

'We're your friends. We'd like to know.'

'Why don't you try guessing?' Neil said as if disdainful, though actually trying to hide the fact that he did not have a clue, for he had never got that far and assumed the other three had.

'We'd like you to tell us,' Frankie insisted, artfully hiding the fact that he, too, was a virgin and had only ever used a condom to protect his rifle.

'I respect my girl too much,' Neil lied shamelessly.

'Do you *know* what to do without a johnny? Have you ever unwrapped one, kid?'

'Aw, come on, Jimbo! Knock it off! Of *course* I've unwrapped one. I just don't like to use them, as I said, and that's all I'm saying.'

'So what do you do?' Jimbo insisted. 'Pull it out before you come? Do you squirt it all over her lovely belly and make a right bleedin' mess?'

'God, you're disgusting! I'm not listening to this.' Neil stood up and glanced across the desert like a man deep in thought. 'I think I'll go for a piss.'

Neil snorted, then stomped away from the camp to take a leak out in the desert, well away from the mocking laughter of his mates. 'Filthy-minded bastards!' he muttered as he stepped into darkness, suddenly filling up with visions of his girlfriend back home in Blackburn. A pleasingly plump lass who worked in the cotton mills, she had frequently let him feel her breasts in the back row of the local cinema, but had never let him go any farther, always whispering, 'Not until we're married, luv!' Neil was not sure that he loved her, but he certainly wanted to marry her, if only to feel more of her, and now all that talk about johnnies was making him think of her.

Suddenly he felt very far from home and yearned to be back there, even if only for a short while, back in the back row of the cinema, feeling Florence's soft breast.

'Those bastards!' he muttered as he spread his legs and irrigated the sand of the vast, moonlit darkness just outside the perimeter of the camp. 'They've got no sensitivity.' Nevertheless, he felt an awful lot better when he had emptied his bladder.

Meanwhile, the navigators were using the abundance of stars to check their position and plot the next day's course. Their calculations would, however, be double-checked at first light the next day with the aid of a compass and sextant.

Bored out of their minds with no one to torment, Jimbo and Frankie, having been taught a few things by their LRDG navigator, the amiable Rhodesian, Mike Sadler, watched him at work with his sextant. Inspired by his performance, they decided to experiment with improvised compasses by stropping razor blades against the palms of their hands, as Mike had taught them, and dangling them on lengths of thread to see if they pointed north.

'Mine's stopped,' Jimbo said. 'It's pointing north.'

'How do *you* know?' Frankie asked. 'Could be south, for all you know.'

'Wherever it stops is north, you bleedin' berk!'

'So how do you know?'

''Cause Mike told us so.'

'Mike's a bloody Rhodesian,' Frankie said, 'and they're all mad as hatters and born liars. He was pulling your leg.'

'It's fucking north,' Jimbo said. He studied the dangling razor blade for a moment, not really seeing it, his thoughts focused on sex, this having been brought on by all that talk about contraceptives.

Now, with a hard-on, brought on by sexual taunts, Jimbo suddenly realized that he had not had it for a long time – certainly not since leaving Cairo a couple of months ago. Instead, he had been forced to toss off a lot and make his own right bleedin' mess in the desert sands. Bloody shameful, when you thought of it, what a man had to do, no matter how hard he tried avoiding it. Human nature was base, all right.

Still tormented by his hard-on, which was only made more insistent by recollections of the many delicious little whores he had had in Tiger Lil's in the Sharia el Berka (all the time trying desperately not to think of his wife in Wapping), Jimbo tried to distract himself by recollecting how, during one weekend in Cairo, he had tried to distract himself from the temptations of Tiger Lil's by visiting the Great Pyramid of Cheops, located on the west bank of the Nile.

'Pretty bloody mysterious, isn't it?' he said, tapping the dangling razor blade with his forefinger and watching it slowly spin before pointing north. 'I mean, the way a magnetized razor blade will always point north.'

'I wouldn't know if it's mysterious or not,' Frankie responded pragmatically. 'I just know it does.'

'Bloody funny things, razor blades,' Jimbo said, trying to lose himself in higher thoughts. 'Remember that day I visited the Great Pyramid?'

'No.'

'Well, I did, see? And you know what I found out?'

'No.'

'Well, I visited the Great Pyramid because I'm interested in certain mysteries, see? Like Ancient Egypt and the stars and what have you. And when I visited the Great Pyramid I learnt, from this old Arab who guided me, that if you put a razor blade inside the pyramid between shaves, it'll never go blunt. In fact, if you keep puttin' the razor blade in there between shaves, you could use the same razor blade for ever. Bloody amazing, isn't it?'

'Fascinating,' Frankie replied. 'I'm amazed that half the population of Egypt isn't lining up every night to leave their razor blades in the pyramids and save themselves a fortune in the long term.' He tapped his dangling razor blade and watched it spinning. 'Fucking rubbish!' he said.

Later that evening they stretched out on their groundsheets, but found it next to impossible to sleep, being tormented by buzzing flies and whining mosquitoes, as well as haunted by the thought of creepy-crawlies, particularly snakes and scorpions.

'I keep thinking I can feel things crawling over me,' Frankie complained. 'I'm not scared of the Krauts, I don't mind dying by the bullet, but I have to confess my nerve collapses completely when I think there's something crawling up my leg, heading straight for my balls.'

'Stop being so bleedin' childish,' Jimbo remonstrated. 'You're supposed to be superior to common soldiers, so try to act like you're . . . *Christ, what's that?*'

'What?'

'Fucking hell!' Jimbo frantically rolled off his groundsheet and turned back to examine it. 'Something nipped me,' he said. 'A bleedin' scorpion! I'll be dead by first light . . . Whoops!' He reached down and snatched at it. 'Here's the little bugger! A stone as sharp as a fucking razor. All right, Frankie, stop laughing.'

Later, when it grew colder and even the flies and mosquitoes had settled down, they were kept awake by the bass rumbling of heavy bombers overhead and, for an hour or so, by a *son et lumière* spectacle of tracer shells and bomb explosions illuminating the north-western horizon over what they could only assume was El Agheila, where the Afrika Korps had dug in.

'War can be so beautiful,' Captain Halliman said to Stirling where they lay side by side under a triangular poncho tent strung between their lorry and the ground.

'You think so?'

'Yes. It has a kind of terrible beauty, but the beauty of it can't be denied. I suppose that's what makes war so seductive – it startles and stuns. Rather strange, don't you think?'

'No,' Stirling replied. 'I don't think it's strange at all. Everything seductive is dangerous – and that's what war is.'

'Seductive?'

'Yes. It's rather like mountaineering, which I've done quite a bit. The higher you go, the more dangerous it becomes. The more dangerous it becomes, the more beautiful the world looks and the more heightened your senses become. I would call that seductive.'

'You've climbed some dangerous mountains, haven't you?'

'Yes,' Stirling replied.

'Those climbs must have heightened your senses in a truly dramatic way.'

'They did. They made me feel supremely alive. The desert can do that as well – as can the war we're conducting here.' He glanced at the horizon, where explosions and burning fires were streaking the sky with criss-crossing lines of red, yellow and purple, now visible between pyramids of pulsating, silvery, eerie light. 'That spectacle on the horizon is part of all that. It means death, but it's beautiful.'

Halliman sighed. 'It certainly reminds me that they're dying while we live . . . and *that* certainly makes life seem all the sweeter.'

'You only truly appreciate life when you've come close to losing it,' Stirling said. 'Few are privileged to do so.'

They both slept on that notion.

Up at first light the following day, the men had a quick breakfast of wads and hot tea, then dismantled their shelters, rolled up and packed their groundsheets and ponchos, poured petrol on their own waste and burned it, and in general removed all traces of the camp.

Moving out with the vehicles spaced well apart, in single file, just like a foot patrol, the column soon reached the southernmost tip of the Western Desert, where many battles had raged back and forth over the past few months. It was therefore no accident that the men soon found themselves passing through an eerie flat, white landscape littered with the blackened wreckage of bombed tanks, armoured cars, troop lorries and half-tracks, both Axis and Allied, with whole areas of flatland given over to mass graves covered with hundreds of crude white crosses.

'We're south of El Agheila,' Captain Halliman explained. 'We're now heading north to Sirte and Tamit. We'll be there quite soon, David.'

Surprisingly, though the sky overhead was filled with aircraft, both Axis and Allied, the column was not attacked and eventually, just before last light, they reached the DZ for the first raiding party, to be led by Stirling.

After clambering down to join the rest of his group, Stirling walked over to Callaghan's lorry to wish him good luck.

'Don't forget,' he added, 'that even as we speak, General Ritchie's Eighth Army is advancing on Benghazi and might, indeed, wrest it back from the Afrika Korps today. Because of this, our recent intelligence will be relatively useless. What I mean is that the situation will be changing every minute and we've no way of knowing whether or not the planes we've targeted are going to be called into action, thus leaving us again with empty runways. Also, more importantly, we've no way of keeping in touch with the Axis troop movements, which means we could run smack-dab into them. For this reason, then, no matter what happens, just try to do as much damage as you can, as best you can, wherever you can, then get the hell back to the desert RV. That's it, Paddy, good luck.'

'The same to you, David.'

The LRDG lorries moved off across the desert, churning up clouds of sand that obscured the sinking sun. Stirling waited until they had disappeared completely, then turned to his men.

'Right, chaps, let's get going. Irregular single file behind me. Jimbo, you're out on point as lead scout. You, Frankie, are coming up the rear as our always dependable Tail-end Charlie. Does that sit well with you?'

'Yes, boss,' Private Turner replied, pleased to be called by his first name and to use the word 'boss' in return, instead of the usual 'sir'. Frankie had never liked the rigidity of normal Army protocol, which is why he had applied for L Detachment.

This new, informal approach, particularly when combined with the unusual nature of the work, made him feel pretty good. 'Tail-end Charlie it is,' he said, then turned away and went to the back of the column to take up his position.

Captain Stirling raised and lowered his hand, indicating 'Move out'.

Beginning the hike at sunset, they arrived in protective darkness at the road that ran west of Sirte, beyond which lay the airfield. Once there, Stirling's luck, if such it could be called, changed for the worse yet again.

Just as they approached the road, advancing in single file, intending to cross it one by one, the lights of a slow-moving vehicle appeared in the north, where the coastline lay, and came inexorably towards them.

Stirling signalled immediately for the men behind him to lie down, then he too fell to the sand, just behind Jimbo Ashman. The latter, being an experienced soldier, was already flat on his belly by the edge of the road, holding his Sten gun at the ready.

The lights came towards them, advancing along the road. As they came closer, other lights floated into view behind them, then more lights behind those. They floated eerily in the darkness, beaming down on the road. Gradually gaining in definition, they turned out to be the lights of troop lorries. The first rumbled past, then the next, a third and fourth. Behind the fourth lorry was a German armoured car, followed by a tank.

Stirling sighed in despair. His raiding party was trapped at the side of the road by an Afrika Korps armoured column moving up to the front. It was composed of hundreds of vehicles, including tanks, armoured cars, half-tracks and troop lorries, and it was carrying thousands of men.

It took four hours to pass.

Lying there belly-down by the side of the road, Stirling was convinced that he was going mad. The armoured column passed at a snail's pace, hundreds of vehicles, one by one, and he checked his watch compulsively, obsessed by the time, realizing that *his* time was running out and that soon he would have none left to spare. The strain was almost intolerable, but he had to bear it, wondering meanwhile what the men behind him were thinking as they, too, lay flat on the ground and watched their opportunities slip away.

When, four hours later, the last of the German vehicles had passed, Stirling realized that there was not enough time left to go on to the airfield. He had been foiled again.

'Damn, damn, damn!' he whispered, hammering his fist into the sand.

'You said it yourself, boss,' Sergeant Lorrimer consoled him. 'The Crusader battle has made everything unpredictable and we've no way of knowing what to expect. Let's do what we can, while we can, wherever we can, then get the hell out of here.'

Charmed to have his own words flung back at him, Stirling smiled again.

'Damned right,' he said.

'So?' Lorrimer asked, always keen to present a challenge.

Stirling checked the time again. 'Because that bloody armoured took four hours to pass, we have approximately sixty minutes left to cause some mayhem and madness. Let's do it, Sergeant.'

'I'm here to obey orders, boss. Just give me the word.'

'Weaponry?'

'This time, just in case, we brought along a Browning 0.5-incher and a Bren light machine-gun. The men, apart from those, are reasonably well equipped, with a combination of bolt-action rifles, tommy-guns, and that new thing, the 9mm Sten sub-machine-gun. Not too many worries in that direction, boss. No need to sweat.'

'Land-mines?'

'Absolutely.'

'Hand-grenades.'

'Naturally.'

'You've just made my day, Sergeant Lorrimer. Let's get set to hit and run.'

'It's as good as done, boss.'

'We need transport.'

'I'll call it up.'

Having brought along a No 11 radio set, Lorrimer used it to recall one of the LRDG lorries that had gone on to Tamit. Twenty minutes later, even before the arrival of the vehicle, a German staff car came along the road with a full complement of top brass. Placed in charge of the Browning 0.5-inch machine-gun, Jimbo had no hesitation in squeezing the trigger and sending a hail of bullets into the German officers. They died amid a convulsion of flailing limbs as their vehicle, also peppered with bullets, careered off the road, dived nose-first into the sand and exploded when its petrol tank was punctured.

'We've just given our position away,' Stirling said, sounding pleased, 'so let's hope that LRDG lorry gets here and takes us elsewhere.'

Luckily, it did. Five minutes after the destruction of the German staff car, which had burst into flames and was pouring oily black smoke, an LRDG lorry arrived to hurry them out of the area.

'Take us ten miles down the road,' Stirling said, 'towards the enemy lines. That way, we can pick the bastards off before they get this far. Nipping them in the bud, as it were. A bit like gardening, really.'

Once driven along the road by the LRDG corporal, they planted some land-mines across the desert road, actually an MSR, then spread out again belly-down on the ground and waited for more Axis traffic to pass. The next time it was a troop lorry packed with Italian soldiers. It was blown up by the land-mine, flipped onto its side, and started burning as the unfortunate troops spilled out onto the road. There, before they could even scramble onto their feet, they were chopped to pieces in the triangular fusillade of bullets from Jimbo's 0.5-inch Browning and the Bren light machine-gun being fired by Frankie.

The Italians ran left and right, dropped to their knees, crawled on their bellies, some trying to unsling their weapons, many shouting curses or orders, but the triangular hail of bullets made the ground spit and explode, first around them, then between them, filling the air with swirling sand, and they screamed, convulsed and jerked like demented puppets, then fell back into the murk, their clothing in tatters, punched with holes, torn to shreds, and often died beneath the bodies of their comrades, who were falling like nine-pins.

'You're not bad at all,' Jimbo said to Frankie, both men oblivious to the screams of the wounded scattered around the blazing Italian troop lorry. 'You're pretty good really.'

'Those two bastards are born killers,' Lorrimer told Stirling. 'I'm not suggesting it's good, I'm not complaining that it's bad, but I'm certainly saying they're the kind we're looking for. Take that as you may, boss.'

'I take it as read,' Stirling replied. 'Now let's move on, Sergeant.'

They moved on along the road, heading towards the enemy lines, and again took up their positions on both sides of the road. This time they hit an Italian tank, first stopping it with land-mines, which blew its treads off, then punching holes in its side armour and fuel tank with a combined burst from the Browning 0.5-incher and a Bren light machine-gun, and finally slaughtering the crew in a hail of fire from their combined bolt-action rifles, tommy-guns, and 9mm Sten sub-machine-guns as the unfortunate men, some on fire and already screaming dementedly, tried to escape the series of convulsions that were filling the interior with flames and smoke.

When the attack was over, with nothing left alive in the pall of smoke covering the burning tank and road, the SAS men moved on again.

So it went for the next few hours, a precise routine repeated constantly, with the men attacking Axis transports along the MSR, using a combination of land-mines, machine-guns, and automatic and semi-automatic rifles which, between them, created a devastating cross-fire. Tanks exploded internally. Lorries burst into flames. Staff cars careered off the road and rolled over in clouds of dust, the officers inside peppered with bullets that ricocheted off the doors, shattered the windows, and in general created a bedlam that drowned out the screams of the dying. Other soldiers, not so lucky, were incinerated in the flames, choked in the dense smoke, or expired slowly in the agony of amputated limbs and punctured stomachs. Very few survived.

Leaving the smouldering wreckage and its dead, Stirling's group advanced even closer to the Axis lines to attack again, exactly as previously – land-mines for the vehicles, machine-guns and small arms for the troops – before those travelling in the direction of Sirte could find the previous victims.

As the vehicles included tanks, armoured cars, half-tracks, staff cars and lorries, the results of Stirling's attacks along the MSR, moving ever closer to the front, were more impressive than even he realized at first. Certainly, by the end of the few hours left to him after being stopped by the four-hour-long convoy, he had caused an enormous amount of damage to the Axis transports attempting to move along the MSR.

'I couldn't have picked them off easier at a funfair in Brighton,' Jimbo said to Frankie as they packed up their machine-guns and moved out. 'A regular little duck-shoot, that was. We should do it again sometime.'

They moved out with minutes to spare, heading back across the desert, leaving their last victims sprawled across the wide MSR in a welter of burning petrol, melting rubber, buckling perspex, smouldering upholstery, shattered glass, and red-hot, twisted metal. They also left the stench of cordite and scorched flesh, heading gratefully back into the pure air of the clean, silent desert. The buzzing of flies and the whining of mosquitoes did not count in this reckoning. Now the desert seemed pure to them.

Four hours later, in the early hours of the morning, Stirling arrived back at the desert RV, where Callaghan, already sitting in his poncho tent with a glass of whisky and cigar, told him that his group had destroyed a whole squadron of aircraft on the airfield at Tamit.

'A real fireworks display,' he told Stirling. 'Flame and smoke to the heavens.'

'That sounds like Irish hyperbole,' Stirling replied, 'but being Scottish, I'm pleased to accept it. Pour me a whisky, thanks.'

'L Detachment, SAS, has earned its wings,' Callaghan told him. 'You need doubt it no longer.'

Stirling looked up at the vast, starlit sky and asked his one, burning question: 'Where are the others?'

17

Dropped off by T2 Patrol at Nofilia, over 120 miles east of Sirte, Lewes made for the airfield under cover of darkness with Lieutenant Greaves and his troopers, including Corporal Taff Clayton and Private Neil Moffatt, determined to prove the worth of his bombs. Unfortunately, as before, the problem was not the bombs, but the shortage of targets and the lack of adequate prior intelligence.

With the best will in the world, Lewes could do little at Nofilia because there were only a few Axis planes on the runway, so widely dispersed that it took an age to get from one to the other. To make matters worse, the need to tie the SAS raids to General Ritchie's advance on Benghazi had left no time to correct the erratic timing of the Lewes bomb fuses. Thus, the bomb on the first plane, timed to ignite in thirty minutes, went off much earlier, before the raiders were even clear of the second plane.

That first bomb exploded as the men were making their getaway, thus drawing the Axis sentries to the airfield. Even worse: the second bomb never went off – either because the fuse had malfunctioned or, just as likely, because the early explosion of the first bomb had given the enemy warning in good time to either defuse, or remove completely, the second bomb.

In any event, by the time the single explosion erupted behind them, illuminating the night sky with jagged fingers of yellow flame that were almost instantly smothered in a blanket of ink-black smoke, Lewes and Greaves were already racing away from the airfield, to begin their trek back across the desert to the RV. Glancing back over their shoulders, they saw the flames and smoke of the burning plane, with Axis troops converging from all sides to the scene of the blaze.

'Only one!' Lewes exclaimed bitterly. 'Not even two!'

'It's the luck of the draw,' Greaves responded. 'Come on, Jock, keep running!'

They fled from the unguarded perimeter as fast as their legs would carry them, glancing repeatedly back over their shoulders to check that the Axis troops now surrounding the blazing plane had not decided to follow the saboteurs. In the event, none of them did, which made the getaway easy. Nevertheless, the SAS men slowed down to a quick march only when the airfield behind them was out of sight beyond a line of smooth, wave-like sand dunes painted pale white by the moonlight. When the dunes too had disappeared, the men slowed down to a normal walk.

'What a bleedin' cock-up!' Taff said to Neil, just before they broke into single file. 'I thought we'd really bought it that time, mate, what with all those bleedin' Germans flooding over the runway when that bomb went off early.'

'I was saying my prayers, I can tell you,' Neil replied solemnly. 'Nearly shitting my pants, I was. We were lucky they all went for that burning plane and didn't come after us.'

'One fucking bomb! It breaks your bleedin' heart.' Taff could hardly believe they'd had such bad luck. 'So much for so little!'

'Not as bad,' Neil said. 'One bomb's better than none – and it kept the Germans and Eyeties busy, at least.'

'Look for the silver lining, right? You're a bloody optimist, Neil.'

'I like to look on the bright side, that's true. So what happens now?'

'We're going to the RV. Linking up with Captain Stirling and other raiding parties that were sent off on raids in the same area at approximately the same time. Then the LRDG lorries will take us back to base and a nice cup of char.'

'I can't wait,' Neil said.

In fact their jocular manner hid a bitter disappointment that nagged remorselessly at all of them as they made their long march through the night.

The desert's darkness was deep, though a pale moon shone down, and the silence had an unreal, eerie quality that made some of the men uneasy. Planes often flew overhead, obviously heading for Benghazi, and occasionally lorries were heard in the distance, taking troops to the front. Lights fanned up in the distance, illuminating the northern horizon, reminding the men that the war was still engaged and that the planes overhead were on bombing runs against the beleaguered Axis forces.

'It looks pretty from here, doesn't it?' Taff said. 'But I bet it's hell over there.'

'We're marching in the right direction,' Neil told him. 'Well away from that shit.'

'Poor bastards,' Taff said.

'Move apart, you men!' Lewes snapped. 'You're supposed to be marching in single file, not bunched up like Girl Guides.'

'Sorry, boss!' Taff responded, then fell back to where he was supposed to be – as Tail-end Charlie. He felt isolated back there, cut off by the moonlit darkness, too aware of the vastness of the desert and its lack of identifiable features. He felt minute and vulnerable.

Lewes, meanwhile, though second in the group, now marching behind Neil, was emotionally isolated by his nagging sense of failure, unable to believe that they had managed to bomb only one Axis plane. Even worse: either one of his bombs had failed to go off or the early ignition of the first one had given Jerry time to defuse the second. Either way, Lewes had little to be proud of and was feeling extremely bitter about it. He marched, then, in disconsolate isolation, blaming himself, but also gearing himself up for further research into explosives and other tactical matters when he got back to the base camp at Kabrit.

L Detachment, SAS, is now a functioning, worthy unit, he thought, but it's not perfect yet. Making it perfect is the next job on my list. I must keep this in mind.

That his interest was returning already had to be a good sign.

They marched for six hours, but still arrived at the desert RV in darkness, just before first light. As usual, they made contact with the LRDG by using a series of whistling sounds, which both groups recognized, then by shining their torches at those shining at them. Eventually, the lorries of the LRDG took shape in the darkness and the other men, including those of the SAS, came forward to greet them.

Stirling, towering over most of the others, was the first to emerge from the darkness, holding his hand out and smiling. He shook Lewes's hand and asked, 'How did it go?'

'Badly,' Lewes replied bluntly.

He told Stirling what had happened. Stirling listened thoughtfully, then smiled even more widely and patted Lewes on the back. 'Nothing to be ashamed of, old boy,' he said. 'These little mishaps are bound to happen and have to be lived with. Look at us, after all. We didn't even get as far as the airfield.'

'But you made up for it,' Lewes said, 'by attacking Jerry along that MSR.'

'We were in the right place at the right time.

That's all there was to it. Come on, Jock, cheer up! It's Christmas morning, after all. Also, we've just heard on the radio that General Ritchie's Eighth Army marched into Benghazi yesterday. Our raids, so I'm told, had a lot to do with that – reducing the number of enemy aircraft and distracting their troops – so we've finally proved our worth to the sceptics. L Detachment, SAS, is now a viable entity. They won't stop us now.'

'Well, that's something,' Lewes said.

Feeling a lot happier when he climbed up into the heavily armoured, four-wheel-drive Chevrolet, behind Sergeant McGee and his driver, Corporal Cook, he was glad to take his usual seat right beside the Boyes anti-tank gun mounted in the rear and manned by Private Sammy Bakewell of the LRDG.

The rest of the men were still greeting each other, shaking hands and slapping backs, trading compliments or amiable insults, when Stirling took his place in the lorry of the LRDG commander, Captain Halliman.

'Looks like we're leaving straight away,' Jimbo said, where he stood with Frankie, Taff and Neil near the lorry that was taking them back.

'Without even breakfast,' Taff complained.

'You didn't earn breakfast,' Jimbo told him. 'I mean, one plane for Christ's sake!'

'You didn't get *any*,' Neil reminded him.

'So? At least we shot up a lot of bleedin' Krauts and Eyeties, as well as their tanks, armoured cars and troop lorries. That's more than *you* did.'

'You bastards just struck it lucky,' Taff insisted. 'It's as simple as that.'

'Right!' Jimbo said. 'Begrudge us our dues. Just because you can't face the fact that your own raid was a bloody balls-up. It's understandable, really.'

'One plane,' Taff insisted, 'is one more plane than *you* bastards got.'

'Don't come it, m' darling!'

'Get up on your trucks, you bloody men!' Sergeant McGee bellowed. 'We haven't got all day!'

Startled, Jimbo and the others hurriedly climbed up into their lorries to a round of sardonic applause from the other men.

'Thank you, folks,' Jimbo said, taking a bow. 'And now for our next act!'

Up in the leading vehicle, the LRDG commander, Captain Halliman, with Captain Stirling by his side, raised his right hand and waved it forward, indicating that the convoy should move out. The engines roared into life, the wheels churned up clouds of sand, and the lorries headed across the flat plain, towards the first gold-and-crimson tendrils of the rising sun.

Within half an hour the sun was a huge red-and-yellow ball in a whitening sky. An hour later, it was just a fierce whiteness in a sky of the same colour. The cold of night was burned away, the heat was rising rapidly, and the air was filling up with the usual buzzing flies and whining mosquitoes. These came swarming around the troopers every time the trucks stopped for their hourly checks. They got under the men's *shemaghs*, into their cups of tea, and covered their uniforms and weapons. A normal day in the desert.

'Open your mouth to drink your char and you're going to have *these* bastards for breakfast,' Jimbo said, swatting flies and mosquitoes from his cup. 'I can take anything the desert throws at me except these bloody insects.'

'You've just managed to speak without swallowing them,' Frankie replied, 'so they can't be that bad.'

Frankie never bothered swatting them away; he seemed to think they were natural.

'You're a walking dung-heap,' Jimbo told him. 'That's why they don't bother you.'

Frankie grinned and patted Jimbo on the shoulder. 'My old mate,' he said.

They had stopped for one of their hourly vehicle

checks when Sergeant McGee, hawk-eyed as ever, spotted a plane glinting in the sky and bawled a warning to everyone.

It was an Italian Savoya SM 79 Sparviero, a light bomber with three 12.7 Breda machine-guns and a Lewis gun, as well as over a ton of bombs. It flew directly over them, circled back, then banked and flew at them.

'He's attacking!' Captain Halliman bawled.

The Italian pilot flew in low, all his guns spitting fire, stitching lines of exploding sand across the desert, running at tremendous speed towards the parked trucks. The men in the trucks returned fire with their Boyes anti-tank guns and Lewis light machine-guns, but the Savoya was already releasing its first bombs and climbing as the bullets from its guns ricocheted noisily off the lorries and wounded some screaming men.

The bombs seemed to drop slowly, turning over like black slugs, then hit the ground and exploded, one slightly behind the other. The earth erupted into two roaring mushrooms of sand, soil and smoke.

When the smoke and raining sand had thinned out, the blackened, mangled remains of an LRDG lorry was revealed. It had been blown up, set on fire, and turned upside down, with its passengers either killed by the blast, burned alive or crushed to death.

'Bastards!' Jimbo bawled, standing up in the rear seat of his own vehicle, beside the Boyes gun, and shaking his fist at the Savoya as it circled around in the distance, coming back to attack again. 'Fuck you!' he screamed, unslinging his Sten gun and preparing to fire at the oncoming plane. 'Have a mouthful of this!'

The Boyes and Lewis guns roared again as the Savoya banked towards the column and began its second descent. The yellow flickering along its wing edges indicated that its guns were firing, then two more bombs dropped from its belly and fell like black slugs as the lines of spitting sand, kicked up by bullets, raced towards the column.

Jimbo was not alone in opening fire with his Sten gun. Most of the SAS men were on their feet, in the lorries or beside them, adding the roar of their rifles, semi-automatics and even handguns to that of the LRDG machine-guns.

The second pair of bombs exploded as the Savoya roared overhead, its bullets peppering more of the men and ricocheting off the lorries. The earth erupted again, one explosion following the other, to pick up two vehicles, smash them together, and throw the passengers in all directions, like rag dolls, before the lorries crashed back to the ground.

The mushrooming clouds of sand, soil and smoke briefly blotted out the sky, eventually rained back down, and drifted away on the wind, revealing more death and devastation, with charred bodies smouldering in the wreckage.

When the Savoya circled around and banked for another attack, Lewes, enraged, took charge of the pintle-mounted Lewis light machine-gun. After swinging it expertly onto what he deemed to be the proper elevation, he waited until the aircraft was virtually roaring straight at him with yellow fire spitting from its wings.

Lewes opened fire as twin lines of spitting sand raced up to his lorry, ricocheted off its bonnet, and blew the back of McGee's head off. Perhaps Lewes saw the spewing brains, blood and bone of the sergeant's exploded head before bullets punched through his own body like a series of red-hot rivets, throwing him violently backwards off the lorry and into the sand. After that, he saw nothing.

The two bombs from the Savoya, which roared overhead and away, exploded in front of the truck, picking it up and flipping it over, to smash back down in geysering sand that covered Lewes like a blanket.

Stirling jumped from his truck and ran back to examine Lewes. Discovering that he was dead, he shuddered helplessly with grief and shock, then managed to regain control of himself, clenching and unclenching his fists repeatedly, letting the tension flow out of him. Finally, breathing deeply and wiping some tears from his eyes, he stood up over the dead body of Captain Lewes and scanned the silvery-blue sky.

The Savoya had gone but he knew that it would return, almost certainly bringing other aircraft with it.

Possibly reading his mind, Sergeant Lorrimer said, 'I think we should move on.'

'Yes,' Stirling said. 'I agree. However, I fear we can't take the dead with us. It's too hot for that.'

Lorrimer snapped his fingers at a group of SAS troopers standing nearby. 'You men,' he said. 'Get some shovels and bury these dead men – and be quick about it.'

'Yes, boss!' two of the men said simultaneously. Then they all went off to one of the trucks to get a couple of shovels. The six men were able to dig two shallow graves in a relatively short time. While they were digging, another couple of troopers wrapped the dead bodies of Captain Lewes and Sergeant McGee in tightly bound canvas sheeting.

Eventually, when all was ready, the bodies were lowered into the shallow graves and covered up again. After the men had solemnly gathered around the graves, Captain Stirling, clearly trying to hide his overbrimming emotions, conducted a brief, moving ceremony, completing it with an unsteady voicing of The Lord's Prayer.

Raising their heads after the prayer, the men saw Captain Stirling wiping another tear from his eyes before composing his features.

'That's it,' he said, trying to sound gruff. 'All right, men, let's go.'

The men piled back onto their lorries and continued the long drive due east, towards Jalo Oasis.

Unfortunately, as anticipated by Stirling, two German Me 109F fighters appeared on the horizon to finish the work begun by the Savoya. Suddenly roaring in overhead, one after the other, they turned the desert floor into a sea of spitting sand, then tore the earth up in a series of roaring eruptions when two sticks of bombs were dropped in close succession. The bombs exploded even as the jagged lines of spitting sand raced through the column and peppered the lorries with bullets that ricocheted off into the wild blue yonder, miraculously without hitting any of the SAS or LRDG troopers, most of whom were trying to bring the departing aircraft down with their small arms. The combined noise of the exploding bombs, roaring machine-guns, and automatic and semi-automatic weapons was ear-shattering, with the men continuing to fire even after the Messerschmitts had flown off, letting the swirling, billowing sand settle down around the still-moving convoy.

The men in the trucks cheered when they saw the planes flying off. They stopped cheering when they turned around and headed back towards them.

'They're coming back!' someone bawled.

A running game of hide-and-seek then began between the lorries and the aircraft and continued for the next few hours.

At times the lorries would try to race away from the planes with the LRDG gunners firing on the move; then the lorries would be called in to form a defensive laager, when the fire of the LRDG gunners would be joined by a fusillade of fire from the small arms of the defiant SAS troopers.

The tyres of one vehicle exploded, making it sink to the ground to be obscured in billowing clouds of sand. Another was peppered with bullets, was hit in its petrol tank, and exploded into flames as the last of its crew jumped to safety. Another lorry was picked up and flipped over by a bomb explosion, tipping its crew out, then finally crashing upside down, practically bouncing off the desert floor, and finally grinding to a halt in a hole created by its own weight, like a dying animal digging its own grave.

Eventually most of the lorries were damaged one way or another by the enemy aircraft, but miraculously no more men were hit and the drivers kept going.

Running out of ammunition, the Messerchmitts flew off.

They were replaced, however, forty minutes later by the original Savoya, which again caused havoc with its deadly combination of spitting machine-guns and exploding bombs.

Knowing that a defensive laager would be a sitting duck for the Savoya's bombs, Captain Halliman ordered the other drivers to scatter as widely as possible across the desert, thus forcing the Italian pilot to choose between individual targets.

He was, in fact, coming in on a low sweep over Halliman's lorry when six RAF Hurricane II fighters, probably en route to El Agheila, spotted him and banked to attack him. Four of them bore down upon him, one after the other, all with guns roaring, and the Savoya shuddered violently, belched out oily black smoke, lost pieces of one wing, then went into a spinning, shuddering, whining dive to the desert floor, where it exploded in a spectacular ball of vivid-yellow fire surrounded by boiling black smoke.

As the scattering Chevrolets of the LRDG came back together again, the Hurricanes flew over them, dipped their wings in salute, then flew on towards the coast, eventually disappearing beyond the horizon.

'We all complain about the RAF,' Lieutenant Greaves said to Jimbo, 'but sometimes, you must admit, they're worth waiting for.'

'I hate to admit it,' Jimbo replied, 'but those bastards *did* warm my heart.'

Lorrimer, listening in on the conversation, just shook his head wearily.

The LRDG lorries continued on towards Jalo Oasis, though by now they were all virtual wrecks that began breaking down, one after the other. As each vehicle expired, its passengers would clamber out, strip the vehicle of anything of value – usually tyres, petrol cans and water –

and distribute themselves and the spare parts as evenly as possible between the others lorries. Then the ever-diminishing convoy would trundle on across the flat, sun-scorched plain.

Gradually, however, the remaining lorries also broke down, until, by the late afternoon, there were only three left, with fifteen men on each, balanced precariously and holding on to each other in a pile of salvaged tyres, petrol cans, water bottles, and weapons. Another vehicle then broke down, leaving only two, which meant that a lot of the men had to start walking, though mercifully now in cooling darkness.

By the time the cool air had turned to rapidly chilling night wind, another lorry had broken down and the sole remaining one, sagging under the weight of its fifteen men, was squeaking in protest as it crawled on.

Stirling and Greaves, though offered a lift on the last lorry, still in the charge of Captain Halliman, decided to set a good example to their men by rejecting the offer and joining the others on the arduous march through the freezing night.

After four hours, they caught up with the remaining lorry, which had expired trying to climb a slight slope, beyond which lay a broad swathe of perfectly flat, hard terrain, perfect for driving. The passengers were nowhere in sight, which meant they had marched on.

'If this was daylight,' Lorrimer said, 'you'd see their footsteps all the way across the desert, heading towards the horizon. They aren't waiting for anyone.'

'Good on 'em,' Taff replied. 'They've set a shining example.'

'Damned right,' Lorrimer said.

By first light, a total of forty-five men were spread out across the desert, all heading in their separate ways for Jalo Oasis. Though ragged, numb with cold, hungry and thirsty, none showed the slightest sign of wanting to give up.

'Not now,' Jimbo gasped. 'Not after all this shit. I'm only going down when I'm in my grave and that's a long way off yet . . . Come on, Taff, stay awake!'

'It's my eyes,' Taff replied, croaking out of a ravaged throat. 'They're hurting so much from the sun, I can't keep them open. It's not tiredness – I don't think it's that – it's just my eyes that are giving in.'

'Your eyes? Shit! You're swaying like a reed in the wind and wandering left, right and centre. You're about to collapse, Taff.'

'I won't fall until you do.'

'We all heard you making that bold statement,' Frankie told him, 'so now you're going to have to live up to it.'

'Right,' Neil said. 'Here, put your arm around my neck . . . That's it, Taff! Now lean on me.'

'I'm all right, I tell you . . . Thanks, Neil. God, I'm so bloody tired!'

'We're *all* tired,' Jimbo said.

'Shut your mouths, conserve your breath and keep marching,' Lorrimer told them. 'That way you might make it back.'

So saying, he hurried on ahead, swinging his arms as if marching to a brass band, setting a shining example. It was his way of helping them.

Thus they helped one another, supporting each other, taking turns, and so managed to get through another night and into the second day. It was worse than the day before. The heat was like a furnace. The flies and mosquitoes, smelling sweat, sensing weakness, went into a veritable frenzy around the men, attacking in swarms. The light dazzled and blinded.

Sometimes a man collapsed. When this happened, others supported him. When that man recovered, smiling sheepishly, maybe shaking, he took his turn in supporting another man – and so it went on for many hours – even when the dazzling light and fierce heat of the day had returned to blister the skin around their eyes and drain them of strength.

It was only the *shemaghs* that prevented their faces from being blistered and gave them protection from the frenzied swarms of flies and mosquitoes. They marched, walked, stumbled and sometimes crawled through those noisy swarms, those veritable clouds of insects, emerging from them, as if from dark rain clouds, to the sun's dazzling light and the heat haze shimmering up from the desert floor. Scorched and consumed by the sun, they gradually merged with the featureless desert, becoming part of its landscape.

They were ghosts in the haze.

Captain Stirling stayed out in front. He felt that it was his duty. Already a tall man, he grew taller as the day began, letting his stature, both real and imagined, give strength to his men. They followed as best they could, some close behind him, others straggling, and were proud to see that the other officers – Captain Callaghan and Lieutenant Greaves – were marching as resolutely as himself, though now looking like scarecrows.

This is the final testing ground, Greaves thought, recalling the great battle outside Mersa Brega and thinking it child's stuff compared to this. If we finish this hike, if we survive, we'll have proved we are worthy. L Detachment, SAS, will exist and go on to better things. Keep walking. Don't stop.

Greaves did not stop. Marching into the heat haze – or, more accurately, dragging his feet behind him, through the heavy, burning sand – he kept himself going by dwelling on where he had come from and what the end of his bitter journey might bring him.

He recalled his elegant family home in Hanover Street, Edinburgh, his student days at the University, romance with his girlfriend, now fiancée, Mary Radnor; then recruit training and his first years with the Scots Guards; and, finally, his baptism of fire in Sicily with 8 Commando, leading to that unforgettable day when, outside Mersa Brega, the awesome might of Rommel's Afrika Korps – hundreds of tanks, thousands of men – had swept over the British defences and pushed them all the way back to Tobruk and the Mediterranean.

Whether a defeat or not, that last adventure had been the most exciting time of Greaves's life to date.

Disturbing though it was to acknowledge the fact, Greaves had enjoyed the experience, had taken pride from surviving it, and was still feeling proud when recuperating from his painful wounds in the hospital in Alexandria, where he had first met Captain David Stirling, likewise Scots Guards, who had led him to where he was this very moment.

That pride sustained him even now as, scorched by the sun, his throat dry, his head aching, his eyes bloodshot and practically blind, he continued to stumble on towards that dazzling horizon.

He would not stop. He had a lot to look forward to. He would drink a cooling beer, eat a decent meal, be flown out to Cairo and, if he was lucky, even be reunited with Nurse Frances Beamish in the relative luxury of Shepheard's Hotel. Life was for the living, he realized, and he wanted to live.

That romantic notion kept Greaves going when his exhausted body begged him to give in.

Nor did any of the others stop. Captains Stirling and Callaghan, Corporal Clayton, Privates Ashman, Privates Turner and Moffatt and all the others. Though hungry and thirsty, though burnt and blistered, though mentally and physically exhausted, they refused to give in. They hiked, marched, walked and, in some cases, eventually crawled, until they saw what some of them thought was a mirage: the palm trees, green grass and pale-blue water of Jalo Oasis.

Jimbo was on his hands and knees. Having collapsed, he had started crawling. After crawling on his belly for what seemed like an eternity, he had risen back onto his hands and knees. He was wearing shorts and his knees were blistered. The blisters burst and were scraped by sand. The raw flesh of Jimbo's knees poured blood that soaked the sand and the pain, which was beyond his imagining, made him shed silent tears.

His hands were blistered, too. The burning sand burst those blisters. When the pus poured out, the hot sand scorched his raw skin and made him almost cry out with the pain. Almost, but not quite. Jimbo gritted his teeth instead. He advanced on blistered hands and knees, in the agony of the damned, leaving a trail of blood behind him, towards what he was convinced was a mirage of cool water and shade.

'Won't give in,' he gasped. 'Never!'

Someone walked out towards him, stopped above him, looked down at him. He was a very big man in an immaculate uniform, his arms folded across his broad chest as he gazed down in wonder.

'You're a right bloody mess,' LRDG Sergeant

'Wild Bill' Monnery said with a widening grin. 'Welcome home, trooper.'

Jimbo smiled and collapsed.

18

The SAS raids of December 1941 had accounted for ninety-seven aircraft, according to L Detachment's meagre records. Also destroyed, however, were at least forty vehicles, including fuel tankers invaluable to the Axis forces.

In March, June and December of the following year, having learnt from their good and bad experiences, the SAS mounted a number of successful raids around Benghazi and Tobruk, destroying shipping and supply dumps as well as airfields.

When Rommel's Afrika Korps advanced into Egypt, L Detachment, SAS, by then equipped with its own jeeps armed with mounted Vickers and Browning machine-guns, destroyed many enemy aircraft with Lewes bombs and machine-gun fire in raids against the airfields of Bagoush and Sidi Haneish.

Whatever the precise number of Axis losses, General Auchinleck, the British Commander-in-Chief of Middle East Forces, was satisfied that L Detachment had indeed proved its worth. Captain Stirling was therefore promoted to Major and allowed to recruit a further six officers and up to forty other ranks.

The deeds of L Detachment, and of Captain Stirling, soon became legendary, particularly in the folklore of service bars throughout the Middle East.

In October 1942, L Detachment, now 500 strong, was officially listed as 1st Special Air Service (SAS) Regiment.

Though the creator and official head of the SAS, Captain Stirling did not stay with it for long, being captured by the Germans in January 1943, during Operation Torch in Tunisia, then incarcerated in Gavi prison, Italy, from where he escaped four times, before being sent to the high-security Colditz Prison, where he remained as a POW for the rest of the war.

The future of the SAS Regiment was, however, assured when, in 1943, Captain Stirling's brother, Lieutenant-Colonel William Stirling, then with the British First Army, formed 2 SAS and, with the Special Raiding Squadron (SRS) – which was 1

SAS temporarily renamed – performed invaluable work in the Allied capture of Sicily.

In October 1945 the SAS was officially disbanded because the War Office saw no future need for it. However, in 1947, the War Office, changing its tune, established a Territorial Army raiding unit attached to the Rifle Brigade, which was then merged with the Artists Rifles and renamed 21 SAS (Artists).

In 1950, during the so-called 'Emergency' in Malaya, Colonel 'Mad' Mike Calvert, veteran of the Chindit campaigns in Burma, formed the Malayan Scouts, which included a detachment from 21 SAS (Artists). In 1952, at the recommendation of Colonel Calvert, 22 SAS was created from the Malayan Scouts as a special counter-insurgency force.

Many of those who had fought with Stirling during World War Two rushed to join 22 SAS, serving with it during many remarkable campaigns in many parts of the world.

Within a decade, the SAS became the most famous regiment in the world. Whether reviled or admired, criticized or deified, it remains that way still.

SOLDIER H: SAS

THE HEADHUNTERS OF BORNEO

Shaun Clarke

Prelude

The landscape consisted of dense, often impenetrable jungle, swamps, rivers so broad and deep that they were frequently impassable and aerial walkways created at dizzying heights over the rapids by the primitive tribesmen. Snakes, scorpions, lizards, poisonous spiders and dangerous wild pigs infested the whole area. Though seemingly uninhabitable, the jungle was home to many native settlements, or kampongs, most located either by the river or on a hillside, where the inhabitants tilled the land around them or hunted for fish, lizard, boar, deer, baboon, porcupine or the ever-present snake.

These primitive peoples were Land Dyaks, Ibans, Muruts and Punans, who lived in longhouses made of atap wood, with sloping roofs of tin or thatch. The longhouses were apt to creak balefully on the stilts that had kept them out of the water for decades. Inside they were unhygienic and usually fetid because as many as fifteen families would live in a single dwelling at any given time, using the slatted floor as a communal lavatory. Small and indolent, the natives wore nothing above the waist, regardless of sex, wore their hair long, often tattooed themselves against evil spirits, and lived off rice, tapioca, vegetables and curried meat. Before being killed for eating, their prey was first stunned by a virulent nerve poison borne by on a slim bamboo dart shot from a blowpipe.

Early morning in the jungle and swamps was often misty. The strong sun did not break through until at least mid-morning and most afternoons brought a torrential deluge of rain, accompanied by spectacular electrical storms. As a result, the water often rose 30 feet in a single day, slopping and splashing around the stilts of the longhouses, making them groan in protest.

Because certain of the tribesmen, notably the headhunters among them, thought the creaking and groaning were the whispering of bad spirits, they attempted to keep the spirits at bay by stringing up shrunken human heads on the doorposts atop the entrance stairways.

Many of the primitive Iban tribesmen, being experts in jungle tracking, had been employed by the British during the Malayan Emergency of 1948–60 as Army trackers, and were dubbed the Sarawak Rangers. Now, in 1963, having been trained by the SAS, they had been recruited again as an irregular force, the Border Scouts, used mainly as trackers, but also armed and trained as paramilitaries. Increasingly under the command of, and working alongside, the Gurkha Rifles, they were engaged in the 'secret' war being waged to protect Sarawak, Borneo, from the forces of Indonesia's ambitious President Sukarno, who were striking from neighbouring Kalimantan.

Enlisting the aid of the indigenous population, and with the additional reconnaissance and intelligence support of the men of A Squadron, SAS, the Gurkha-led patrols made cross-border raids against the Indonesians, worked at winning the hearts and minds of the jungle dwellers, and set up many Scout posts and observation posts (OPs) in the kampongs and along the densely overhung river banks.

At Long Jawi in Sarawak, 30 miles from the border with Kalimantan, the Gurkhas had established a Scout post consisting of twenty-one trained locals, or Border Scouts, two Police Field Force signallers and a six-man Gurkha team headed by SAS corporal, Ralph Sanderson, on loan to A Squadron from D Squadron. Operating from their own riverside longhouse just outside the village, the members of the border team had spent weeks making friends with the tribesmen in the other longhouses in the area, training certain of them to be armed Border Scouts, and patrolling the valleys, not only for intelligence about Indonesian Army or CCO – Clandestine Communist Organization – troop movements, but also to map out a possible route across the jungle-covered mountains between Sarawak and Kalimantan.

Nominally in charge of such missions, Corporal Sanderson had immersed himself in local culture to such an extent that he was treated by the natives as one of their own and was told all they knew about Indonesian activities in the valley and across the hills, where the build-up of uniformed enemy forces was increasing daily.

Though the SAS were not yet under orders to take aggressive action against such forces, they were allowed to embark on reconnaissance and intelligence-gathering (R & I) missions and, if they sighted the enemy, to inform the Gurkhas and guide them and the armed Border Scouts back across the border. The Gurkhas and Border Scouts would then attack the enemy and make a subsequent hasty retreat back to the Scout post on their own side of the border.

These experiences had filled Sanderson with admiration for the skill and courage of the Gurkhas, but left him with mixed feelings about the Border Scouts. Although fond of the tribesmen, who were superb as trackers and good-natured as comrades, he was convinced that training them as paramilitaries was a waste of time. As well as lacking any sense of discipline, they simply could not learn to handle their weapons properly, and were always pointing them accidentally at one another when they were cocked and loaded. It was the corporal's belief, therefore, that while the Border Scouts were dependable as trackers, they could not be relied on in a fire-fight and might even be a liability.

Sanderson did not know it, but he was about to be proven right in a most forceful manner.

Just before dawn one day in September 1963 a well-equipped company of Indonesian regulars made an attack by river on Long Jawi, emerging from the early morning mist. The Border Scouts manning the GPMG (general-purpose machine-gun) in a protective sangar at the edge of the river, just outside the Security Forces longhouse and the kampong 500 yards east of it, had been drinking *tapai*, a potent local cider, the night before and were sleeping soundly at their gun when the Indonesian boats slid into the river bank. The Border Scouts were still sleeping it off when the enemy troops, all wearing jungle-green fatigues and carrying Armalite M16 5.56mm and Kalashnikov AK47 7.62mm assault rifles, slipped off the boats, spread out in a broad firing arc and advanced quietly on the longhouse. While they were doing so, more troops disembarked behind them to set up two 7.62mm RPK light machine-guns spaced so as to cover both lines of retreat from the longhouse.

The first of the Border Scouts was awakened by the snapping of twigs on the jungle floor as the Indonesian troops stealthily approached his sangar. Looking up and seeing two of them practically on top of him, he managed to let out a shrill cry of warning before the enemy guns burst into action with a deafening roar and a combined hail of 5.56mm and 7.62mm bullets tore the sangar apart, turning the Scout into a convulsing rag doll of torn clothing, punctured flesh, exposed bone and pouring blood. The guard next to him suffered a similar fate before even lifting his head, expiring in an explosion of swirling thatch, bamboo and dust from the exploding walls of the devastated sangar.

The Security Forces men also inside the longhouse were rudely awakened by the roaring of the guns outside. First out of his hammock was Corporal Sanderson, who almost in one movement rolled off the bed and landed on his feet on the slatted floor. Picking up his self-loading rifle, he rushed to the veranda while the two Police Field Force signallers and a six-man Gurkha team sharing the longhouse were still struggling to get their wits together. Running at the crouch out through the entrance and along the veranda raised high above the ground, he saw that the Border Scouts who had been sleeping around the longhouse were perishing in a hail of bullets from the Indonesian raiders. The latter were spread out across the clearing between the river and the longhouse and firing their weapons on the move.

The combined roaring of the two Indonesian RPK light machine-guns, fired simultaneously to spray the front of the longhouse, filling the air with flying splinters of bamboo and thatch, merely added to the general bedlam of gunfire, ricocheting bullets, shouting and screaming.

Realizing instantly that there was no hope of defending the longhouse, Sanderson fired a couple of bursts from his SLR. He had the satisfaction of seeing a couple of enemy troops fall down, then he bolted around the corner of the longhouse – the veranda ran right around it – as some Gurkhas emerged from inside, bravely firing their SLRs from the hip. More Indonesians were cut down, but the Gurkhas were punched back by a fusillade of enemy gunfire and collapsed with pieces of clothing and bloody flesh flying from their torn bodies. Even as they were dying, their killers were racing up the steps of the longhouse, still firing on the move.

Now at the side of the longhouse, Sanderson saw one of the two Police Field Force signallers frantically working the radio on the communal table while the other shouted instructions in his ear and the remaining Gurkhas fired their weapons at the entrance. In a futile gesture of defiance, he aimed his SLR through the window-shaped opening in the wall and opened fire as the Gurkhas were cut down by a hail of enemy bullets and the first of the Indonesians burst into the room. The slaughtered Gurkhas were still being bowled backwards by the bullets, knocking chairs and tables over, as the Indonesians shot by Sanderson quivered and collapsed. Those behind them, however, either opened fire on the hapless signallers – blowing the radio to bits and turning one of the signallers into a shuddering quiltwork of shredded cloth and spurting blood – or turned towards Sanderson, trying to locate the source of his gunfire.

The second signaller was still tapping the Morse code keys frantically when a *parang* swept down through striations of sunlight and sliced off his hand. Before he had time to feel the pain and scream, he was shot through the head with a pistol. The man who had shot him was in turn dispatched by a burst from Sanderson, before the SAS corporal turned away from the window – the other Indonesians too were now aiming at him –

and vaulted over the bamboo wall of the veranda as bullets whistled past his head.

A former paratrooper, Sanderson landed on his feet, let his legs buckle, rolled over a few times and jumped back up as a group of Indonesians, one carrying a flaming torch, raced around the corner of the longhouse. A short burst from Sanderson's SLR bowled over a couple of them, including the one carrying the flaming torch. Falling, the man set fire to himself and started screaming dementedly, his feet frantically kicking up loose soil as some of his comrades tried to put out the blaze.

Meanwhile Sanderson had slipped into the jungle and crept around the back of the longhouse, carefully covering his tracks, while the Indonesians who had seen him plunged on ahead without checking, assuming he would flee in a straight line. As they disappeared into the undergrowth, Sanderson kept circling around the back of the building and saw, through the dense undergrowth, that the Indonesians were setting fire to it. Moving further away, still concealing his own tracks and footprints, he headed for the kampong, to where the sounds of shooting and screaming had spread. Through a window in the undergrowth he saw the Indonesians throwing blazing torches onto the verandas of the simple houses while the natives, men, women and children, fled into the jungle.

Having seen enough, and aware that there would be no survivors in the longhouse, Sanderson turned away and headed deeper into the jungle.

When he glanced back for the last time, he saw, through the narrowing window in the undergrowth, that the raiders were looting the kampong and destroying it by fire. When they were finished, he knew only too well, they would withdraw in their boats, leaving nothing but smouldering ruins. As there was nothing he could do to prevent it, Sanderson looked back no more.

He moved at the crouch deeper into the jungle, weaving broadly between the trees, stopping every few minutes to concentrate on the silence and allow any enemy troops in the vicinity to give themselves away by their movement. As he had anticipated, the group pursuing him had broken up to fan out, hoping to find him sooner that way.

One of them materialized straight ahead, his presence made known only by the slight shifting of foliage. Not wishing to give his presence away by firing his SLR, and also in need of rations for what he knew would be a long hike, Sanderson very carefully lowered his SLR to the jungle floor, unsheathed his Fairburn-Sykes commando knife, and inched forward to the shifting, whispering foliage. Rising up silently behind where the foliage was moving, he saw the shoulders and back of the head of the enemy soldier in jungle-green fatigues.

Sanderson stepped forward without hesitation, letting the bushes part noisily, to cover the soldier's mouth with one hand, jerk his head back and slash across his throat with the knife, slitting the jugular. As the man went into a spasm and his throat gushed warm blood, Sanderson kept his mouth covered and held him even tighter, ensuring that his convulsions did not make too much noise. The dying soldier struggled very briefly, choking on his own blood, and eventually went limp in Sanderson's arms.

Lowering the dead man gently, almost tenderly to the ground, though this was solely to keep the noise down, Sanderson removed the webbed belt containing his victim's survival rations and placed the belt around his own body. Then, after going back to pick up his SLR, he headed carefully into the jungle once more.

Four days later, after an epic journey through jungle and swamp, across rivers, through uncharted valleys and over densely wooded hills, using nearly invisible tracks and dangerously swaying aerial walkways, braving snakes, scorpions, wild pigs, charging boar and headhunters, Sanderson – slashed by thorns and palm leaves, bitten by mosquitoes, drained of blood by leeches, a stone lighter and almost starving, his uniform in tatters and his feet badly blistered – stumbled out of the jungle in the early-morning mist of Kuching, Sarawak, and staggered up to the guarded main gates of SAS HQ.

'I have something to report,' he croaked to the astounded trooper on duty. Then he collapsed.

1

The briefing took place in the new SAS headquarters, a large house lent to them by the Sultan of Brunei and known as the 'Haunted House' because during the days of the Japanese occupation, when it had been used as an interrogation centre, a young British woman had been tortured to death there and was now said to haunt the place. Even so, it was a great improvement on the makeshift headquarters the SAS Squadrons had been using previously, containing as it did a communications centre (COMMCEN), sleeping quarters, showers, recreation room, and other rooms such as the lecture hall where the briefing was given.

Leading the session was the Squadron Commander, Major Patrick 'Paddy' Callaghan, who felt completely at home in Borneo after having served his stint in Malaya during the Emergency. Also, though many SAS officers felt ill at ease when first confronting their notoriously critical troopers

– it was the SAS NCOs, after all, who picked the officers during Initial Selection and thereafter judged them sternly – Callaghan felt comfortable because of his lengthy experience with the SAS since its inception in World War Two.

In fact, Callaghan had been one of the very first officers to work with the regiment's founder, Captain David Stirling, alongside the Long Range Desert Group in North Africa. After a few years back with his original regiment, 3 Commando, he had been one of the first chosen to take part in the regiment's re-formation during the Emergency in Malaya. From there he had returned to Bradbury Lines, then still located at Merebrook Camp, Malvern, where he had worked with his former Malayan Squadron Commander, Major Pryce-Jones, on the structuring of the rigorous new Selection and Training programme for the regiment, based mostly on ideas devised and thoroughly tested in Malaya. Promoted to the rank of Major in 1962, shortly after the SAS had transferred to Bradbury Lines, Hereford, Callaghan had been pleased to be offered the leadership of D Squadron just before its assignment to the Borneo campaign in 1964.

It is possible, therefore, that he felt even more at peace with the world because some of his former troopers, including the so-called 'troublemakers'

Pete Welsh and Alf Laughton, both since promoted to corporal, and Corporal (now Sergeant) Richard Parker, were here with him, impatiently waiting for the briefing while wiping sweat from their faces and swatting away swarms of flies and mosquitoes.

'Piggin' fucking flies and mosquitoes,' Alf Laughton said. 'They only send me to countries filled with the bastards. It's their way of tormenting me and driving me loopy.'

'You buzz like a fly and whine like a mosquito,' his good mate, Pete Welsh, replied sardonically. 'That's why they send you to places like this. They think they're sending you home.'

'Fuck you an' all,' Alf grunted.

'All right,' Callaghan said firmly, picking up a pointer, tapping it noisily on his lectern, then pulling the cloth covering off the blackboard behind him to reveal a large map of Borneo. 'Pay attention now. This,' he continued when the men had settled down, 'is what we're protecting.' He tapped the word 'Sarawak' with his pointer, then 'Kuching' and 'Brunei' and finally ran the pointer along the red-dotted line marking the border. 'Regarding the required background . . .'

He was interrupted by the customary moans and groans, since this was always the least popular part of an initial briefing, when the men had to listen, rather than taking part in the SAS custom of the

'Chinese parliament', or free exchange of ideas between officers and men.

'I know you all find this boring,' Callaghan said, grinning, 'but it's necessary, so kindly be quiet.' When they had settled down again, he continued: 'Brunei is one of three British dependencies in Borneo; the others are the colonies of North Borneo, now known as Sabah, and Sarawak. These territories, though extensive, represent only a quarter of the island. The rest belongs to Indonesia, whose head of state, President Sukarno . . .'

'The Mad Doctor!' Alf bellowed, winning a few laughs. With flaming red hair and a face pitted by acne, the corporal looked like a wild man. He had served twice in Malaya. The first time was in 1953 with the King's Own Yorkshire Light Infantry – when he had spent most of his time having a good time in Penang, rather than fighting. The second was in 1958, when, as a recently badged SAS trooper, he had been forced to stop fooling around and, instead, faced the horrors of the Telok Anson swamp alongside Sergeant Parker, Corporal Pete Welsh and a good many other, now dead, friends. Once considered a troublemaker and almost thrown out of the SAS, Alf had been saved by his exemplary behaviour in that dreadful swamp and went on to become a ruthlessly efficient member of the Directing Staff at 22 SAS Training

Wing, Hereford. Now considered an 'old Malayan hand', he was indisputably a good man to have in Borneo.

'Yes,' Callaghan agreed, acknowledging the nickname bestowed by British troops on Indonesia's ambitious leader. 'The Mad Doctor . . . Anyway, on 8 December 1962 an internal rebellion in Brunei was organized and led by a young sheikh named Azahart, who wanted to unite the three dependencies. This he did by launching simultaneous guerrilla attacks against police stations, government buildings and other strategically important targets. Obliged to put this revolt down, the British quickly sent in troops stationed in Singapore, including the Queen's Own Highlanders, the Royal Marine Commandos and the Gurkhas. Eight days later the rebellion was over and most of the rebels had fled into the jungle.'

'Where they remain to this day,' Pete Welsh said.

'More or less,' answered Callaghan.

Another old Malayan hand, Londoner Pete Welsh was an explosives expert who had been trained at No 101 Special Training School Singapore during World War Two, transferred as a sapper to 3rd Corps, with whom he had fought the Japanese during the occupation, then finally became an SAS trooper with D Squadron, returning to Malaya to take part in the Emergency with Alf Laughton, as well as some other good friends, who were killed in the Telok Anson swamp. Like Alf, regarded at that time as troublesome, he had, just like his mate, been matured by his experiences in the swamp and emerged to become an exemplary member of the Directing Staff at 22 SAS Training Wing. He was glad to be in Borneo, back in the thick of things.

'Which brings us to the Mad Doctor,' Alf said.

'Correct,' Callaghan replied. 'President Sukarno, a great fan of the Japanese, is now driven by the dream of unifying south-east Asia under a single leadership – naturally, in this case, his own – and has cast his greedy gaze on Borneo. For this reason, when Britain backed the proposed formation of a new political entity in the region, comprising Malaya, Singapore, Sabah, Sarawak and Brunei, Sukarno opposed it, did everything in his power to wreck the plan and, in December 1962, just after the Brunei Revolt had been put down, infiltrated insurgents from Kalimantan into Borneo. When, in September 1963, Sabah and Sarawak were officially incorporated into the new Malaysian Federation, Sukarno's forces dramatically increased their activities, with more attacks along the border. The British response was, again, immediate: to fly a force of Malaysian, British and Commonwealth troops in to contain the insurgents. You men are a further part of that force.'

The last comment was followed by a round of applause, handshaking, mutual backslapping and mutual congratulation. Callaghan let the hubbub die down before continuing: 'The jungle war, or so-called "Confrontation", between Britain and Indonesia is being fought on our part with a mixed force of Gurkhas, Australians and New Zealanders, totalling about 28,000 men. It's being fought in an area as intractable as Vietnam or – for those old hands present – Malaya.'

'If we did it in Malaya,' Pete Welsh said, 'we can do it here.'

'Hear, hear!' a few of the men chimed.

Callaghan grinned and nodded, acknowledging what they were saying, before adding a more cautious note. 'Let's hope so. However, please bear in mind that just as the CTs [communist terrorists] in Malaya were wizards in the jungle, so President Sukarno's Indonesian troops are seasoned experts in this largely unexplored jungle region.'

'Not as expert as us,' Pete said stubbornly. 'We can match anyone in the *ulu*.'

'Right,' Alf agreed.

Callaghan grinned, then continued: 'The original purpose of Sukarno's troops was to destabilize the fledgling Federation of Malaysia through clandestine guerrilla warfare and terrorism. However, when that failed, Sukarno's generals turned to all-out invasion and blatant warfare, including air attacks on the Malay Peninsula and incursions along the border between Indonesian-held Kalimantan and Sarawak. Our job is to stop that.'

'How?' Sergeant Richard Parker asked in his chillingly quiet manner. Glancing down from the dais, Callaghan saw the grey eyes of Parker gazing up at him, unblinking and, to some, unnerving.

Parker was universally known as 'Dead-eye Dick' or simply 'Dead-eye' because of his exceptional marksmanship – displayed not only during his three years with the 2nd Battalion, Royal Regiment of Fusiliers, but also on the firing range of the SAS base at Merebrook Camp, Malvern, and then, most notably, during the Malayan Emergency of 1958. As Callaghan knew only too well, Dead-eye had gone into that campaign a rather quiet, serious young man who desperately wanted to be a good SAS trooper and had emerged, after some dreadful experiences in the Telok Anson swamp, an even quieter, emotionally withdrawn man but a superlative soldier.

Promoted to corporal as a reward for the bravery and skill he had displayed in Malaya, particularly in the swamp, Dead-eye had moved with the Regiment from Malvern to Hereford, where he acted as a somewhat restless member of the Directing Staff, clearly yearning for another war to fight. Bored with the peace-time fighting force, he had married a girl he met in Hereford, but separated from her three years later. By 1963, when he had been posted with the squadron to Borneo, the marriage was over.

Callaghan thought he knew why. For a long time after returning from Malaya, Dead-eye had been haunted by his appalling experiences in the Telok Anson swamp, in particular the death of the man he had most respected and tried to emulate, Sergeant Lorrimer, whose head had been guillotined by a female CT wielding a *parang*, a machete-like jungle knife. This gruesome scene had taken place right in front of Dead-eye.

Subsequently, back in Malvern, then in Hereford, Dead-eye had suffered repeated nightmares about the severed head of Lorrimer, whose eyes (so Dead-eye reported to the SAS psychiatrist) had kept moving frantically left and right in his head for some time after it had been severed. This bizarre phenomenon had been caused by a final, perfectly natural, nervous spasm of the muscles controlling the eyeballs, but to Dead-eye it had seemed that Lorrimer was still alive in some way and desperate to know what had happened to him – or, worse still, pleading for release from his nightmare.

More than anything else, it was the recollection of that severed head and its desperately swivelling eyes that had haunted Dead-eye for years afterwards and probably made him impossible to live with. It could not have helped the marriage; in fact, it had almost certainly ended it.

'The main problem facing Major-General W. Walker, the British commander in Borneo,' Callaghan replied, speaking directly to Dead-eye, 'is that he has only five battalions to cover more than 1000 miles of jungle-covered border. Also, in addition to Sukarno's Indonesian insurgents, he has to contend with an internal threat in the shape of the Clandestine Communist Organization, composed mainly of Chinese settlers from Sarawak. Initially, General Walker wanted us to act as a kind of mobile reserve, dropping onto the jungle canopy by parachute, as we did in Malaya, but this was deemed too dangerous and unlikely to produce worthwhile results. Instead, we'll be operating in small patrols along the border, not engaging with the enemy unless absolutely necessary, but providing early warning of any Indonesian or CCO incursions.'

As most of the men hated R & I, as distinct from direct engagement, this announcement received the expected moans and groans, eventually silenced by a question from Pete Welsh.

'We've virtually just arrived here,' he said, 'so know little about what's going on. Who else is involved in this conflict? Sorry, boss, *confrontation!*'

Callaghan grinned at Pete's mockery of the official term, then became serious again. 'As Malaysia is a member of the South-East Asia Treaty Organization, the Aussie and Kiwi SAS have each sent us a squadron. The Kiwis, in particular – perhaps because of the large number of Maoris in their ranks – are the best jungle trackers we've got. I would ask you men of D Squadron – fresh as you are from training in West Germany and Norway and, in many cases, experienced as you are from your excellent work during the Emergency in Malaya – to be on your best behaviour with them.'

This was greeted with hoots of derisive laughter, which Callaghan deliberately ignored.

'Also, having arrived here a few months before us, A Squadron has renewed old friendships with veterans of the Sarawak Rangers, Iban tribal trackers and headhunters brought to the Malay Peninsula in the 1950s as teachers and pupils of the SAS during the campaign.'

One of the new men, Private Terry Malkin,

nervously put his hand up, cleared his throat and said, ''Scuse me, boss!'

'Yes?'

'What did you mean when you said that the natives were teachers *and* pupils?'

Malkin, only recently badged and still nervous with the old hands, was a Signaller. As he came from Northern Ireland, the other troopers often joked that he should be particularly good as a radio operator, blessed as he surely was with Celtic intuition and 'second sight'. A lot of jokes bounced off Malkin's hide on those spurious grounds.

'We taught them about modern firearms and soldiering; they taught us about tracking in the jungle. Since coming here, A Squadron has been using them as a paramilitary force, the Sarawak Rangers, later known as the Border Scouts, but that's being changed. From now on they'll be used solely as trackers and support units to SAS-led Gurkha teams.'

'Why?' Dead-eye asked.

'Last September our Scout post at Long Jawi, located near the border of Sarawak, was attacked and destroyed by over a hundred Indonesian soldiers who'd crossed the border from Kalimantan. Most of those men approached the post by boat, but according to the sole survivor of the attack, Corporal Ralph Sanderson, some of them emerged from the kampong itself, which they must have infiltrated days before.'

At the mention of Sanderson's name, practically everyone in the room glanced automatically at the lean-faced soldier sitting in the back row, ignoring the flies and mosquitoes swarming around him. He was obviously used to them.

'Though he came to Borneo with A Squadron,' Callaghan explained, 'Corporal Sanderson has been transferred to D Squadron to give us the benefit of his experience. If any of you men have any questions to put to him at any time over the next few months, don't hesitate. For the moment, however, please limit yourselves to any questions you might have for me regarding the briefing so far.'

'How did we react to the attack against Long Jawi?' Dead-eye asked.

'Swiftly and effectively,' Callaghan replied without hesitation. 'We flew Gurkhas to cut-off points on the Indonesians' line of retreat, where most of the enemy were killed in ambushes. Nevertheless, the fact that the Dyaks had not mentioned their presence, and that the Border Scouts failed to lend adequate support to the few Gurkhas in the post, made it perfectly clear that we can't depend on the former for anything other than tracking and intelligence gathering. Their training has therefore been taken over by the Gurkha Independent Parachute Company. Also, they no longer wear uniforms, which makes them less obviously members of the Security Forces. Naturally, we'll still use them as porters or to fell trees to clear helicopter LZs, as they're expert at both those tasks.'

'What about us?' Alf asked.

'Since the Indonesian forces are making more frequent incursions into Sarawak and Sabah, we'll be living almost entirely in the jungle, this time relying on our Border Scouts only for local information or when visiting a longhouse for a brief stay. Once we've settled in among the indigenous population, our function will be to patrol the areas where the Indonesians are most likely to cross the border. These include the comparatively flat plains along Sarawak's western border; the valley tracks leading through Stass, about 30 miles from Kuching, the capital of Sarawak; the previously mentioned Long Jawi in the 3rd Division; the valleys south of Pensiamgan; and the waterways of eastern Sabah.'

Dead-eye turned his flat, grey gaze on Corporal Sanderson. 'Speaking from experience, what's your judgement on the Indo incursions?'

Sanderson smiled slightly, recognizing a kindred soul. 'It's my belief,' he replied with confidence, 'that small Indonesian patrols also infiltrate by other, less visible routes, particularly in the unexplored stretch of jungle known as 'the Gap', lying east of the Pensiamgan valleys of Sabah.'

'Precisely,' Callaghan interjected. 'The Gap! Though largely unexplored territory, therefore particularly dangerous, that area will become your main battle zone.'

'I thought we weren't engaging the enemy,' Alf said sarcastically.

'You know what I mean, Trooper. If engagement is unavoidable, you engage; otherwise these are R & I patrols.'

'How do we insert?' Terry Malkin asked.

'A good question from our most recently badged member!' Callaghan responded, only half joking and going on to give a serious explanation. 'We insert in small groups by chopper to an LZ within yomping distance of the respective target kampongs. From there we march the rest of the way. Once at their selected kampong, the individual small groups will ingratiate themselves slowly but surely, adopting a hearts-and-minds approach, as we did in Malaya. Finally, when the trust of the aboriginals has been gained, you will persuade them to let us bring more troops in by helicopter – the regular Army, Royal Marine Commandos and Gurkhas – to turn the kampongs into fortified camps. Once that's done, we start sending

SAS-led R & I patrols out into the surrounding jungle – either with or without the help of the natives.'

'What are the hazards of this particular jungle?' Terry asked, obviously taking this, his first campaign, very seriously.

Callaghan simply glanced at Sanderson, who said without a trace of irony: 'Snakes, lizards, leeches, wild pigs, aggressive boar and primitive peoples: Land and Sea Dyaks, Muruts and Punans. Some of them are headhunters and don't take too kindly to strangers.'

'And we're using them as trackers?' the trooper asked doubtfully.

Sanderson grinned. 'Only the ones we know and have personally trained. Others, when not actually headhunting, work for the Indos or CCO, so you have to be careful.'

'*When* do we insert?' Dead-eye asked.

'The day after tomorrow,' Major Callaghan replied. 'Today you rest; tomorrow you prepare; the next day you leave. The flight is only twenty minutes. When you reach your LZ, an NCO from A Squadron will be there to take you in to the selected kampong and guide you through the hearts-and-minds requirements for this particular area. Any more questions?'

'Yes,' Pete Welsh said. 'I'm told that the natives

often offer their bare-breasted daughters as gifts. Are we allowed to accept?'

'The elders are genuine when they offer,' Sanderson replied from the last row, 'but if you accept the offer, you're liable to offend the young men of the kampong. The short answer, then, is a categorical no!'

A loud chorus of exaggerated groans filled the room, followed by Alf's melodramatic: 'War is hell!'

'You should know,' Callaghan responded. 'That's it. Class dismissed!'

The men gratefully pushed back their chairs and hurried out of the briefing room, determined to enjoy their last day of rest before the hard work began.

2

Selected as one team were Sergeant Parker, Corporals Welsh and Laughton, Private Malkin, all of D Squadron, and A Squadron's Corporal Sanderson, who would be their general guide and adviser, both in the jungle and regarding their relationship with the Dyaks.

After their day of rest, which took the form of a lengthy booze-up in the NAAFI, they arose at first light to shower, shave, dress, have a hearty breakfast, then get kitted out with proper jungle wear. This included 'olive-greens'; a soft, peaked hat with sweat-band and a yellow marker inside for identification; and rubber-and-canvas jungle boots with a metal plate inserted in the sole to prevent sharp objects, such as vicious *punji* stakes, going through the sole and into the foot. The kit consisted of ammunition pouches; two external water bottles; and the usual bergen rucksack including, in this instance, a useful bamboo carrier, two spare water bottles, a rolled-up sleeping bag, canvas sheeting and camouflaged hessian for setting up a temporary 'basha', and an escape belt holding high-calorie rations, hexamine fuel blocks, a fishing line and hooks, a small knife, waterproofed matches, a button-compass and a small-scale map.

Private Malkin was given a standard-issue Armalite M16 5.56mm assault rifle with 20-round box magazine, Corporal Sanderson opted for the generally less popular 7.62mm SLR, which he insisted he was used to, and the rest selected the 7.62mm Armalite assault rifle, which was light and compact, and therefore ideally suited to the jungle. Each man was also given a good supply of '36' hand-grenades and '80' white-phosphorus incendiary grenades, which were clipped to the webbed belts around their chests and waist. All of them were also given a standard-issue 9mm Browning High Power handgun with 13-round magazines and a Len Dixon holster. They were also given two knives, a Fairburn-Sykes commando knife and a *parang*.

'Shit,' Terry said, swinging the Malay jungle knife experimentally from left to right, 'this thing looks pretty dangerous.'

'We first had these in Malaya,' Alf told him, 'and a lot of us badly cut ourselves while learning to use them. It isn't as easy as it looks, so handle that item with care, kid.'

'Yes, boss.' Terry clipped the sheathed *parang* to his belt, beside the commando knife. 'I feel as heavy as an elephant with all this gear.'

'You'll soon get used to it, Trooper.'

Though every member of the four-man patrol had been trained in signals, demolition and medicine, and was presently undergoing training in the local language, each individual had to specialize in one of these skills. Trained to Regimental Signaller standard in Morse code and ciphers, the team's specialist signaller was responsible for calling in aerial resup (resupply) missions, casualty evacuations and keeping contact with base. While all had been trained in demolition work, the team's specialist in this field was responsible for either supervising, or carrying out, major sabotage operations. The job of the language specialist was to converse with the locals, to both gain their trust as part of the hearts-and-minds campaign and gather any information he could glean from them. Last but not least, the specialist in medicine would not only look after the other members of his patrol but also attempt to win the trust of the locals by treating them for any illnesses, real or imagined, that they might complain of.

As the team's demolition expert, Pete Welsh was placed in charge of their single crate of mixed explosives, mostly of the plastic type such as RDX and PETN, along with both kinds of initiator: electrical and non-electrical, with the relevant firing caps and time fuses. As signaller, Terry was not asked to depend on his Celtic clairvoyance but instead was given an A41 British Army tactical radio set, which weighed 11lb excluding the battery and was carried in a backpack. Each of the men was supplied with a SARBE (surface-to-air rescue beacon) lightweight radio beacon to enable them to link up with CasEvac helicopters should the need arise.

Having been trained in first-aid and basic medicine, each man in the patrol was obliged to carry an individual medical pack that included codeine tablets and syrettes of morphine; mild and strong antiseptics (gentian violet and neomycin sulphate); chalk and opium for diarrhoea and other intestinal disorders; the antibiotic tetracycline; and an assortment of dressings and plasters. However, as the team's medical specialist, more extensively trained with the US Army's special forces at Fort Sam, Houston, Texas, and Fort Bragg, North Carolina, Alf was in charge of a comprehensive medical pack that included all the above items, but also a greater selection of drugs and dressings, as well as surgical equipment and a dental repair kit.

'I wouldn't let that butcher near *my* mouth, Pete

said, 'if my teeth were hanging out by the roots. I'd rather pull 'em myself.'

'Any more sarcastic remarks,' Alf retorted, 'and I'll practise my surgery on your balls instead of your teeth. I'm pretty good when it comes to the cut and thrust, so don't cross me, mate.'

'Another mad doctor,' Pete replied. 'We should call you Sukarno.'

As the team's linguist, Dead-eye carried the lightest load. But once in the jungle, which was usually known by the native word *ulu*, he would compensate for this by being out front on 'point', as scout – the most dangerous and demanding job of them all.

Sanderson, as their guest, or rather guide, carried only his personal weapons and kit.

Kitted out just after breakfast, the men were then compelled to spend the rest of the long, hot morning on the firing range, testing the weapons and honing their skills. This was not as easy as it sounds, for the heat soon became suffocating, sweat ran constantly down their foreheads and into their eyes when they took aim, and they often choked on the dust kicked up by the backblast of the weapons. On top of all this, they were tormented by the usual swarms of flies and mosquitoes.

'I give up,' Alf said. 'I can't even see along

the sights with these clouds of bloody insects everywhere. Let's just call it a day.'

'Get back on your belly on the ground,' Dead-eye said. 'And don't get up till I say so.'

'Yes, Sarge!' Alf snapped.

They came off the firing range covered in a fine slime composed of their own sweat and the dust. After a refreshing shower, they washed the clothes they had used on the firing range, hung them up to drip dry in the still-rising heat, dressed in their spare set of olive-greens, then hurried to the mess for lunch. This was followed by an afternoon of lessons about the history, geography and culture of Borneo, with particular emphasis on the border between Sarawak and Kalimantan, where most of their operations would take place.

By the time the lessons had ended, in the late afternoon, the men's clothes had dried and could be ironed (which they did themselves), then packed away in the bergens. When their packing was completed, they had dinner in the mess, followed by precisely one hour in the bar, which ensured that they could not drink too much.

Back in the spider, or sleeping quarters, each man had to take his place beside his bed, while Dead-eye inspected his kit and weapons, ensuring that no bergen was too heavy and that the weapons were immaculately clean and in perfect working order.

Satisfied, he told them to be up and ready to leave by first light the following morning, then bid them goodnight and left the barracks.

When Dead-eye had gone Terry exhaled with an audible sigh. 'Blimey!' he almost gasped. 'That Sergeant Parker scares the hell out of me. He's so bloody expressionless.'

'A born killer,' Alf said gravely.

'Heart of stone,' Pete added.

'He eats new boys like you for breakfast,' Alf warned. 'I'd be careful if I was you.'

'Aw, come on, lads!' Terry protested, not sure if they were serious or not. 'I mean . . .'

'Never look him directly in the eye,' Pete said firmly.

'Never speak to him unless spoken to,' Alf chipped in.

'If you see him take a deep breath,' Pete continued, 'hold onto your balls.'

'He'll bite them off otherwise,' Alf said, 'then spit them out in your face.'

'Leave off, you two!'

'It's the truth,' Pete said.

'Cross our hearts,' Alf added. 'Old Parker, he'd cut your throat as soon as look at you, so it's best to avoid him.'

'How can I avoid him?' Terry asked. 'He's our *patrol leader*, for God's sake! I mean, he's going to be there every minute, breathing right in my face.'

'And he *does* so hate new troopers,' Pete said. 'You can take that as read.'

'You poor bastard,' Alf said.

Terry was starting to look seriously worried when Alf, able to control himself no longer, rolled over on his bed to smother his laughter in his pillow.

'Night-night,' Pete said chirpily, then he switched out the lights.

At dawn the next morning, after a hurried breakfast, they were driven in a Bedford RL 4x4 three-ton lorry to the airfield, where they transferred to a stripped-out Wessex Mark 1 helicopter piloted by Lieutenant Ralph Ellis of the Army Air Corps. Some of them knew Ellis from Malaya five years before, when he had flown them into the Telok Anson swamp in his Sikorsky S-55 Whirlwind.

'You men haven't aged a day,' Ellis greeted them. 'You *always* looked like a bunch of geriatrics.'

'Listen who's talking,' Pete countered. 'Nice little bald spot you've developed in five years. Soon you'll be nothing but ears and head while we remain beautiful.'

'The girls still love the pilots,' Ellis replied. 'They

don't view us as hooligans in uniform. They think we have class.'

'And what's this?' Alf asked, poking Ellis in the stomach with his forefinger. 'A nice bit of flab here.'

'It's the easy life the bastard lives,' Pete informed his mate. 'He'll soon look like a cute little blancmange with a billiard ball on top.'

'Very funny, I'm sure,' Ellis replied. 'Just get your fat arses in the chopper, thanks.'

'Yes, mother!' Alf and Pete replied as one, grinning wickedly as they clambered into the Wessex, followed by the others. Once inside, the men strapped themselves in, cramped together among the mass of equipment. The engines roared into life and the props started spinning. The helicopter shuddered as if about to fall apart, rose vertically until it was well above the treetops, then headed west, flying over a breathtaking panorama of densely forested hills and mountain peaks, winding rivers, waterfalls, swamps, aerial bridges and shadowy, winding paths through the *ulu*.

'That jungle looks impenetrable from here,' Terry observed, glancing down through the window in disbelief.

'In many places it is,' Alf replied, 'but we'll manage somehow.'

Twenty minutes later the Wessex landed in

a jungle clearing and the men disembarked, to be greeted by another member of A Squadron, Sergeant Alan Hunt. Dropped on his own a week ago, he was living in the clearing, close to a stone-filled, gurgling river, his basha a poncho pegged diagonally from the lowest branch of a tree to the ground with his kit piled neatly up inside. Hunt was wearing jungle-green trousers and a loose shirt that seemed far too big for him. A Browning High Power handgun was holstered on his hip.

'Hi, boss,' Sanderson said, shaking the sergeant's hand. 'Boy, have *you* lost a lot of weight already!'

The sergeant grinned and shrugged. 'Three stone fell off me just living here for two weeks. You'll all look the same soon enough.' He indicated the clearing with a wave of his right hand and all of them, glancing around at the oblique beams of sunlight streaking the gloom, realized just how hot and humid it was. 'Ditch your gear and fix up your bashas. This is home for the next week or so. I'm sure you'll enjoy it. When you're ready, gather around my lean-to and I'll tell you what's happening.'

When the helicopter had taken off again and its slipstream had died down, the men followed Hunt's example by constructing triangular shelters with their waterproof ponchos, first hammering two

Y-shaped sticks into the ground about six feet apart, running a length of rope between them and tying the rope tight, then draping the poncho over the rope and pegging the ends down to form a triangular tent. A groundsheet was rolled out inside the tent and covered with dry grass to make a mattress. A sleeping bag was then rolled out on the grass to make a soft bed. All of the lean-tos were well hidden by clumps of bamboo and screened from above by the soaring trees.

When their kit had been placed carefully around the inner edges of the tent, the men lit their hexamine stoves outside and brewed up. They drank their tea gathered around Hunt, hearing what he had been up to since arriving there a fortnight earlier.

'As most of you know,' he began, 'when waging our hearts-and-minds campaign in Malaya, we transplanted the aboriginals from their original kampongs into new, fortified villages, well out of reach of the CTs. Given the nature of the locals, as well as the terrain, there's no possibility of doing that here. In any case, most of the tribesmen are well disposed towards the British and we have to capitalize on that by relying on non-violent persuasion and using them where they live, rather than attempting to move them on. To this end I've already made contact with the elders of the nearby kampong, which is about five minutes from here.'

He pointed at the dense jungle to his left.

'My first step towards penetration was to build this hide within walking distance of the kampong. From here, I kept the village under observation long enough to ensure that neither guerrillas nor Indonesian regulars were already established there. Once I was sure that they weren't, I walked in, all smiles, and made contact through a combination of basic Malay and sign language. Gradually, they came to accept me and I started helping them with modest medical aid and by bartering some of my possessions for some of theirs. Now that I've been accepted, I can introduce you as friends and hopefully you'll win their trust the same way, gradually becoming part of the village and sharing their lifestyle. Once that's been accomplished, we'll persuade them that our other friends should be invited in, too. If they agree, we can then call in the regular Army and Gurkhas – all one big happy family. We then use the village as a Forward Operating Base, moving out on regular patrols into the *ulu*, hopefully with the help of the villagers.'

'What are they like as people?' Dead-eye asked.

'Physically small, generally cheerful, and lazy.'

'Sounds just like me!' Pete quipped.

'They don't cut their hair,' Hunt continued,

ignoring the quip. 'Nor do they dress above the waist – neither the men nor the women – so you'll have to learn not to let the females distract you too much.'

'I'm willing to die for my country,' Alf said, 'but what you're asking is too much.'

'I'm very serious about this,' Hunt said sharply. 'Certain proprieties have to be maintained here, no matter how you might feel to the contrary. For instance, the village elders have a tendency to offer their daughters as a gesture of goodwill. You won't get into trouble if you politely refuse. However, you *may* get into trouble if you accept.'

'My heart's breaking already,' Pete said. 'I know just what's coming.'

'Although, as I've said, the natives are generally cheerful, the young men suffer jealousy like the rest of us mere mortals and could take offence if you take their girls. In short, if you receive such an offer, make sure you refuse.'

'What kind of gifts should we give them?' Terry asked, as solemn as ever.

'You don't. Generally speaking, the Malay system of giving gifts doesn't work here, though bartering of a minor nature is enjoyed. Instead, what you do is be mindful of their pride, showing tact, courtesy, understanding and, most of all, patience regarding all aspects of their lifestyle.

Also, it's vitally important that you show respect for the headman, whose dignity and prestige have to be upheld at all times. Obey those few simple rules and you should have no problems.'

'So when do we start?' Dead-eye asked.

'Today,' Hunt replied. 'At least one man has to stay here to guard the camp at all times – this will be a rotating duty – while the others go into the kampong. As Corporal Sanderson is already familiar with the Indians, he'll stay here today and the rest of you can come in with me. Leave your weapons here in Sanderson's care, then let's get up and go.'

'We're going straight away?' Terry asked, looking uneasy.

'That's right, Trooper. What's your problem?'

'He's embarrassed at the thought of seeing all those bare boobs,' Pete said, making Terry blush a deep crimson.

'Cherry-boy, is he?' Hunt asked crisply.

'No!' Terry replied too quickly. 'I'm not. I just . . .'

'Think you'll get a hard-on as soon as you see those bare tits,' Pete interjected, giving form to Terry's thoughts. 'Well, no harm in that, son!'

'Just keep your thoughts above the waist – yours, that is,' the sergeant said, 'and you should be all right. OK, men, let's go.'

As Sanderson stretched out on the grassy ground beside his basha and lit up a cigarette, the others extinguished the flames from the burning hexamine blocks in their portable cookers, then followed Hunt into the dense undergrowth. Surprisingly, they found themselves walking along a narrow, twisting path, barely distinguishable in the gloom beneath the overhanging foliage.

Terry, the least experienced in the group, immediately felt oppressed and disorientated by the *ulu*. He had stepped into a vast silence that made his own breathing – even his heartbeat – seem unnaturally loud. Instead of the riot of birds, wildlife, flowers and natural colours he had expected, he found only a sunless gloom deepened by the dark green and brown of vine stems, tree-ferns, snake-like coils of rattan, an abundance of large and small palms, long, narrow, dangerously spiked leaves, gnarled, knotted branches – and everywhere brown mud. Glancing up from the featureless jungle, he was oppressed even more by the sheer size of the trees which soared above the dense foliage to dizzying heights, forming vertical tunnels of green and brown, the great trunks entangled in yet more liana and vine, disappearing into the darkness of their own canopy, blotting out the sunlight.

Looking up, Terry felt even more dizzy and disorientated. In that great silent and featureless gloom, he felt divorced from his own flesh and blood. His racing heart shocked him.

Though the hike took only five minutes, it seemed much longer than that, and Terry sighed with relief when the group emerged into the relative brightness of an unreal grey light that fell down through a window in the canopy of the trees on the thatched longhouses of the kampong spread out around the muddy banks of the river. The dwellings were raised on stilts, piled up one behind the other, each slightly above the other, on the wooded slopes climbing up from the river. Some, Terry noticed with a tremor, had shrunken human heads strung above their doors. The spaces below and between the houses, where the ground had been cleared for cultivation, were filled with the Iban villagers – also known as Sea Dyaks because they had once been pirates – who, stripped to the waist, male and female, young and old, were engaged in a variety of tasks, such as cooking, fishing, laundering, picking jungle fruit – figs, durians, bananas and mangos – or working in a small, dry *padi*, where their basic food, rice and tapioca, was grown. This they did with no great expenditure of energy, except when playing odd games and giggling. Their longboats were tied up to a long, rickety jetty, bobbing and creaking noisily in the water. Buffalo and pigs also congregated there, drinking the water or eating the tall grass as chickens squawked noisily about them.

'They fish in that river,' Hunt explained. 'They also hunt wild pig, deer, birds, monkeys and other animals, using traps and the odd shotgun, but mostly blowpipes that fire poisoned arrows. Annoy them and they'll fire them at you – so don't steal their women!'

Terry was blushing deeply, Pete and Alf were gawping, and Dead-eye was staring impassively as a group of bare-breasted women, giggling and nudging each other, approached behind a very old, wizened man who was naked except for a loincloth and, incongruously, a pair of British army jungle boots. Obviously the headman, he raised a withered arm, spread the fingers of his hand, and croaked the one word of English he had learned from Sergeant Hunt: 'Welcome!'

Two weeks later, Terry had stopped blushing at the sight of the bare-breasted women, but felt even more disorientated and removed from himself. This had begun with his first short trek through the awesome silence and gloom of the *ulu*, but was deepened by his daily visits to the kampong and his increasingly intimate interaction with the Ibans. They were so gentle and good-natured that he could not imagine them as pirates, let alone as the headhunters they obviously were, judging by the shrunken heads on prominent display. Certainly, however, they lived a primitive life of fishing in the rivers, hunting animals with blowpipes, tilling the kampong's one rice-and-tapioca *padi*, and constantly maintaining their longhouses with raw materials from the jungle. They also engaged in amiable barter, trading jungle products such as timber, rattan, rice, tapioca, fruit, fish, even the swiftlet's nests used for Chinese soup, in return for clothes, boots, rifles, tins of baked beans, chewing gum and cigarettes. Bartering, from the point of view of the SAS troopers, was the easiest way to the affections of the villagers, leading to much giggling and backslapping.

Once this had become commonplace, however, the men started winning the hearts and minds of the Ibans in other ways: Pete showed them how to use explosives for various small tasks, such as blowing fish out of the water; Alf ran a daily open-air clinic to deal with their real and imagined illnesses; Terry entertained them by tuning his short-wave radio into various stations, which invariably reduced them to excited giggles; Dead-eye trained some of them in the selective use of weapons; and Hunt and Sanderson took turns with Dead-eye to teach English to the more important men of the kampong.

The SAS men spent most of their waking hours with the Ibans, which made for a long and exhausting day. Invariably, this began at first light when, just after breakfast, they would make the short hike through the *ulu* from their hidden camp to the kampong. After an average of twelve hours in the kampong, eating their lunch with the Ibans, they would make their way back to the camp, invariably at last light and concealing their tracks as they went, to have a brew-up and feed gratefully off compo rations.

The Ibans were very sociable, and often, in the interests of good manners and improved relations, the troopers would be obliged to stay in one of the longhouses to partake of native hospitality. For all of them, this was pure torture, particularly since the villagers' favourite meal was a stinking mess called *jarit*, which they made by splitting a length of thick bamboo, filling it with raw pork, salt and rice, and burying it for a month until it had putrefied. Indeed, while Dead-eye and Hunt were able to digest this stinking mess without bother, the others could only do so without throwing up by washing it down with mouthfuls of *tapai*, a fierce rice wine which looked like unfermented cider, scalded the throat and led to monumental hangovers. Nevertheless, when drunk through straws from large Chinese jars, it was potent enough to drown the stench and foul taste of the *jarit*.

The eating and drinking, combined with the accompanying entertainments, in which the SAS men were obliged to dance for the villagers, was made no easier by the fact that many families shared a single longhouse and the air was fetid not only from their sweat and the heat. Also, because they used the floor as a communal toilet, urinating and defecating through the slatted floor onto the ground below, the purgent air was thick at all times with swarms of flies and mosquitoes.

Luckily for the SAS men, they were called upon to explore the surrounding area and fill in the blank spaces on their maps, showing waterways suitable for boat navigation, tracks that could be classified as main or secondary, distances both in linear measurements and marching hours, contours and accessibility of specific areas, primary and secondary jungle (*belukar*), and swamps, and areas under cultivation (*ladang*). They also filled their logbooks with often seemingly irrelevant, though actually vitally important, details about the locals' habits and customs, their food, their state of health, the variety of their animals, their weapons and their individual measure of importance within the community. Last but not least, they marked down potential ambush positions, border crossing-points, and suitable locations for parachute droppings and helicopter landings. While this work was all conducted in the suffocating humidity of the *ulu*, it was preferable to socializing in the fetid longhouses.

By the end of the two weeks, close relationships had been formed between the villagers and the SAS men, with the former willing to listen to the latter and do favours for them.

'The time's come to bring in the regular troops and fortify the kampong,' Sergeant Hunt informed Dead-eye. 'Then we can go out on proper jungle patrols, using the village as our FOB.'

'Do you think the locals will wear it?'

'That depends entirely on how we put it to them,' Hunt said with a relaxed grin. 'I think I know how to do that. First we tell them that evil men from across the mountain are coming and that we're here to protect the village. Then we explain that although our group is only five in number, we have many friends who'll descend from the sky, bringing aid. It would be particularly helpful, we'll then explain, if the necessary space could be created for the flying soldiers to land safely. I think that might work.'

'Let's try it,' Dead-eye said.

That afternoon they approached the village elders, joining them in the headman's longhouse, where they were compelled to partake of the foul-smelling *jarit*, mercifully washing it down with the scalding, highly alcoholic rice wine. After four hours of small talk, by which time both troopers were feeling drunk, Hunt put his case to the headman and received a toothless, drunken smile and nod of agreement. The headman then also agreed to have a landing space cleared for the flying soldiers to land on. Indeed, he and the others expressed great excitement at the thought of witnessing this heavenly arrival.

Immediately on leaving the longhouse, Hunt, trying not to show his drunkenness, told Terry to call up A Squadron and ask them to implement the 'step-up' technique devised by their brilliant commander, Major Peter de la Billière. This entailed warning a full infantry company to be ready to move by helicopter to a remote forward location for a demonstration of quick deployment and firepower.

The following day, when Hunt and Dead-eye were sober, the tribesmen expertly felled a large number of trees with small, flexible axes, dragged them away with ropes, then flattened the cleared area, thus carving a helicopter landing zone out of the jungle. When they had completed this task and were waiting excitedly around the edge of the LZ for the arrival of the 'flying soldiers', Hunt ordered Terry to radio the message: 'Bring in the step-up party now.' About fifteen minutes later the helicopters appeared above the treetops, creating a tremendous din and a sea of swirling foliage, before descending vertically into the clearing and disgorging many small, sombre Gurkhas, all armed with sharpened *kukris*, or curved machetes, and modern weapons. The next wave of choppers brought in Royal Marine Commandos, the regular Army, and the remainder of D Squadron, SAS, all of whom were armed to the teeth.

The Ibans giggled, shrieked with excitement, and finally applauded with waves and the swinging of their blowpipes. They viewed the arrival of the Security Forces as pure entertainment.

3

With the arrival of the full Security Forces complement, the fortification of the kampong was soon accomplished and it became, in effect, a Forward Operating Base complete with landing pads for the resup Wessex Mark 1 helicopters; riverside sangars manned with Bren light machine-guns and Gurkhas armed with 7.62mm SLRs; and defensive pits, or 'hedgehogs', encircled by thatch-and-bamboo-covered 40-gallon drums, bristling with 4.2-inch mortars and 7.62mm general-purpose machine-guns, or GPMGs.

The bartering of portable radios, simple medical aid and other items beloved by the villagers rapidly ensured that the SF troops became a welcome body of men within the community – so much so that eventually the natives were making endless requests for helicopter trips to outlying kampongs and help with the transportation to market, also by chopper, of their rice and tapioca, timber and even pigs and chickens. In short, they came to rely more on the soldiers and airmen than on their own civilian administration.

'Like living in fucking Petticoat Lane,' Alf said. 'If you don't know how to barter you're doomed. A right bunch of Jew-boys, this lot are.'

'Jew-boys in loinclothes,' Pete added. 'With long hair and a lot of weird tattoos. They'd look pretty normal in the East End, peddling their wares.'

'Do you mind?' Terry said.

'What's that, Trooper?' Pete asked.

'I don't think you should use terms like 'Jew-boys'. I think it's offensive.'

'But you're Irish!' Alf exclaimed.

'Just born there,' Terry corrected him.

'If you were born there, that makes you fucking Irish, so don't come it with me, Pat.'

'Don't call me Pat.'

'His name's *Paddy*,' Pete exclaimed.

'He must be an Irish Jew,' Alf responded, 'to be so concerned about this lot.'

'I'm not Jewish,' Terry said. 'I'm not really Irish either. I just happened to be born there, that's all, but my family moved to Liverpool when I was three, so I don't know any more about Ireland than you two. I'm not Irish, really, and I'm certainly not a Jew. I just dislike anti-Semitism, that's all.'

'The cocky bastard's just picked up his winged

dagger and already he thinks he can give us lectures. Makes you wonder, doesn't it?' said Pete.

'I just meant . . .' began Terry.

'Don't worry, kid,' Alf said in his kindly manner, 'we're not remotely offended. We just think you're a dumb prat.'

'Hear, hear,' Pete agreed.

Despite the sentiments of Alf and Pete, the SAS troopers, being already experienced in hearts-and-minds work, were very skilled at it. Major Callaghan, who loved life in the jungle and had revelled in kampong life ever since his Malayan days, made his contribution by flying out, at his own expense, hampers of Christmas food from Fortnum and Mason's of London, to supply the natives. Not surprisingly, Pete's only comment was: 'They eat better than we do. Spoiled rotten those Indians are.'

'Fortnum and Mason's, no less!' Alf exclaimed, his normally pink cheeks more flushed than normal. 'And here we poor bastards sit, getting sick on raw pork and tapioca. Makes you want to puke, doesn't it?'

Sergeant Hunt, on the other hand, being of a practical bent, made his personal contribution to village life by constructing a water-powered generator to provide the only electric light in thousands of square miles. This thrilled the villagers.

Not to be outdone, Corporal Sanderson, whose four-day trek through the jungle after the attack on Long Jawi the previous year had already gained him a great deal of respect among his fellow SAS troopers, dismantled his bergen and converted its metal frame into a still for making alcohol.

'He may be from A Squadron,' Pete said, 'but he's all right with me. Any man who can make a still from a rucksack has to be A1.'

'I'll drink to that,' Alf replied, sampling the brew from Sanderson's still. 'But then I'll drink to anything!'

While most of the men clearly enjoyed making such contributions to village life, they never lost sight of precisely why they were making them: to win the hearts and minds of the Ibans, and persuade them to favour the SF forces over those of President Sukarno or the CCO. The message that accompanied their contributions was therefore always the same.

'The Indonesians and the CCO are on the other side of the mountains and one day they'll cross them to destroy you,' Dead-eye, the language specialist, would solemnly inform the locals in their own tongue. 'We are here to protect you.'

Once they had managed to convince the villagers of this, the SAS men were able to convince them also that they must help themselves by staying alert for anything unusual seen in the *ulu*.

'Particularly the marks of rubber-soled boots,' Hunt explained to them. 'The sign of the Indo invader. If you see those, please tell us.'

'Yes, yes,' the village elders promised, perhaps not quite understanding what they were being asked to do. 'We understand. Welcome!'

They did, however, know enough to understand that they were receiving the good things of life from people who feared the Indonesians and CCO. For that reason, when asked if they could select certain of their number to be 'link-men' with the soldiers, they were quick to comply. Callaghan then placed those selected as link-men in the charge of the Gurkhas, who trained them in the use of certain weapons, but mainly used their natural talents for tracking and intelligence-gathering in the jungle. Though called the Border Scouts, like those who had gone before them, they were not destined to be used as fighting soldiers, but as aids on the reconnaissance and intelligence-gathering missions. Given modern weapons to carry – mostly World War Two 0.3-inch M1 carbines – they were more than happy to take part.

'They love those fucking rifles,' Pete observed, 'but they forget to keep them out of your face when they're loading and cocking.'

'Too right,' his mate Alf agreed. 'If they actually get to shoot the bloody things, they'll be shooting themselves.'

'Or us,' Pete replied.

'In the meantime,' Terry said, 'I'm keeping out of their way.'

'Very wise,' Pete told him.

The bare-breasted Iban women brought daily presents of fruit and vegetables, the men arrived to gossip and swap news, the children looked on, hoping for sweets or chewing gum, and the leaders of the community came to ask for, and offer, advice. The SF men therefore slipped as easily into the primitive rhythms of the day and seasons as the people themselves. Soon the cycle of planting, seeding and harvesting became part of the soldier's life itself, and the native customs, rites and celebrations as familiar as Bank Holidays back home.

'I can't really complain about all these holidays,' Alf said, 'but three days of drinking that awful *tapai* shit doesn't quite compensate for the loss of a good pint of bitter.'

'Between the *tapai* and that *jarit*,' Pete said, 'I've more snot coming out of my arse than coming out of my nose. These bloody Ibans don't know shite from shinola, but what can you do? I mean, we have to be nice to them.'

'Yeah,' Alf grunted. 'Keep them smiling or lose your head. Those primitive bastards collect human heads like we collect postage stamps. So be nice to them. Yes, sir!'

'It's your job,' Terry said.

'What?' Alf asked, puzzled.

'It's part of the hearts-and-minds campaign,' Terry explained with studied patience, 'so it's part of your job. Apart from that, they good people and don't need your insults.'

'Insults?' Pete was outraged. 'Who the fuck's insulting them? We're just saying that they're primitive bastards and a pain in the arse.'

'That's the *jarit*,' Alf reminded him.

'Goes straight through you,' Pete said.

'Three days of eating *jarit* and drinking *tapai* and your guts are turned inside out.'

'Primitive bastards,' Pete repeated.

'Shit through the floorboards,' Alf reminded him.

'Of course, Paddy here – sorry, I mean Terry – thinks all that is wonderful.'

'The real world,' Alf said.

'Back to nature,' Pete explained.

'I'm just saying . . .' Terry began, then gave up. 'Oh, fuck off the pair of you!'

'We're corporals,' Alf said.

'And you're just a trooper,' Pete informed him.

'That means you're being insubordinate,' Alf explained, 'and could go up on a charge.'

'Up you an' all,' Terry said.

While the SAS were attempting to win hearts and minds, Gurkha teams of five or six men were training ten or twenty times their own number of tribesmen in counter-terrorist reconnaissance, intelligence gathering and, less comprehensively, warfare. The Gurkhas shared their own longhouse near to those of their many trainees, which enabled them to live exactly the same life and forge closer bonds.

Also included in the training were basic military disciplines, such as team spirit, mutual dependence, and endurance. Though language presented difficulties, this was solved with pantomime. This novel method of communication even extended to helicopter training without helicopters, throwing hand-grenades without live grenades, and hand-to-hand fighting with invisible enemies. These activities led to both frustration and laughter, but they certainly worked.

At all times, however, as Sergeant Hunt had said they should, the men treated the Ibans with the utmost respect and were particularly reverential to the headman. This even extended to letting the latter take the salute at Retreat each evening.

The hearts-and-minds campaign required time and patience but eventually it paid off.

By now the SAS team had its own quarters in a separate longhouse on the edge of the village, from where they were broadcasting daily reports to Squadron Headquarters in Brunei, the 'Haunted House', on a more powerful PRC 320 Clansman radio flown in by Army Air Corps Lieutenant Ralph Ellis.

'You've all lost a lot of weight already,' Ellis noted when they had been there for six weeks.

'The *ulu's* like a fucking steam bath,' Alf replied. 'It just strips a man down.'

This was true. Living in the longhouse for weeks at a time, leaving it only to watch, listen, patrol and report, meant the men were constantly dripping sweat and gasping for air. Even when making the shortest hikes through the jungle, they often found themselves dragging their booted feet laboriously through mud as thick and clinging as quicksand, or wading chest-deep through swamp water covered with sharp, heavy palm leaves and broken branches. These physical demands were in no way eased by the constant strain of trying to look and listen for signs of the enemy, who was known to be able to blend with the *ulu* as well as the animals. Their first two months, then, of living with the Ibans, placed a tremendous physical and mental strain on them, which led to a further loss of weight, in addition to that caused by the oppressive heat and humidity.

'It's fucking tension,' Alf explained, not joking any more. 'It's doing everything for nothing. We yomp through the fucking *ulu*, we wade through the fucking swamps, we get eaten alive by mosquitoes and midges and tormented by flies – and what's it all for? You don't see a thing out there. You hear nothing but the fucking birds. You keep looking over your shoulder for an enemy that isn't there and you start wanting to shoot your best friend just for something to do. Then you come back here. You're stuck in this fucking longhouse. There are more flies and midges and mosquitoes, plus the stench of your own shit and piss coming up through the floorboards. This is life in the raw in the fucking jungle and it's driving me crackers.'

While the hearts-and-minds campaign was not without interest, living on their own just outside the kampong in their own, now crowded, fetid longhouse was both uncomfortable and boring, making each man feel increasingly alienated from himself, forcing him back into his private thoughts and making him dwell on the past.

Being in the jungle reminded Alf of his two trips to Malaya, first in 1953 with the regular Army and then five years later with the SAS. Born in Birkenhead, one of the five children of publicans who worked night and day, Alf felt at home as one of a large group and had therefore taken naturally to the Army. Destined for National Service anyway, he had decided that enlisting would give him certain advantages and, true enough, his first posting overseas, to Butterworth, Malaya, had turned out to be the best experience he had ever had. Depressed when his tour of duty was over, he had signed on for the newly re-formed SAS, gained his winged badge, and soon found himself back in Malaya, this time fighting the communist terrorists in the jungle. Having survived that experience, he was flown back with the others to England, then seconded to the US special forces for advanced medical training in America. He had enjoyed that period, but, for all his moaning, preferred being back in the jungle with his best friend, Pete Welsh, by his side.

Pete was thinking pretty much the same thing. In fact, ever since arriving he had found himself thinking repeatedly of how, when he had first joined the SAS, he had had a chip on his shoulder the size of the Rock of Gibraltar and nearly been thrown out of the regiment because of it. An illegitimate child, he had been raised in London's Finsbury Park by an lone, alcoholic mother who earned her crust as a prostitute and took her revenge out on men by beating her only child, Pete, badly throughout most of his childhood. Joining the Army to escape her, Pete had been trained as an explosives expert and posted to No 101 Special Training School, Singapore. From there he transferred to the 3rd Corps where, with other sappers, he harassed the Japanese by blowing up railways and bridges of strategic importance. He then joined the SAS, and served in Malaya.

Though an excellent soldier, Pete had still got a chip on his shoulder at that time. He only lost it when, in the Telok Anson swamp, actually planning to indirectly kill a fellow trooper who had humiliated him, he realized what he was doing and saved the man's life instead.

Rather like Pete, Dead-eye had joined the Army to escape life at home and had found there a new pride and confidence. Born and bred in West Croydon to a violent lorry driver and a brow-beaten mother, Dead-eye had grown up to be a relatively withdrawn individual, but he had gone even more deeply into himself after witnessing Sergeant Lorrimer's death. Posted to the 2nd Battalion, Royal Regiment of Fusiliers, where his prowess on the firing range soon became a talking point, he realized that he loved being a soldier but wanted an even greater challenge. This led him to apply for a transfer to the SAS when it was re-formed to combat the Emergency in Malaya. He had met Lorrimer there.

Dead-eye had respected Lorrimer more than any other man he had ever known. A veteran of World War Two, a former member of the legendary Long Range Desert Group and the original 1 SAS, also in North Africa, as well as Force 136 – the clandestine resistance unit set up by the British Special Operations Executive (SOE) during World War Two for operations in Japanese-occupied Malaya – then again with the SAS in Malaya during the Emergency, Lorrimer was a legendary old hand who had taught Dead-eye everything he now knew. They had often spent weeks together in the jungle, fighting the CTs with a deadly combination of the Browning autoloader shotgun, the 0.3-inch M1 carbine, No 80 white-phosphorus incendiary hand-grenades, home-made bombs, and even, when silent killing was necessary, with their Fairburn-Sykes commando knives or a crossbow. That had been one of the greatest experiences of Dead-eye's life to date, cementing his friendship with Lorrimer for all time.

Now, in this jungle in Borneo, which was strikingly similar to the jungles of Malaya, Dead-eye was recalling his old friend with particular, deeply wounding clarity. Only work could assuage his pain.

Luckily, the work was plentiful. Once the Gurkhas, Royal Marine Commandos, British Army and other D Squadron, SAS, personnel had moved into the kampong and completed its fortification, the smaller SAS patrols were able to move deeper into the jungle on R & I missions. Eventually, when four villagers who were clearing another landing zone for the SF helicopters were shot by a passing Indonesian or CCO patrol – no evidence of their identity was left behind – which led to the other Ibans becoming more fearful and less cooperative than they had been, Major Callaghan decided to send patrols even deeper into the *ulu* to seek out the enemy and, if necessary, engage with them.

Often augmented by one or two members of the local Police Field Force, these teams made circular tours of the area, some lasting up to five days and including visits to many other kampongs en route. Before moving out, the men painted their weapons with quick-drying green camouflage paint, then wrapped them in strips of cloth specially dyed to match the jungle background and disguise their distinctive shape. In both instances, the men were particularly careful not to let the paint or strips of cloth interfere with the weapons' working parts or sights. After wrapping masking tape around the butts, pistol grips and top covers, they replaced the noisy sling swivels with para-cord, which made no sound at all.

Once the weapons were disguised, they camouflaged themselves, applying 'cam' cream and black 'stick' camouflage to the exposed areas of their skin, including the backs of their hands, and their wrists, ears and neck. The facial camouflage was applied in three stages: first dulling the features with a thin base coating diluted with water (they would use their own saliva when in the jungle); then making diagonal patterns across the face to break up the shape and outline of the features; and finally darkening the areas normally highlighted, such as forehead, nose, cheek bones and chin. To complete this effect, areas normally in shadow were left a lighter shade.

When applying personal camouflage the patrol members paired up to check each other's appearance and ensure that nothing had been missed.

'You look beautiful,' Pete said.

'Not as lovely as you,' Alf said.

'You're just saying that to make me blush, but I think you're sweet anyway.'

'*Terry* looks sweet,' Alf said.

'And he's blushing,' Pete noted. 'Pay a virgin a compliment and she'll blush. It's just one of those things.'

'I'm not blushing,' Terry said.

'Yes, you are,' Pete replied. 'We just can't see it because of the cam cream, but you're blushing, I'll bet.'

'Just shove off,' Terry said.

'He's so bad-tempered,' Alf told Pete, looking deeply, seriously wounded. 'He's a virgin, so you try to be gentle and that's how he behaves. What's the world coming to?'

'Just knock it off,' Terry said. 'Go and look in the mirror and get excited and have a good wank. It's all you're fit for.'

'What a foul mouth!' Alf said.

They moved out on patrol, relieved just to get out, each carrying a bergen packed with enough food and water to last a minimum of five days, each carrying his own personal weapons, including their semi-automatic rifle, commando knife and *parang*, the latter used to hack a path through the dense, often lacerating, undergrowth. Like kampong policemen, they moved on foot. Unlike kampong policemen, they moved unobtrusively, in single file, the lead scout of the patrol followed by the commander and his radio operator, with a gun carrier at the rear playing Tail-end Charlie.

When Dead-eye went out with his three chosen men – Pete, Alf and Terry – as well as three Ibans and five constables from the Police Field Force, they found only signs that some Muruts had been hunting there. Leaving the three tribesmen and the five Police Field Force constables to construct a thatch-and-bamboo observation post overlooking a winding path through the *ulu*, which they suspected was an Indonesian supply route, Dead-eye and his three SAS men tracked down the Muruts just for the practice. A few hours later, they found them in a jungle hide where they were lying up with their blowpipes and dead pigs scattered around them, eating *jarit* and getting drunk on *tapai*. Being friendly, hardworking people who had taken to the British presence in the *ulu*, they invited the SAS men to join them. The subsequent socializing went on for three days, as to leave early would have been impolite. During that time, while the men forced down the vile food and became increasingly light-headed from the alcohol, they picked the brains of the Muruts and learnt a lot about Indonesian and CCO troop movements. Though drunk more often than not, Dead-eye managed to keep his head enough to jot down everything he was hearing.

When, at last, the Muruts moved on, the SAS men felt as if they had been poleaxed. Nevertheless, they made their way back to the rest of the group, who were worried that they had been ambushed by the Indonesians or the CCO.

Returning from the mission, the men, led by Dead-eye, learnt that the threat they had been instilling in the natives was real enough. That very day a force of thirty guerrillas had surrounded the police station at the border town of Tebedu in West Sarawak. After a brisk battle in which a police corporal was killed and two others wounded, the raiders had looted the bazaar. When the news reached the local military HQ, a troop of Royal Marine Commandos was sent to the scene, but the raiders had already disappeared back into the *ulu*, leaving leaflets which stated that the action was a continuation of the earlier revolt in Brunei.

Because of this surprise attack, Major Callaghan ordered all his four-man SAS teams in the area to dig in where they were and await further instructions.

'That's it,' Dead-eye said with no attempt to conceal his pleasure. 'The hearts-and-minds campaign has come to an end. The real war is beginning.'

4

With his SAS patrols dug in over a broad defensive arc, Major Callaghan began sending out more ambitious patrols, trying to track down the infiltrators and put a stop to them. To give Dead-eye more experience, Callaghan placed him in a patrol with Sanderson as his second in command and including Pete Welsh and Alf Laughton, as well as the new man, Terry Malkin, and the same three Ibans they had used before. The patrol was to hike into the high jungle hills of the Pueh Range, which had a peak of nearly 5000 feet and was believed to be a favourite route for CCO agents infiltrating through the jungle to reach Lundu, where the police Special Branch knew a number of communist cells were active.

'Your purpose,' Callaghan informed them, 'is to explore along the mountain range and back down to the lowlands, to locate the CCO forward base used by those terrorists being infiltrated from

Kalimantan. It's in a place called – so the Special Branch believes – Batu Hitam, or Black Rock. A nice, simple job, lads.'

'I'll bet,' Terry murmured.

For this patrol they had to avoid kampongs and any contact with local people, so they carried in their bergens all they might need for two weeks in the *ulu*. This, however, had been limited to 50lb since an excessively heavy bergen in tropical heat could overtax the strength of even an SAS trooper. Their rations would provide only 3500 calories a day (or as little as 2000 for those who chose to make the standard fourteen-day pack last twenty-one days), to save weight in their bergens. Yet to stay fully fit on such active patrols a man needs 5000 calories per day.

'We've lost so much weight already,' Alf observed, 'we'll probably look like ghosts when we get back, after these bloody rations.'

'And nothing from Fortnum and Mason's,' Pete complained. 'That's been reserved for the Ibans.'

'Complain to your squadron commander,' Dead-eye told them. 'Now shut up and let's hump it.'

Before moving out, each man smeared his face and other exposed skin with the usual 'cam' cream and black 'stick' camouflage. Their clothing consisted of a long-sleeved shirt and lightweight trousers tucked into gaiters above standard-issue boots, which had moulded composition soles, cunningly doctored to leave the pattern of an Indonesian, rather than a British, footprint on the jungle floor. They also wore a soft, long-peaked, close-fitting cap or the 'floppy' hat that was standard Army issue, with only a yellow band sewn in the lining as a recognition sign to friendly forces when the hat was put on inside out.

'Just imagine,' Alf said sarcastically. 'You're hiking through the jungle, leaving Indonesian boot marks instead of British, so you're tailed by a couple of your own men. You see them coming up on you, Armalites blazing, so you turn your fucking hat inside out and hope for the best. Some fucking hope!'

Their personal weapons – mainly the 7.62mm Armalite, but with Sanderson carrying his usual 7.62mm SLR and Terry given an M16 5.56mm assault rifle – were also camouflaged with strips of cloth dyed to match the jungle. When Pete held his camouflaged Armalite up to his 'cam'-painted face, the match was perfect.

'The fucking Black and White Minstrel Show,' Alf said. 'Let's all sing *Swanee*!'

Already feeling heavily burdened, Terry was weighed down even more with the PRC 320 Clansman radio, weighing 11 1/2lb, which he carried on his back, allowing him the use of both arms. The Clansman had a hand generator system, an alternate, or emergency, rechargeable nickel-cadmium battery, and a sky-wave facility of 30–1200 miles, with a ground-wave range of over 25 miles. It could also be operated by remote control from a distance of up to two miles.

'That's a damned good radio,' Pete told Terry, 'if a bit on the heavy side.'

'Right,' Terry said.

'The last man we had humping that fucking thing,' Alf contributed, 'collapsed after a four-hour hike with a heart attack. Went down like a log, he did.'

'Thanks a lot,' Terry said.

'He was older than you, though,' Pete said.

'By two years,' Alf added.

'Won a silver cup for running,' Pete said, 'but that bloody radio did him in.'

'If I'd wanted Morecambe and Wise,' Terry said, 'I'd have asked the BBC. Let's just call it a day, guys.'

'Such spirit!' Alf sang.

The patrol was escorted by five Police Field Force scouts as far as the border, which ran north–south along the mountain ridge. There the men moved out on their own, striking west from the border, heading into Indonesian jungle where they could as easily be ambushed as ambush an Indonesian patrol.

Within minutes of hiking into the dense jungle of the mountain range, Terry again experienced that oppressive awareness of vast silence combined with a chilling absence of colour and light. Mercifully, as they were already high in the hills, they had no swamps to brave, but almost as frightening to him were the many aerial walkways that swayed in the wind high above the gorges where, in the dizzying depths, streams wound, often violently over sharp rocks, between the high, muddy walls.

The aerial walkways were like miniature suspension bridges, but made of bamboo instead of steel. The walkway itself was constructed from only three lengths of thick bamboo, wide enough to span the gorge and laid down side by side to form a dangerously narrow path. The gaps in the bamboo uprights on either side of the walkway were three to four feet wide, with other lengths of bamboo running along them to be used as handrails.

Treading along the walkway, holding onto to the bamboo handrails on either side, a man was exposed to the full force of the wind blowing along the gorge. This was only made worse by the wide spaces between the uprights, which forced him to look down on the frightening, dizzying drop on either side. Nor could he ignore the constant, sickening swaying of the wind-blown walkway, often suspended a good hundred feet or more above the torrential river sweeping through the narrow gorge on a bed of sharp stones. There was no way to survive such a fall and all the men knew it.

Crossing the walkways was a stomach-churning experience and there were many to cross in the mountain range. Immensely relieved each time they stepped off a creaking, swaying aerial walkway, the men were then faced with yet another steep climb through the dense, often impenetrable undergrowth on the face of the steep hills. Their aching, forward advance often involved hacking away the undergrowth with their *parangs*, a task rendered even more difficult and dangerous by the steep fall of the hills, the loose soil underfoot and the lack of something to cling to if they slipped, since many of the branches were covered with sharp spikes and razor-edged palm leaves. The men therefore often slipped back, even fell and rolled down, while desperately trying to keep the blade of the *parang* away from their face and hands as they reached desperately for a hold on something that would stop them from rolling further.

All of this was made even more frustrating by the almost suffocating humidity, the sweat dripping constantly in their eyes, and the usual swarms of bloated flies and mosquitoes which frenziedly tried to feed off the sweat. They were also faced with a disturbing number of snakes, some venomous, which slept coiled around branches or slithered across the jungle paths, often hidden under the leaves on the ground, appearing as long, narrow mounds that moved magically forward while curving sinuously from left to right. Also, spiders and stinging ants often fell on them when the branches of trees were shaken accidentally.

'Christ!' Terry hissed, breathing heavily, when something large and hairy fell on him and bounced off his shoulder. 'That bastard was as big as my fist!'

'It was only a tarantula,' Pete replied. 'Its bark is worse than its bite.'

'It's the bleedin' *ants* that have the bite,' Terry said, 'and I'm black and blue.'

'No more talking from this moment on,' Deadeye told them, 'unless it's absolutely necessary. This is a silent patrol.'

Terry shivered, remembering the enormous spider, then he filled up with gloom at the prospect of not being able to break the suffocating silence of the jungle with conversation. Nevertheless, he moved on with the others, his face, shirt and trousers soaked with sweat.

Their routine was to march for an hour before

breakfast, which consisted of dried biscuits and tinned sardines, washed down with water. The water was usually drawn from a fast-flowing stream. If taken from a pool or slow-flowing stream, it would be purified with dissolving tablets before being used. Dead-eye would not even permit them to brew tea in case the smoke gave away their position.

For lunch they might have a few more biscuits and a tin of cheese, keeping the meatier items in their ration packs for supper just before nightfall.

Dead-eye permitted no cooking on this patrol. Though they might go cold and hungry, he explained, they were definitely a lot safer not attracting the attention of an Indonesian patrol, or even the region's headhunting Land Dyaks, to the sight of camp-fire smoke or the smells of cooking.

Halting either for a short break on the march or for one of their three miserable meals of the day, the men sat on their bergens, resting their rifles across their laps or cradling them in their crooked arms, either way always alert. If they talked, it was only to exchange brief sentences in a whisper. Meanwhile, as scout Dead-eye scanned the jungle ahead, while the navigator, the more experienced Sanderson, rechecked his route with a combination of map, magnifying glass and compass. The rest periods were therefore not all that restful and by last light all the men were exhausted.

After the draining heat and humidity of the day, the high mountain range could be surprisingly cold at night. Their lying-up positions, or LUPs, consisted mainly of uncovered shallow 'scrapes' in which they unrolled their hollow-fill sleeping bags on plastic sheeting. Above these simple bedding arrangements they raised a shelter consisting of a waterproof poncho draped over wire stretched taut between two Y-shaped sticks, making a triangular tent with the apex pointing into the wind. Sometimes, if camping out beneath the trees, they would construct a fresh-leaf shelter consisting of a low framework with a sloping roof. After collecting the largest leaves available, they thatched them into the bamboo framework of the roof. The four sides were made from bamboo and thatch woven together and lashed firmly in place with rattan vines. They then made a huge pile of branches and leaves as a mattress, put on all their clothes, smeared themselves with mud, if available, to keep away the insects, and finally covered themselves with groundsheets. Though taking longer to make, the fresh-leaf shelter afforded more protection than one made from a poncho.

Before moving on the next morning, just before first light, they meticulously removed all signs of their overnight bivvies. Even branches and leaves that had been disturbed were pushed back into their natural positions. This was a tedious, but vitally necessary routine.

As they moved further west, cresting the summit of the mountain range, exploring along it, then circling back down to lower ground, the need to be alert to a chance meeting with a Land Dyak became more pronounced. The Land Dyaks were not familiar with white men and tended to be suspicious of all strangers, including the Ibans from the coastal areas, such as the three travelling with the SAS patrol. Given that they were skilled at jungle warfare and still practised headhunting, they were a breed of native best avoided.

As Sanderson helpfully informed the rest of the group, smiling only slightly, the Land Dyaks were likely to come out of the wilder jungle heading towards the settlements along the Sempayang River, where there were many paddy-fields (as distinct from dry *padi* fields) for the growing of rice in traditional watery beds. The men saw the paddy-fields soon enough when they reached the lower slopes and began their sweaty hike along the river. The crops of seedlings, which would not be harvested until April, gave no cover, so the patrol kept mainly to a jungle-covered spur from which there was a view of the river.

In the event, the only Land Dyak they met was one they saw ankle-deep in the river, fishing with a blowpipe and darts smeared with a substance that paralysed the fish without leaving poison in its system.

Leaving the rest of his group hiding in the shelter of the trees, Dead-eye sneaked up on the tribesman, aimed his Armalite at him, and called out in Malay for him to turn around. Startled, the man did so, then studied Dead-eye with a gaze more considered than afraid. He did not put his hands up – the gesture was probably unknown to him – but simply stood there, holding the blowpipe by his side, staring at Dead-eye as if studying some new breed of animal.

'You are stranger,' he said, speaking in Malay.

'Yes,' Dead-eye replied, still aiming his weapon at the long-haired, half-naked native and keeping his eye on the blowpipe. 'I am a visitor here and wish you no harm. I look for the Indonesian soldiers. Have you seen any?'

The tribesman nodded and pointed along the river with his blowpipe. 'Batu Hitam,' he said.

'Anywhere else?' Dead-eye asked.

The Dyak shook his head from side to side, indicating no.

'And Batu Hitam is straight along the river?'

This time the Dyak nodded, again without speaking. He then pointed upriver.

'Thank you,' Dead-eye said, then backed away to where the rest of his group were hidden, crouched low at the edge of the *ulu*. He did not remove his gaze from the Dyak's blowpipe, but by the time he reached the shelter of trees, the native had already returned to his work, blowing his poisoned darts into the water, then reaching down to snatch up the immobilized fish.

'Learn anything?' Sanderson asked.

'Only that the Indos are in Batu Hitam, further upriver. He says he hasn't seen them anywhere else.'

'Then let's head upriver,' Sanderson said, 'and find their camp.'

'Right, men,' Dead-eye said, glancing at the others. 'Let's haul out.'

Heading upriver, sticking close to the bank, they reached Batu Hitam in two hours. There, from where they were hiding at the edge of the forest, they saw a Dyak settlement, clearly filled with headhunters, judging from the number of shrunken skulls strung over the doors of the thatched longhouses. But there was no trace of the Indonesians. Circling around the settlement, crouched low, weapons at the ready, taking note of the fact that the male Dyaks were armed with spears and blowpipes, they carefully checked every aspect of the village, but still saw no sign of either Indonesian soldiers or the CCO.

Just as they were about to turn back, however, one of the Iban trackers, Ejok, raised and lowered his clenched right fist repeatedly, indicating that the rest of the patrol should join him. When they did so, he showed them a lot of footprints in the swampy ground near the river, leading from the settlement to the river bank. All the footprints were of men who had been wearing Indonesian jungle boots.

'They must have been here,' Ejok said in Malay, nodding back in the direction of the settlement. 'These bootprints are fresh, so they must have left only recently, maybe this morning, taking boats from here and heading upriver. As they have left no sign of their presence in the camp, they don't intend coming back.'

'Damn!' Dead-eye said softly.

Sanderson sighed. 'We've lost them. We're not allowed to stay out longer than two weeks. We'll have to go back empty-handed.'

Dead-eye was visibly frustrated. He ordered the patrol to turn around and go back downstream. They crossed the river two hours later, just before reaching the spot where the Dyak had been fishing, then they began the long hike to the forward operating base, three days' 'tab' away.

During that sweaty, exhausting hike they lost even more weight when, wading chest-deep through the swamps of the humid lowland forests, they were covered in leeches that greedily fed off them. By the time they had reached dry land again, where they could burn them off, they had all lost a lot of blood, as well as more weight.

On reaching the FOB, still without having made contact with the enemy, let alone a sighting of them, they were even more frustrated to learn that another SAS-led patrol had successfully ambushed a Chinese party on the mountain six miles west of the Bemban where an Indonesian base was known to be located. A second patrol had found a deserted Indonesian fort with mortar pits and well-sited defences. A third patrol, waiting to ambush a CCO patrol, had themselves been attacked by a 100-strong Indonesian platoon on the Bemban track. The SAS men suffered no casualties and managed to kill at least eleven of them before making a quick withdrawal.

'We're the only ones who saw and did nothing,' Dead-eye said bitterly. 'What a waste of time!'

'Everything comes to him who waits,' Major Callaghan replied with a teasing grin. 'Now go and get some sleep, Dead-eye.'

Dead-eye joined the others back in the spider, where he slept like a log.

5

'In the words of our commanding officer,' Major Callaghan said in the briefing room of the Haunted House, 'this is the year that began with the end of a revolution and ended with the beginning of an undeclared war.'

Pausing to let those words sink in, he wiped sweat from his forehead and waved flies away from his face. A large fan whirred above his head.

'That undeclared war has commenced along the frontier,' he continued, 'so you men will be moved back to the unmapped mountain border of Sarawak – the so-called 'Gap' – also known as the 3rd Division. You will concentrate your efforts on the shorter frontier between Indonesia and Brunei, which has chosen to remain a British Protectorate rather than join the new Federation. There you will engage in aggressive raids into enemy territory.'

The men sitting in rows of hard-backed wooden chairs under two more large rotating fans cheered and applauded. Callaghan waited for them to settle down before he continued.

'The object of the raids is to pre-empt any likely Indonesian build-up or attack; to harass the Indonesians on patrol and in their camps; and to gradually compel them to move their forces away from the border. As the major purpose, then, is to deter or thwart aggression by the Indonesians, no attacks will be mounted in retribution or with the sole aim of damaging the enemy. The enemy is only to be engaged as a last defensive resort. Where this is the case, minimum force should be used, rather than large-scale attacks, to avoid escalation.'

Seeing the expression on the faces of his men, Callaghan felt a certain regret. It was obvious from their faces that they were delighted to be back in action; and Callaghan, who himself liked nothing better than action, wanted to go with them. Unfortunately, as Squadron Commander, he was going to be kept back at HQ, mapping out the campaign, analysing the intelligence, and controlling the various patrols by radio based on that information. It was an exciting job in its own way, but not quite what he wanted.

'Collectively, the raids will be known as "Claret" operations and classified "Top Secret",' he told them. 'Initial penetration distance into Indonesian territory will be 5000 yards, though this may be extended to 20,000.'

'I could piss 5000 yards,' Alf said. 'It's not worth considering.'

'Yes, it is,' Callaghan said firmly when the laughter had died down. 'Your primary function will be deep penetration and the gathering of intelligence across enemy lines, engaging the enemy if necessary.' The latter part of that remark raised a few more cheers. 'This penetration will include the river routes used by the Indonesians as military supply routes, to move men and equipment up to the border. You will count the boats and the men on those MSRs, and map suitable areas from which they can be ambushed from the river bank. Last but not least, you'll locate the kampongs and bases from which the boats are coming and, if at all possible, enter them without alerting the sentries or dogs, recce them, then slip back out into the jungle.'

'Sounds better than suffering the horrors of *jarit* and *tapai* in order to win hearts and minds,' Pete said tartly. 'Count me in, boss.'

'It's *because* you drink *tapai*,' Alf told him, 'that you can fart from your mouth. Can we get on with the briefing, thanks?'

'OK, men, let's dampen it.' Though smiling, Callaghan sounded serious, so the men quietened down again. 'The first cross-border patrols,' the major informed them, 'will be made by two- to five-man teams *not* accompanied by local guides. You'll carry exactly the same equipment and weapons as you've used in Sarawak, with the main small arm being the Armalite rifle.'

'Why the Armalite?'

'It's presently viewed as the perfect jungle weapon, being portable and powerful. Also, though used widely around the world, it isn't standard issue to the British Army. Therefore, if wounded or taken prisoner, you can attribute your presence in Indonesian territory to a map-reading error, which should sound, in the circumstances, reasonably plausible.'

'It might if we're caught on the river banks,' Dead-eye pointed out. 'But it certainly won't if we're caught near their kampongs or training bases.'

Callaghan sighed. 'No, I'm afraid that in those circumstances you won't have a leg to stand on and will be treated rather harshly by your captors.'

'The understatement of the year,' Alf said.

'Fat chance of *me* being caught,' Pete added.

'Don't treat the possibility lightly,' Callaghan warned him. 'Having already been out there, the 1st/2nd Gurkha Company has discovered that a lot of the approach tracks to the camps and kampongs are mined. Also, outlying machine-gun positions add considerably to the overall camp defences.'

'I'll piss on them from 5000 yards,' Alf said, 'and put out their fire.'

'I wouldn't call him a boastful man,' Pete said, 'but there are those who are humbler.'

'How do we navigate?' Dead-eye asked in a sombre tone when further ribald remarks had faded away.

Callaghan was prompt and precise in his response. 'Through the scrutiny of air photographs; cultivation of a photographic memory of topographical features such as rivers and ridges, as well as their compass bearings; and a precise sense of distance walked to calculate a dead reckoning of mileage covered by reference to time-on-march. You will also use jungle tracking as a means of following the enemy to their kampongs or bases.'

'How do we engage?' Dead-eye asked, getting to the heart of the matter.

'Mainly the shoot-and-scoot standard operating procedure.' This meant breaking contact with the enemy as soon as possible, whenever contact occurred, and making themselves scarce again, disappearing like ghosts. Some of the men groaned aloud when they heard this approach proposed, voicing their disapproval, but Callaghan waved them into silence. 'I know this particular SOP isn't popular with many of you, but it's our belief that it'll keep casualties to a minimum, while simultaneously disorientating the enemy. I know you'd rather stay and fight it out, but shoot-and-scoot it will have to be.'

'Whoever devised that SOP,' Pete said, 'should be hung, drawn and quartered.'

'I devised it in Malaya,' Callaghan responded, 'with your old friend Sergeant Lorrimer.' He waited for the embarrassed silence to grip the room, then moved in for the kill. 'It's already proved its effectiveness more than once, in circumstances similar to the ones you'll soon find yourselves in, so while your moans and groans are acceptable, don't try refusing.'

'No, boss!' Alf said, knowing when he was beaten.

Now confident that he had the upper hand, Callaghan smiled again – a merciless smile – as he gave them even worse news. 'Please bear in mind, also, that if you get lost, or are captured, no rescue will be attempted by the other men in your patrol.' When he felt that they had digested this harsh fact, he explained: 'Nothing is to be left in enemy territory that will betray our presence there. No casualties, dead or wounded, to be left behind. No identity discs, photos or letters from home. No cigarette stubs. No spent cartridge cases.

Not even the prints of your boots. Regarding the latter, you will be asked to wear irregular footwear, with sacking or hessian over your boots, shoes and sandals to blur all marks indicating their origin. You will check every leaf and spider's web, leaving absolutely no trace of your movements. Any questions so far?'

Corporal Sanderson put up his hand. 'How long will the individual raids last?'

'Approximately three weeks each.' Someone gave a low whistle of surprise. 'Yes,' Callaghan said, 'it's a long time. And as you'll be obliged to live on dehydrated rations based on a relatively meagre 3500 calories per day instead of the recommended minimum of 5000, you can expect to lose a considerable amount of weight.'

'We've already lost that,' Terry informed him.

'You're going to lose even more,' Callaghan responded bluntly. 'On your return, *if* you return, you'll have a one-day debriefing, followed by a two-day period of total rest, then a two-day briefing for the next patrol. You move out again after a total of five days back here, during which time you should have put your lost weight back on.'

'Only to lose it again on the next patrol,' Sergeant Hunt said sardonically from the back of the room.

'Given your impressive paunch, Sergeant, I don't think it will harm you.'

The men had a good laugh at that, but Hunt took it in good part. 'What about air support?' he asked when the laughter had died away.

'It will only be given in cases of extreme emergency. Otherwise, forget it.'

Callaghan glanced left and right, from one row of faces to the other, trying to glance at each trooper in turn, even if only for a few seconds. 'Any more questions?' When most of the men shook their heads, Callaghan nodded.

'Some points to note,' he said, wrapping it up. 'For these particular raids, the important thing is not how much you can carry, but how far you can travel with the minimum of equipment. You can't go head down, arse up in this kind of situation, so prior to your departure we'll be weighing your bergens to check that they're not a single ounce over the maximum weight of 50lb. If they are, certain items will be taken out, no matter how much you value them, until the weight is reduced to the permitted level.' He ignored the groans of disgust. 'Also, between now and when you leave, your NCOs will be making random urine and blood tests to ensure that you're all taking your Paludrine against malaria. I don't care if you wash them down with beer, but make sure you take them.' He grinned at the rolling eyes and murmurs of protest. When these had subsided, he raised his hands, calling for complete silence. 'All right, gentlemen, I think I've had my turn. Now it's yours. Good day and good luck.'

The men applauded him unreservedly.

6

The first cross-border raids were tentative probes over the ridge into Indonesian territory by unaccompanied groups of between two and five men carrying exactly the same equipment and weapons they had used before. The same team that had made the unproductive hike to Batu Hitam, still under the command of Dead-eye with Corporal Sanderson as his second in command, was given the task of reaching the River Koemba, which ran for three miles parallel to the border of western Sarawak.

'This border from Cape Datu in the north,' Captain Callaghan explained to Dead-eye in his private office in the Haunted House, 'crosses the coastal plain where Gurkhas and Royal Marines of the Special Boat Squadron have patrolled from time to time. It then runs north–south along the Pueh Range,' he continued, tracing a line with his forefinger on the map spread out on his desk, 'and turns south-eastwards across the flat lands north of the Sentimo marshes.' He tapped the marked area with his forefinger, looking rather distracted. 'Here the Sarawak border runs across trading tracks leading to Stass. The only major routes crossing the border for the next 30 miles of frontier run along mountain ridges north of the Koemba and further eastwards parallel to the Sentimo marshes.'

'So, the obvious, if not necessarily easy, crossing for any Indonesian invasion,' Dead-eye replied, looking down at the map, 'is still through Stass and on to the Sarawak capital of Kuching.'

'Exactly,' Callaghan said, always pleased by Dead-eye's quick, intuitive grasp of military strategy. 'So that's where we want you to cause your little disruptions.'

'No problem,' Dead-eye said.

'Unfortunately, there *is* a problem. SAS patrols sent out earlier this year reached the edge of the Sentimo marshes and the headwaters of the Koemba, but were unable to penetrate the marshes north of the river. You might come to the same grief.'

In fact, Dead-eye's group did. They spent over a week trying to reach the upper part of the river and the mountain plateau separating it from the Sentimo marshes. This involved hiking through dense primary and secondary jungle. In the latter, known as *belukar*, the foliage had been cleared and was growing back again, thicker than ever, to form an often impenetrable tangle of palms, tree-ferns, bracken, seedling trees, rattans and other sharp thorns. Here, too, the moss-covered tree trunks often soared to over 100 feet, wrapped in another tangle of huge leaves, thick creepers and liana, forming an almost solid canopy above which blotted out the sun. Because of this lack of light the ground was wet and often slippery with mud, making progress slow and dirty; it also reminded the already struggling men that the actual swamps could not be far away.

This turned out to be true. Finally emerging from a gruelling struggle through a stretch of *belukar*, the men found themselves faced with primary jungle filled with large swamps. These were hell to cross. The muddy water often came up to the waist, and sometimes the chest. It was covered with drifting debris, including large, razor-sharp leaves, thorny brambles, broken branches, seedlings, and spiders' webs succumbing to the slime. This debris was in turn covered with dark swarms of flies and mosquitoes that buzzed and whined frantically around the men, covering their unprotected eyes, lips and noses. The men were further tormented by this because they could do nothing to prevent it, being forced to hold their weapons above their heads while trying to feel their way with their booted feet over an underwater bed rendered treacherous by shifting mud, tangled weeds, sharp or rolling stones, thorny branches that also moved when stepped on, and unexpected holes that could trap the feet.

Nor could the troopers prevent themselves being covered by the slimy, worm-like leeches that crawled onto them from wet vegetation and sucked their blood as they waded through the swamp holding their weapons aloft. But even more tormenting was the fact that in many areas of the swamps the lower branches of the trees stretched out across the water, often practically touching it, forcing the men to either work their way around them, which could double the distance travelled, or duck under them. This latter course of action presented the risk of being cut by thorns and sharp palm leaves or, even worse, could cause them to accidentally shake more leeches, poisonous snakes or spiders off their wet leaves, branches or glistening webs filled with trapped insects.

In fact, one of the main dangers of wading through the water was the possibility of an encounter with venomous sea snakes, which had flattened, paddle-shaped tails and, being the same brownish colour as the broken branches, could easily be mistaken for them until it was too late. Luckily, no one was attacked.

Nevertheless, it took a few more days to make it through the swamps and marshes, which meant that they had to sleep there as well. Sometimes, if they were lucky, they could sling hammocks between tree trunks. But when this was not possible they were forced to sleep standing upright, often waist-deep in water, usually tying themselves to a tree trunk to prevent themselves falling over. While acutely uncomfortable, this did allow them a little sleep, though it was rarely deep or truly restorative.

If the jungle's silence was oppressive during the day, by night it gave way to an eerie cacophony of croaking, hissing, flapping, snapping, rustling, squawking, buzzing and whining that penetrated the senses of those sleeping and frequently jerked them awake. To this kind of disruption of normal sleep was added their own fear, which also kept them awake, of slipping out of their ropes and sinking into the water, too tired to realize what was happening before they drowned; or of being bitten by venomous snakes or eels while their bodies sagged in the water. The leeches fed off their blood all night, but this no longer concerned them.

Finally, after five days of such horrors, already exhausted and only halfway through the patrol, the men reached the upper part of the river – only to find that the sheer cliffs of the plateau offered no possible route to the jungle over 800 feet below, on the other side of the mountain range.

They had to turn back.

To make matters worse, on their return journey across the border, through the hellish swamps, then the dense *belukar*, and finally the dark, humid primary jungle leading to the rendezvous point, they almost shot up some of their own men, when, hiding at night in the jungle, they heard what they could only assume was an Indonesian or CCO patrol coming along the path they were overlooking.

Immediately they dropped low and took aim with their Armalites, preparing to open fire. The first 'enemy' troops appeared around a bend in the path, not attempting to hide themselves, and only when Dead-eye recognized the 0.3-inch M1 carbines they were carrying did he realize that they were actually a patrol of Dyak Border Scouts, coming to meet up at the wrong RV.

'Don't fire!' Dead-eye bawled instantly, then he leapt out upon the startled Dyaks, some of whom nearly opened fire at the sight of him. After an acrimonious exchange, Dead-eye's group joined the confused tribesmen on the short hike back through the darkness to their correct RV.

Frustrated by the failure of his SAS groups to get beyond the Sentimo marshes and still constrained by not being permitted to use them for overtly aggressive actions, Major Callaghan revised his strategy and, instead, concentrated on planning offensive cross-border operations by the Gurkha battalions, with the SAS acting as scouts.

While this still led to a certain amount of frustration for some of the SAS men, notably those such as Dead-eye, they all conceded that it was better than doing nothing and could even be quite relaxing, particularly after the relative isolation of the earlier patrols, which had emotionally drained many of them.

Terry Malkin was one of those convinced that scouting for the Gurkha battalions was almost pleasant when compared to the R & I patrols through the *ulu*, when the silence and gloom, combined with the frightening isolation of the five-man team, had given him more than one bad night.

Not that the scouting work was not demanding, both physically and mentally. Certainly, in the windless, silent days in the jungle, being a scout had its own difficulties and discomforts. For instance, no trooper was allowed to eat, smoke or unscrew his water bottle without his platoon commander's permission. At night, sentries checked any man who snored or talked in his sleep. Whenever the company was on the move, a recce section led the way, their packs carried by the SAS men behind. Because of the long approach march, each man carried six days' basic rations together with various lightweight additions and a small reserve in a belt pouch, but these were barely sufficient for his needs.

Nevertheless, even more demanding than the marches were the many periods when the scouts had to remain stationary to watch and listen for the enemy.

As Dead-eye explained to Terry when he had complained about such stops: 'The man who's stationary in the jungle has the tactical advantage. Not moving himself, making no sound of his own, he can see and hear a lot more of the enemy movements. That gives him the upper hand.'

It was for that reason, therefore, that the SAS scouts were compelled to spend as much as twenty minutes in every half hour sitting and listening, only marching during the other ten minutes. It made for slow, frustrating progress, but it kept them alive.

Nevertheless, if scouting for the Gurkha battalions had its own share of danger, tension, isolation and frustration, Terry noticed the difference in the evening when, having completed the day's recce in the *ulu*, he could return, not to a tiny, cramped jungle hide with his small, relatively defenceless team, but to a whole battalion of Gurkhas in their camp. This tended to make him feel a lot safer and, in many ways, more human. It was a good feeling to be in the middle of their perimeter, warmed by a camp-fire, eating decent food, and surrounded by so many small, cheerful, brown-faced men, whom he knew were actually ferocious fighters. To see them at night in their sangars, spaced evenly around the perimeter, with their GPMGs aiming out in all directions, made the novice SAS man feel safe.

He even felt safer than normal when, just before he was due to return with the rest of Dead-eye's team, the SAS led the Gurkhas to an Indonesian camp they had found recently. To reach the camp, they had to hike through the night, arriving just after dawn.

Completely surrounded by thick undergrowth, the camp consisted of a few thatched huts on stilts, some open latrines covered with clouds of flies, and a protective ring of sunken gun emplacements and defensive trenches. The Indonesian soldiers were seated in large groups around smoking open fires, breakfasting on roast pig, when the Gurkhas arrived and spread out in a great circle around the camp, though remaining well hidden in the forest. In that same thick undergrowth, the Gurkhas and

SAS men quietly brought into position British 3-inch mortars, Soviet RPG-7 rocket launchers, M79 single-shot, breech-loading grenade-launchers, and GPMGs and Bren light machine-guns. The gun and mortar teams were in touch with one another through their small, backpacked A41 radio sets and, at the command from the Gurkha commander, they would fire simultaneously.

Kneeling in the darkness with Pete and Alf on one side of him and the inscrutable Dead-eye on the other, Terry, as signaller, was listening to his A41 with a racing heart and sweat on his brow. Though five years in the Irish Guards, he had not actually seen combat before, and realized that at last he was about to take part in a fire-fight. Any advances to be made would, he knew, be made by the Gurkhas, with the SAS giving covering fire; but that in itself was close enough to the real thing to make him feel simultaneously nervous and excited. He would be, after all, in the line of enemy fire and therefore in considerable danger. Yes, this *was* the real thing.

Glancing to the left, past Dead-eye's granite profile, Terry saw the Gurkha commander raise his clenched fist, preparing to give the order to fire. Glancing back at the enemy camp, he saw the many soldiers in their jungle-greens still squatting around the open fires, waving smoke from their faces, eating roast pork and rice, laughing, joking and relaxing as if they had all the time in the world. They were inside the perimeter. Around the perimeter in the sunken gun emplacements, the sentries were, in many instances, also paying more attention to food and drink than they were to what was happening in the jungle.

Terry studied them intently. They seemed very unconcerned. He was in a trance of watchfulness, studying the soldiers around the fires, when the voice of the Gurkha commander snapped 'Open fire!' in Malay, his voice reverberating eerily in Terry's headset, followed almost simultaneously by the crump-crump of mortars and the sudden, savage roar of the combined rocket-launchers and machine-guns.

Even before Terry had quite grasped what was happening, the first mortar shells were exploding in and between the gun emplacements and defensive trenches, as well as among the Indonesians around the camp-fires. At the same time, a barrage of 2.25kg missiles, 40mm fin-stabilized grenades and 7.62mm tracer bullets was flaring across the clearing and disappearing into the flames and boiling smoke caused by the first mortar explosions.

Some gun emplacements and slit trenches were destroyed instantly in violent eruptions of spewing soil, with broken bodies hurled upwards and out like burning rag dolls; but others returned the fire, their guns spitting fire and smoke, causing different-coloured tracers to race outwards from the perimeter and into the jungle.

One of the huts inside the camp exploded in flames as the jungle around Terry went wild, with shells and tracers zipping past on both sides and foliage being blown to shreds all around him.

'Open fire!' Dead-eye bawled.

Just about to hug the ground to avoid the return fire of the enemy, Terry instead found himself firing his Armalite at the men jumping up from their camp-fires, grabbing their weapons and running left and right to find cover as the huts blazed behind them and more shells and bullets cut them to pieces.

Another hut exploded, disintegrating in a ball of fire, with the men nearby, also on fire, hurled in all directions. Within seconds the camp had been obscured in a grim pall of smoke through which shadowy figures and brighter flames could just about be discerned; though the screams of the wounded and dying actually rose above the deafening bedlam of the roaring guns and explosions.

Terry kept firing, feeling as if he was dreaming but vividly aware of the return fire flashing and snapping angrily on both sides, kicking up the soil in front of him, then blowing apart the foliage directly above to make it rain down on him. He kept his finger on the trigger until the magazine was empty, ejected it, loaded another, and continued to fire at the shadowy figures running and falling in that hellish tapestry of flame and smoke.

He did not know if the men falling in his sights had been hit by him or by some of those firing methodically around him; nor did he care. He just could not stop. The men around him also continued firing with everything they had – mortars, rocket launchers, machine-guns, sub-machine-guns and rifles – until the return fire from the enemy camp had diminished considerably and, eventually, started to taper off altogether.

Terry was not sure if he had heard the second command on his headset or not, but suddenly, as the smoke cleared, two assault platoons of Gurkhas moved in to clear the camp, advancing at the crouch, firing on the move, and not stopping to take prisoners or ask questions.

'Selective firing only,' Dead-eye ordered, switching to single-shot and starting to give selective covering fire by picking off individuals who looked like being a threat to the advancing Gurkhas. 'We want no own goals,' he added, meaning that they were not to accidentally shoot any of their own men, in this case the Gurkhas. 'Do it right or stop firing.'

Terry did not stop firing. Now, for the first time,

with the smoke clearing and the enemy thinning, he knew exactly which falling men had been shot by him and felt better about it. It was an odd, uncomfortable feeling, perhaps even shameful, but it filled him with an odd kind of pride as well – odd because tinged with fear.

Though most of the soldiers in and around the camp had been put out of action, either dead or seriously wounded, a number of naked, panic-stricken Indonesians suddenly rushed out from around the burning ruins of a hut demolished by mortar fire. Not waiting to find out if they had arms or booby-traps behind their backs, the ferocious little Gurkhas dealt with them quickly and ruthlessly, cutting them down in a hail of fire from their SLRs and M16s. When the last of the naked men had fallen, all resistance ended.

'Cease fire,' Dead-eye said to the men beside him.

Standing up beside the impassive Dead-eye and his two more excited corporals, Terry saw that most of the enemy gun emplacements and defensive trenches were now blackened shell holes, that most of the camp-fires had been blown apart by gunfire, that all of the huts hit by the mortars were either still blazing or smouldering, and that the dead and wounded were scattered all around the clearing in an unholy mess of other shell holes, spent shells, buckled weapons, shreds of clothing, dismembered limbs and spreading pools of blood. Turning away from that ghastly sight, he met the fathomless grey gaze of Sergeant Parker.

'You did pretty good,' Dead-eye told him. 'You've just earned your winged dagger.'

Young Terry was too numb to respond.

'You'll recover,' Dead-eye said.

7

Terry recovered. Six weeks later he was kneeling with the other members of a five-man group that included another new man, Trooper Kenneth Burgess, Welsh Guards, in the dense foliage at the side of a jungle track known to be used as an Indonesian military supply route. This was at the tail end of a four-week period in which many small groups of SAS men, having finally received formal approval to do more than 'watch and count' or act as scouts for the Gurkhas, had broadened the scope of the 'Claret' raids to include attacks on enemy approach routes and MSRs, either by road or water, ambushing tracks and rivers, and setting booby-traps where it was known that the Indonesian or CCO raiders would pass. The range of penetration across the border had therefore been greatly increased and the pre-emptive actions undertaken by the unaccompanied SAS groups had increased in both frequency and ferocity.

Basing most of their attack methods on Major Callaghan's 'shoot-and-scoot' SOP, the groups had made the essence of their ambushes speed of movement and reaction: hitting the enemy from close range with a brief, savage fusillade of small-arms fire, including hand-grenades, then vanishing speedily, leaving the counter-attackers to find nothing but apparently empty jungle. These tactics were highly successful, causing a lot of damage, and soon the SAS were getting tales back from the Dyaks and other aboriginals about how the Indonesians and CCO were whispering fearful stories about their 'invisible' attackers.

For this reason the SAS troopers started calling themselves the 'Tiptoe Boys'.

At other times, however, the attacks would be lengthier, more sophisticated affairs with electronically detonated Claymore mines catching an enemy's front and rear, while the SAS troopers' automatic fire raked the centre.

Which is what Terry's group were planning this very minute, as their last and largest attack before heading back to the RV. So, while Terry, Dead-eye and Alf knelt in the firing position in the shadow of the trees by the side of the road, spaced well apart to give a broad arc of fire, their demolition expert, Pete Welsh, quickly and expertly laid his four Claymores approximately equidistant along the centre of a 100-yard stretch of road, placed so as to catch the front and rear of the Indonesian column, as well as the middle.

Invented by the Germans during World War Two, the Claymore anti-tank mine consists of a round, flattish dish with a concave plate of steel on its face. It is filled with explosive. When detonated, the plate is blown off and can go through the side or front of a Panther tank at a distance of 80 yards. After the war the Americans modified the Claymore to fire metal spikes, or 'slugs', instead of the plate. When this modified Claymore is exploded, its 350 razor-sharp slugs will fly out over a sixty-degree arc to a range of 100 yards, shredding anyone unfortunate enough to be within its range. It is a terrible weapon.

Pete was wiring his Claymores for detonation by remote control. This enabled him to bury them in the ground, face up, resting on their spiked base, with earth and leaves thrown over them to disguise their presence.

As he watched Pete lay the Claymores and, at the same time, kept his ear cocked for the sound of advancing Indonesians, Terry thought with pride of the many attacks he had made with this small group since his baptism of fire with the Gurkhas near the River Koemba. Though not exactly frightened by that attack, he had been shocked by the results of it, dwelling for days on the carnage it had caused. Nevertheless, as Dead-eye had promised him, he had recovered soon enough and gone on to his other fire-fights with more confidence and a necessary pragmatism. Distancing himself from the bloody results of what he was engaged in, he had learned to treat it as a job, in a professional manner, and eventually, after three or four more attacks with this five-man team, had even started taking pride in a job well done.

Luckily, their personal attacks had so far been uniformly successful, which had helped Terry build up his confidence. However, as they had learnt over the past six weeks through radio communications, other patrols had not been so lucky. Inevitably, some had been ambushed *en route* to ambush the Indonesians or CCO. In those attacks, all the SAS men had died. The sergeant leading another group had contracted the jungle disease leptospirosis, which meant that the whole group had to turn back, carrying him all the way while he suffered from a 105-degree temperature and other, more agonizing symptoms. Even more bizarrely, an Australian SAS trooper was gored by an elephant and had to be left in the jungle, on the Indonesian side of the border, while the rest of his group made a two-day trek back across the border to obtain help from a Gurkha camp. Unfortunately, the wounded

Aussie had died by the time he was found by a casualty-evacuation helicopter pilot determined not to let the man be found by the enemy, dead or alive. As for the others who had died, all identifying items had been removed from their bodies, after which there was a quick burial in an unmarked grave. It was a brutal business.

As Pete started scattering leaves and twigs over the buried Claymores, Terry glanced in both directions, seeing Dead-eye and Alf on one side of him and the newcomer, Ken Burgess, on the other, all of them braced on one knee, the other foot braced on the ground, their Armalites already aimed in different directions at the jungle track. With their faces striped with 'cam' cream and their weapons and clothes also camouflaged, they merged almost perfectly with the tall foliage in which they were hidden.

Dead-eye looked as impassive as ever, Alf looked reasonably intent, and the newcomer, Ken, was the only one showing any tension. So far, Ken had shown his mettle and made no mistakes, but undoubtedly the jungle had taken its toll on him, making him more nervous than he might otherwise have been and causing the others to keep their eyes on him. Some men, no matter how good they were as soldiers, were destroyed by the jungle. Terry had likewise suffered when first exposed to it, but now he was used to it.

After hiding the last of his Claymores, Pete checked the whole area, making doubly sure that it looked absolutely normal, then backed towards the other men, brushing dust, leaves and twigs over his own tracks as he went. When he had finished, the track looked like it had not been trodden on since the dawn of time.

No one spoke. Dead-eye merely acknowledged the thoroughness of Pete's work by silently giving him the thumbs up. Nodding and grinning, Pete knelt in the flattened grass beside the plunger he would use for the detonation of the mines. As SAS troops on patrol were not allowed to leave their weapons at any time – even when sleeping – Pete's Armalite had been slung over his shoulder all the time he was laying the mines. It was still there when he checked the plunger, then rested one hand on it and glanced along the jungle track, to where it disappeared between the trees.

They had neither seen nor heard the Indonesian foot patrol, which was known to be carrying supplies to a full battalion camped north of the River Koemba, but had learnt about it from another SAS patrol, who had caught a glimpse of it from a distant plateau and tracked its direction and speed of movement for over an hour. From those calculations, communicated to this patrol by radio, Dead-eye had been able to calculate the Indonesians' estimated time of arrival at this location. Allowing approximately two hours extra for rest stops and, possibly, an early breakfast, he reckoned that they were due to arrive any time within a two-hour period starting thirty minutes from then.

The wait was tortuous because the men could neither speak to one another nor move from their firing positions. In the absolute silence of the windless *ulu*, the sound of even the slightest movement could carry a long way. Therefore the men had to be ready to fire and to remain in that position, frozen like statues, but with their muscles under strain and rapidly becoming painful, until the action could begin. Luckily, they heard the sounds of distant, advancing movement forty minutes later.

With their weapons already cocked, the SAS troopers did not have to make even that sound. They merely pressed the triggers down slightly and took more careful aim.

The few minutes it took for the Indonesian patrol to appear seemed longer than the previous forty minutes, but eventually the first troops rounded the bend in the path, emerging slowly from the trees and tendrils of early-morning mist, wearing jungle-green fatigues, soft peaked caps and jungle boots.

All of them were slim and had delicate, handsome features. As the rest advanced around the bend, about forty in all, it became clear that they were carrying a variety of weapons, mostly of World War Two vintage, such as Lee-Enfield .303-inch bolt-action rifles and the Soviet PPSh-41 7.62mm sub-machine-gun. They also had hand-grenades clipped to their belts and bandoliers criss-crossing their chests in a manner viewed by the SAS men as suicidal.

The SAS group hidden in the trees did not stop breathing, but each man concentrated on breathing slowly and evenly as he applied a little more pressure to the trigger of his Armalite.

The first of the Indonesian troops reached the first buried Claymore.

Pete placed his free hand beside the other on the detonating plunger, and bunched up his shoulders.

The lead soldier stepped on the buried mine, walked over it and kept walking, kicking up the loose leaves, followed by the others, spread foolishly across the track in twos and threes, treading on one mine, then another, now passing the hidden SAS men, until the last man had stepped on the first mine, buried at a forty-five degree angle from where Pete was leaning forward to press on the plunger.

Pete pressed the plunger all the way down.

The explosions were like thunderclaps, four

mighty roars in one, blowing the soil up and outwards in great fan shapes that spewed smoke and fire. The Indonesians were blown apart, picked up and slammed back down, or slashed to ribbons by the hundreds of razor-sharp slugs that flew with the speed of bullets in all directions.

That the SAS men should open fire with their Armalites simultaneously was almost an act of mercy, since many of the Indonesians not instantly killed were staggering about in the swirling smoke, or writhing on the dust-choked ground, with their skin either scorched and blistered or slashed to the bone and, in many cases, stripped right off the rib cage or limbs, exposing bloody intestines and naked bone.

The hail of SAS bullets stitched through these unfortunates, silencing their demented screams, then moved left and right in a broad arc that took in those who had escaped the blasts of the Claymores and were now retreating into the jungle, firing on the move. Still confused by the explosions, some of them raced straight towards the hidden SAS men, only to be bowled over by another sustained fusillade from the Armalites. Dust billowed up around their falling bodies and blended in with the swirling smoke.

Even before the smoke had cleared, the Indonesians now hidden at the far side of the devastated track

– the soil upturned and blackened, filled with dead men, dismembered limbs, pieces of uniform and broken weapons – were opening fire with their small arms, aiming blindly across the road, through the smoke, and hoping to hit the enemy by accident.

'Bug out!' Dead-eye roared.

Since they were carrying no machine-guns or support weapons, the men were able to jump up and beat a retreat immediately. But as they were doing so, the jungle behind them exploded, showering them with foliage and almost bowling them over.

In fact, Terry *was* bowled over and found himself rolling on the ground until stopped by a tree trunk. Shaking his head to clear it, he glanced to the side, back towards the obliterated path, and saw an enemy soldier rising spectrally from one of the holes caused by a Claymore, his uniform in tatters, pus dripping from blinded eyes, his chest slashed from the left shoulder to just below the right hip, with the skin hanging down like a towel dipped in blood, revealing the rich fruit of his intestines. Obviously sightless, in terrible pain and terrified, he advanced a few feet, waving his scorched hands as if in search of something to cling to, then was cut down by a blast from an Armalite held close to Terry's ear.

Startled, Terry looked up just as Dead-eye grabbed his shoulder, hauled him roughly to his feet, and bawled, 'Run!' Terry ran, holding his own Armalite at the ready, following Dead-eye away from the smoke of the mortar shell, deeper into the jungle. They all kept running for some time, away from the sound of gunfire, weaving between liana-covered tree trunks, changing direction many times, and only stopped when they were sure that the Indonesians would not know where they were. Mortar shells continued to explode well behind them, close to where they had hidden to set up the ambush.

They glanced at one another, then Alf whispered: 'Where's Ken?'

They all looked in different directions, but Ken was nowhere in sight. They waited for a whole minute, but neither saw him nor heard him.

'Damn!' Dead-eye whispered. 'I'd better go back and find him. If he's dead, I have to strip him of identification. If he's alive . . .' Dead-eye shrugged.

Alf glanced at his watch. 'Leave it, boss,' he said.

'No,' Dead-eye replied. 'Wait here. Give me ten minutes. If I don't return, move out.'

'Let's all go,' Pete said. 'If he's wounded, we'll have to try to get him out. If he's dead, we can give you protection while you strip him and bury him.'

'Right,' Dead-eye said.

Without another word, he led them back to where they had come from, hoping that the new man, if still mobile, would have had the sense to follow their tracks. These they had not bothered to cover, knowing that the Indonesians, devastated by the attack, would have followed them only a short distance into the *ulu*. In the event, when they got back to where the enemy mortar shell had exploded (by which time the Indonesians had stopped firing), they found only a small pool of blood and a trail of broken foliage that obviously led directly to where the ambush had taken place. The ground beneath the broken foliage showed the marks of boot heels, indicating that the unfortunate trooper had been wounded by the exploding mortar shell, then captured and dragged away by the Indonesians.

Realizing they were possibly surrounded by Indonesian troops, Dead-eye communicated with sign language, indicating that Ken had been captured and that nothing more could be done for him. Clearly upset, he nevertheless turned back, indicating with another hand signal that they should follow him.

Only when they were well away from the Indonesians did they stop for a rest.

'They'll give Ken a hard time,' Pete said.

'Let's hope he was badly wounded,' Dead-eye

replied, 'and won't last too long. He'll suffer less that way.'

Realizing what they were talking about, Terry shivered involuntarily and made a point of checking his Armalite.

'Time's up,' Dead-eye said crisply.

Badly shaken by Ken's fate, they began the long trek back to the RV, speaking little, staying well spaced apart, and never relaxing for a moment. They did not aim directly for the border, which the Indonesians would have expected, but instead headed south to where the Rivers Sentimo and Koemba met. Dead-eye was out on point, the experienced Alf was Tail-end Charlie, and Terry was behind Pete, his job not only to scout the jungle on both sides, but also to protect the vitally important radio operator or, failing that, the actual radio, which was even more important.

In fact, without the A41 many of the men in the small patrols might have gone mad in the jungle. It was the radio that kept them in touch with one another and removed much of the burden of what might otherwise have been an intolerable burden of isolation. Also, through the radio they could pass on to one another details of enemy troop movements which, for some tactical reason or other, they could not interfere with. It formed a common bond that few wanted to lose.

Four hours later, with the sun high in the sky, they found themselves in the jungle swamps near the confluence of the two rivers. Just before making another hellish slog through waist-deep water, with all the horrors it contained, they contacted other patrols on the A41 and learnt from one of them that according to some Dyaks, the captured SAS trooper had been alive when taken, though suffering from minor wounds to one arm. He had been seen in the enemy camp to which the supply patrol had been heading, lying on the ground with his hands behind his back and tied to his ankles, doubtless awaiting questioning. More news was to be relayed as it came in.

Now even more shaken, Dead-eye's patrol kept on the move, wading through the greenish-brown water while assailed by swarms of flies and mosquitoes. By last light they were in a state of familiar exhaustion, but managed to keep going for another couple of hours until they had reached a dry islet. There they had a meal of dry biscuits, tinned sardines and water, though smoking was not permitted and the hexamine stoves could not be lit for a warming brew-up.

The islet was large enough for them all to sleep on, which was an unexpected luxury that allowed them to awaken relatively refreshed. They moved on for another hour, again wading waist- and sometimes chest-deep through the water, then stopped to have a cold breakfast and try contacting the other groups with the A41. When they did so, they learnt that another Dyak had reported seeing an SAS trooper, obviously Ken Burgess, still bound as before, being dragged roughly across the clearing of the enemy camp and into one of the thatched huts raised on stilts. The tribesman said that he had then heard the soldier screaming for a long time, before being dragged back out again and thrown, still bound, off the veranda of the raised hut. It would have been a long drop.

'Poor bastard!' Alf whispered when Terry, in charge of the radio, had recounted this information to all of them.

'Let's get moving,' Dead-eye snapped.

By noon that day they were out of the swamp and hacking their way through more *belukar* while their booted feet slipped in deepening mud. Now knowing that they were well away from any Indonesians or CCO terrorists, they were able to talk more freely and used the opportunity to express their bitterness over Ken's ordeal.

Dead-eye soon put a stop to it.

'What the fuck do you expect?' he asked contemptuously. 'We chopped those Indos to pieces with our Claymores and bullets, then took off before they could retaliate. Can you imagine what the survivors felt like when they found Burgess wounded? What did you *expect* them to do? Give him a medal?'

'That's no reason to . . .'

'Some of those Indos lost their limbs,' Dead-eye said, cutting Terry off in mid-sentence. 'Others had the flesh stripped off their bones. Still others had burns so severe they couldn't possibly live. That isn't just dying, Trooper. It isn't heroics. It's fucking terrible, it's happening to your friends, and the bastards who did it have disappeared. Then you find one of those bastards. He was left behind by the *other* bastards. He's lying there, wounded, at your feet, and you're not inclined to admire him. Also, you want to find out where his friends are, so you go to work on him. What would *you* have done, Trooper?'

Terry had no answer to that, so he just lowered his eyes.

'Right,' Dead-eye snapped. 'Subject closed. Let's move out, men.'

By last light they had reached a suitable hiding place near Poeri, still on the River Koemba, from where they intended heading north, first to Stass, then on to the RV between Bau and Kuching.

Despite Dead-eye's outburst, the rest of the group was slowly burning up with the thought of what was happening to Ken. Subsequently, when they had made camp, eaten and bedded down in their bashas, they had a night made even more restless by anger and bitterness than it was by the usual flies, mosquitoes, spiders, ants, and the jungle's customary nocturnal cacophony. Their mood was in no way improved when, the following morning, they learnt over the radio that according to the most recent Dyak reports, Ken had been tortured so appallingly that he died before his captors could 'break' him.

'Bastards!' Pete whispered.

'Cunts!' Alf exploded.

'What a shitty thing to do,' Terry said, wiping tears from his eyes. 'I mean . . . Jesus! We can't just forget this. We must *do* something.'

'What we do is head back to the RV,' Dead-eye said firmly. 'Now let's pack up and move out.'

Nevertheless, as they made the short hike to Poeri, from where they intended branching north, Dead-eye knew that what had happened would rankle with the men and maybe make them lose focus. He was therefore almost relieved when, just before they reached Poeri, a longboat containing three uniformed Indonesian soldiers came along the river, heading upstream.

Dead-eye plunged into the shelter of the trees by the river bank, followed immediately by the others.

Kneeling there in the firing position, they watched the boat approaching.

'Well?' Pete asked, his finger itchy on the trigger. 'Do we just let them waltz past?'

'They're not waltzing,' Alf retorted. 'They're rowing like fucking Cambridge dons . . . And that boat's filled with weapons.'

'*And* a dead pig,' Terry observed. 'That means food for a lot of men.'

The three of them turned to stare at Dead-eye. He stared back, then shrugged.

'Let's not argue,' he said.

While Dead-eye, Alf and Terry took aim with their Armalites, Pete unclipped an '80' white-phosphorus incendiary grenade from his webbed belt. 'Let's not take any chances,' he said with grim satisfaction. After unpinning the grenade, he stepped forward for a better view, though still protected by the trees, waited until the boat was abreast of his position, then hurled the grenade.

That movement was enough to attract the attention of the Indonesians in the boat. They glanced up just as Pete stepped back into the trees, raised their eyes even higher when they saw the grenade, then, shouting frantically, threw themselves face-down in the boat as the grenade fell towards them. It actually bounced off the stern, exploding with a thunderous clap, creating a great fountain of rushing, roaring water and smoke illuminated by silvery phosphorus. The stern of the boat was thrown high in the air, forcing the prow down into the water and throwing the soldiers forward, one into the other, with the third one – the one nearest the explosion – bursting into flames and catapulting over his tangled friends, into the river.

Even as the remaining two were struggling to right themselves, one reaching for his rifle, the SAS men on the river bank opened fire with their Armalites, peppering the boat from front to rear, making the soldiers spasm epileptically in a dreadful dance of death as fragments of wood exploded upwards and rained back down over them.

In seconds the two soldiers were dead and the hull of the boat was disintegrating and starting to sink as the SAS men continued firing in an orgy of vengeance. A minute later, when they had finally stopped firing, the boat was practically in pieces, taking in water and going down as the water turned crimson with the blood of the dead men.

The dead men drifted with the boat's debris in swirling blood-red currents, then all evidence of the attack – the wooden flotsam, the bodies, the bloody water – was carried away downstream and eventually disappeared.

'Satisfied?' Dead-eye asked his men.

'Yes, boss!' they replied, one by one.

'Right,' Dead-eye said. 'Let's go.'

As the dead men drifted down river, being swept towards their living comrades in some far off, hidden camp, the SAS patrol headed back across the border, beyond which were more hellish swamps, *belukar* and primary jungle. They tried not to think ahead.

8

Further along the border, on the lower slopes of Gunong Rawan, near Tebedu in the 3rd Division, Sergeant Alan Hunt and Corporal Ralph Sanderson, at the head of their patrol, were moving down from a ridge on a jungle track towards an old Indonesian border-terrorist camp that had been discovered the day before and appeared not to have been used for many months. Nevertheless, as both men knew by now, appearances could be deceptive, so they both advanced on the camp with great care, with Sanderson at the front as lead scout and Hunt second in line.

Hunt was an amiable giant of a man from rural Oxfordshire, with thinning red hair, a constantly flushed, blue-veined face (his heavy drinking only showed there; certainly not in a drinker's paunch) and a body which, for all of its weight, was pure muscle and bone. Thirty-four years old, he had been wounded when engaged with the Gloucestershire

Regiment in their epic battle on the River Injon in Korea, damaging his right arm so badly that it became paralysed and required four years to repair. Once recovered, however, he had applied to the SAS, got in with flying colours, and sustained his already admirable reputation with his work during the Malayan Emergency. Now, here he was, big and wind-blown, yet oddly graceful, moving down the densely forested slope with all the stealth of a tribesman, holding his Armalite at the ready and expert in using it. He was a man worth admiring.

Sanderson admired him. Up at the front on point for the sergeant he knew so well, aware that Indonesian troops could be hiding anywhere, ready to spring an ambush, Sanderson was glad to have Hunt backing him up. Ever since the disaster at Long Jawi, when everyone but Sanderson had lost his life, Sanderson had been more aware than ever of how easy it was to die in this war. A product of the Fifeshire coalmines and the Queen's Own Highlanders, he took pride in being a good soldier and respected only those who felt the same way. Being a good soldier was being a worthy man and Sanderson wanted to be just that.

Reaching a curtain of bamboo, he knelt on the ground and listened intently for any unfamiliar sounds. As no breeze could penetrate the dense canopy of the jungle, let alone reach the ground, and since the animals were always careful to conceal their presence from alien presences, such as humans, Sanderson heard nothing other than the occasional cry of a long-armed gibbon or the squawk of a distant hornbill. Apart from that there was nothing but a total, oddly disturbing silence.

Staring carefully between gaps in the bamboo curtain, he saw the Indonesian camp stretched out just below. Built in a clearing between the jungle and a stream that flowed down to the River Sekayan, it consisted of many bamboo-and-thatched lean-tos without roofs, obviously used as bashas; open-air latrines now covered with swarms of flies; and a series of sunken rectangles that had clearly been gun emplacements and defensive slit trenches. The Indonesians had not bothered to fill in any of these when they moved on. Also, as Sanderson saw when he used his binoculars for a closer inspection, they had not bothered to clean up their debris, which included the black ash of camp-fires, hundreds of cigarette butts, the bones from cooked chicken and pigs, and a lot of rusty food tins with labels stating in Malay that they contained rations for the Indonesian Army. A very careless commander, Sanderson realized, had made no attempt to cover his battalion's tracks.

Lowering his binoculars, Sanderson glanced back

up the wooded slope to see Hunt keeping him covered with his 5.56mm Armalite light automatic rifle. Unseen, because carefully hidden in the jungle behind the sergeant, was the rest of the patrol – three SAS troopers and two Border Scouts – armed with 7.62mm SLRs and now experienced at using them, after four weeks of successful 'Tiptoe Boys' raids. During that time they had travelled light, with no bergens; only their belts and personal weapons. This had made the 'shoot-and-scoot' standard operating procedure much easier and the raids more successful.

Before returning his gaze to the Indonesian camp, Sanderson sniffed the air, trying to catch a tell-tale whiff of anything that would give away another human presence: scent, cigarette smoke or even hair-cream. In the windless jungle such aromas could hang around for hours, which is why the SAS men were careful not to smoke or pamper themselves with hair-creams or aftershave when on patrol. Indeed, so still was the air in this jungle that a man could avoid having his throat cut by smelling the sweat of an approaching enemy. That, in fact, had been the case with Sanderson and he had never forgotten it; no more than he had forgotten his narrow escape at Long Jawi. He considered himself a very lucky man and hoped it would stay that way.

Looking to the front again, Sanderson surveyed the open slope between himself and the camp, which had obviously been cleared by the Indonesians to give their sentries a better view. Seeing no movement, he jumped up and ran forward at the crouch, then dropped down behind another screen of bamboo. As he did so, Hunt advanced behind him, taking up the position Sanderson had just left. The rest of the group then advanced as well, until they were spread out around the position formerly held by their sergeant. They had advanced this way for the past hour, which made the going slow and extremely frustrating.

Again Sanderson looked out between the tall bamboo stalks. At first he saw nothing. Then he thought he saw a slight movement 45 degrees to his right. Turning in that direction, he was startled to see an Indonesian soldier five or six yards away, lying down beside a tree, taking aim with what looked like a Lee-Enfield .303 bolt-action rifle.

Before Sanderson could move the Indonesian opened fire, followed almost simultaneously by a fusillade from his hidden fellow soldiers. Something smashed into Sanderson's leg, bowling him over. Falling, he hit the ground hard, then found himself lying behind a small rock to his left with blood spurting up into his face from a dreadful wound in his left thigh.

'Shit!' he whispered from between clenched teeth, hardly able to hear his own voice above the racket of the battle suddenly raging in front and behind him.

Where the hell was his rifle? Unable to sit upright, he twisted to the side and saw his Armalite just as another Indonesian, who had been lying concealed in the tall grass beyond the rock, also sat up, aiming his Lee-Enfield. The man was so close that Sanderson even saw the tiger's-head emblem on the shoulder of his jungle-green uniform and the panic in his youthful brown eyes.

With no time to spare, Sanderson grabbed his Armalite, blinked blood from his eyes, and fired a short burst that punched the soldier backwards and threw him into the tall grass. He fired another burst to be sure, then wiped more blood from his face and glanced back up the slope.

Hunt was running to his rescue, zigzagging at the crouch between the clumps of bamboo as purple tracers from enemy machine-guns arced past him on both sides. Halfway down, he jerked wildly, dropped his weapon and collapsed, even as Sanderson saw the cloth of his trousers exploding and spitting twin streams of thick blood.

The sergeant fell face-down, but rolled onto his back. He tried to sit up but failed, his shattered legs useless. So, ignoring the bullets stitching the ground on both sides, he rolled back onto his belly, aimed his Armalite and opened fire again, determined to give Sanderson cover.

Behind him, but further up the hill, the rest of the patrol were trying to keep the Indonesians pinned down with a sustained fusillade.

Unable to walk, but still with one good leg, Sanderson managed to stand upright and hop awkwardly up the hill towards Hunt, who was too busy firing to notice his ungainly progress. Once parallel with his friend, but about five yards away, Sanderson dropped to his belly again, gritting his teeth against the pain, and joined the fire-fight.

The Indonesians were spread out on the ground in an arc covering the approach to the empty camp. Lying belly-down, half hidden by the tall grass and clumps of bamboo, they were keeping up a relentless barrage of fire.

Hunt stopped, glanced back over his shoulder, up the hill, and bawled, 'Bug out!' He then turned back and continued firing, enabling the rest of the patrol to make their escape and return to the RV, where they could get help.

As the patrol stopped firing and disappeared over the crest of the hill, one of the Indonesian soldiers, not noticing the wounded men, jumped to his feet and started racing up the hill, heading straight for Hunt. The big, cool-headed sergeant, his hips and legs drenched in blood, fired a short burst from his Armalite and felled the running man. When a second Indonesian stood up, Sanderson put a lethal burst into him, too. The rest of the Indonesians remained on the ground, but kept firing up the hill.

Letting them get on with it, Sanderson rolled onto his back, managed to sit upright, protected by the rock, and examined his wounded leg. It was a mess. In fact, he could not feel it, nor see the wound for the blood still pumping out of it, and so was not sure if the leg was still fixed to his upper thigh or had been torn off by bullets. Delicately wiping away the blood with his fingers, he saw that the bullet, or bullets, had severed the large femoral artery and shattered the femur, though the leg was still joined to the thigh.

Realizing that if he did not stop the bleeding immediately, he would be dead in no time – the blood was pumping out in sprays about fifteen inches long – he hurriedly removed the sweat rag from his forehead, tied a knot in the middle of it, pressed the knot firmly against the artery in the groin, tied the rest of the sweat rag around the limb, wrapped the ends of the rag around the handle of his commando knife and then twisted the knife until the cloth had tightened painfully, with the knot pressed like a vice on the artery, cutting off the supply of blood. When the blood had stopped pumping, he tied another knot in the cloth, completing the makeshift tourniquet, then injected himself with a shot of morphine and heaved a sigh of relief.

Looking up, he saw that the Indonesians were still firing at him and Hunt. Though the bullets were turning the ground into a convulsion of boiling dust and spinning foliage, Sanderson crawled over to his friend, who, when he saw him coming, rolled onto his back and gazed up at the sky.

'I can't move my damned legs,' he said.

Hunt's face was a white mask glistening with sweat. He had been shot in the hip, though his wound was much worse than Sanderson's. The bullet had entered the left hip, almost severing the sciatic nerve, thereby paralysing and rendering numb that leg. While the hole punched in the front of the thigh had been only slightly larger than the .303-inch bullet that caused it, it had enlarged as the bullet passed through the pelvic opening, destroying a fist-sized mass of muscle in the right buttock and therefore paralysing that leg as well. Besides losing a mass of blood, Hunt had lost the use of both legs.

'Fucking mess, eh?' he said, gritting his teeth.

''Fraid so, boss,' Sanderson replied.

Another sustained burst of fire came from the

Indonesian positions and more green tracer shot upwards and whipped past them, just a few feet away.

'Russian RPD machine-gun,' Hunt said. 'I know. I saw the whites of his fucking eyes. Then he copped me.' He winced and looked down at the blood soaking his trousers around the tattered hole. 'Christ!' he said softly. 'At least it's not a tourniquet job.' He had not noticed the crude tourniquet on Sanderson's leg. 'I think I can fix this.'

While Sanderson kept the Indonesians pinned down with single shots from his Armalite, thus conserving ammunition while remaining a viable threat, Hunt removed two shell dressings from his first aid kit, worked them in and under the torn cloth around the bloody wound, gritted his teeth and pressed them into the hole, then held them in position by wrapping his sweat rag around the thigh. After completing the job with a shot of morphine, he rolled onto his belly, beside Sanderson, and picked up his Armalite to fire on the Indonesians.

'Shoot-and-scoot,' he said.

'What does that mean?' Sanderson asked him.

'It means we have to prevent casualties when there's no point in fighting to hold ground. It means that in a situation like this, you pocket your pride and piss off. It means that we all scoot independently for the RV and that if a man is incapacitated, you have to leave him, at least temporarily, to prevent further casualties.'

'Piss on that,' Sanderson said.

'No,' Hunt replied. 'We don't piss on that. You go back to the RV and join up with the others. If you find enough men for reinforcements, you can come back to find me. If you still find the Indos here, you piss off and leave me to my fate. If, on the other hand, the Indos have gone you can pick me up for the CasEvac and early pension.'

'I don't like it,' said Sanderson gloomily.

'It's not a request. Get going, Corporal.'

Sanderson squeezed the sergeant on the shoulder, then, reluctantly, started crawling up the hill, dragging his wounded leg. As he did so, Hunt opened fire with his Armalite, still on automatic, laying down a sustained burst that would ensure the enemy kept their heads down for a short while. Sanderson used that brief lull in their fire to get up the hill as quickly as possible, though his numbed leg did not make it easy for him. He did, however, manage to clear the breast of the hill just as Hunt stopped firing to reload and the Indonesians let rip again.

Glancing back over his shoulder, Sanderson saw the ground around Hunt turned into a nightmarish convulsion of spitting dust and exploding foliage. Then Sanderson crawled away, down the other side. The sudden silence from the other side of the hill convinced him that Hunt had been killed in that final fusillade. Shocked, but determined to survive, Sanderson crawled on.

It was not an easy journey. Unable to stand, he had to crawl most of the way, stopping at intervals to loosen the tourniquet and let the blood flow a little, thus diminishing the chances of gangrene. Then he tightened it and moved on again.

Just as he had to keep stopping to loosen and tighten the tourniquet, so he had to stop to give himself repeated injections of morphine, which eased the excruciating pain when the crawling made the pieces of the shattered femur grind together. He could even hear them grinding, which made the pain seem worse, and he also knew that the sharp-edged, broken bones could, when grinding together, sever more arteries and kill him that way.

Nevertheless, he kept crawling back towards the RV, through mud, over felled logs, between tangled clumps of thorny bushes, stopping only to attend to the wound, then starting forward again.

By nightfall, he had managed to crawl only 500 yards, though each yard had seemed like a mile. Finding a pig hole beneath a fallen tree, he crawled into it, deep into the pools of mud, and took another shot of morphine before falling asleep.

Sergeant Hunt had not been killed by the Indonesians. In fact, after that final fusillade, they gave up, assuming the enemy was gone, and retreated back across the empty camp, then into the jungle. They did not reappear.

Seeing that they were gone, Hunt pulled himself into the cover of a clump of bamboo, injected himself with more morphine to combat the pain, checked that the bandages in his enormous wound were still stemming the blood, then passed out.

He was unconscious most of the night. Just before first light, after breakfasting on chocolate from his escape belt, he injected himself yet again, then began to crawl up the hill, determined to follow Sanderson to the RV. So bad was his leg that he could only do this by using his elbows: digging them into the soft earth and pulling himself forward, inch by inch. This he did until, by late afternoon, he had managed to drag himself to the top of the ridge, which was only 400 yards from the scene of the fire-fight. Exhausted, he lay there face-down for a couple of hours, then rolled over and studied the afternoon sky. Seeing no friendly choppers up there, he rolled back onto his stomach and recommenced his dreadful journey.

This time he was forced to elbow his way through a stretch of *belukar*, which was filled with thorny undergrowth that cut him all over, depriving him of more blood. As secondary jungle is the haunt of wild pigs, Hunt soon found himself crawling through a maze of runs where the pigs had rooted in the soil for food. These runs were filled with mud containing many leeches, which were attracted by the smell of his thorn wounds and attached themselves to him to drink the blood. Too weak to fend them off, Hunt soon found himself covered in mounds of writhing leeches and knew that he was losing more blood than he could reasonably afford, given what he was also losing from the gruesome bullet wound.

Still he crawled on until, like Sanderson, he found a pig hole into which he could crawl for the night. There, while he tried to sleep, swarms of fat, shiny bluebottles clustered on his wound and laid eggs that turned into grubs to make the wound fester. If he did not get the wound tended to soon, he would be in serious trouble.

Using his elbows for leverage, though the skin there was rubbed raw and giving him more agony, the next morning he managed to crawl another 1000 yards. What kept him going was the knowledge that the rest of the patrol would have gone to find the infantry – the 1st Battalion of the 6th

Gurkha Rifles – and bring them back to find him, and perhaps Sanderson too.

In fact, he thought that he might come across Sanderson at any moment, which was another incentive to keep going. In the event, neither Sanderson nor the Gurkhas materialized.

That night, now even more exhausted, as well as being in agony, Hunt injected himself with another shot of morphine and fell into the sleep of the dead. He was not dead, however, and next morning awakened to the distinct smell of coffee. Not realizing at first where he was, and imagining that he was awakening in his own basha in the spider at Kuching, he turned his head and saw an Indonesian soldier climbing a nearby durian tree.

Freezing cold where he was lying, suddenly remembering where he was and that he was seriously wounded, he watched as the Indonesian soldier, having gained his desired position, stretched out along the branch of a tree and picked off some of its spiky fruit, the flesh of which was edible. Lowering his gaze, he saw a whole group of enemy soldiers squatting at the base of a nearby tree, around a communal pot of rice or tapioca. Looking up again, he saw the first soldier staring straight at him from the tree.

Hunt froze. He had to force himself to remember

that although he was looking up into the eyes of the man in the tree, that man could not necessarily see him where he was lying in a hollow in the ground, caked as he was with mud and covered with foliage. And yet he could not be sure of that, so his heart started racing.

At that moment a British Army Air Corps Sikorsky S-55 Whirlwind helicopter appeared in the sky, flying in low over the jungle, obviously searching for the two missing SAS men. Seeing it, Hunt was flooded with relief and reached automatically for the SARBE rescue beacon on his webbed belt. As he was doing so, the Indonesian in the tree and his friends on the ground all glanced up at the helicopter. Some of them pointed at it, chattering excitedly, then bent over to pick up their weapons.

Suddenly realizing that the Whirlwind would be in danger if he fired his SARBE beacon and encouraged it lower, Hunt removed his hand from his belt and decided to take his chances.

When the Whirlwind passed overhead without coming within firing range, the Indonesians put down their weapons and returned to their breakfast. Eventually, the soldier in the tree, who clearly had not seen the SAS man, clambered back down to the ground, where he passed out the durian fruit to his friends.

Hunt lay there and watched them, gritting his teeth against the pain of his wounded leg, but not daring to risk the movement required to inject more morphine. Eventually, after what seemed like hours, but was in fact an hour later, the Indonesians completed their breakfast, picked up their weapons and marched away, quickly melting back into the *ulu*.

Sighing with relief, Hunt injected himself with more morphine, cleaned his wound of pus and maggots, finished off the last of his chocolate, then began crawling forward again, using his bloody elbows as leverage. By noon he had managed a few hundred yards more, but was stopped by exhaustion. Falling asleep, or perhaps rendered unconscious by the return of the pain, he woke in the late afternoon, feeling weaker and more disorientated.

Though now convinced that he was fading fast, he had enough strength of mind to inject himself with more morphine and start another exhausting forward crawl. Convinced as he was that he could not survive another night without aid, he was not encouraged by the fact that the jungle here was *belukar*, so dense with tree stumps, felled logs, saplings, thorns and general undergrowth that a helicopter would not have been able to land.

Nevertheless, he kept going and, two hours later,

as the sun was beginning to set and the nocturnal chorus of the insects was building, he came out of the *belukar*, into more accessible terrain. There, however, beyond the darkening mountain, black rain clouds were spreading across the sky, threatening a tropical storm. No helicopter could fly through such weather.

Hunt was silently praying that the storm would not begin when he heard distant thunder. No, it was not that. It was another, more constant sound. He glanced up as the sound grew louder, becoming a rhythmic throbbing, then an actual roaring. Something blotted out the sinking sun and cast its shadow over him as a violent wind tore leaves off the trees and whipped the leaves off the ground. It was the same chopper, coming back to find him.

Knowing that the Indonesians were nowhere near this territory, he unclipped the SARBE beacon from his belt and sent up a rescue signal. Hearing the SARBE's bleep, the pilot descended vertically, wobbling from side to side, but could find no space clear enough for a landing.

Like a blood-splattered crab, Hunt crawled out on bent elbows to where he could be seen, then raised his right hand to wave frantically.

The pilot dropped until he was almost touching the trees, with the rotor blades actually chopping leaves off. While the chopper hovered there, in danger of crashing, a crewman threw the rescue strop out on its lengthy cables. It plunged to just above the ground, jerked back up, then bobbed in mid-air, just above the wounded man.

Still unable to move his legs, Hunt had an agonizing time with the strop, which kept swinging to and fro just above his outstretched fingers; but eventually he managed to grab it and twist himself around until he could fit it under his armpits. Still holding his Armalite in one hand, he signalled with the other for the crewman to winch him up. The helicopter ascended as he was being winched up and soon he found himself swinging in the sky above the vast, darkening jungle.

Up there he was as free as a bird.

As Sergeant Hunt was being flown to the Gurkhas' jungle post at Sain, from where he would be casualty-evacuated to Kuching Hospital, 45 miles away, Corporal Sanderson was sleeping in another pig hole not far from where his friend had been rescued.

Dangerously weak from loss of blood, pain and the exhaustion of having to crawl for miles on his belly, Sanderson had a very troubled sleep and woke at dawn feeling dreadful. Nevertheless, he kept going. He was only 5000 yards from the Gurkha camp at Sain, but it might as well have been that number of miles. After another 200 yards, he was in a state of almost total exhaustion, bordering on hallucination, and felt even more unreal when he came across the bergens that the team had left behind to make the 'shoot-and-scoot' operation easier. By now the bergens were rotted by damp and fungus, with what little food remained after the ransacking of pigs and honey-bears as rotted as the rucksacks themselves.

Sanderson did, however, find a water bottle filled with drinkable water and used this to quench his raging thirst. Then, forgetting in his rising delirium that the most likely place the choppers would look for him would be where the bergens had been left, he crawled on, determined to find the RV.

By last light he had covered 1000 yards, a mere fifth of the distance he had to go. Not knowing where he was, and increasingly delirious, he did not even bother trying to find a pig hole for the night, but just crawled to a moss-covered tree and propped himself upright, surrounded by thick liana, under a great umbrella of razor-sharp palm leaves. There he finished off the last of his chocolate, washed it down with the last of his water, then closed his eyes and tried to sleep, reconciling himself to death and crazily amused at the thought of his corpse being eaten by wild pigs or other jungle animals.

Better than compo food, he thought as the darkness descended. I can take pride from that.

Either dreaming or hallucinating, he was jerked back to reality by a faint thrashing sound not far away. Opening his eyes, he saw only the gloomy *ulu*, but then he heard the thrashing sound again. It was not very loud – it was almost stealthy – but it was coming towards him.

Instinctively trying to move, Sanderson was whiplashed by the pain in his wounded leg and had to stop himself from crying aloud. Nevertheless, the sudden, stabbing pain, accompanied by a spurt of leaking blood where he had loosened the tourniquet, had the virtue of making him more alert. Still sitting upright against the trunk of the tree, he pulled the Armalite off his shoulder, rested it on his knees, then held it up with the stock pressed against his right hip.

Glancing down, he saw that his sudden movement had loosened the tourniquet more and now blood was pumping out at a dangerous rate. Glancing to where the thrashing sound was growing louder, he saw branches being parted in a way that suggested he was not faced with an advancing animal, but an army patrol.

Sanderson set the Armalite to automatic, then cocked the weapon.

The foliage just ahead parted and the first of

the soldiers emerged – small, brown-faced men, carrying Armalites and SLRs, all with familiar yellow flashes on their soft jungle caps. It was the Gurkhas from Sain.

Sanderson smiled and lowered his Armalite, letting it rest in the grass beside him, though still under his hand. His other hand was covered in his own blood, but he raised it in welcome.

'Hi, there!' he said.

He passed out when they picked him up, placed him on a stretcher and carried him the remaining 4000 yards back to the base camp at Sain.

9

'You have to return to the River Koemba north-west of Poeri,' Major Callaghan insisted, sitting behind his desk in his office in the Haunted House in Kuching, smoking a cigarette, blowing smoke rings and watching them disappear. 'It's there that the Indonesians are believed to have one of their main staging posts for men and supplies going eastward to Seluas, a good-sized trading settlement where the Indonesian Division has its base. That longboat you shot up on your way back was probably heading for there.'

'Why us?' Dead-eye asked, unwrapping some chewing gum and popping it into his mouth.

'What's the matter, Sergeant Parker? Don't you *want* this lovely job?'

'I'll do any job you give me,' Dead-eye replied. 'I just wondered if we were picked for a specific reason when we've just got back from there.'

'Not quite the same area, but close enough.'

Callaghan pursed his lips and blew another smoke ring. Even in the afternoon, with the sun blazing outside, he had the shutters down to keep the sunlight out. It made the office pretty dark, Dead-eye thought. Like a haunted house, in fact. 'Six other patrols attempted to reach specific points on the river near Poeri, but failed because the river marshes were too deep. You lot actually made it. So I'd like you to go back there, but this time to find that staging post at Seluas and put a stop to it. You can choose your own spot for setting up a river watch and causing a little mayhem near the town. I'm sure you'll enjoy it.'

Dead-eye grinned slightly, then glanced at the maps spread out on Callaghan's desk. 'Can I see those?'

'Of course!' Callaghan dropped his feet off the desk and turned the maps around to enable Dead-eye to study them. This Dead-eye could do because he had been briefed at West Brigade's HQ, where, as a trained reader of aerial photographs, he had been able to spot the spur that had enabled the recent patrols to recce the unexplored territory known as the Gap. Now, studying the aerial pictures laid out before him, he was soon able to find another spur of the low border hills. It pointed towards a broad bend in the river.

'There,' he said, putting his finger on the spot as

Callaghan stood up and walked around the desk to peer over his shoulder. 'This finger of dry ground here. It appears to peter out three quarters of a mile short of the river, but it might actually reach it. Usually, when it's this close on the map, there's a dry strip somewhere. I'll opt for that route.'

'I'm sure you're right,' Callaghan said. 'You usually are.' He went back around his desk and sat down again. 'So who do you plan to take? Sergeant Hunt and Corporal Sanderson are obviously out of the picture – both back in Blighty, badly hurt, up for commendations and/or medals – so you'll have to be the man in charge and pick your own team.'

'That's nice,' Dead-eye said. He was not too concerned about the loss of Sanderson and Hunt, since both of them actually came from A Squadron and he had never got to know them all that well. He had, however, respected them and visited them at the Kuching Hospital when he was there for a couple of days of so-called recuperation leave. While in reasonably good spirits, both men had been in a bad way physically, with Sanderson likely to lose a good inch or so off his wounded leg and neither man likely to continue to serve with the SAS in their original capacity. More likely they would be given some kind of desk job in the 'Kremlin' in Hereford, which was not the kind of thing that would satisfy them. Still, they had been stoical about it and Dead-eye admired them both.

'I want the same men,' he told Callaghan. 'Welsh as demolition expert and number two; Laughton as medical specialist and photographer; young Malkin as signaller and for general back-up.'

'I'm not sure I want someone so inexperienced for this job.'

'He's not inexperienced any more. He's been through a lot.'

'No problems?'

'None.'

'I thought at first he was showing signs of instability – particularly regarding the *ulu*.'

'He was, but he got over it and has certainly proved himself since then. Not just once – a lot more than that – so he's shown some consistency. He's earned his winged dagger, boss.'

Callaghan smiled. 'Anything you say, Dead-eye. If you want him, you've got him.' He stubbed his cigarette out, clasped his hands behind his head, placed his feet back on the desk and gazed reflectively at the large wooden-bladed fan turning above them. 'God!' he exclaimed softly. 'Remember Welsh and Laughton in Malaya? A right pair of wide boys, troublemakers, always right on the edge there. Neither I nor Sergeant Lorrimer – God rest his soul – thought they'd last another year with the regiment. In fact, both of us were preparing to RTU them, but that didn't happen.'

'The Telok Anson swamp,' Dead-eye said, recalling its singular horrors and how it had matured Welsh and Laughton, instead of destroying them. All bad things had their good side.

Callaghan sighed. 'God, yes. What a hole! And those two came good in the end, which just goes to show.' He continued to study the fan for a while, then lowered his gaze again, grinning at Dead-eye. 'Still miss Lorrimer?'

'Yes.'

'He *was* a good man.' Callaghan glanced down at the maps spread out on his desk, then ran his forefinger lightly, with barely concealed yearning, along the dotted line that indicated the River Koemba. 'I wish I was going with you,' he said. 'I'm not keen on desk jobs.'

'You're good at it, boss.'

Callaghan nodded, but his face revealed his feeling of loss. 'Yes, I'm good at it. I'm a wizard at intelligence. I'm even better at planning and strategy, which makes me invaluable . . . But I'd rather be out there in the field, doing what I was born to do.'

'Maybe you'll get back to it.'

'We both know that's not true. This will be my last tour with the regiment, then it's back to 3 Commando and another promotion.'

'What's wrong with promotion?'

'It leads to even more administration and a lot of rather boring socializing in the name of public relations. I'll be a stuffed dummy for the Army, attending functions, shaking hands, signing the odd document – in fact, doing all the things I detest. That's what's wrong with promotion.'

'Refuse.'

'I can't. It's my age. It comes to us all.'

'Me as well, boss.'

'But you're luckier, Dead-eye. *You're* an NCO. That means you can stay with the SAS for as long as you like – at least until your retirement. Even when it gets to the stage where you can't fight, you can stay with the Training Wing in Hereford, doing good work.'

'To me, doing good work in the Training Wing is the same as you shaking hands. It's just not my style.'

Callaghan grinned in that same sad way. 'No, I suppose not. I just can't imagine it.' As if troubled by his own words, he glanced down at the maps, then looked up again and changed the subject, trying to sound lighter. 'So Laughton's your photographer.'

'Yes,' Dead-eye said.

'Can he actually handle a camera?'

'Yes.'

'Make sure he takes a lot of pictures.'

'I will, boss. Don't worry. So when do we leave?'

'First light.'

'Tomorrow?'

'You've had your leave, Dead-eye. You *hate* leave. So it's first light tomorrow.'

'Right, boss, that's fine. I'd better go and brief the men.'

'Yes, Dead-eye, you do that.'

Dead-eye left Callaghan's office and stepped onto the veranda outside, where he had to shade his eyes against the morning's fierce light. Adjusting to the glare, he saw the trees of the jungle rising in a rich green tangle above the loose scattering of longhouses and warehouses along the dusty road leading into the town. While most of the regular Army, Marine Commandos and Gurkhas in the area were living in converted warehouses and even less comfortable accommodation, Callaghan had cleverly outflanked the billeting arrangements by murmuring about lack of space for his men, the possible requirement for unnecessarily expensive hotels, and so forth, with the result that his men now had their bashas in a large and comfortable Chinese merchant's house.

Entering the building, which was not far from the Haunted House, Dead-eye made his way to the rear, where the men had turned the largest room into their spider. He found Pete Welsh, Alf Laughton and Terry Malkin in there, the first two sitting together on one bed, smoking, drinking beer and playing cards, the latter listening to the BBC World News Service while reading James Joyce's *Ulysses*.

'How can you do both?' Dead-eye asked him.

Terry swung his legs off the edge of the bed and sat up, almost at attention. Although he had proved himself as a soldier, he was still in awe of Dead-eye.

'Don't know, boss. Just can.'

'You understand that *Ulysses*, do you? I heard it was difficult.'

'I don't really understand it all, but I like the bits I *do* understand.'

'That sounds logical, Trooper. We're going back on patrol tomorrow morning, so come and hear what it's all about.'

Dead-eye walked over to where Pete and Alf were playing cards in a haze of cigarette smoke, only breaking their concentration long enough to swig some more beer. However, they did look up when Dead-eye stopped beside the bed with Terry beside him.

'Oh, oh,' Pete said. 'It's Sergeant Parker.'

'This can only mean trouble,' Alf added.

'It's work,' Dead-eye told them, then filled them in at length on the situation, ignoring the other men in the long room, most of whom were listening to the radio, playing cards, reading or writing letters home. When he was finished, he asked, 'Any questions?'

'Yes,' Alf said. 'How come we only got a weekend off after all that shit?'

'We didn't want to spoil you,' Dead-eye said.

'Spoil me?' Alf replied. 'I hardly had time to dip my wick before I had to pull it out again and hurry back to the base. Two days, meaning one night, in that town doesn't do you much good, boss.'

'I'm amazed you could get it in,' Dead-eye said. 'I think that calls for a Mention in Dispatches. Remind me to remind Major Callaghan when he's nothing better to do.'

'*Terry* got it in,' Pete said, grinning slyly at Alf as the butt of their humour blushed deep crimson. 'At least we saw him leave the bar with a whore who had her hand on his arse.'

Terry blushed even more. 'Come on, fellas, knock it off! I didn't tell them anything, Sarge. What I do is my business.'

'Was this a whorehouse?' Dead-eye asked.

'You might call it that,' Alf said. 'It was a bar with a couple of rooms at the back and bedsprings that made too much noise. That's how we know

Terry dipped *his* wick: we could hear all the squeaking.'

'From him,' Pete said.

'That's a lie!' Terry burst out.

'I hope you used a rubber,' Dead-eye said. 'The whores here are diseased.'

'She wasn't a whore!' Terry protested.

'She was *nice*,' Pete said. 'She was so nice she let us share her around when Terry walked out the door.'

'That's not true!' Terry exploded again.

'He's in love,' Alf explained.

'He'll get her out of his system,' Dead-eye said, 'when we're back on the border.'

'When?' Pete asked.

'Tomorrow.'

'What time?'

'Don't tell me,' Alf said wearily, blowing smoke. 'We move out at first light.'

'What a bright boy you are,' Dead-eye told him. 'First light it is. In fact, I'm letting you sleep till then, just to prove I'm a nice guy. You can get out of your bashas at first light and have a quick shower and shave. Breakfast at six-thirty sharp, then a line-up at the quartermaster's stores at seven, on the dot. You'll have one hour to get kitted out, collect your weapons and get to the chopper. We lift off at eight. Any questions?'

'Yes,' Pete said. 'Is Terry in love with his whore? Has he picked up gonorrhoea or syphilis? What do you think, Sarge?'

'I think your two-day leave was two days too many and that bastards like you are safer up on the border, fighting the Indos. Tomorrow you'll all be back where you belong and I think you should thank me.'

'Thank you, Sarge,' Pete said.

'I kiss your feet,' Alf added.

'I think you're *all* bloody disgusting,' Terry said, then returned to his bed.

'He'll make a good trooper,' Dead-eye told the other two, then he grinned, turned away and walked out of the barracks, back into the scorching sun of noon. He could hardly wait to get out of there.

10

Dead-eye's patrol checked their weapons and drew ammunition. This was limited to the amount they could comfortably carry when engaged in 'shoot-and-scoot' operations. Each man therefore packed in his bergen only the clothes he considered vitally essential for this patrol, as well as his basic rations: oatmeal blocks, sardines, Oxo cubes, small tins of cheese, biscuits, a little sugar, tea or coffee, milk in a tube, and twenty-four blocks of dehydrated meat – in all weighing less than 1lb for each day's meals. Permitted by Dead-eye were the little extras personally preferred by each man to add taste to the basic rations, such as curry powder, cigarettes or sweets. All of them carried a piece of strong nylon cord, which could be used for many things, including rigging up hammocks in the swamps and making tourniquets. They also carried a parachute-silk sleeping bag with a poncho to keep out the worst of the tropical rainstorms.

Since streams are obvious camp-sites, always under surveillance, invariably a patrol makes its hides a good distance from water. For this reason, each man was given a large water bottle which he could fill up in a stream and then carry to the hide, where he would purify the water with tablets before drinking it or otherwise using it.

As photographer, Alf naturally had high-power binoculars and a camera, a robust 35mm SLR, with which he would take shots of men, boats, vehicles, military camps, longhouses and even areas likely to be of interest to the staff of military intelligence, who could study the photos later at their leisure.

'If I get enough practice,' he informed Pete, 'I'll be a pin-up photographer when we get home – all bare arse and tits.

'I'm a knickers and bra man myself,' Pete confessed as he manoeuvred some more kit into his packed bergen. 'It's my little perversion.'

'I'll be catering for all kinds,' Alf assured him, 'so you've no need to worry there. I'll even photograph some whores for young Terry here to fall in love with.'

'You pair are sick!' Terry snapped.

In fact, it was Terry who had the heaviest load, because, besides the A41 radio set and spare battery, its aerials and the code-books, he also carried on his belt the SARBE radio beacon. To compensate for this, his rations were divided among the others, purely for the purpose of transportation.

'The things we have to do for these newcomers,' Pete complained melodramatically, trying to find some spare space in his already packed bergen for his share of Terry's rations.

'I didn't ask you to,' Terry said. 'It was Dead-eye. He said . . .'

'Sucking up to Sarge goes a long way,' Alf interjected, holding a bar of Terry's chocolate in front of his groin and pantomiming the act of masturbation over it. 'If you're willing to get down on your hands and knees, sweet things will come your way.'

'I want my rations back,' Terry said, outraged by the others' attempts to humiliate him.

'You're not getting them,' Dead-eye said. 'I've weighed everyone's kit and you're overweight, so these lads have to share the weight.'

'Then tell them to shut up.'

'My lips are sealed,' Pete said. 'I try to be nice and I'm rejected and struck dumb by grief.'

'If you don't seal those lips,' Dead-eye said, 'I'll do the job for you. So seal them and shut up.'

'Yes, boss!' Pete said briskly.

For this particular mission, each man was given a 7.62mm SLR instead of the 5.56mm Armalite assault rifle. This caused a lot of 'honking', or complaining.

'Bloody useless,' Alf grumbled.

'A fucking toy,' was Pete's verdict.

'You're wrong,' Dead-eye insisted. 'Its hitting power is more likely to damage river craft than higher-velocity bullets from an Armalite. That's why we're switching.'

'I still prefer the Armalite,' Pete said. 'It's smaller and lighter and fully automatic. The SLR is only semi-automatic and an awful lot heavier.'

'I agree,' Alf said.

'That doesn't change the fact,' Dead-eye informed them, 'that the SLR has a more powerful cartridge and bullet, which makes it better for long-range firing and penetration. It'll therefore be a lot more effective when attacking the river boats.'

'Not so effective in a fire-fight,' Pete persisted.

'We shoot and scoot, Pete,' Alf said.

'I hate that,' Pete objected. 'I like to stand and fight.'

'We're not concerned with body counts,' Dead-eye told him. 'We want to stop their supplies. So stop whinging and get on with your packing. We haven't got all day.'

Once equipped, they applied the usual camouflage to themselves and their weapons, checked each other's camouflage and kit – ensuring in the latter case that nothing was loose – then strapped their bergens on their backs, picked up their weapons, and left the spider.

Once outside the Chinese merchant's house, in the early-morning mist, they were driven in a Bedford RL 4x4 three-tonner along a road lined with *belukar* and soaring trees to Kuching airfield, where they boarded an RAF Twin Pioneer for the short flight to Lundu.

'I seem to have spent half my life in fucking aeroplanes,' Alf complained as he strapped himself into his seat.

'Better than public transport,' Pete replied. 'And certainly better than walking.'

'This is the part I hate most,' Terry chipped in. 'I hate being cooped up.'

'Except in cramped rooms on squeaking beds with delectable little Indonesian whores.'

'Oh, shut up, Pete!' Terry said, flaring up again. 'You've got a mind like a sewer.'

'And a nose for the dirt.' Dead-eye was looking grimly at Pete. 'Why not can it, Trooper?'

'My silence is now guaranteed, boss. Whoops! There she blows!'

The engines of the Pioneer had just roared into life. Less than a minute later she was taxiing along the runway, preparing to take off. Within minutes she was in the air, flying over another spectacular panorama of jungle, mountains, winding rivers and aerial bridges spanning deep, narrow gorges with torrents raging through them. A fine curtain of silver-grey mist covered the green splendour of the *ulu* and made it seem dreamlike, reminding all of them, except Terry, of their days in Malaya. They were memories of heroism and horror, of friendship and grief. The men were silent throughout the flight.

The journey was short, twenty minutes, and soon they were disembarking at Lundu, where another Bedford was waiting to transfer them to a familiar Wessex Mark 1 helicopter, piloted by their old friend, Lieutenant Ralph Ellis of the Army Air Corps. Ellis was biting into an apple and grinning sardonically.

'This is getting to be a bad habit,' he told them. 'Dragging me out of bed at this ungodly hour. This,' he added, waving the apple, 'is the only breakfast I've had.'

'We haven't *had* breakfast yet,' Pete reminded him. 'You fly-boys have got an easy life – even apples for breakfast!'

'He's a healthy lad,' Alf said.

'With a little paunch,' Pete pointed out.

'And a little bald spot on his head, getting bigger each day.'

'It's the shock of being dragged out of bed this

early,' Alf explained to his friend. 'He's not used to the hard life.'

'And you jokers,' Ellis said, wrapping the apple core in a piece of paper and putting it into his tunic pocket, 'have forgotten how to show respect for an officer. So shut up and get in.'

'Yes, dear!' Alf and Pete sang, clambering into the chopper, with Dead-eye and Terry right behind them.

The lift to the LZ took less than thirty minutes, and took them over the sheer green canopy of the jungle in brightening sunlight. Ellis dropped them near the frontier with Kalimantan, due north of Achan. Unable to land, he descended between the trees, dangerously close to their branches, and hovered there, creating a storm, just above the jungle floor.

The men jumped out one by one, burdened with weapons and bergens, and melted into the *ulu* before the Wessex had even started climbing. Already hidden by the soaring trees, the men grouped together near the LZ, whiplashed by the slipstream of the rotors but waiting until the helicopter had ascended and was heading away from them. Only when it had disappeared beyond the jungle canopy, into the silvery-blue, cloud-smudged sky, did they prepare to move off.

'I think it's highly fucking unlikely,' Alf said,

'that the Indos and CCO won't have seen that chopper drop us off.'

'I've no doubt that they saw us,' Dead-eye replied calmly, 'but since we're still on our own side of the border, they'll assume we're just another bunch of reinforcements moving up to join the border battalions. They won't suspect for a moment that we're planning to cross into Kalimantan.'

'Still, the quicker we get out of here the better,' Pete said.

'I agree,' Dead-eye replied quickly, 'so let's hit the road, lads.'

They marched away from the clearing, heading into the *ulu*, on the first leg of the route that Dead-eye had mapped out.

It would not be an easy route.

11

They headed roughly due south, following Dead-eye's compass bearings, intending to turn due west seven days later, which would lead them to the finger spur seen on the maps. The first day's march was uneventful and relatively easy, through primary jungle that did not require hacking, even though it was as humid as always and oppressively dark. During this first day's hike they stopped frequently to rest and listen for enemy movements, broke for a lunch of water and dried biscuits, but otherwise kept going until nightfall, trying to get as far as they could while they felt reasonably fresh.

After selecting a suitable LUP, they had supper, which was another cold and unedifying meal. Then, while Pete and Alf sat out on point, keeping their eyes and ears open for enemy movements, Dead-eye gave Terry the first of his daily reports, to be transmitted, encoded, to Major Callaghan back at HQ.

They moved on at first light the following morning. Dead-eye was out in front on point as the scout, followed by Pete as his number two, then Terry with the radio, and Alf as Tail-end Charlie. Each man was concentrating intently on his individual defensive arc, holding his SLR at the ready and prepared to use it.

This constant watchfulness was more stressful than expected, though their arduous SAS training had prepared them for it. Though less burdened with kit than the others, Dead-eye had the most demanding job, being far ahead of the main group and therefore dangerously isolated. He needed to be constantly vigilant, and could not relax for a second as he watched and listened for likely ambush positions or signs of enemy movements up ahead. As he also had to check the jungle floor and the lower branches of the trees for mines or booby-traps, he was always under great stress, though he handled this better than most, in his deadly calm, cold-blooded way.

Pete had a dual role. His first function was to give the point man cover should the enemy attack. The second was to glance back over his shoulder every few minutes to ensure that the signaller, carrying the all-important radio, was still in sight and unharmed. In conducting this visual check, he constantly alternated from left to right, and so also managed to scan the *ulu* on both sides of the track. This ceaseless vigilance – to the front, to both sides, and to the rear – was also more demanding, both physically and mentally, than it would have appeared to an inexperienced onlooker.

Terry's primary function was to transmit messages, check constantly whether there were any incoming ones, and to protect the radio with his life. But he, too, had to keep his eyes on the men ahead, on the *ulu* on both sides of the track, and on the Tail-end Charlie, a good distance behind him, to ensure that he had not been picked off quietly by a silenced rifle, a knife, a garrotte, or even a booby-trap.

Bringing up the rear, Alf's primary duty was to check every few minutes that no Indonesians were stalking the patrol. This he did by turning his back on the patrol and walking backwards at regular intervals, scanning the *ulu* on both sides as well as directly behind him. As it is with the scout on point, so the most stressful part of the Tail-end Charlie's job is being relatively isolated from the main group, always wondering if someone is sneaking up from the rear to dispatch you with a bullet in the spine or slit your throat with a dagger. The Tail-end Charlie also has to keep a keen eye on the signaller directly ahead of him, and ensure that even if he is killed, the radio is saved.

By noon of the second day, which was the first full day of hiking, they had crossed the border north of Achan and started to circle around it, heading, through a combination of primary jungle and *belukar*, for the swamps that lay between it and the River Koemba. The primary jungle was tolerable, if not exactly an easy hike, but the *belukar*, having been cleared and grown again, more dense than ever, required backbreaking work with the *parangs* and great patience.

Once they had to scatter to avoid the charge of a wild pig. Another time they had to move off the only track they had found for hours and circle around it, through even worse *belukar*, because a giant king cobra was coiled in the middle of the track and rose up hissing, preparing to attack, each time they tried to approach it. This simple detour cost them another hour, though it certainly saved lives.

That evening, when they lay up in their latest LUP, their poncho tents close together to discourage animal intrusions, Pete and Alf discussed the snake at great length, comparing it with similar reptiles they had seen in Malaya, and grossly exaggerating their recollections for the sake of young Terry.

'Snakes 20 feet long they had there,' Pete said with relish. 'They sting their victims, paralysing them but leaving them fully conscious, then swallow the poor fuckers whole.'

'I don't believe that,' Terry said.

'It's true,' Alf told him. 'Cross my heart, hope to die. A snake 30 feet long swallowed one of our mates and we could see the poor sod struggling inside its body, kicking and punching frantically, before that bastard finally digested him.'

'I can't see how a snake could digest a fully grown man,' Terry said rationally, determined not to be sent up, 'when he's kicking and punching its insides. That doesn't make sense.'

'They say it's got acids in its stomach that just melt you down,' Pete explained. 'A dreadful way to die, that.'

'You two should have been novelists,' Dead-eye said quietly. 'You both invent such wonderful stories.'

'Right,' Terry said. 'It's all bullshit.'

'You be cynical, then,' Alf said. 'Just choose to ignore us. But if one of them king cobras gets near you, you'll soon know different, kid.'

'You'll be swallowed whole, paralysed, fully conscious,' Pete solemnly informed him, 'then dissolved in its stomach juices. You won't sneer at us then!'

But Terry had rolled over in his sleeping bag and

was pretending to sleep. When eventually he did fall asleep, he had very bad dreams.

Luckily for Terry, given the horror of his dreams, he had to rise with the others at dawn and begin another day's march. An hour after setting off they stopped for breakfast. It was cold and unsatisfying. Four hours later they stopped for a late lunch that was not much better. To frustrate them even more, no one could 'honk', because now that they were deep in enemy territory, they were only allowed to speak – and then only in whispers – at night, in their isolated, hidden LUPs, while they were forcing down their awful grub. So after finishing this dismal cold lunch, they marched on again.

They had hiked for no more than an hour, through dense primary jungle, when Dead-eye heard the sound of axe blows up ahead. Signalling silently with his hand, he stopped the three men marching behind him. When they had all dropped to one knee with their weapons at the ready, Dead-eye listened intently. He heard the sound of axes on wood, then the faint murmur of distant voices speaking Malay. Indicating with another hand signal that the rest of the group should remain where they were, he slipped out of his bergen, uncocked his SLR and advanced at the crouch, weaving as quietly as possible from tree to tree, stopping when he could see exactly where the noises were coming from.

About 20 yards away, visible in a fragmented way through irregular windows in the undergrowth, a few Indonesian soldiers were at work, chopping down saplings and smaller trees. Out of sight, though heard distinctly, were many more men, maybe a whole platoon, clearly busy making jungle shelters.

Instinctively, Dead-eye started raising his rifle to the firing position, then realized what he was doing and lowered it again. His mission was to get to Seluas and attack Indonesian supply boats, not to engage the enemy in the jungle, let alone tackle a much larger force, which could be suicidal. Reminding himself of this, he turned around and headed back where he had come from.

The other men were still kneeling where he had left them, watching him intently. Using hand signals – one to say 'Enemy ahead', the other 'Follow me' – Dead-eye led them in a wide detour, avoiding the clearer passages through primary jungle, edging as quietly as humanly possible into an area of chest-high tropical ferns and an undergrowth filled with large, sharp-edged palm leaves and thorny bushes. As they went, they all took particular care lest signs of their passing – awkwardly bent fern stems, upside-down leaves, or even threads from their uniforms – should be noticed by any patrol from the enemy platoon. Thus it took the rest of that day to cover a mere three miles towards their objective.

By noon the next day they had reached a broad track running north-west from Poeri and almost certainly used regularly by soldiers going to Achan. Checking the actual track against his much-folded map, Dead-eye recognized it on the map from the faint blurs with which he had marked it and which he alone could see. In line with SAS thinking, he had not plastered his map with chinograph symbols indicating key points. He had also deliberately folded the map much more than necessary to prevent the enemy, if capturing it, from guessing which section had been used, as this in turn would have indicated to the enemy his main area of interest.

Satisfied that the track was clear, the men crossed it swiftly and vanished again into the *ulu*, now heading on a direct line for the swamps that led east to the River Koemba.

That afternoon they came to a recently cleared track running compass-true parallel to the river – so straight, in fact, that it would not only give a cut-off party a quick route to some border ambush, but also provide a devastating line of fire for enemy machine-guns.

Dead-eye silently indicated that Alf should photograph this particular part of the track from a few different angles. When Alf had done so, then written down the details of the location in his notebook, they crossed the track unnoticed. Even so, they were uncomfortably aware that in such a clearing there was always the possibility that the occupant of some unseen observation post had spotted them and, even worse, radioed in patrols to block their routes of advance and retreat.

In the event, no patrols appeared – nor were they likely to – for not too far ahead, just beyond some bamboo screens and a tangle of *belukar*, stretching away as far as the eye could see, was the dreaded swamp.

12

Knowing that it would be suicidal to enter the swamp at night, they searched around its edge for a suitable hide. Finding one, they quickly made up their bashas, trying to beat the sinking sun, rolling their sleeping bags out on leaves scattered under ponchos strung to the lower branches of the trees, stretched taut at an angle of 45 degrees, and fixed to the ground with rope and pegs.

Before supper could be enjoyed, Terry had to transmit Dead-eye's daily report back to Major Callaghan at SAS HQ, Pete had to check his explosives and Alf had to carefully annotate all the rolls of film he had shot so far. The sun was still sinking when each man quickly checked his rifle, removing the mud, twigs, leaves and even cobwebs that might have got into it; oiling the bolt, trigger mechanism and other moving parts; then rewrapping it in its jungle-coloured camouflage. They had to do all this before the sun sank, leaving them in complete darkness.

As they ate their cold supper of tinned sardines, biscuits and water, battling every second to keep off the flies, midges and mosquitoes, the sun set as a great ball of crimson-yellow lava behind the mountains west of the River Koemba. The lower it sank, the more it spread out along the alluvial top of the wooded mountains, until it resembled a great urn turned on its side and pouring molten metal which, hitting the mountain top, flooded north and south along its black summit. When the sun finally disappeared, vast clusters of opulent stars appeared over the soft peaks. Within minutes, however, those stars had been blotted out by gathering clouds darker than the sky and pregnant with rain.

In the event, the storm did not reach the SAS hide, though it created a magnificent *son et lumière* spectacle of light and sound. Fingers of lightning – accompanied by impressive rolls of thunder – clawed through boiling clouds, illuminating them from within with a magical radiance, and causing the stars to disappear and reappear in the pitch-black sky.

The storm went on for a long time, as if the jungle was exploding, yet there, near the swamp, from where they were seeing it so clearly, the SAS men felt it only in the form of teasing gusts of wind and a gradual lowering of temperature from the day's fierce heat to severe cold. Such cold they would have felt in any event with the coming of night.

The next morning, at dawn, with tendrils of mist hanging over the jungle and clinging like mournful ghosts to the tree trunks, the men broke up the hide, carefully hiding all traces of their presence, then embarked on the usual hour-long, pre-breakfast hike.

Moving into the swamp from north-east of the river bend, they quickly found themselves knee-deep in slimy, debris-covered water and assailed by madly buzzing insects. Though the bed of the swamp was soft and yielding – a combination of mud and small stones, dangerously cluttered with larger stones, fallen branches and other debris – they were able to push on towards Dead-eye's spur until, in the early afternoon, the water became too deep to cross and the mud too soft to walk on, particularly when carrying 50lb of bergen and 11lb of loaded SLR.

In this area gigantic bright-green palm leaves floated on the swamp and lay on small islands of firm ground, covered with seedlings and brown leaves. Surprisingly hard, they split if stepped on, giving off a loud crack that could have drawn attention to the wading men. For this reason, the men tried avoiding them, but even when they were pushed gently aside in the water, they often split with what seemed in the stillness a very loud noise, like a distant pistol shot.

'These leaves will do for us,' Pete whispered. 'They'll have the Indos all over us.'

'I think you're right,' Dead-eye replied. 'Let's call a halt for a moment.'

Leaning against the hard earth of one of the many small dry islands, though still waist-deep in water, the men wiped sweat from their faces, waved the swarms of flies and mosquitoes away, burned the leeches off their skin with cigarettes, and tried to catch their breath and relax in general.

'Dump your bergens on that dry ground behind you,' Dead-eye told the others. 'Might as well relax properly.' He waited until they had done so, then said: 'I don't see any point in all of us going on until we know exactly what's ahead. The maps don't help us here. There are no markings for the swamp. All I've got to go on is the general direction, but that doesn't tell me where we are now or how far away the river is. This water is getting deeper. The mud is getting thicker. If Terry slips, or simply sinks too deep in water, the radio will get damaged and we'll lose touch with HQ. Also, if present indications are anything to go by, this swamp will get worse the further south we go and we may find we have to dump the bergens. Without them we'll be lost, so I suggest that we keep them here, with two of us watching them and the other two advancing into the swamp to try finding that river.'

'Seems sensible,' Alf said.

'I agree,' Pete said.

'What about you?' Dead-eye asked Terry, taking him by surprise, but making him blush with pleasure.

'I agree as well,' he said. 'I'm getting worried about the radio. Wading here is like walking on quicksand and it's getting more dangerous. Your plan sounds good to me.'

'Good,' Dead-eye said. 'So you stay behind with the radio. As Alf's our medical specialist and photographer, he can stay here as well. Pete and I will leave our bergens here with you and go on without them. While we're gone, I want you to contact HQ every night and give them some kind of report – if only to tell them that we're still exploring the region. If we're not back within three days, assume we're casualties and return to the RV. Any questions?'

'No, boss.'

'Ok, Pete, let's go.'

Having already dumped their bergens on the small, dry island, Dead-eye and Pete started wading away from the others. Before disappearing around a screen of bamboo, they glanced back to see Alf and Terry clambering gratefully up onto the island.

Practically swimming, but holding their weapons above their heads, they headed south-east, hoping to catch a glimpse of the river and calculate where they were. They waded for a long time and saw nothing but more swamp, and when the sun started sinking they both realized that they could be in danger in more ways than one.

In fact, they were in a frightening position, for they had only one spare magazine apiece, plus their *parangs* and escape kit. This would not help them much if they could not find their way back through the tangle of rank vegetation in the late afternoon's fading light.

As Dead-eye and Pete waded forward, the latter distanced himself from the former to reduce their chances of being killed by a single burst of gunfire. This could well happen. The water, as Dead-eye noticed, was swishing quietly past them, leaving a tell-tale trail across the surface scum. An enemy soldier could follow that watery trail right to its source and blow their brains out.

Dead-eye knew the risks and did not give in to fear, instead giving most of his concentration to his compass and the rest to his wading, making sure that each footstep among the submerged tangle of roots was reasonably secure. To break an ankle here would be a disaster, possibly fatal.

Following Dead-eye, Pete was both fascinated

and repelled by the sight of slimy marsh bugs racing on their numerous legs across the weed-covered surface. Magnified, he realized, they would look horrible. The thought made him shiver.

Just before darkness fell, they clambered onto a small strip of dry land under a natural umbrella of large palm fronds, where they laid up for the night, first having a basic snack of blocks of dry meat washed down with water. They slept as best they could beneath the overhanging palms, surrounded by the scum-covered swamp, numbed by the cold, tormented by numerous, unseen creepy-crawlies, to wake black and blue from insect bites.

'We've been eaten alive,' Pete whispered grimly, studying the bites and stings on his arms and chest. 'We've probably picked up every disease known to man – and some unique to this swamp. Fuck this for a lark, boss.'

'Keep your voice down,' Dead-eye whispered. 'We still don't know what's out there.'

'We don't even know where we are,' Pete whispered even softer than before. 'We're just wandering blind.'

'No, we're not,' Dead-eye told him, checking his compass. 'The map may be useless, but at least we know the river's south, and according to this compass that's where we're heading, so let's keep going, Corporal.'

'Anything you say, boss.'

For the rest of that day they roamed on a south-easterly arc across the swamp, trying to find the River Koemba. Failing, they grew frustrated and discussed heading back to the others. But then, just as they did so, they heard the heavy throb of diesel engines, coming from no more than two or three miles further south.

'That's it,' Dead-eye said. 'That's the sound of a supply boat. It can only be travelling along the River Koemba. That's where we have to go.'

'Are you sure, boss?'

'Yes, Pete, I'm sure. And it can't be too far away.'

Yet even though they waded south-east for another hour, they saw nothing beyond an almost solid wall of bamboo and tall reeds, thrusting up from water so deep and muddy that it could not be crossed.

'Fuck it,' Dead-eye said, even as he heard the throb of another diesel engine in the distance, beyond that impenetrable wall of tightly tangled bamboo and reeds. 'There has to be another way. Let's backtrack north-west to the firm ground where we left the others. They must be getting lonely by now.'

They managed to make it back to the others before last light the same day. That night, making themselves as comfortable as best they could on the same small island, the four men had a 'Chinese parliament' to pool suggestions. Out of this came the simple plan to continue south-east, following the line of the River Sentimo until they reached the River Koemba. They could then follow the latter due east until it took them to Seluas.

Having agreed on that, they all sighed with relief, then turned into their bashas to endure another night as best they could in a nightmare of whining insects, stinging creepy-crawlies, and unseen birds and animals that only made their presence noisily known when a man was trying to sleep.

They felt like hell the next morning.

13

As agreed, they moved out early the next day, heading south, wading waist-deep in the water for what seemed like an eternity, though it actually took them only three miles, to the confluence of the Rivers Poeteh and Sentimo. As Dead-eye had predicted, the water here was deeper, the foliage more impenetrable, but when they tried following the river, wading through even worse swamps, they soon lost it in dense jungle. Doggedly wading on, they found themselves emerging to relatively clear, swampy land which Dead-eye predicted was due north of the River Koemba.

Pressing on, they came to a series of slow-flowing tributaries that wound their way between a maze of dry banks and curtains of bamboo. They were trying to cross this maze, up to their waists in water, when a large boat, judging by the sound of its engine, swished by on the other side of a high bamboo curtain. Its wash lifted the flotsam of leaves so high that Alf was practically submerged, though he managed to hold his SLR above his head until he had surfaced again, spitting water and weeds from his mouth, then cursing angrily.

No one ribbed him; they dared not speak. Unable to see through the curtain of bamboo, beyond which was the channel along which the boat had passed, Dead-eye decided to change direction and head back into the swamp to avoid accidentally emerging into the river just as another boat was passing.

The change of direction turned out to be the SAS men's first lucky break, since after wading for another four hours, hidden in the swamp but following the line of the river, they reached firm ground. It was, Dead-eye was convinced from its appearance, the fingertip of the spur he had been seeking.

'No doubt about it,' he said, checking his map against a compass reading. 'This is the spur.'

Pleased, Dead-eye put the map and compass away, then took in the scene as they knelt on the edge of the narrow strip of dry jungle, hidden by tall grass, looking at the broad sweep of the River Koebma where it curved around the well-spaced trees of a rubber plantation. On his left the strip of jungle continued right up to the river bank. He pointed to it with his forefinger. 'That could make an OP.'

He was right: it was just right for an observation post. In the centre of the strip of dry jungle a large tree spread its branches above dense scrub and a shallow ditch, but with open ground surrounding both – as open as it was to his right, where the rows of rubber trees spread along the river bank. The trees were being 'rested', with no sign of recent tappings, though Dead-eye saw that there were some well-used paths through the plantation, indicating that it was still being worked.

As a site for their OP, Dead-eye plumped for the lone tree and its scrub-covered, shallow ditch. Feeling exposed where he was kneeling, and having made sure that there were no enemy troops in the immediate vicinity, he ordered the patrol into the scrub surrounding and covering the ditch.

'Make four scrapes under the scrub,' he said. 'Two men facing the river, two facing the jungle. And be quick about it.'

'Anything for a kip,' Alf said. 'Even building an OP.'

'A little home from home,' Pete added, 'with a view of the river.'

'Shut up and start scraping.'

'Yes, boss!' they both chimed.

The simple OP was made up by digging four shallow depressions in the soft earth for their bashas – two facing the river for the purposes of observation, the others facing the jungle behind: one for observation, the second for sleeping in, with one man sleeping at a time. The scrapes were filled with a bed of leaves and the sleeping bags were then rolled out on the leaves. Another shallow scrape, placed in the centre of the four larger ones, was used as a well for kit and weapons. To help keep out the rain, ponchos were raised on forked sticks above the scrapes and pegged to the ground. The scrub was pulled closely over the ponchos and in turn covered with more leaves and foliage. Narrow 'windows' were made to the front and back of the foliage to give the men an adequate view of the river and jungle.

When the OP was completed, they settled down to wait, though they did not waste their time while doing so. Dead-eye updated his logbook and also redrew his map in the light of his recent explorations through the swamp, marking accessible routes, good lying-up positions, and average time-to-distance figures for the various routes recommended. Alf photographed the river and any traffic on it, whether civilian or military, and made notes on the shots he was taking, including the date, the time of day and a written description of the contents of the passing traffic and the direction in which it was cruising. Terry, as well as acting as the sentry facing the jungle behind the OP, checked through the various wavebands of his radio in hopes of picking up enemy transmissions as well as encoded news of other SAS patrols. Last but not least, Pete kept his eye on the river and his SLR aimed and ready to fire. His specialist skill, demolition, was of no use here.

They had not been in the OP for long when the first military launch chugged past, crewed by six half-naked Dyaks. Two uniformed Indonesian soldiers were sitting on the deck with their legs outstretched and their backs resting against tarpaulin-covered supplies. Their idea of protecting the cargo was to idly watch the river bank slip by. The boat flew the red-and-white ensign of Indonesia.

'Let's finish them off,' Pete whispered.

'No,' Dead-eye replied. 'First, we have to spend a few days just watching, photographing and taking notes on the traffic to establish just how much of it there is. We need permission from HQ to attack, and that'll only be received when we're ready to bug out.'

'Shit!' Pete whispered in frustration, then rolled away from the window in the foliage and said to Alf: 'It's all yours, mate.'

Alf immediately took his mate's position and began to take photos of the passing launch. When he had done so, he quickly jotted down as many of its details as he could manage before it disappeared from view.

No other military craft passed that afternoon. By nightfall the SAS men had to fight a combination of boredom and exhaustion. Once darkness fell, however, they were able to slip down to the water's edge to fill the large communal bottle, as well as their personal canisters. They purified the water with tablets before drinking it. Supper was a choice between dehydrated meat and tinned sardines, supplemented for some with cheese. Dead-eye spiced his sardines with curry powder, the smell of which nauseated the other three, who said it was putting them off their desserts of chocolate or sweets.

Finally, before settling down for the night, Terry transmitted, encoded, Dead-eye's daily report to HQ. Receiving an acknowledgement, he was reminded that the real world still existed. But for now he was in this alien, unreal world, the light fading, the river gurgling in front of him, the jungle whispering behind him, the nocturnal chorus of the birds and animals steadily rising in the trees to deprive him and the others of sleep.

In fact, they all slept well that night, waking refreshed.

Shortly after a breakfast of oatmeal blocks washed down with cold tea, they had a bit of a scare when two Indonesian soldiers appeared around the bend in the river and paddled up to a tree on the bank, very close to the OP. Wondering if this seemingly innocent act was in fact a diversionary move to cover an attack on the OP across the open ground behind it, Dead-eye decided to take no chances and ordered his men to adopt firing positions front and rear, cautioning them not to shake the scrub as they did so.

Rolling belly-down into the scrapes and gently easing the barrels of their SLRs through the scrub, the men took aim. Dead-eye and Pete covered the men in the boat; the other two covered the jungle behind the OP.

They lay like that for some time, not moving, hardly breathing. Though it seemed like an eternity, it was, in reality, only the few minutes it took for the Indonesian soldiers in the boat to empty a fish trap and go back down the river, rowing casually and chatting and laughing in loud, high voices.

'They don't seem too concerned about being overheard,' Pete observed.

'A good sign,' Dead-eye replied. 'That means they don't suspect we're in the area. They've just made my day.'

The rest of the day was equally busy, with a little local traffic in the morning followed by a greater number of military supply boats flying the Indonesian flag and manned by armed troops. Obviously they were cruising to and from the trading settlement at Seluas, which Dead-eye estimated was about five miles downstream.

With so much traffic passing, Alf was kept busy with his camera, and Pete had to take over the job of entering details of the traffic in the logbook. So busy were they that they had no time for lunch.

By early afternoon, with the sun high in the sky, the OP was intoleraby hot, full of buzzing flies and whining mosquitoes, and smelt of sweat and piss. Unable to leave their cover, the men urinated and defecated into plastic bags, in full view of each other, then sealed the bags and buried them in the mud. To make them even more uncomfortable, ants were hurrying back and forth in long lines across the bottom of the ditch, invading the kit well and crawling over food and weapons alike.

Even worse, spiders the size of an outspread hand occasionally emerged from holes in the mud and clambered fearlessly over the men's boots. Unsettled though the men were by the experience, they had to resist the impulse to violently kick or swipe the giant spiders off, since this would have disturbed the foliage, possibly attracting the attention of the armed sentries on the Indonesian launches passing by less than 20 yards away. Instead, the harmless, though hideous spiders had to be removed with a gentle brush of the hand, which meant touching them longer than the men would have liked.

Terry, in particular, poured sweat each time a spider crawled over his booted foot or trouser leg. He shuddered each time he had to perform the ghastly task of brushing it off.

'Are you all right?' Dead-eye asked, obviously concerned.

'Yes, Sarge, I'm OK.'

'Are you sure?'

'Yes. They just give me the willies.'

'They're harmless.'

'They still give me the willies, but I'm all right.'

'Good. Stick it out, Trooper.'

By late afternoon the SAS men were growing frustrated at their inability to attack the passing supply boats. Their frustration was increased by the sheer number of vessels on the river, most of them piled high with supplies for the Indonesian battalions.

Just before dusk, as storm clouds were gathering over the jungle canopy and great striations of light were streaming across the dimming sky, the men's frustration dissolved into an almost hallucinatory state of disbelief as a large, immaculate cruising yacht approached around the bend in the river, passing only fifteen yards from the men.

As the vessel approached, a beautiful Indonesian girl in a white swimsuit stepped out of the deckhouse, draping a bathing towel over one arm. With shapely legs, full breasts, a flawless, high-cheekboned face, and long, ebony hair cascading down to the small of her back, she was a rare, unexpected vision of loveliness who took each man's breath away.

After walking along the side of the yacht, ignoring the helpless, nervous stares of the Indonesian sentries, she spread out the towel on the deck, put on a pair of sunglasses, then stretched out on her back on the towel, raising an elegant leg and turning her face to the side. She lay there, frozen in crimson twilight, as the yacht passed the SAS men, so close that its wash splashed over the bank just below the OP.

'I don't believe it!' Pete whispered.

'Christ, she's beautiful!' Terry murmured.

'She isn't sunbathing. She's just cooling down,' Pete fantasized. 'She must have worked up a sweat in that cabin with some fat-bellied bastard.'

'I'm coming just thinking about it,' Alf informed them, then released a soft, melodramatic groan. 'Oh, God help me!'

'Forget the girl,' Dead-eye said in his more

pragmatic way. 'That boat makes a great target. It obviously belongs to a high-ranking civilian official – not a military officer.'

'Military officers don't get women like that,' Pete said as the yacht passed. 'That's some wonderful whore, boss.'

'It could have been his daughter,' Terry said, his face filled with yearning as the vessel moved on and the girl disappeared out of sight behind the bulwark.

Alf rolled his eyes, then shook his head in disbelief. 'Innocence is surely bliss!' he exclaimed. 'His *daughter*, for God's sake!'

'Quieten down, you men,' Dead-eye growled. 'The way you're talking, you might as well get a megaphone and announce our presence up and down the river. We're here to recce that river, not ogle corrupt local officials' bints. Now let's get back to business.'

After another minute or so of moans, groans and excited whispers, the men quietened down and went back to their work.

The sun started sinking. Darkness crept across the jungle. Lightning flashed through the dark clouds in the distant sky, followed by thunder.

Twenty minutes passed. Another launch came along the river with seven soldiers spread carelessly under its fixed canopy, eating and smoking in an unconcerned manner. Alf took the last photograph of the day and Pete logged the details. Then darkness fell.

'Day's work done,' Alf whispered, removing the roll of film from his camera.

'A lot of traffic in this little logbook,' Pete informed them. 'It certainly wasn't time wasted.'

'That girl was gorgeous,' Terry reminded them. '*That's* why the time wasn't wasted. I'd lie here for another couple of days just to see her again.'

'He's a romantic,' Alf said.

'For lithesome whores,' Pete corrected him.

'You don't have to be sarcastic,' Terry said. 'I'm just saying she was gorgeous to look at. No harm in that.'

'Shut up!' snapped Dead-eye in a hoarse whisper, glancing up and down the dark river, clearly frustrated. 'I've had enough of this. Get on that A41, Terry, and tell those bastards at HQ that Sergeant Parker requests permission to fire on any suitable target, starting tomorrow. You get that? *Now do it!*'

Terry transmitted the message and they all sat back and waited, gorging on their personal preference among tinned sardines, blocks of dehydrated meat, cheese, dry biscuits, chocolate, sweets, cold tea and plain water. Though Alf and Pete were gasping for cigarettes, Dead-eye refused to let them light up lest the glow be seen by the enemy.

Forty minutes later, when the distant electrical storm had arrived at the river and was pouring rain on the OP to the accompaniment of thunder and lightning, Terry received a transmission from HQ granting immediate permission to attack suitable targets.

If the men had been allowed to make a sound, they would have leapt up and cheered.

14

Now that they could attack suitable targets, the men felt more enthusiastic when they woke the next morning. Shortly after completing their usual dismal breakfast, they saw two Indonesian soldiers passing by in a canoe with their Lee-Enfield .303-inch bolt-action rifles lying on the crossboard between them. While they could have been snatched as useful prisoners, Dead-eye refused the men permission to do so, insisting that sinking a launch would be much more effective.

'Apart from depriving the Indos of supplies,' he explained, 'the loss of a whole boat might frighten the river community into not cooperating with them in general.'

'The other side of the hearts-and-minds coin,' Terry said.

'Thanks a million for that clarification, Mr Einstein,' Pete said.

'It's good to have a brilliant tactician in the

OP with you,' Alf added. 'Sort of fills you with confidence.'

'Just kill the sarcasm, you two,' Dead-eye told them. 'And as a matter of fact, Terry's right. He knows more than you two arseholes put together.' Then suddenly his voice dropped to a whisper: 'Keep your voices down. That canoe's coming closer.'

The two soldiers in the canoe rowed right past the OP, hardly glancing at the high banks, both apparently lost in their thoughts as they studied the river. If it had not been for their uniforms and the rifles lying between them, they would have seemed like two men on a fishing trip. They rowed slowly, lazily, as if they had all day, and eventually disappeared around the bend where the river turned due east.

'They'll never know how lucky they were,' Terry whispered.

'Luck has a way of running out,' Dead-eye replied in his soft but oddly chilling manner. 'Their day might yet come.'

A longboat with a thatched canopy followed shortly after, poled by half-naked, colourfully tattooed Ibans, who were helped by the swiftly flowing current pushing them downstream. This was followed by another canoe, also rowed by Ibans; then by a couple of motor launches crewed by Iban traders and piled high with supplies for their kampongs. After that, for the next five hours, only the usual small boats passed the OP, some carrying Indonesian soldiers, but most not.

As the day wore on, the men grew impatient and started begging Dead-eye to let them make a strike.

'You said any suitable target,' Pete reminded him, 'and these are suitable targets, boss.'

'No, they're not,' Dead-eye insisted. 'They're mostly just locals. When we *have* seen Indo soldiers, they've been in boats too small to bother with. We need something bigger.'

'How big, for Christ's sake?' Alf was close to the limit of his patience. 'The *Ark Royal* won't be coming along, so let's settle for something less.'

'We can't hit anything less,' Dead-eye told him. 'We'll only get one shot at it. Once we mount an attack, the word will go up and down the river and we'll have to clear out of here. So the first one is the last one and it has to be worthwhile. That's why we have to be patient and wait for the right one. Understood?'

Alf sighed. 'Yes, boss.'

Nevertheless, his frustration was almost palpable, as was that of the others. The enthusiasm with which they had greeted the dawn began to disappear and was in no way improved when the rising heat brought back the flies and mosquitoes, the stench of sweat and piss, and the huge spiders that emerged from the mud to crawl relentlessly over them.

Nor did their mood lighten when the afternoon rain clouds darkened the sky and suddenly burst over them, the rain making a deafening drumming sound on the camouflaged ponchos and hitting the palm leaves so hard that they quivered rhythmically and, in some cases, were torn from their stems. So heavy was the rain that it flooded the ponchos and made them sag with the weight of water, which then poured off the edges of the ponchos and down into the OP. More water poured in from the surrounding earth and gradually flooded the ditch where Alf and Terry were lying belly-down, trying to watch the jungle.

'It's covering us!' Alf complained. 'We'll soon have to sit up. We'll probably have to get out of here.'

'It's already up to my nose and rising damned quickly,' confirmed Terry.

Though Dead-eye and Pete were kneeling at the front of the OP, to get a good view through the windows, the water was rising there, too, and already washing around their boots.

'The whole OP's flooding. We'll have to evacuate,' Pete said to Dead-eye.

'Damn!' Dead-eye muttered.

At that precise moment, above the roar of thunder and the fearsome crack of lightning, he heard the distant chugging of what sounded like a large launch approaching through the downpour.

Wiping the rain from his eyes and looking up in disbelief, Dead-eye saw what was indeed a very large motor launch coming upriver around the western bend. When it had rounded the bend and was approaching him, he saw that it was crowded with enemy soldiers and piled high with supplies.

'Perfect!' he exclaimed, not bothering any longer to whisper, since no one other than those with him in the OP could hear him. 'Just what I was waiting for.'

'I'm drowning!' Terry shouted, trying to keep his face out of the water rising rapidly in the ditch.

'Get up, you stupid prat,' Pete told him. 'What the fuck are you doing down there? Playing with your toy submarine?'

Terry rolled onto his back, then quickly sat upright, shaking the water off him like a dog as Alf, also grateful to get out of the rising water, slithered up the muddy side of the ditch and stared over the river.

'Wow!' Alf exclaimed softly, seeing the boat for the first time. 'What a fucking beauty!'

The big launch was now coming level with the

OP, allowing them to get a good look at its cargo, as well as the men milling about on deck. The men were all fully uniformed soldiers and the cargo was mostly in large wooden crates, suggesting weapons and ammunition. The rain obscured other details.

'I've got to get a picture of this,' Alf said, removing the camera from his bergen, where he had stowed it to protect it from the rain. '*If* I can get one in this light.'

'Then be quick about it,' Dead-eye said. 'It'll pass any moment now.' While Alf was frantically snapping away, not expecting good results, Dead-eye was squinting through the rain at the approaching boat. 'Ok,' he said as he checked his rifle, then uncocked it and switched to automatic fire. 'It's a shoot-and-scoot job. We wait until she's passing the OP – right there in front of us – then we rake her from prow to stern. The intention is not only to finish off the troops, but also to smash the boat to hell. When she's passed – or when what's left of her has passed – we bug out and don't look back. Now go to it, men.'

As the launch approached, the rain was lashing down so hard that the drops bounced off its cabin roof as well as off the river's rushing surface, where it formed a dazzling silvery tapestry. The canvas side screens of the cabin were closed against the storm, but Dead-eye knew that there were more men behind them, most of them officers.

Them and their whores, he thought cynically. But that's not my concern.

Having come up from the ditch, Alf and Terry spaced themselves about eight feet apart, one either side of Pete. Dead-eye then moved to direct the fire-fight from their left, on slightly lower ground that was covered by the water pouring noisily into the OP. From there, though ankle-deep in water and pounded by the rain, he had a clear view of the river as it swung downstream to the right, flowing to the south-east, past the Indonesians' trading settlement at Seluas.

As the launch drew level with the OP and then passed it like a great whale strung with glowing oil lamps obscured by the heavy rain, the rest of the men checked their weapons, cocked them, switched to automatic fire, then braced themselves and took aim.

'The rest of you fire when I do,' Dead-eye told them, squinting along the sights of his SLR.

He saw the prow of the launch through his night-vision sight, with the enemy soldiers gathered near it, staring along the river, some shielding their eyes against the rain with cupped hands, others huddled under their ponchos, playfully punching one another and giggling. Other men, the heavily armed crack troops, were, like their officers, hidden by canvas screens over the open deck near the stern.

The prow slipped out of view and the main deck appeared, packed with soldiers huddled around the piles of crates, most leaning against the tarpaulins, with their ponchos wrapped tightly about them to keep out the rain. That picture also moved on, slipping out of sight, ghostlike in the eerie green glow of Dead-eye's night-vision sight.

Then the bulwark came into view, in the dead centre of his sight, with more soldiers, obviously officers, standing near the steering wheel and pointing at the jungle, where the thunder was rumbling and the lightning was daggering through black clouds. They were obviously concerned more about the storm than anything else, which was fine by Dead-eye.

He got one officer dead in his sights, then pressed the trigger of his SLR, which roared in his right ear. The officer went into a convulsion, frantically throwing up his arms, then spun backwards, almost somersaulting, and fell out of sight.

Dead-eye kept firing as the bulwark moved on and was replaced with the stern. By this time Pete, Alf and Terry had also opened fire and the boat, while slipping past his line of vision, was turned into a hell of exploding wood, flying shards of smashed glass, running, ducking, falling, screaming men, and expanding, dazzling balls of fire from exploding oil lamps.

Within the space of thirty seconds Alf and Terry had each put their full twenty rounds into the launch, one magazine full, just as Dead-eye had ordered. Dead-eye had added fifteen rounds of his own and Pete had fired half a magazine before Dead-eye called 'Stop!'

All four immediately reloaded with a full magazine, as was the standard drill. Though he had half a magazine left, Pete did the same because he did not want to be caught in another action with only ten rounds.

When Dead-eye opened fire again, the rest followed suit.

While Dead-eye continued taking out the soldiers still on deck, Alf and Terry hammered away at the launch's waterline, hoping to either tear it to shreds or put enough bullets into it to flood it and sink it.

Meanwhile, Pete's SLR jammed. Cursing, he checked the weapon and cleared the stoppage in seconds. He began firing again as some of the soldiers, who had been laughing happily just a few seconds before, were set on fire by the burning oil from the exploded lamps and threw themselves screaming over the side of the boat, preferring to drown rather than burn to death.

By now the sustained fire aimed at the waterline had begun to have its desired effect and the launch had begun to list, with flames dancing up from the spilled oil blazing on the decks, black smoke billowing up and blowing backwards on the wind, and burning men pushing aside the canvas screens to jump over the side. Splashing into the river, which was now torrential because of the torrential rain, they were either swept downstream, fighting to stay afloat, or smashed into the high, muddy banks, where they were knocked unconscious and sank.

Smoke hung low in the heavy rain as it spread from beneath the canvas screens now flapping loose on the deck of the burning, listing, sinking launch.

Knowing that the boat's signaller had almost certainly transmitted an alarm call as soon as he heard the firing, and not wanting to be around when enemy choppers arrived to rake the vicinity with their guns or deposit troops sent to find the SAS ambush party, Dead-eye stopped firing and waved at Alf and Terry to withdraw.

After locking their SLRs and slinging them over their shoulders, Alf and Terry picked up their bergens, strapped them to their backs, then made a dash for the rubber trees, covered by Dead-eye and Pete, who watched the river, blinking repeatedly and squinting into the rain to check that no enemy patrols were coming along the bank.

Once in the relative safety of the jungle, Alf and Terry adopted firing positions, ready to give covering fire if any Indonesians appeared, while Dead-eye and Pete clambered out of the flooded, muddy OP and ran for the trees.

Suddenly, Dead-eye darted back to the ditch.

'What the fuck . . .?' Imagining that Dead-eye had seen enemy riflemen in the plantations, Pete, as number two, followed him back to the OP. Dead-eye, however, had only gone back to retrieve the large communal water bottle.

'We've a long way to go,' he explained, 'Besides, we don't want to leave anything that might help the Indos identify us. That's it, Pete. Let's go.'

Glancing back at the river, they saw the Indonesian boat, now listing heavily and on fire from prow to stern, sinking into the river, while the soldiers still alive were either burnt to death in the blazing oil slicks spreading out from the sinking vessel or were swept away in the swift waters, now merely part of the debris.

Satisfied, Dead-eye led Pete back to Alf and Terry, then the four men fled into the jungle.

15

As they moved back into the *ulu*, Dead-eye and the others saw the light of an explosion through the mist and rain, flaring up over the river and the rubber plantation, indicating that the launch had rolled onto its side and was finally sinking.

'We did it,' Pete said. 'The fucker's gone down. We pulled it off, boys.'

'Which is exactly why we have to keep moving,' Dead-eye said. 'That boat will have sent out an SOS the minute we opened fire on it. The Indos are going to be on our tail, so we've no time to waste. Let's get the hell out of here.'

Burdened down with their bergens, they embarked on the short, difficult hike back over the maze of watery channels, dry banks and curtains of bamboo until they reached the southern tip of the swamp, bordered by a dense tangle of *belukar*. Forced to stoop down under the lower branches and palm leaves, they had an arduous trek for the next hour, their backs breaking and every muscle taut. It was therefore a relief when they could straighten up again and advance like human beings, even though each step took them deeper into the scum-covered water.

As Dead-eye led them along at a pace that showed no mercy, with each man distanced safely from the one ahead, a king cobra hidden in a branch about four feet above the water suddenly reared its large, plate-shaped hood and started hissing aggressively, ready to strike at Dead-eye's chest.

Almost as quick and as deadly as the snake, Dead-eye aimed his SLR at its swaying head, then froze motionless, holding the barrel absolutely steady, practically touching the snake's open, salivating jaws and darting forked tongue.

The rest of the men, spaced well apart behind Dead-eye, froze as well, not knowing why he had stopped.

Still standing there frozen, with the barrel of his SLR practically down the great snake's throat, Dead-eye did not know quite what to do. Certainly, he knew that to fire the rifle might give away his patrol's position.

Pete, standing a few yards behind him, knew this also, which explains why, though having seen the snake, he was aiming at it, but not actually firing. In fact, Pete was not only worried about a shot alerting the enemy. He was concerned that, since his two friends behind him could not see what was happening, they might think the shot was from an Indonesian patrol and therefore take the required evasive action, breaking away from the single-file formation and melting into the *ulu*, possibly to never be seen again.

So for those two reasons, though seeing the snake spitting and hissing only inches from Dead-eye's face, Pete could not bring himself to press the trigger.

As for Alf and Terry, neither knew why Dead-eye had stopped, so they prepared for any eventuality and were ready to fire.

Dead-eye did not move a muscle. He out-stared the hissing creature. Eventually, the snake, having no cause to strike the rock-still sergeant, retracted its hood, slid away and disappeared behind a log in the muddy ground.

Dead-eye heaved a sigh of relief. He hurried up to Pete, who shook his head in disbelief, then they both glanced back in the direction they had come from. Even here, a good half mile from the river, they could still smell the smoke and burning oil from the sinking launch.

'Let's go,' Dead-eye whispered.

They waded deeper into the swamp, forced as usual to endure the swarms of flies, mosquitoes and midges, constantly alert for sea snakes, concentrating at all times on not breaking an ankle on one of the many large stones on the swamp bed, or losing balance by treading on an underwater log, or sinking or slipping in the clinging mud. Also forced as usual to carry their SLRs above their heads to keep them dry, they soon had badly aching muscles and sharp, stabbing pains between their shoulder blades.

This time, at least, Dead-eye was using a map annotated by himself from the previous journey, so he had only to retrace his own footsteps, as it were, to get them back to the RV on the other side of the border. The enemy, however, had other ideas.

The SAS men's first indication that they were being followed was when an Indonesian Army helicopter flew low overhead, obviously searching the swamp. Seeing it, they froze where they where, hoping that their camouflaged clothes would make them merge into the swamp and that their lack of movement would leave no rippling wake on the water that could be seen from above.

When the helicopter disappeared, the men moved on again, but less than twenty minutes later a second helicopter appeared, this time suddenly roaring out of the southern sky and hovering right above where they were wading through a stretch of swamp covered with tangled, obstructing vegetation. Holding their rifles up with one hand and hacking at the dense foliage with a *parang* held in the other, they were taken by surprise and had no time to freeze before the pilot saw them and brought the chopper down to hover right over them.

An enemy soldier was kneeling behind a machine-gun fixed to the floor at the open side door of the helicopter. When he saw the men struggling through the swamp, he opened fire on them. With the helicopter hovering dangerously close to the trees and swaying slightly from side to side, the gunner had difficulty in keeping his aim steady. His first burst therefore went wide, making the water boil violently some yards from the men. This gave them time to wade behind the nearest tree trunks, from where they were able to fire back with their SLRs switched to automatic. Instead of ascending, the chopper actually dropped lower to give the gunner a better view of his target.

Now Pete and Alf appreciated having the more powerful SLR, rather than the lighter Armalite, for they were able to put some bullets into the helicopter, stitching a line just above the door and hitting something inside that burst into flames.

Sucked out on the helicopter's own slipstream, the flames roared through the open door to engulf the unfortunate gunner, whose screams were like nothing remotely human. As the helicopter ascended, still on fire and pouring smoke, a crewman inside, attempting to put out the flames, kicked out the blazing, screaming gunner. He fell like a blazing projectile, kicking and screaming, leaving a vertical stream of smoke to mark his downward course, and was only silenced when he plunged into the swamp a good distance away. The helicopter turned around and headed back the way it had come, still pouring smoke.

'He'll tell the others where we are,' Dead-eye said. 'Now they'll start coming after us. We'd better make tracks.'

They continued wading through the swamp, passing the dead pilot, whose charred, smouldering body was sinking slowly, then heading deeper into an area covered with overhanging *belukar*. When another helicopter flew overhead, the *belukar* hid them from view, but half an hour later they saw another chopper behind them, this one a larger transport, hovering low enough to enable a good dozen troopers to climb down a rope ladder into the swamp where the first pilot had seen them.

'Shit!' Dead-eye softly exclaimed. 'That's what I feared. We'd better move faster.'

They continued their laborious, exhausting advance through the swamp, now desperate to get out of it and onto dry land, even if it was *belukar*, before the Indonesians caught up with them. Unfortunately, about fifteen minutes later, another transport helicopter flew overhead and deposited a second group of enemy troopers about a mile directly ahead of them.

'They know where we are,' Dead-eye said, 'and what direction we're heading in. They're going to cordon off the whole swamp and move in on all sides.'

Now it was Pete's turn to softly whisper, 'Shit!' He glanced about him, in every direction, as if expecting to see the enemy burst out of the undergrowth. 'What the fuck do we do?'

'We keep going,' Alf said. 'We don't have a choice. We can't go back and we can't detour, because no matter which way we go, we're going to have to fight our way out. So we might as well keep advancing.'

'I second that,' Terry said, also glancing about him, wondering just how fast their pursuers would close in.

'I agree,' Dead-eye said. 'We don't have a choice. If they're going to cordon off the whole swamp, we might as well keep going and be prepared for a fire-fight. At least the swamp from here on is relatively clear of dense undergrowth, so our hands will be free.' He held up his SLR to show them what he meant. 'Be prepared,' he said. 'Release the safety-catch. OK, let's go.'

They marched without incident for about half an hour, then stopped when they heard movement ahead. Quickly taking up positions, each man behind a different tree, they waited until the foliage just ahead parted and the first man in an enemy patrol emerged, waist-deep in water, holding a Lee-Enfield .303 bolt-action rifle across his chest at an angle.

Relatively safe hidden in this lengthy stretch of *belukar*, Dead-eye did not want the sound of shots to give away their position. Working on the assumption that the lone soldier was a scout, out on point and well away from the main patrol, he gave a hand signal, indicating that no one should fire, then carefully slung his SLR by its strap over his left shoulder. With his right hand he withdrew his commando dagger from its sheath and pressed himself against the trunk of the tree, waiting for the soldier to pass him. He did so a few seconds later, his left shoulder actually brushing the branches around Dead-eye's face.

The Indonesian looked about eighteen and had large brown eyes and delicate features slightly marred by tension. Dead-eye saw the beads of sweat gleaming on his brown skin. Without taking a step – since the soldier would have heard the moving water – Dead-eye leaned forward, slapped his hand around his mouth, silencing him, then jerked his head back and swiftly drew the blade across his taut throat, slashing through to the windpipe. Blood shot out in a long, thin arc, squirting through Dead-eye's fingers, as the soldier released a strangled, gargling sound, convulsing and dropping his rifle. The weapon splashed into the water being kicked up by his convulsions. When the man was still, Dead-eye lowered him gently into the swamp, where his blood poured out, turning the water red.

Dead-eye cleaned his bloody left hand on some leaves, cleaned and sheathed the knife the same way, then removed his SLR from his shoulder and waved the others forward. Knowing that the rest of the enemy patrol would not be far ahead, they moved with particular care, stopping every few minutes to watch and listen. Their patience was rewarded when they heard the sound of movement directly ahead.

Spreading well out and melting back into the trees on either side of what they assumed would be the enemy's path, they were rewarded when the six-man patrol emerged from the foliage, wading carefully through the water, and passed by without noticing their presence.

The SAS men waited for five minutes to ensure

that the patrol was well out of earshot, then started to move on. But they were stopped by a hand signal from Pete.

When Dead-eye looked enquiringly at Pete, the latter walked up to the sergeant and whispered, 'Once those six Indos find the body of their dead scout, they'll turn back to get us. I think we should give them a little surprise.' When Dead-eye again stared at his number two, saying nothing, Pete grinned and removed a Claymore anti-tank land-mine from his bergen. 'I've been keeping this for a rainy day,' he whispered. 'Obviously I can't bury it in the ground, but I *can* put it up there as a booby-trap.' He pointed to the lower branches of the trees.

'Do it,' Dead-eye said.

Pete waded through the water, pushed the foliage aside, then clambered up to the lower branches of the nearest tree, checking carefully that there were no snakes sleeping up above. Sitting on the thickest branch, which was just above the surface of the plant-covered water, he tied one of the Claymores to its underside with the cord from his bergen, then attached a lengthy piece of trip-wire to it. Clambering down again, he let the trip-wire run out through his fingers as he waded across the route taken by the enemy patrol, which he treated as an imaginary 'path' about ten feet wide. He stopped at a tree well to the other side of the 'path'. After tying the wire to the tangled roots of the tree, he tugged it until it was tight enough to trip the mine if moved by the passage of a human body or leg. As the wire was just under the surface of the water it would not be seen by its potential victims.

'Job done,' he whispered, proudly surveying his handiwork.

'How many have you got?' Dead-eye asked him.

'Four.'

'Let's set the other three up the same way at intervals of about a mile. We've about three miles of swamp still to cover before reaching the *ulu* proper, so the mines might hold them back long enough to let us get through.'

'That still leaves the problem of the Indos ahead of us,' Alf pointed out.

'Solving half a problem is better than nothing,' Dead-eye informed him. 'We can deal with the ones in front of us a lot easier than we can with the lot coming up on our backsides. So it's one mine each mile, Pete.'

'I'm your man, Sarge.'

They advanced through the swamp at the usual laborious pace, dragging their feet through the mud, pushing the drifting debris aside, swatting the flies and mosquitoes, and being constantly on the alert for sea snakes or the spiders that often dropped off branches when they were brushed. The leeches they could not avoid or combat in any way; they simply had to let them cling there, sucking their blood, until they next stopped to let Pete set another booby-trap with his Claymores. While Pete was doing this, the men burned the countless leeches off themselves with the lit end of a cigarette. However, once Pete had done the same and they were on the move again, more leeches came off the wet leaves to attach themselves to their already ravaged skin. Within half a mile each man would be covered yet again in a mass of slimy leeches, all sucking his blood.

The first Claymore exploded well behind them when they were nearing the end of the swamp. Even from this distance the noise was shocking, a mighty clap of thunder, and when they glanced back they saw a cloud of black smoke boiling up from the area. They even heard men screaming from this distance, but those sounds were much fainter.

Dead-eye grinned at Pete and stuck his thumb in the air. Then they moved off again.

The second Claymore exploded behind them about an hour later. Again, when they glanced backwards, they saw a cloud of black smoke billowing up from the swamp and heard the faint sounds of men screaming. It took little imagination to visualize the devastation caused to the patrols by the explosion, as well as by the dreadful shredding effect of the mine's 350 sharp-edged, red-hot, flying metal slugs.

More concerned for themselves than they were for the enemy, the SAS men moved on, gradually reaching higher ground, where the water only came up to their knees.

Knowing by this that they were almost at the end of the swamp, they stopped for a rest – and to look and listen for the sounds of the enemy. They were lucky to have done so, for they heard the sounds of movement directly ahead, which encouraged them, as usual, to melt into the trees at both sides of the imaginary path, two men to each side, with each man hiding behind his own chosen tree.

Again, a lone soldier emerged from the foliage ahead – a scout out on point – and again Dead-eye slashed his throat with his commando dagger, then lowered his convulsing body into the blood-reddened water.

Knowing that the full patrol would not be far behind, he decided to keep the men where they were and deal with the patrol when it appeared. While they were waiting, the third Claymore exploded behind them, creating another billowing cloud of black smoke and producing more distant screams.

Those booby-traps would ensure that if the Indonesians took any of the SAS troopers alive they would show them no mercy. This merely convinced Dead-eye even more that they should attempt to fight their way out of the swamp, giving no quarter.

Within a few minutes the first members of the patrol emerged from a clear path running through the *belukar* straight ahead. It consisted of ten men.

Dead-eye raised his hand, preparing to give the signal to fire, but did not lower it until the rest of the patrol had emerged from the undergrowth. Meanwhile, Pete Welsh had taken an '80' white-phosphorus incendiary grenade from his webbed belt and was preparing to pull the pin. Alf and Terry were squinting through the sights of their SLRs, but they did not fire when Dead-eye dropped his hand.

Instead, they let Pete throw the grenade. It arced through the air, seeming to travel very slowly – certainly slow enough for one of the enemy to look up, see it coming and shout a warning. That warning came too late. The grenade bounced off a tree right behind the patrol and exploded with a mighty roar, filling the air with silvery-white streams of phosphorus and swirling black smoke, tearing the foliage to shreds, and bowling over two or three of the men. Even as the latter were splashing into the boiling water, Alf and Terry were opening fire with their SLRs, pouring it into the enemy in short, savage bursts that tore them to pieces. Dead-eye and Pete then opened fire as well, firing single shots at selected targets – notably those men who had broken away from the main group and were rushing to take cover behind the trees.

The combined roar of the four SLRs reverberated through the trees, shockingly loud, but could not drown the screams of the men dying and splashing into the swamp. The greenish-brown water was boiling furiously, being kicked up by the hail of bullets, but in less than half a minute it had settled down again, the SAS guns had ceased firing, and ten dead Indonesians were floating and gradually sinking in spreading pools of blood.

'Let's get out of here,' Dead-eye said.

Advancing, they were forced to wade through the blood-reddened water, pushing the drifting, lacerated corpses aside until they had passed through and could enter the same clear path that the enemy had emerged from. They had just done so when an Indonesian helicopter, obviously drawn by the sounds of the fire-fight, flew overhead, hovered above the floating or sinking bodies, then moved on until it was hovering right over Dead-eye and the others.

They froze immediately, glancing up at the helicopter, preparing to fire at it with their SLRs if the actions of the pilot indicated that he had seen them. Obviously knowing that they could not be far away, he flew to and fro over the general area, coming down as low as he dared – so low, in fact, that the slipstream of the rotors was creating a minor hurricane around the hiding men, tearing leaves and branches off the trees. Eventually, however, the pilot gave up and flew off, letting them move on again.

They were just reaching the end of the swamp when the fourth and last Claymore went off behind them, creating the by now customary din and producing more screaming. Elated that the booby-traps had done their job by delaying the advance of the troops behind them, the four men grinned at one another, then waded on. Gradually they came up out of the scum-covered water until it was splashing only around their ankles.

It was just before dusk when they crossed the fire-lane track and Dead-eye decided they should lie up. Slowing down, they turned right, off their route, and moved, continually covering their tracks, into a thick patch of jungle.

Working on the assumption that they were still being followed, Dead-eye left Alf behind as the sentry between their old route and this new hide.

It would be a lonely duty for Alf, but someone had to do it. Once in the hide, with bashas laid out under the trees, Dead-eye gave his report to Terry for transmission to the Haunted House.

As Terry was transmitting, Dead-eye and Pete were diverted by the sounds of distant mortar explosions from an area much further east, which suggested that the Indonesians had gone off in search of them elsewhere.

'Don't believe it for a second,' Dead-eye said. 'That's what the Indos want us to think, but it's just an old trick of theirs. The CTs did the same thing in Malaya: sent some of their men off a good distance to set off some explosions, making you think that's where they were. Then, while you were relaxing, maybe even stopping to rest, thinking the enemy was far away, the main body of men would catch up with you and wipe you off the map. I'd say those mortar explosions are serving the same purpose for the Indos. They want to make us believe they're miles away, but they're right there behind us. That's why Alf is sitting out there on his lonesome: to make sure they don't take us by surprise. We move on at first light.'

They had been out on patrol for little more than a week, but had carried enough rations for two. Therefore, because so much had happened in this single day, and as they were now within a day's march of the border, Dead-eye allowed them to eat as much as they wanted. When they had done so and were settling down, satiated, he ordered them to bury the rations they did not need. This, he explained, would lighten their load on the last leg of the hike. The men did as they were told, then gratefully stretched out on their bashas under the trees.

They slept soundly that night.

16

Rising at first light the following morning, they had a cold breakfast with the last of the rations they had kept, then carefully cleaned up, removing all traces of the hide, and marched back to collect the frozen Alf, who had survived his lonely vigil without incident.

Immensely relieved to be out of the swamp, but still convinced that the Indonesians would not give up the chase until they reached the border, they marched on. The hike took them into the relative ease of primary jungle, though also into a series of high ridges and forested hills, criss-crossed with sparkling streams and deep, dangerous gorges, only some of which had aerial walkways spanning them.

Foiled by a bridgeless gorge not shown on the map, they had to make a detour and found themselves at a location different from the one through which they had entered enemy territory. Here the low hills, with no clear contour lines or outstanding features, made navigation especially difficult. Also, though all of them except Alf had had a decent night's sleep, they were suddenly attacked by the psychological effects of their arduous and brutal flight through the swamp. Alf was edgy and snapped at the others; Pete was slightly disorientated and slow to respond to orders; and Terry, in particular, was showing signs of distress, manifested in his refusal to let anyone else carry the radio, even though he was clearly exhausted.

'I'm the only one who can use it quickly in an emergency,' he said, speaking nonsense. 'And besides, I feel fine.'

The only one not affected appeared to be Deadeye, though he saw what was happening to the others. Familiar with this syndrome from Malaya, particularly from his experiences in the dreadful Telok Anson swamp, he called more rest periods than normal and gently coaxed the men into eating the high-calorie rations in their escape belts. The chocolate, in particular, would give them back some of the strength they had lost not only through sheer exhaustion, but also by being drained of so much blood by the countless leeches that had fed off them for days.

Just after noon, when the *ulu* was like a steam bath, they saw an enemy soldier in the branches high up a tree, looking directly at them, then signalling frantically with both hands, clearly telling his friends he had seen them. Dead-eye picked off the soldier with a single shot from his SLR, making him spin backwards off the tree and plunge screaming to the ground, smashing through, and snapping off, many branches as he fell. Nevertheless, within minutes, a helicopter was rising from the jungle nearby, from where the soldier had been signalling to. It headed straight towards the SAS men.

'They know where we are,' Dead-eye said. 'That means they'll come after us again. Let's skedaddle as fast as we can.'

Given a positive incentive to keep moving, the men did so, now more alert than they had been in the morning. The helicopter roared overhead, descending vertically, creating a storm, and then hovered directly above them, dangerously close to the trees.

A gunner was kneeling at the side door, taking aim with his Chinese 7.62mm gas-operated machine-gun.

The roar of the gun added to the deafening noise of the helicopter, then the vegetation around the running men went crazy, with palm leaves, thorny branches and splinters of bark exploding from the trees and cascading out in all directions.

'Shit!' Alf exclaimed angrily, his cheek slashed

by a thorny branch, the wound dripping blood. He dropped to one knee beside a screen of bamboo, took aim with his SLR and fired a sustained burst at the helicopter. The gunner fired back, aiming at Alf, who threw himself to one side as a line of bullets ran at him and blew the bamboo screen apart. The flying bamboo cut him even more, making him curse as he rolled away. When he clambered back to his feet, he was bleeding from more cuts to his face, as well as from both hands.

'You look like a pin-cushion,' Pete said, tugging Alf forward. 'Come on! Let's get going.'

The machine-gun was blowing the clearing all to hell as the men melted into the trees beyond it. The pilot, seeing where they had gone, advanced to locate them.

'Fuck this for a lark,' Pete said. He stopped, tugged an '80' grenade from his belt, pulled the pin, then swung his arm and hurled the grenade as hard as he could, on a very high arc. It exploded like a thunderclap in front of the chopper, filling the air with streaming silvery-white phosphorus and billowing smoke. Though it did not damage the helicopter, it either shocked or temporarily blinded the pilot, making him briefly lose control.

The chopper tilted violently sideways, its nose inching through the cloud of phosphorus and smoke, its rotors, which had been spinning close to the trees, now actually hitting them. First they chopped off branches, then they buckled badly, and finally one of them broke off completely and fell to the ground. Crippled, the helicopter leaned sideways and plunged to earth, smashing down through the branches, bringing whole trees down with it, and then exploding into a fierce ball of yellow-and-blue fire that engulfed the surrounding trees and foliage, creating an even bigger blaze.

Pete raised his right fist and shook it, grinning like a loon, then he and the others hurried away from the inferno before the smoke choked them.

Infuriated, the Indonesians redoubled their efforts to either destroy or capture the SAS patrol. Shortly after another helicopter had skimmed over the jungle canopy, staying well out of gunshot range and merely tracking those below, relaying their position to the soldiers on the ground, enemy mortars started firing repeatedly. The explosions erupted all around the fleeing SAS men, showering them with soil and vegetation, but not actually hitting them. While the explosions continued, the enemy troops advanced faster than ever, zigzagging from one tree to the other and gradually catching up.

Not willing to call for a helicopter lift while they were on the Indonesian side of the border and the enemy were so close, but determined to protect the radio at all costs, Dead-eye urged the patrol on while he took up the rear and picked off the soldiers as they appeared. One went down, then another, a third and a fourth. Temporarily foiled, the remainder stopped advancing and took cover behind the trees, only reappearing long enough to fire short bursts at Dead-eye, where he was kneeling behind a bamboo screen.

One of the Indonesians climbed up a tree to try and locate Dead-eye's precise position. Dead-eye accounted for him with a single shot and the man spun off the branch and plunged screaming to the jungle floor, smashing through branches and kicking up a cloud of soil and mud when he thumped into the ground. Another started climbing and was also picked off, likewise crashing down through the trees.

Seeing the futility of what they were doing, the Indonesians remained in hiding, but unleashed a concentrated barrage of mortar shells on the general vicinity as determined by the sound of Dead-eye's gunfire. They were not too far off. The forest around Dead-eye became a hell of exploding earth and foliage, with trees set on fire and the smoke gradually swirling around Dead-eye.

Choking, he jumped up and ran, following the rest of the patrol. Seeing him, the Indonesians released a fusillade of fire that had bullets whipping past his head and blowing lumps of bark off the trees. He dropped low, turned around, fired a short burst, then jumped up and ran again, repeating this time and again until he was within sight of the patrol.

As Dead-eye approached, Pete and Alf knelt facing him, shielding Terry and the radio, and laid down a fusillade of fire that forced the enemy to take cover again. When Dead-eye reached them, he saw Terry standing nervously at an aerial walkway that spanned a deep gorge. Looking down, momentarily dizzy, Dead-eye saw a river squeezing through a bottle-neck of large rocks and emerging at the other side, directly below the walkway, as a raging torrent.

'Christ!' he whispered involuntarily.

'My knees are shaking, boss,' Terry said, wiping sweat from his face. 'I don't think I can cross this.'

'You have to. We all have to.'

'It makes me dizzy just to look down.'

'Don't look down. Look straight ahead. Keep your eyes fixed on the jungle at the other side and pretend you're on solid ground. Do it now, lad. Don't hesitate.'

Terry wiped sweat from his face, took a deep breath, stepped forward and then stopped again.

'I can't!'

'Yes, you can.' Dead-eye pushed him gently, but

Terry still would not move. Only when bullets started whipping around them did he step onto the walkway, taking one tentative step, then stopping again to grab the horizontal bamboo railing on his right, the other hand being engaged with his SLR.

This simple movement caused Terry to glance sideways, probably to check that he was really holding the railing; but then his gaze took in the wide spaces between the uprights, the fragile look of the bamboo walkway, and the raging torrent that wound between the rocky walls of the gorge a good 100 feet down.

Terry started sweating and shaking. Clearly, he was more frightened at being on the swaying walkway than he was of the bullets still whistling about him. Pete and Alf, meanwhile, were still facing the Indonesians, keeping them pinned down as much as possible with short bursts of fire.

'Get moving, Terry,' Dead-eye said.

'This bridge is moving, boss!'

'It moves, but it's not about to break apart. It's just the way they're built, Terry. Start walking. Don't look down.'

'I can't move, boss. I'm sorry.'

Dead-eye turned around and saw the enemy in the *ulu*, either lying in the tall grass and only jumping up to get off a quick shot or sticking their heads out from behind the trees for the same reason. Pete and Alf were still kneeling by the walkway, their SLRs roaring in turn as they kept the Indonesians pinned down.

'I'm going to take Terry over the walkway,' Dead-eye told them. 'Try to keep those bastards back until we get to the other side. When we do, I'll give you covering fire until you get across.'

'Right, boss,' Pete said.

Dead-eye stepped onto the walkway. As soon as he did so, it moved, swaying a little from left to right. It was being shaken constantly by the wind sweeping through the gorge, but it swayed more with each move Dead-eye took, which made it seem very dangerous.

Dead-eye grabbed the bamboo support on his right. Looking down, he felt dizzy. The walkway itself was only the width of its three lengths of thick bamboo, laid down side by side and strapped together with rattan. It was hardly much wider than two human feet placed close together. The uprights angled out and in again overhead, bending where they were strapped with rattan to the horizontal holds.

You could slide your hand along the holds only as far as the next upright. Once there, you had to remove your hand for a moment and lift it over the upright before grabbing the horizontal hold again.

That was what had done Terry in, Dead-eye

realized. He had automatically looked down when he took hold of the upright and now he was afraid to let go and move further along.

Knowing this, Dead-eye carefully made his way forward, along the narrow, swaying, creaking walkway, until he was standing right behind Terry. He slung his SLR over his shoulder, then placed his free hand on Terry's elbow, holding him steady.

'Start walking,' he said. When Terry did not move immediately, apart from visibly shaking, Dead-eye pushed him forward gently, but insistently, by the elbow and he took his first step. 'That's it,' Dead-eye said in a soft, mesmeric tone of voice. 'Easy does it. Don't look down. Keep your eyes on the trees straight ahead. It's not too far to walk.'

In fact, the walkway was about 150 feet in length, though being so narrow it looked a lot longer. Its swaying was visible, its creaking constant, and the wind blowing along the gorge had the force of a hammer blow.

Given the wide spaces between the uprights, Dead-eye realized, a man could be blown off the walkway with nothing to stop him falling to his doom. Terry must have been aware of this fact, also, but prompted by Dead-eye, he did at least keep going forward, only hesitating when he had to let go of the horizontal bamboo and stand unsupported for the second it took to lift his hand over the upright and take hold again.

Those moments always seemed like an eternity, but they had to be braved.

'That's it,' Dead-eye said. 'Good.'

They were about halfway across when the walkway, already swaying noisily, shook suddenly and swayed even more.

When Terry's knuckles whitened over the bamboo, displaying his panic, Dead-eye glanced backwards and saw that Alf had jumped onto the walkway. Amazingly, Alf was moving backwards, holding the horizontal bamboo with one hand and firing short bursts from his SLR with the other, keeping the barrel steady by pressing the stock into his hip. Alf was giving covering fire to Pete as he, in turn, did the same for Terry and Dead-eye. Pete was still kneeling in the tall grass near the edge of the gorge, firing his SLR, reloading, firing again, and occasionally jumping up to hurl a hand-grenade. The explosions tore the shrubbery apart and obscured the advancing soldiers behind veils of white-phosphorus dust and smoke.

'It's only Alf,' Dead-eye explained to reassure Terry. 'He's jumped onto the walkway. Keep going. You're over halfway. You'll soon be on the other side. Take it slow and steady.'

Understandably, Terry was feeling more tension

because he was also humping the radio on top of his heavy bergen. This made his balance more precarious when the walkway swayed from side to side, as it was now doing more than ever as Alf backed across it.

At that moment, the enemy started firing their mortars at the walkway. The first explosion erupted near Pete, almost bowling him sideways and certainly covering him in showering soil and foliage. The second shell looped down past the walkway and exploded against the side of the gorge just below it, hurling rocks and soil into the rapids far below.

The walkway shook violently again. This time, when Dead-eye glanced back, he saw that Pete had also jumped onto it and was, like Alf, moving backwards while firing his SLR at the troops advancing out of the undergrowth.

'Faster!' Dead-eye snapped at Terry, wanting to leave the walkway free for the other two. 'Damn it, Terry, get going!'

Impelled by the urgency in Dead-eye's voice, Terry gathered his courage and practically ran the rest of the way across, jumping gratefully onto the solid ground at the far side. Even as Dead-eye followed him, Terry was turning around and unslinging his SLR to give covering fire to Alf and Pete. He had already opened fire as Dead-eye jumped onto the ground and also turned back to add to their fire.

Two more mortar shells exploded on the far bank, dangerously close to the pinions of the walkway. A third shell looped down over the walkway, narrowly missed the bamboo uprights, and continued down into the gorge, exploding in the rapids and creating a great mushroom of boiling water.

Alf was, by now, halfway across, still moving backwards and firing at the same time. Pete had just commenced his own, painfully slow, backwards crossing while firing short but effective bursts at the soldiers who were emerging from the *ulu*. Hit by Pete's bullets, but only wounded, one of the Indonesians fell, rolled off the edge and plunged screaming down into the rapids. Others convulsed and fell along the grassy, irregular edge of the gorge. More emerged from the *ulu* and risked Pete's bullets to try and reach the end of the walkway. Some finally made it.

Running out of time and now protected a little by the covering fire of Dead-eye and Terry, Alf turned around and hurried towards them. By the time he left the walkway, jumping onto the solid ground beside the other two, Pete was halfway across, though still walking backwards and firing at the same time.

Four enemy soldiers started onto the bridge, but were cut down by the combined fire-power of Dead-eye, Terry and Alf. The soldiers crumpled in a heap, one practically on top of the other, effectively blocking access to the walkway. Seeing this, the other soldiers retreated back behind the trees along the edge of the gorge and fired a sustained fusillade at Pete, who was now just over halfway across. The hail of bullets tore the bamboo uprights and horizontals apart, with pieces of bamboo sailing down into the rapids and sharp splinters showering over Pete.

'*Run!*' Dead-eye bawled.

Pete was turning around to do just that when he jerked epileptically, dropped his SLR, and fell chest-first against a horizontal length of bamboo. Hanging there for a second, he watched his rifle fall down into the rapids, then he straightened up again, holding his left arm, and staggered on across the bridge toward his comrades. His arm was a bloody mess, with blood spurting out of punctured veins and dropping like rain into the gorge.

'Jesus!' Alf whispered, then fired a savage burst across the gorge, hoping to hit one of the many soldiers hiding behind the trees at the other side. He did little good. More bullets were punching into Pete, making him jerk and quiver and almost fall over toward the spaces between the uprights.

A machine-gunner, also well hidden in the trees, started firing at the spot where the walkway was fixed to the side of the gorge. He was trying to blow it apart.

'Faster!' Dead-eye bawled at the now badly wounded, bloody and staggering Pete. 'Faster, damn it! *Faster!*'

But Pete could go no faster. He was losing blood too rapidly. He managed to remain upright, holding onto the handrail, but he was swaying dangerously from side to side and jerking spasmodically as more bullets punched into him – even as the hail of bullets from the machine-gun was blowing asunder the supports at the side of the gorge.

'Come on, Pete!' Alf screamed, then fired another angry burst across the gorge.

But Pete fell on his hands and knees in the middle of the walkway, looking straight down that dizzying drop as his blood squirted out from the bullet holes in his body and shattered arm to rain down on the rapids.

Alf dropped his SLR and nearly jumped onto the walkway, intent on rescuing his friend, but Dead-eye grabbed him by the shoulders and jerked him back, practically slamming him face-down into the dirt. 'No, Alf! It's too late!'

As Alf sat up again, the supports savaged by the

machine-gun finally came away from the gorge wall and the whole walkway started breaking up, with great lengths of bamboo sailing down into the gorge. The rest of the fragile construction soon followed, breaking up like the pieces of a gigantic jigsaw puzzle. The three lengths of bamboo that had formed the actual walkway were the last to break apart, with the separate pieces slipping out of their rattan ties and falling into the rapids far below.

Still fixed to the side of the gorge where Dead-eye, Terry and Alf were kneeling, the remaining half of the walkway started tilting down, tearing away from the rocks in which it had been embedded, then breaking up even as Pete, still on his hands and knees, slid backwards to the broken end, wrapped his arms around a crossbeam, then found himself hanging from it with his legs kicking frantically in mid-air.

He did not hang there long. The pain from his wounded arm made him scream and let go. A final burst from the machine-gun tore him away for good and he fell, screaming louder, tumbling like a wind-blown leaf, to the bottom of the gorge, where he splashed into the raging rapids, was smashed against the rocks, and then was swept away out of sight to a watery grave.

'*Bastards!*' Alf screamed. He stood up to fire his

SLR at the soldiers over the gorge, but Dead-eye jerked him back down, pushed him towards the trees, and bawled, 'Go! They can't get at us now. Let's get the hell out of here!'

The three men picked themselves up and hurried into the trees, away from a final, frustrated volley of fire from the other side of the gorge.

They had made it back.

Late that afternoon, when they had crossed the border and Dead-eye was certain that the Indonesians would not pursue them by helicopter, he told Terry to radio for one of their own choppers, asking the pilot to home in on the SARBE beacon and fix their position relative to the LZ. The message transmitted back was that the pilot was going to do more than that: he was going to save them from the long hike to the RV by picking them up.

While they waited for the chopper to arrive, the distraught Terry and, particularly, Alf, finished off the last of the high-calorie rations in their escape belts, then distracted themselves by cleaning and oiling their much-used weapons. Meanwhile, Dead-eye kept himself busy by making the last entries in his notebook, detailing everything about the mission for later analysis by the 'green slime', the officers of SAS intelligence.

Forty minutes later, a Wessex Mark 1 helicopter

arrived overhead, making a lot of noise and whipping up the foliage when it hovered just above the treetops, about 90 feet up. Unable to land, the pilot had his crewman lower his winch wire with two harnesses attached. The harnesses fell down through the trees, bouncing off the branches, and finally dangled, bobbing up and down, a few inches above their heads.

The three men piled their bergens into one of the winches, Terry took the second, and the wires were then rapidly reeled in. Alf went up next. Finally, Dead-eye was pulled up and scrambled gratefully into the chopper, which was piloted by his old sparring partner Army Air Corps Lieutenant Ralph Ellis.

'Had a nice ten day's jaunt in the countryside, did you?' he asked.

'Very nice, thanks,' Dead-eye replied deadpan. '*You* should try it some time.'

The helicopter ascended towards the crimson sun, then turned north and flew above the jungle canopy, heading for Kuching. By nightfall the men were being debriefed in the Haunted House.

The mission was over.

17

Sergeant Richard Parker, Corporal Alf Laughton and Trooper Terry Malkin were returned with the rest of D Squadron to the SAS base in Hereford, but the war in Borneo did not end with their departure.

Following their successful patrol to the bend in the River Koemba, other patrols retraced their route and photographed the fire-track they had crossed. Further 'Claret' raids were mounted a few months later and, greatly aided by the intelligence brought back by Dead-eye's team, were even more successful.

D Squadron was replaced by the returning A Squadron, led by Major Peter de la Billière, who would eventually become the commander of the SAS. Under his brilliant leadership, A Squadron forged a closer relationship with the border battalions, made great improvements in the organization for supplying patrols in the field, and worked closely with the 1st/2nd Gurkhas in a series of highly successful cross-border operations. These included intelligence-gathering forays west and south of Stass; tapping Indonesian telephone lines 10 miles inside enemy territory, which produced invaluable taped conversations between various high-ranking Indonesian Army officers; snatching top-secret documents from an Indonesian Army building; and laying minefields in Sabah's formerly unexplored jungles.

Plans were being drawn up for even more ambitious 'Claret' raids when, in March 1966, a military government replaced the aggressive President Sukarno and the war eased a little. The war ceased completely when a treaty was concluded between Indonesia and Malaya the following August. This brought to a definite end the 'undeclared' war that had lasted nearly four years, killing 114 Commonwealth soldiers, including Corporal Pete Welsh and six other SAS men. The Indonesians suffered five times that number of casualties.

The so-called 'Confrontation' in Borneo had shown the necessity of having troops who could solve the unique problems raised by an 'undeclared' war where British forces could not overtly take the fight into enemy territory. It also confirmed once and for all that the kind of hearts-and-minds campaign devised by the SAS in Malaya could work wonders where direct military action was not a viable option.

As with every SAS campaign, the men who took part in the Confrontation in Borneo were affected by it in different ways.

The 'newcomer', Terry Malkin, returning from Borneo as a toughened, experienced trooper, was sent almost immediately to take part in the counter-insurgency campaign in Aden. There he became one of that legendary group of men who, disguised as Arabs, infiltrated the souks and bazaars to assassinate leading members of the National Liberation Front by use of the 'double tap' – firing a 9mm Browning High Power handgun at close range – as part of the daring 'Keeni Meeni' operations.

Corporal Alf Laughton, who had survived the horrors of the Telok Anson swamp in Malaya approximately five years before his Borneo experience, was deeply shocked by the loss of his best friend, Pete Welsh, and emotionally drained by his two gruelling campaigns. At his own request he was sent for treatment to 'the thinking man's Belsen' – Ward 11 of the British Army Psychiatric Unit – where he was gradually coaxed out of his depression and returned to the regiment to become a ruthlessly efficient member of the Directing Staff at 22 SAS Training Wing, Hereford.

Like Corporal Laughton, Sergeant Richard Parker

had physically survived the horrors of both jungle campaigns, but was psychologically scarred by his experiences, as well as by the loss of so many good friends. Eschewing psychiatric help, Dead-eye solved his problems in his own way, mainly by spending most of his spare time alone, reading books on military theory, and by training himself to live without the need for friends who might be killed in battle. In 1972, by then dubbed 'Soldier C' by some snooping journalists, he was one of those who took part in the fight to clear the fanatical Adoo guerrillas from the summit of the mighty Jebel Dhofar in Oman. He survived that as well.

'Tell me in one sentence,' Terry Malkin said in the Paludrine Club in the SAS base at Hereford, just before they were shipped out to Aden, 'how you've managed to survive all that shit.'

'Who dares wins,' Dead-eye told him.

SOLDIER J: SAS

COUNTERINSURGENCY IN ADEN

Shaun Clarke

Prelude

The port of Aden is located on a peninsula enclosing the eastern side of Bandar at-Tawahi, Aden's harbour. It is bounded to the west and north-west by Yemen, to the north by the great desert known as the Rub' al-Khali, the Empty Quarter, to the east by Oman, and to the south by the Gulf of Aden and the Arabian Sea. Though a centre of trade since the days of antiquity, and mentioned in the Bible, the city in 1964 looked less than appealing.

Standing beside his wife, Miriam, on the deck of the P & O liner *Himalaya*, Norman Blakely, emigrating to Australia from Winchester, where he had taught ancient history at the renowned public school, realized he had known all these facts since his own school days. He certainly recognized the features he had often read about, yet he felt a certain disappointment at what he was seeing, not least the surprising modernity of the place.

Even from this distance, beyond the many rowing boats and motor launches dotted about the mud-coloured waters of the harbour, Aden was no more than an untidy sprawl of white-painted stone tower buildings and warehouses surrounded by an ugly clutter of jibs and cranes, immense oil tanks and huge lights raised high on steel gantries – all hemmed in on two sides by the promontories of Jebel Shamsan (Aden) and Jebel Ihsan (Little Aden). Both of these short necks of bleached volcanic rock thrust out from, and were dominated by, an equally unattractive maritime mountain range that varied from 1000 to 2000 feet and was constantly shadowed by depressing grey clouds.

Rising up the lower slopes of the mountains behind the town, about a mile beyond it, was a roughly triangular maze of low, white-painted buildings, which Norman assumed was the old commercial centre known as the Crater. What he did not know – even though he and the other passengers had received a leaflet gently warning them of the 'occasional' dangers of Aden – is that it was the home of the most dangerous anti-British terrorists in that troublesome country.

'If the town's as depressing as it looks from here,' Norman said to Miriam, 'we'll take a taxi up to the Crater. It's almost certainly less commercialized than Aden proper – and hopefully more like the real thing.'

'That leaflet said not to wander too far from the port area,' Miriam reminded him.

'The authorities *always* exaggerate these situations for their own reasons,' Norman said with conviction. 'In this instance, they doubtless want us to remain in the port area because that's where all the duty-free goods are sold. They just want to make money. Such goods aren't sold up in the Crater, so that's where we'll go.'

Trade in a particular kind of duty-free goods was already taking place in the water below them, where the 'bum boats' were packed tightly together by the hull of their ship and stacked high with a colourful collection of souvenirs and other cheap merchandise piled high in wooden crates and cardboard boxes. On offer were 'hand-tooled' – in fact, mass-produced – leather purses and wallets; cartons of Senior Service, Players, Woodbine and Camel cigarettes; Zenith 8 x 30 binoculars, sold in sealed boxes, many of which were fake and did not work; 35mm SLR cameras; transistor radios; counterfeit Rolex wristwatches; and even cartons of Colgate toothpaste. The goods were being sold by shrieking, gesticulating Arabs dressed in a colourful variety of garments, from English shirts and trousers to sarongs and turbans, though all wore thongs about their legs.

The Arabs were bartering by shouting preliminary prices and sending their wares up for inspection in baskets tied to ropes that had been hurled up to the passengers, who had obligingly tied them to the ship's railing. The individual passenger then either lowered the goods back down in the basket or removed them and deposited the agreed amount of money in their place.

While this noisy, good-natured barter was being conducted between the passengers and the Arab vendors below, other passengers were throwing coins into the water between the bum boats and watching Arab children dive from the jetty for them.

Ignoring these activities, Norman led his wife down the swaying gangplank to embark on the sixty-man transit boat that would take them the short distance to the quay. The latter was guarded by uniformed British soldiers, some in shorts, others in lightweight trousers, some armed with

Sten guns or self-loading rifles, others with pistols holstered at their hips.

The sight of the soldiers made Miriam more nervous.

'Are you sure this is wise?' she asked Norman.

'Of course,' he said resolutely, but with a hint of irritation, for his wife was the anxious type. 'Can't let a few tin soldiers bother us. Besides, they're here for our protection, so you've no need to fear.'

'There's a war going on here, dear.'

'Between Yemeni guerrillas and the British army, mostly up in the mountains. Not down *here*, Miriam.' He tugged impatiently at her hand. 'Come on! Let's explore.'

Walking through the arched entrance of the Aden Port Trust, which was guarded by more British troops, Norman and Mariam stepped into Tawahi Main Road, where they were suddenly assailed by the noise of traffic and a disorientating array of signs in Arabic and English. Stuck on the wall by the entrance was a small blue rubbish bin with a notice saying, in English only: Keep Your Town Clean. Another sign said: Aden Field Force – Forging an Empire. Left of the entrance, lined up against a wire-mesh fence surmounted by three strands of menacing barbed wire which protected the building, was a taxi rank whose drivers, all Arabs wearing a mixture of sarongs, turbans and loose shirts, were soliciting custom from the *Himalaya*'s emerging passengers. Other Muslims were carrying with one hand trays piled high with bananas, selling steaming rice-based dishes from blue-painted, wheeled barrows, or dispensing water for a price, dishing it out by the ladleful from a well-scrubbed steel bucket.

An enthusiastic armchair traveller on his first real trip away from home, Norman was keen to see the harbour area, which he knew was called Ma'alah. Politely rejecting the services of the beaming, gesturing taxi drivers, he led his wife through the teeming streets. He was instantly struck by the exotic variety of the people – mostly Sunni Muslims, but with a smattering of Saydi Muslims from the northern tribes of northern Yemen, as well as small groups of Europeans, Hindus and Yemeni Jews.

However, the history teacher was slightly put off by the sheer intensity of the noisy throng, with its cripples, blind men, thieves with amputated hands, grimy, shrieking children, armed soldiers, both British and Federation of South Arabia, along with goats, cows and mangy dogs. He was also disillusioned by the forest of English shop signs above the many stores stacked with duty-free goods. Everywhere they looked, Norman and his increasingly agitated wife saw signs advertising Tissot and Rolex wristwatches, Agfa and Kodak film, BP petrol.

A soldier from the Queen's Own Highlanders, complete with self-loading rifle (SLR), water bottle and grim, watchful face, stood guard at a street corner by the Aden Store Annexe – the sole agent for Venus watches, proudly displayed in their hundreds in the shop window – under a sign showing the latest 35mm cameras. In another street, the London Store, Geneva Store and New Era Store stood side by side – all flat-fronted concrete buildings with slatted curtains over window-shaped openings devoid of glass – with buckets, ladders and the vendors' chairs outside and the mandatory soldiers parading up and down. In a third street, the locals were practically jammed elbow to elbow under antique clocks and signs advertising hi-fi systems, televisions and photographic equipment, while the tourists, either seated on chairs or pressed back against the walls by the tide of passers-by, bartered for tax-free goods, oblivious to the armed troops standing watchfully beside them.

As well as blind and crippled beggars, including one who hopped along on his hands and knees like a human spider, the streets were packed with fast-talking Arabs selling phoney Rolex wristwatches and Parker pens. Honking Mercedes, Jaguars and more modest Volkswagen Beetles all had to make their slow progress not only through the teeming mass of humans, but also through the sea of livestock and undernourished dogs.

Towering over the town, the mountains appeared to run right down to the streets, sun-bleached and purplish in the grey light, with water conduits snaking along their rocky slopes.

Stopping by the Miramar Bazaar, Norman wiped sweat from his face, suddenly realized that the heat was appalling, and decided that he had had enough of this place. Apart from its few remaining Oriental features, it was all much too modern and commercialized for his liking.

'Let's take a taxi to the Crater,' he said.

'It's called Crater,' Miriam corrected him pedantically. 'Not *the* Crater . . . And I don't think we should go up there, dear. It's supposed to be dangerous.'

'Oh, tosh!' Norman said impatiently, eager to see the *real* Aden. 'It can't be any worse than this filthy hole. Besides, you only live once, my love, so let's take our chances.'

So packed was the street with shops, stalls, animals and, above all, people, that the cars could only inch forward, their frustrated drivers hooting relentlessly. It took Norman some time to find a vacant taxi, but eventually the couple were driven out of town, along the foot of the mountains, to arrive a few minutes later at the foetid rabbit warren of Crater.

Merely glancing out the window at the thronging mass of Arabs in the rubbish-strewn street, wreathed in smoke from the many open fires and pungent food stalls, was enough to put Miriam off. She was disconcerted even more to realize, unlike in the harbour area, there were no British soldiers guarding the streets.

'Let's go back, dear,' she suggested, touching Norman's arm.

'Rubbish! We'll get out and investigate,' he insisted.

After the customary haggling, Norman paid the driver and started out of the taxi. However, just as he placed his right foot on the ground, a dark-skinned man wearing an Arab robe, or *futah*, and on his head a *shemagh*, rushed past him, reaching out with his left hand to roughly push him back into the cab.

Outraged, Norman straightened up and was about to step out again when the same Arab reached under his *futah* and took out a pistol with a quick, smooth sweep of his right hand. Spreading his legs to steady himself, he took aim at another Arab emerging from the mud-brick house straight ahead. He fired six shots in rapid succession, punching the victim backwards, almost lifting him off the ground and finally bowling him into the dirt.

Even as Miriam screamed in terror and others bawled warnings or shouted out in fear, the assassin turned back to the deeply shocked couple.

'Sorry about that,' he said in perfect English, then again pushed Norman back into the taxi and slammed the door in his face. He was disappearing back into the crowd as the driver noisily ground his gears, made a sharp U-turn and roared off the way he had come, the dust churned up by his spinning wheels settling over the dead Arab on the ground.

Shocked beyond words, no longer in love with travelling, Norman trembled in the taxi beside his sobbing wife and kept his head down. Mercifully, the taxi soon screeched to a halt at the archway leading into the Aden Port Trust, where their ship was docked.

'He was English!' Norman eventually babbled. 'That Arab was *English*!'

Miriam sobbing hysterically in his arms, he hurried up the gangplank, glad to be back aboard the ship and on his way to Australia.

'He was English!' he whispered, as they were swallowed up by the welcoming vastness of the *Himalaya*.

1

The Hercules C-130 transport plane bounced heavily onto the runway of Khormaksar, the RAF base in Aden. Roaring even louder than ever, with its flaps down, it threw the men in the cramped hold together as it trundled shakily along the runway. Having been flown all the way from their base at Bradbury Lines, Hereford, via RAF Lyneham, Wiltshire, the men of D Squadron SAS were glad to have finally arrived. Nevertheless they cursed a good deal as they sorted out their weapons, water bottles, bergen rucksacks, ammunition belts and other kit, which had been thrown together and become entangled during the rough landing.

'This pilot couldn't ride a bike,' Corporal Ken Brooke complained, 'let alone fly an aeroplane.'

'They're pilots because they're too thick to do anything else,' Lance-Corporal Les Moody replied.

'Stop moaning and get ready to disembark,' Sergeant Jimmy 'Jimbo' Ashman told them. 'That RAF Loadmaster's already preparing to open the door, so we'll be on the ground in a minute or two and you can all breathe fresh air again.'

'Hallelujah!' Ken exclaimed softly.

In charge of the squadron was the relatively inexperienced, twenty-four-year-old Captain Robert Ellsworth. A recent recruit from the Somerset and Cornwall Light Infantry, the young officer had a healthy respect for the superior experience of the troops who had already served the Regiment well in Malaya and Borneo, particularly his two sergeants, Jimmy Ashman and Richard Parker. The former was an old hand who had started as a youngster with the Regiment when it was first formed in North Africa way back in 1941 under the legendary David Stirling. Jimbo was a tough, fair, generally good-natured NCO who understood his men and knew how to get things done.

Parker, known as Dead-eye Dick, or simply Dead-eye, because of his outstanding marksmanship, was more of a loner, forged like steel in the hell of the Telok Anson swamp in Malaya and, more recently, in what had been an equally nightmarish campaign in Borneo. Apart from being the best shot and probably the most feared and admired soldier in the Regiment, Parker was also valuable in that he had spent his time since Borneo at the Hereford and Army School of Languages, adding a good command of Arabic to his other skills.

Another Borneo hand, Trooper Terry Malkin, who had gone there as a 'virgin' but received a Mention in Dispatches for his bravery, was in Aden already, working under cover with one of the renowned 'Keeni-Meeni' squads. As a superior signaller Terry would be sorely missed for the first few weeks, though luckily he would be returning to the squadron in a few weeks' time, when his three-month stint in Aden was over.

Three NCOs who had also been 'broken in' in Borneo, though not with the men already mentioned, were among those preparing to disembark from the Hercules: the impetuous Corporal Ken Brooke, the aptly named Lance-Corporal Les Moody and the medical specialist, Lance-Corporal Laurence 'Larry' Johnson. All were good, experienced soldiers.

Two recently badged troopers, Ben Riley and Dennis 'Taff' Thomas, had been included to make up the required numbers and be trained under the more experienced men. All in all, Captain

Ellsworth felt that he was in good company and hoped to prove himself worthy of them when the campaign began.

The moment the Hercules came to a halt, the doors were pushed open and sunlight poured into the gloomy hold. Standing up with a noisy rattling of weapons, the men fell instinctively into two lines and inched forward, past the stacked, strapped-down supply crates, to march in pairs down the ramp to the ground. Once out of the aircraft, they were forced to blink against the fierce sunlight before they could look about them to see, parked neatly along the runway, RAF Hawker Hunter ground-support aircraft, Shackleton bombers, Twin Pioneer transports, and various helicopters, including the Sikorski S-55 Whirlwind, which the squadron had used extensively in Malaya and Borneo, and the ever-reliable Wessex S-58 Mark 1. Bedford three-ton lorries, Saladin armoured cars and jeeps with rear-mounted Bren light machine-guns were either parked near the runway or cruising along the tarmac roads between the corrugated tin hangars and concrete buildings. Beyond the latter could be seen the sun-scorched, volcanic rock mountains that encircled and dominated the distant port of Aden.

The fresh air the men had hoped to breathe after hours in the Hercules was in fact filled with dust. Their throats dried out within seconds, making them choke on the dust when they tried to breathe, and they all broke out in sweat the instant they stepped into the suffocating heat.

'Jesus!' Ken hissed. 'This is worse than Borneo.'

'I feel like I'm burning up,' Les groaned. 'Paying for my sins.'

'Pay for those and you'll burn for ever,' Jimbo told him, breaking away from a conversation with Captain Ellsworth and Sergeant Parker. 'Now pick up your gear and head for those Bedfords lined up on the edge of the runway. We've a long way to go yet.'

'What?' the newly fledged trooper Ben Riley asked in shock, practically croaking in the dreadful humidity and wiping sweat from his face.

'We've a long way to go yet,' Jimbo repeated patiently. 'Sixty miles to our forward base at Thumier, to be exact. And we're going in those Bedfords parked over there.'

'Sixty miles?' Ben asked, as if he hadn't heard the sergeant correctly. 'You mean *now*?'

'That's right, Trooper. Now.'

'Without a break?'

'Naturally, Trooper.'

'I think what he means, Sergeant,' the other recently badged trooper, Taff Thomas, put in timidly, aware that the temperature here could sometimes rise to 150 degrees Fahrenheit, 'is that a two-week period is normally allowed for acclimatization to this kind of heat.'

Ken and Larry laughed simultaneously.

'That's for the bleedin' greens,' Les explained, referring to the green-uniformed regular Army. 'Not for the SAS. We don't expect two weeks' paid leave. We just get up and go.'

'Happy, Troopers?' Jimbo asked. Both men nodded, keen to do the right thing. 'Right, then, get up in those Bedfords.'

The men did as they were told and soon four three-tonners were leaving the RAF base. They were guarded front and rear by British Army 6×6-drive Saladin armoured cars, each with a 76mm QF (quick-firing) gun and a Browning .30-inch machine-gun. The convoy trundled along a road that was lined with coconut palms and ran as straight as an arrow through a flat desert plain covered with scattered clumps of aloe and cactus-like euphorbia.

As the Bedfords headed towards the heat-hazed,

purplish mountains that broke up the horizon, the coconut palms gradually disappeared and the land became more arid, but with a surprisingly wide variety of trees – acacias, tamarisks, jujube and doum palms – breaking up the desert's monotony.

Once they were well away from Aden, out on the open plain, the heat became even worse and was made bearable only by the wind created by the lorries. This wind, however, churned up dense clouds of dust that made most of the men choke and, in some cases, vomit over the rattling tailgates.

'Heave it up over the back,' Jimbo helpfully instructed Ben as he tried to hold his stomach's contents in with pursed lips and bulging cheeks. 'If you do it over the side and that wind blows it back in, over us, you'll have to lick us clean with your furry tongue. So do it over the rear, lad.'

His cheeks deathly white and still bulging, the trooper nodded and threw himself to the back of the vehicle, hanging over the tailgate and vomiting unrestrainedly into the cloud of dust being churned up by the wheels. He was soon followed by his fellow trooper, Taff Thomas, who picked the exact same spot to empty his tortured stomach, while the more experienced men covered their faces with scarves and either practised deep, even breathing or amused themselves with some traditional bullshit.

'Don't worry about it,' Ken said to Taff as the latter wiped his mucky lips clean with a handkerchief and tried to control his heavy breathing. 'You'll feel better after you've had a good nosh at Thumier. Great grub they do there. Raw liver, tripe, runny eggs, oysters, octopus, snails that look like snot, green pea soup . . .'

Taff groaned and went to throw up again over the back of the bouncing, rattling Bedford, into boiling, choking clouds of sand.

'Bet you've never eaten a snail in your life,' Larry said, more loudly than was strictly necessary. 'That's nosh for refined folk.'

'Refined?' Ken replied, glancing sideways as Taff continued heaving over the tailgate. 'What's so refined about pulling a piece of snot out of a shell and letting it slither down your throat? That's puke-making – not refined.'

'Ah, God!' Ben groaned, then covered his mouth with his soiled handkerchief as he shuddered visibly.

'Throw up in that,' Jimbo warned him, 'and I'll make you wipe your face with it. Go and join your friend there.'

Shuddering even more violently, Ben dived for the tailgate, hanging over it beside his heaving friend.

'A little vomit goes a long way,' Ken said. 'Across half of this bloody desert, in fact. I never knew those two had it in 'em. It just goes to show.'

Men in the other Bedfords were suffering in the same way, but the column continued across the desert to where the lower slopes of the mountains, covered in lava, with a mixture of limestone and sand, made for an even rougher, slower ride. Here there were no trees, so no protection from the sun, and when the lorries slowed to practically a crawl – which they had to do repeatedly to navigate the rocky terrain – they filled up immediately with swarms of buzzing flies and whining, biting mosquitoes.

'Shit!' Les complained, swiping frantically at the frantic insects. 'I'm being eaten alive here!'

'Malaria's next on the list,' Ken added. 'That bloody Paludrine's useless.'

'Why the hell doesn't this driver go faster?' Larry asked as he too swatted uselessly at the attacking insects. 'At this rate, we might as well get out and walk.'

'It's the mountains,' Ben explained, feeling better for having emptied his stomach and seemingly oblivious to the insects. 'This road's running across their lower slopes, which are rocky and full of holes.'

'How observant!' Ken exclaimed.

'A bright lad!' Les added.

'Real officer material,' Larry chimed in. 'These bleedin' insects only go for red blood, so his must be blue.'

'I'm never bothered by insects,' Ben confirmed. 'It's odd, but it's true.'

'How's your stomach?' Ken asked the trooper.

'Feeling sick again?' queried Les.

'I can still smell his vomit from an hour ago,' Larry said, 'and it's probably what attracted these bloody insects. They're after his puke.'

Ben and Taff dived simultaneously for the rear of the lorry and started heaving yet again while the others, feeling superior once more, kept swatting at and cursing the insects. This went on until the Bedford bounced down off the slopes and headed across another relatively flat plain of limestone, sandstone and lava fields. They had now been on the Dhala road for two hours, but it seemed longer than that.

Mercifully, after another hour of hellish heat and dust, with the sun even higher in a silvery-white sky, they arrived at the SAS forward base at Thumier, located near the Habilayn airstrip, sixty miles from Aden and just thirty miles from the hostile Yemeni border.

'We could have been flown here!' Ben complained.

'That would have been too easy,' Ken explained. 'For us, *nothing's* made easy.'

In reality the camp was little more than an uninviting collection of tents pitched in a sandy area surrounded by high, rocky ridges where half a dozen SAS observation posts, hidden from view and swept constantly by dust, recced the landscape for enemy troop movements. There were no guards at the camp entrance because there were no gates; nor was there a perimeter fence. However, the base was surrounded by sandbagged gun emplacements raised an equal distance apart in a loose circular shape and nicknamed 'hedgehogs' because they were bristling with 25-pounder guns, 3-inch mortars, and Browning 0.5-inch heavy machine-guns. Though the landscape precluded the use of aeroplanes, a flattened area of desert near one of the hedgehogs was being used as a helicopter landing pad, on which were now parked the camp's helicopters, including a Sikorski S-55 Whirlwind and a British-built Wessex S-58 Mark 1. The Bedfords of A Squadron were lined up near the helicopters. A line of men, mostly from that squadron, all with tin plates and eating utensils, was inching into the largest tent of all – the mess tent – for their evening meal. A modified 4×4 Willys jeep, with armoured perspex screens and a Browning 0.5-inch heavy machine-gun mounted on the front, was parked outside the second largest tent, which was being used as a combined HQ and briefing room. Other medium-sized tents were being used as the quartermaster's store, armoury, NAAFI and surgery. A row of smaller tents located near portable showers and boxed-in, roofless chemical latrines were the make-do 'bashas', or sleeping quarters. Beyond those tents lay the desert.

'Home, sweet fucking home,' Les said in disgust as he clambered out of the Bedford to stand beside his mate Ken and the still shaky troopers, Ben and Taff, in the unrelenting sunlight. 'Welcome to Purgatory!'

Ken turned to Ben and Taff, both of whom were

white as ghosts and wiping sweat from their faces. 'Feel better, do you?' he asked.

'Yes, Corporal,' they both lied.

'The vomiting's always followed by diarrhoea,' Ken helpfully informed them. 'You'll be shitting for days.'

'It rushes out before you can stop it,' Les added. 'As thin as pea soup. It's in your pants before you even know you've done it. A right fucking mess, it makes.'

'Christ!' Ben exclaimed.

'God Almighty!' Taff groaned.

'Keep your religious sentiments to yourselves,' Jimbo admonished them, materializing out of the shimmering heat haze to study them keenly. 'Are you two OK?'

'Yes, Sarge,' they both answered.

'You look a bit shaky.'

'I'm all right, Sarge,' Ben said.

'So am I,' Taff insisted.

'They don't have any insides left,' Ken explained. 'But apart from that, they're perfectly normal.'

Jimbo was too distracted to take in the corporal's little joke. 'Good,' he said. 'So pick up your kit, hump it over to those tents, find yourselves a basha, have a smoko and brew-up, then meet me at the quartermaster's store in thirty minutes precisely. Get to it.'

When Jimbo had marched away, the weary men humped their 60-pound bergens onto their backs, picked up their personal weapons – either 5.56mm M16 assault rifles, 7.62mm L1A1 SLRs or 7.62mm L42A1 bolt-action sniper rifles – and marched across the dusty clearing to the bashas. Because the two new troopers had been placed in their care, Ken and Les were to share a tent with Ben and Taff.

'Well, it isn't exactly the Ritz,' Ken said, leaning forward to keep his head from scraping the roof of the tent, 'but I suppose it'll do.'

'They wouldn't let you into the Ritz,' Les replied, 'if you had the Queen Mother on your arm. This tent is probably more luxurious than anything you've had in your whole life.'

'Before I joined the Army,' Ken replied, swatting uselessly at the swarm of flies and mosquitoes at his face, 'when I was just a lad, I lived in a spacious two-up, two-down that had all the mod cons, including a real toilet in the backyard with a nice bolt and chain.'

'All right, lads,' Les said to Ben and Taff, who were both wiping sweat from their faces, swatting at the flies and mosquitoes, and nervously examining the sandy soil beneath the camp-beds for signs of scorpions or snakes, 'put your bergens down, roll your sleeping bags out on the beds, then let's go to the QM's tent for the rest of our kit.'

'*More* kit?' Ben asked in disbelief as he gratefully lowered his heavy bergen to the ground, recalling that it contained a hollow-fill sleeping bag; a waterproof one-man sheet; a portable hexamine stove with blocks of fuel; an aluminium mess tin, mug and utensils; a brew kit, including sachets of tea, powdered milk and sugar; spare radio batteries; water bottles; extra ammunition; matches and flint; an emergency first-aid kit; signal flares; and various survival aids, including compass, pencil torch and batteries, and even surgical blades and butterfly sutures.

'Dead right,' Les said with a sly grin. '*More* kit. This is just the beginning, kid. Now lay your sleeping bag out and let's get out of here.'

Jimbo and Dead-eye were sharing the adjoining tent with the medical specialist, Larry, leaving the fourth bed free for the eventual return of their squadron signaller, Trooper Terry Malkin. After picking a bed, each man unstrapped his bergen, removed his sleeping bag, rolled it out on the bed, then picked up his weapon and left the tent, to gather with the others outside the quartermaster's store.

'A pretty basic camp,' Jimbo said to Dead-eye as they crossed the hot, dusty clearing.

'It'll do,' Dead-eye replied, glancing about him with what seemed like a lack of interest, though in fact his grey gaze missed nothing.

'Makes no difference to you, does it, Dead-eye? Just another home from home.'

'That's right,' Dead-eye said quietly.

'What do you think of the new men?'

'They throw up too easily. But now that they've emptied their stomachs, they might be OK.'

'They'll be all right with Brooke and Moody?'

'I reckon so.'

The four men under discussion were already gathered together with the rest of the squadron, waiting to collect the balance of their kit. Already concerned about the weight of his bergen, Ben was relieved to discover that the additional kit consisted only of a mosquito net, insect repellent, extra soap, an aluminium wash-basin, a small battery-operated reading lamp for use in the tent, a pair of ankle-length, rubber-soled desert boots, a DPM (disruptive pattern material) cotton shirt and trousers, and an Arab *shemagh* to protect the nose, mouth and eyes from the sun, sand and insects.

'All right,' Jimbo said when the men, still holding their rifles in one hand, somehow managed to gather the new kit up under their free arm and stood awkwardly in the fading light of the sinking sun, 'carry that lot back to your tents, leave it on your bashas, then go off to the mess tent for dinner. Report to the HQ tent for your briefing at seven p.m. sharp . . . Are you deaf? *Get going!*'

Though dazed from heat and exhaustion, the men hurried back through the mercifully cooling dusk to raise their mosquito nets over the camp-beds. This done, they left their kit under the nets and then made their way gratefully to the mess tent. There they had a replenishing meal of 'compo' sausage, mashed potatoes and beans, followed by rice pudding, all washed down with hot tea.

While eating his meal, Les struck up a conversation with Corporal Jamie McBride of A Squadron, who had just returned from one of the OPs located high in the Radfan, the bare, rocky area to the north of Aden.

'What's it like up there?' Les asked.

'Hot, dusty, wind-blown and fart-boring,' McBride replied indifferently.

'Good to get back down, eh?'

'Right,' the corporal said.

'I note we have a NAAFI tent,' Les said, getting to the subject that concerned him the most. 'Anything in it?'

'Beer and cigarettes,' the weary McBride replied.

'Anything else?'

'Blue magazines and films, whores, whips and chains . . . What do *you* think?'

'Just asking, mate. Sorry.'

Realizing that his fellow soldier was under some stress, Les gulped down the last of his hot tea, waved his hand in farewell, then followed the others out of the mess tent.

'Another fucking briefing,' he complained to Ken as they crossed the clearing to the big HQ tent. 'I need it like a hole in the head.'

'You've already got that,' his mate replied. 'Between one ear and the other there's nothing but a great big empty space.'

'Up yours an' all,' said Les wearily.

2

The men were briefed by their Commanding Officer, Lieutenant-Colonel Patrick 'Paddy' Callaghan, with whom most of them had recently served in Borneo and who was now on his last tour of duty. Wearing his SAS beret with winged-dagger badge, in DPM trousers, desert boots and a long-sleeved cotton shirt, Callaghan was standing on a crude wooden platform, in the large, open-ended HQ tent, in front of a blackboard covered with a map of Yemen. Seated on wooden chairs on the platform were his second in command, Major Timothy Williamson, and the Squadron Commander, Captain Ellsworth. The members of D Squadron were in four rows of metal chairs in front of Callaghan, their backs turned to the opening of the tent, which, as evening fell, allowed a cooling breeze to blow in.

Outside, a Sikorski S-55 Whirlwind was coming in to land before last light, the noise of Bedfords and jeeps was gradually tapering off, NCOs were bawling their last instructions of the day at their troops and Arab workers, and the 25-pounders in the hedgehogs around the perimeter were firing their practice rounds, as they did every evening.

It was a lot of noise to talk against, but after the usual introductory bullshit between himself and his impatient, frisky squadron of SAS troopers, Lieutenant-Colonel Callaghan knuckled down to the business at hand, only stopping periodically to let some noise from outside fade away.

'I might as well be blunt with you,' he began. 'What we're fighting for here is a lost cause created by our lords and masters, who are attempting to leave the colony while retaining a presence here at the same time. Most of you men are experienced enough from similar situations to know that this is impossible, but it's the situation we've inherited and we're stuck with it.'

'We're always stuck with it,' Les said. 'They ram it to us right up the backside and expect us to live with it.'

'Who?' Ben asked, looking puzzled.

'Politicians,' the lance-corporal replied. 'Our lords and masters.'

'All right, you men,' Jimbo said in a voice that sounded like a torrent of gravel. 'Shut up and let Lieutenant-Colonel Callaghan speak.'

'Sorry, boss,' Les said.

'So,' Callaghan continued, 'a bit of necessary historical background.' This led to the customary moans and groans, which the officer endured for a moment, before gesturing for silence. 'I know you don't like it, but it's necessary, so please pay attention.' When they had settled down, he continued: 'A trade centre since antiquity, Aden came under the control of the Turks in the sixteenth century. We Brits established ourselves here by treaty in 1802, used it as a coaling station on the sea route to India, and made it a crown colony in 1937. Because it is located at the southern entrance to the Red Sea, between Arabia and eastern and north-eastern Africa, its main function has always been as a commercial centre for neighbouring states, as well as a refuelling stop for ships. However, it really gained political and commercial importance after the opening of the Suez canal in 1869 and in the present century as a result of the development of the rich oilfields in Arabia and the Persian Gulf. In 1953 an oil refinery was built at Little Aden, on the west side of the bay. Aden became partially self-governing in 1962 and was incorporated into the Federation of South Arabia, the FSA, in 1963, which is when its troubles began.'

Callaghan stopped to take a breath and ensure that he had the men's full attention. Though the usual bored expressions were in evidence, they were all bearing with him.

'Opposition to the British presence here began with the abortive Suez operation of 1956, increased with the emergence of Nasserism via the inflammatory broadcasts of Radio Cairo, and reached its high point with the so-called shotgun marriage of the FSA of 1959–63. This, by the way, linked the formerly feudal sheikdoms lying between Yemen and the coast with the urban area of Aden Colony. Steadily mounting antagonism towards our presence here was in no way eased by the establishment in 1960 of our Middle East Command Headquarters.'

Stopping momentarily to let a recently landed Sikorski whine into silence, Callaghan glanced out through the tent's opening and saw a troop of heavily armed soldiers of the Parachute Regiment marching towards the airstrip, from where they were to fly by Wessex to the mountains of the Radfan. Having served in Malaya and Borneo, Callaghan had a particular fondness for the jungle, but not the desert. Nevertheless, the sight of that darkening, dust-covered ground guarded by hedgehogs bristling with 25-pounders, mortars and machine-guns brought back fond memories of his earliest days with the Regiment in North Africa in 1941. That war had been something of a schoolboy's idea of adventure, with its daring raids in Land Rovers and on foot; this war, though also in desert, albeit mountainous, would be considerably less romantic and more vicious.

'In September 1962,' the CO continued when silence had returned, 'the hereditary ruler of Yemen, the Imam, was overthrown in a left-wing, Army-led coup. This coup was consolidated almost immediately with the arrival of Egyptian troops. The new republican government in Yemen then called on its brothers in the occupied south – in other words, Aden and the Federation – to prepare for revolution and join it in the battle against colonialism. What this led to, in fact, was an undeclared war between two colonial powers – Britain against a Soviet-backed Egypt – with the battleground being the barren, mountainous territory lying between the Gulf of Aden and Saudi Arabia.'

'Is that where we'll be fighting?' Ken asked.

'Most of you in the Radfan; a few in the streets of Aden itself. Aden, however, will be covered in a separate briefing.'

'Right, boss.'

'Initial SAS involvement in this affair took place, with discreet official backing from Whitehall, over the next eight years or so, when the royalist guerrilla army of the deposed Imam was aided by the Saudis and strengthened by the addition of a mercenary force composed largely of SAS veterans. Operating out of secret bases in the Aden Federation, they fought two campaigns simultaneously. On the one hand they were engaged in putting down a tribal uprising in the Radfan, adjoining Yemen; on the other, they were faced with their first battle against highly organized urban terrorism in Aden itself.'

'That's a good one!' Ken said. 'In the mountains of Yemen, a team of SAS veterans becomes part of a guerrilla force. Meanwhile, in Aden, only a few miles south, their SAS mates are suppressing a guerrilla campaign.'

'We are nothing if not versatile,' Callaghan replied urbanely.

'Dead right about that, boss.'

'May I continue?'

'Please do, boss.'

'In July this year Harold Macmillan set 1968 as the year for the Federation's self-government, promising that independence would be accompanied by a continuing British presence in Aden. In short, we wouldn't desert the tribal leaders with whom we'd maintained protection treaties since the last century.'

'However, Egyptian, Yemeni and Adeni nationalists are still bringing weapons, land-mines and explosives across the border. At the same time, the border tribesmen, who view guerrilla warfare as a way of life, are being supplied with money and weapons by Yemen. The engaged battle is for control of the ferociously hot Radfan mountains. There is practically no water there, and no roads at all.'

'But somehow or other,' Dead-eye noted, 'the war is engaged there.'

'Correct. The Emergency was declared in December 1963. Between then and the arrival of A Squadron in April of that year, an attempt to subdue the Radfan was made by a combined force of three Federal Regular Army battalions of Arabs, supported by British tanks, guns and engineers. As anticipated by those who understood the tribal mentality, it failed. True, the FRA battalions did manage to occupy parts of the mountains for a few weeks at a cost of five dead and twelve wounded. Once they withdrew, however – as they had to sooner or later, to go back to the more important task of guarding the frontier – the patient tribesmen returned to their former hill positions and immediately began attacking military traffic on the Dhala Road linking Yemen and Aden – the same road that brought you to this camp.'

'An unforgettable journey!' Ken whispered.

'Diarrhoea and vomit every minute for three hours,' Les replied. 'Will we ever forget it?'

'While they were doing so,' said Callaghan, having heard neither man, 'both Cairo and the Yemeni capital of Sana were announcing the FRA's withdrawal from the Radfan as a humiliating defeat for the imperialists.'

'In other words, we got what we deserved.'

'Quite so, Corporal Brooke.' Though smiling, Callaghan sighed as if weary. 'Given this calamity, the Federal government . . .'

'Composed of . . .?' Dead-eye interjected.

'Tribal rulers and Adeni merchants,' the CO explained.

'More A-rabs,' Ken said. 'Got you, boss.'

'The Federal government then asked for more military aid from the British, who, despite their own severe doubts – believing, correctly, that this would simply make matters worse – put together a mixed force of brigade strength, including a squadron each of RAF Hawker Hunter ground-support aircraft, Shackleton bombers, Twin Pioneer transports and roughly a dozen helicopters. Their task was twofold. First, to bring sufficient pressure to bear on the Radfan tribes and prevent the revolt from spreading. Second, to stop the attacks on the Dhala Road. In doing this, they were not to deliberately fire on areas containing women and children; they were not to shell, bomb or attack villages without dropping leaflets warning the inhabitants and telling them to move out. Once the troops came under fire, however, retaliation could include maximum force.'

'Which gets us back to the SAS,' Dead-eye said.

'Yes, Sergeant. Our job is to give back-up to A Squadron in the Radfan. To this end, we'll start with a twenty-four-hour proving patrol, which will also act as your introduction to the area.'

'We don't need an introduction,' the reckless Corporal Brooke said. 'Just send us up there.'

'You *need* an introduction,' Callaghan insisted. 'You're experienced troopers, I agree, but your experience so far has always been in the jungle – first Malaya, then Borneo. You need experience in desert and jungle navigation and that's what you'll get on this proving patrol. We're talking about pure desert of the kind we haven't worked in since the Regiment was formed in 1941, which excludes most of those present in this tent. Desert as hot as North Africa, but even more difficult because it's mountainous. Limestone, sandstone and igneous rocks. Sand and silt. Lava fields and volcanic remains, criss-crossed with deep wadis. The highland plateau, or *kawr*, has an average height of 6500 feet and peaks rising to 8000 to 9000 feet. The plateau itself is broken up by deep valleys or canyons, as well as the wadis. In short, the terrain is hellishly difficult and presents many challenges.'

'Any training before we leave?' Dead-eye asked.

'Yes. One full day tomorrow. Lay up tonight, kitting out and training tomorrow, then move out at last light the same day. The transport will be 4×4 Bedford three-tonners and Saladin armoured cars equipped with 5.56-inch Bren guns. Enjoy your evening off, gentlemen. That's it. Class dismissed.'

Not wanting to waste a minute of their free time, the men hurried out of the briefing room and raced each other to the makeshift NAAFI canteen at the other side of the camp, where they enjoyed a lengthy booze-up of ice-cold bottled beer. Few went to bed sober.

3

Rudely awakened at first light by Jimbo, whose roar could split mountains, the men rolled out of their bashas, quickly showered and shaved, then hurried through the surprisingly cold morning air, in darkness streaked with rising sunlight, to eat as much as they could in fifteen minutes and return to their sleeping quarters.

Once by their beds, and already kitted out, they had only to collect their bergens, kit and weapons, then hurry back out into the brightening light and cross the clearing, through a gentle, moaning wind and spiralling clouds of dust, to the column of Bedfords and Saladins in the charge of still sleepy drivers from the Royal Corps of Transport. The RCT drivers drank hot tea from vacuum flasks and smoked while the SAS men, heavily burdened with their bergens and other kit, clambered up into the back of the lorries. Meanwhile, the sun was rising like a pomegranate over the distant Radfan, casting an exotic, blood-red light through the shadows on the lower slopes of the mountains, making them look more mysterious than dangerous.

'We should be up there in OPs,' Les complained as they settled into their bench seats in the back of a Bedford. 'Not wasting our bleedin' time with a training jaunt.'

'I don't think we're wasting our time,' Ken replied. 'I believe the boss. All our practical experience has been in Borneo and that won't help us here.'

'I wish *I'd* been in Borneo,' Ben said. 'I bet it was more exotic than this dump.'

'It was,' Larry said ironically. 'Steaming jungle, swamps, raging rivers, snakes, scorpions, lizards, giant spiders, fucking dangerous wild pigs, and head-hunting aboriginals blowing poison darts. Join the SAS and see the world – always travelling first class, of course.'

'At least here we've only got flies and mosquitoes,' Taff said hopefully, swatting the first of the morning's insects from his face.

'*Plus* desert snakes, scorpions, centipedes, stinging hornets, spiders and Arab guerrillas who give you no quarter. Make the most of it!'

Having silenced the new men and given them something to think about, Les grinned sadistically at Ken, then glanced out of the uncovered truck as the Saladin in the lead roared into life. Taking this as their cue, the RCT drivers in the Bedfords switched on their ignition, one after the other, and revved the engines in neutral to warm them up. When the last had done the same, the rearmost Saladin followed suit and the column was ready to move. The Bedfords and the Saladin acting as 'Tail-end Charlie' followed the first armoured car out of the camp, throwing up a column of billowing dust as they headed out into the desert.

The route was through an area scattered with coconut and doum palms, acacias, tall ariatas and tamarisks, the latter looking prettily artificial with their feathery branches. They were, however, few and far between. For the most part, the Bedfords bounced and rattled over parched ground strewn with potholes and stones until, about half an hour later, they arrived at an area bounded by a horseshoe-shaped mountain range. The RCT drivers took the Bedfords up the lower slopes as far as they would go, then stopped to let the men out.

The soldiers were lowering their kit to the ground and clambering down when they saw for the first time that one of the Bedfords had brought up a collection of heavier support weapons, including a 7.62mm GPMG (general-purpose machine-gun), a 7.62mm LMG (light machine-gun) and two 51mm mortars.

'Looks like we're in for a pretty long day,' Les muttered ominously.

'No argument about that,' Ken whispered back at him.

When the Bedfords had turned around and headed back the way they had come, Jimbo gathered his men around him. Dead-eye was standing beside him, holding his L42A1 bolt-action sniper rifle and looking as granite-faced as always.

'The Bedfords,' Jimbo said, 'will come back just before last light. Until then we work.' Pausing to let his words sink in, he waved his hands at the heavy weapons piled up to his left. 'As you can see, we've brought along a nice collection of support weapons. We're going to hike up to the summit of this hill and take that lot with us. I hope you're all feeling fit.' The men moaned and groaned melodramatically, but Jimbo, his crooked lip curling, waved them into silence. 'For most of you,' he said, 'your previous practical experience was in jungle or swamp. A few of us have had experience in the African desert, but even that didn't involve anything like these mountains. You are here, therefore, to adapt to a terrain of mountainous desert, with all that entails.'

'What's that, Sarge?' Ben asked innocently.

'Wind and sand. Potentially damaging dips and holes covered by sand, soil or shrubs. Loose gravel and wind-smoothed, slippery rocks. Ferocious heat. All in all, it calls for a wide variety of survival skills of the kind you haven't so far acquired.' He cast a quick grin at the impassive Dead-eye, then turned back to the men. 'And the first lesson,' he continued, nodding at the summit of the ridge, 'is to get up there, carrying the support weapons and your own kit.' Glancing up automatically, the men were not reassured by what they saw. 'It's pretty steep,' Jimbo said. 'It's also covered with sharp and loose stones. Be careful you don't break an ankle or trip and roll down. And watch out for snakes, scorpions and the like. Even when not poisonous, some of them can inflict a nasty bite . . . So, let's get to it.'

He jabbed his finger at various groups, telling them which weapons and components they were to carry between them. Corporal Ken Brooke, Lance-Corporal Les Moody, and Troopers Ben Riley and Taff Thomas were assigned as the four-man GPMG team. Lance-Corporal Larry Johnson, already burdened with his extra medical kit, got off scot-free.

'We picked the wrong specialist training,' Les complained. 'Johnson gets off with everything.'

'It's not *just* the fact that I'm our medical specialist,' Larry replied, beaming smugly. 'It's because I have charm and personality. It comes natural, see.'

'So does farting from your mouth,' Ken shot back. 'Come on, Les, let's hump this thing.'

The four men tossed for it. Ken lost and became number two: the one who had to hump the GPMG onto his shoulders. Sighing, he unlocked the front legs of the 30lb steel tripod, swung them forward into the high-mount position and relocked them. Then, with Les's assistance, he hauled the tripod up onto his shoulders with the front legs resting on his chest and the rear one trailing backwards over his equally heavy bergen. With the combined weight of the steel tripod, ammunition belts of 7.62mm rounds, and rucksack adding up to 130lb, Ken felt exhausted before he had even started.

'You look like a bleedin' elephant,' Les informed

him. 'I just hope you're as strong.'

'Go fuck yourself,' Ken barked back.

The four-way toss had made Les the gun controller, Ben the observer and Taff the number one, or trigger man. Between them, apart from personal gear, they had to carry two spare barrels weighing 6lb each, a spare return spring, a dial sight, marker pegs, two aiming posts, an aiming lamp, a recoil buffer, a tripod sighting bracket, a spare-parts wallet, and the gun itself.

'This doesn't look easy,' Ben said, glancing nervously up the steep, rocky slope as Les distributed the separate parts of the GPMG.

'It's a fucking sight easier than humping that tripod,' Les informed him, 'so count yourself lucky.'

'Move out!' Jimbo bawled.

The whole squad moved out in single file, spread well apart as they would be on a real patrol, with the men who were carrying the support weapons leaning forward even more than the others. The climb was both backbreaking and dangerous, for each man was forced to navigate the steep slope while looking out for sharp or loose stones that could either break an ankle or roll from under his feet, sending him tumbling back down the mountain. In this, they were helped neither by the sheer intensity of the heat nor the growing swarms of buzzing flies and whining mosquitoes attracted by their copious sweat.

Almost driven mad by the mosquitoes, the men's attempts to swat them away came as near to unbalancing them as did the loose, rolling stones. More than one man found himself suddenly twisting sideways, dragged down by his own kit or support weapon, after he had swung his hand too violently at his tormentors. Saved by the helping hand of the man coming up behind him, he might then find himself stepping on a loose stone, which would roll like a log beneath him, sending him violently forwards or backwards; or he would start slipping on loose gravel as it slid away underfoot.

By now the breathing of every man was agonized and not helped by the fact that the air was filled with the dust kicked up by their boots or the tumbling stones and sliding gravel. The dust hung around them in clouds, making them choke and cough, and limiting visibility to a dangerous degree, eventually reducing the brightening sunlight to a distant, silvery haze. To make matters worse, each man's vision was even more blurred when his own stinging sweat ran into his eyes.

The climb of some 1500 feet took them two

hellish hours but led eventually to the summit of the ridge. This had different, more exotic trees scattered here and there along its otherwise rocky, parched, relatively flat ground, and overlooked a vast plain of sand, silt and polished lava.

Throwing themselves gratefully to the ground, the men were about to open their water bottles when Jimbo stopped them. 'No,' he said. 'Put those bottles away.'

'But, Sarge . . .' Taff began in disbelief.

'Shut up and listen to me,' Jimbo replied. 'As you've all just discovered, the heat in the mountains can wring the last drop of sweat out of you much quicker than you can possibly imagine – no matter how fit you are. If you allow this to happen, you'll soon be dehydrated, exhausted, and if you don't get water in time, dead of thirst.'

'So let us drink our water,' Les said, shaking his bottle invitingly.

'No,' the sergeant replied. 'Your minimum daily intake of water should be two gallons a day, but on a real operation we won't be able to resup by chopper because this would give away the position of the OP. For this reason, you'll have to learn to conserve the water you carry inside your body by minimal movement during the day, replenishing your water bottles each night by sneaking down to the nearest stream.'

'So we should ensure that the OP site is always near a stream,' Ben said, 'and not on top of a high ridge or mountain like this.'

'Unfortunately, no. It's because they're aware of the constant need for water that the rebel tribesmen always check the areas around streams for our presence. Therefore, the site for your OP should be chosen for the view it gives of enemy supply routes, irrespective of its proximity to water. You then go out at night and search far and wide for your water, no matter how difficult or dangerous that task may be.'

'Sounds like a right pain to me,' Ken said.

'It is. I should point out here, to make you feel even worse – but to make you even more careful – that even after dark the exertion of foraging for water can produce a dreadful thirst that can make you consume half of what you collect on the way back. In short, these mountains make the jungles of Borneo seem like sheer luxury. And that's no exaggeration, believe me.'

'I believe you,' Les said, still clutching his water bottle. 'Can I have a drink now?'

'No. That water has to last until tonight and you've only brought one bottle each.'

'But we're all dying of thirst,' Ken complained.

Jimbo pointed to the trees scattered sparsely along the otherwise parched summit of the ridge. 'That,' he said, indicating a tree covered in a plum-like fruit, 'is the jujube. Its fruit is edible and will also quench your thirst . . . And those,' he continued, pointing to the bulbous plants hanging from the branches of a tree that looked like a cactus, 'are euphorbia. If you pierce them with a knife, or slice the top off, you'll find they contain a drinkable juice that's a bit like milk.'

'So when *can* we drink our water?' Taff pleaded.

'When you've put up your bashas, cleaned and checked your weapons, put in a good morning's firing practice and are eating your scran. Meanwhile, you can eat and drink from those trees.'

'Bashas?' Ken glanced down the slopes of the ridge at the barren, sunlit plain below, running out for miles to more distant mountains. 'What are we putting bashas up for? We're only here for one day.'

'They're to let you rest periodically from the sun and keep you from getting sunstroke. So just make triangular shelters with your poncho sheets. Now get to it.'

The men constructed their triangular shelters by standing two upright sticks with Y-shaped tops about six feet apart, running a length of taut cord between them, draping the poncho sheet over the cord, with one short end, about 18 inches long, facing away from the sun and the other running obliquely all the way to the ground, forming a solid wall. Both sides of the poncho sheet were then made secure by the strings stitched into them and tied to wooden pegs hammered into the soil. Dried grass and bracken were then strewn on the ground inside the 'tent' and finally the sleeping bag was rolled out to make a crude but effective mattress.

When the bashas had been constructed, the men were allowed to rest from the sun for fifteen minutes. Though it was still not yet nine a.m. local time, the sun's heat was already intense.

Once rested, the men were called out to dismantle, clean of dust and sand, oil and reassemble the weapons, a task which, with the dust blowing continuously, was far from easy. Jimbo then made them set the machine-guns up on the ridge and aim at specific targets on the lower slopes of the hill: mostly clumps of parched shrubs and trees. The rest of the morning was spent in extensive practice with the support weapons, first using the tripods, then firing both the heavy GPMG and the LMG from the hip with the aid of a sling.

The GPMG, in particular, had a violent backblast that almost punched some of the men off their feet. But in the end they all managed to hold it and hit their targets when standing. The noise of the machine-guns was shocking in the desert silence and reverberated eerily around the encircling mountains.

Two hours later, when weapons practice was over, the men were again made to dismantle, clean, oil and reassemble the weapons, which were then wrapped in cloth to protect them from the dust and sand. By now labouring beneath an almost overhead sun, the men were soaked in sweat, sunburnt and gasping with thirst, and so were given another ten-minute break, which they spent in their bashas, sipping water and drawing greedily on cigarettes. The break over, they were called out again, this time by the fearsome Sergeant Parker, for training with their personal weapons.

Dead-eye's instruction included not only the firing of the weapons, at which he was faultless, but the art of concealment on exposed ridges, scrambling up and down the slopes on hands and elbows, rifle held horizontally across the face. The posture adopted for this strongly resembled the 'leopard crawl' used for the crossing of the dreaded entrails ditch during 'Sickener One' at Bradbury Lines, Hereford. It was less smelly here, but infinitely more dangerous than training in Britain, as the men had to crawl over sharp, burning-hot rocks that could not only cut skin and break bones, but also could be hiding snakes, scorpions or poisonous spiders.

More than one man was heard to cry out and jump up in shock as he came across something hideous on the ground where he was crawling. But he was shouted back down by the relentless Jimbo, who was always watching on the sidelines as Dead-eye led them along the ridge on their bellies.

'Is that what you'd do if you were under fire?' Jimbo would bawl. 'See a spider and jump up like an idiot to get shot to pieces? Get your face back in the dirt, man, and don't get up again until I tell you!'

While some of the men resented having firing practice when most of them had not only done it all before but had even been blooded in real combat, what they were in fact learning was how to deal with an unfamiliar terrain. Dead-eye also taught them how to time their shots for when the constantly swirling dust and sand had blown away long enough for them to get a clear view of the target. Finally, they were learning to fire accurately into the sunlight by estimating the position of the target by its shadow, rather than by trying to look directly at it. By lunchtime, when they had mastered this new skill, they were thoroughly exhausted and, in many cases, bloody and bruised from the sharp, burning rocks. They were suffering no less from the many bites inflicted by the whining mosquitoes.

'I look like a bleedin' leper,' Ben complained as he rubbed more insect repellent over his badly bitten wrists, hands and face, 'with all these disgusting mosquito bites.'

'Not as bad as leeches,' Les informed him smugly as he sat back, ignoring his mosquito bites, to have a smoko. 'Those little buggers sucked us dry in Borneo. Left us bloodless.'

'By the time they finish with us,' Taff said, 'you could throw us in a swamp filled with leeches and they'd all die of thirst. I'm fucking bloodless, I tell you!'

In the relative cool of his poncho tent, Ken removed his water bottle from his mouth, licked his lips, then lay back with his hands behind his head and closed his eyes.

'If you go to sleep you'll feel like hell when you wake up,' Larry solemnly warned him.

'I'm not sleeping,' Ken replied. 'I'm just resting my eyes. They get tired from the sunlight.'

'Getting hotter and brighter every minute,' Larry said. 'It'll soon be like hell out there.'

'We'll all get there eventually,' Les told him, 'so we'd better get used to it.'

'Amen to that,' Ken said.

Immediately after lunch they rolled out of the shade of their bashas to return to the baking oven of the ridge, where, although dazzled by the brilliance of the sky, they took turns to set up, fire and dismantle the 51mm mortar. It weighed a mere 13lb, had no sophisticated sights or firing mechanism, and was essentially just a simple tube with a fixed base plate. Conveniently, it could be carried over the shoulder with its ammunition distributed among the rest of the patrol. The user had only to wedge the base plate into the ground, hold the tube at the correct angle for the estimated range, then drop a bomb into the top of the tube. Though first-shot accuracy was relatively difficult with such a crude weapon, a skilled operator could zero in on a target with a couple of practice shots, then fire up to eight accurate rounds a minute. Most of the men were managing to do this within the first hour, and were gratified to see the explosions tearing up the flat plain below, forming spectacular columns of spiralling smoke, sand and dust.

Even though they had protected their faces with their *shemaghs*, they were badly burnt by the sun, on the road to dehydration, and very close to complete exhaustion when, in the late afternoon, Jimbo and Dead-eye called a halt to the weapons training and said they would now hike back down the hill to the waiting Bedfords.

Believing they were about to return to the base camp, the men enthusiastically packed up their bashas, humped the support weapons back onto their bruised shoulders, strapped their heavy bergens to their backs, picked up their personal weapons and hiked in single file back down the hill. If anything, this was even more dangerous than the uphill climb, for they were now growing dizzy with exhaustion and were forced to hike in the direction of the sliding gravel and stones, which tended to make the descent dangerously fast. Luckily, they were close to the bottom when the first man, Taff, let out a yelp as the gravel slid under his feet, sending him backwards into the dirt, to roll the rest of the way down in a billowing cloud of dust and sand. He was picking himself up when two others followed the same way, either tripping or sliding on loose gravel, then losing their balance before rolling down the hill. The rest of the group managed to make it down without incident, though by now all of them were utterly exhausted and soaking in sweat.

'Right,' Dead-eye said. 'Hump those support weapons back up onto the Bedford, then gather around me and Sergeant Ashman.

The men did as they were told, then tried to get their breath back while wiping the sweat from their faces and, in some cases, vainly trying to wring their shirts and trousers dry. They were still breathing painfully and scratching their many insect bites when they gathered around the two sergeants.

Any hopes they might have held of heading back to the relative comforts of the base camp were dashed when Jimbo gave them a lecture on desert navigation, much of it based on his World War Two experiences with the Long Range Desert Group. The lecture took an hour and, to the men's dismay, included a hike of over a mile, fully kitted, out into the blazing-hot desert. This was for the purpose of demonstrating how to measure distance by filling one trouser pocket with small stones and transferring a stone from that pocket to the other after each hundred steps.

'The average pace,' Jimbo explained, 'is 30 inches, so each stone represents approximately 83 yards. So if you lose your compass or, as is just as likely, simply have no geographical features by which to assess distance, you can easily calculate the distance you're marching or have marched by multiplying the number of stones transferred by eighty-three. That gives the distance in yards.'

Though the exhausted men had been forced to walk all this distance in the burning, blinding sunlight, they had been followed by one of the Bedfords. Fondly imagining that this had come out to take them back, they had their hopes dashed again when some small shovels, a couple of radios and various pieces of wiring were handed down to them by the driver.

Jimbo and Dead-eye, both seemingly oblivious to the heat, then took turns at showing the increasingly shattered men how to scrape shallow lying-up positions, or LUPs, out of the sand and check them for buried scorpions or centipedes. Dead-eye was in charge of this particular lesson and, when he had finished scraping out his own demonstration LUP, he made the exhausted men do the same, kicking the sand back into the scrapes when they failed to do it correctly and making them start all over again. When one of the men collapsed during this exercise, the inscrutable sergeant patiently aroused him by splashing cold water on his face, then made him complete his scrape, which amazingly the man did, swaying groggily in the heat.

A short break was allowed for a limited intake of water, then Jimbo gave them a lesson in special desert signalling, covering Morse code, special codes and call-sign signals; use of the radios and how to clean them of sand; recognition of radio 'black spots' caused by the peculiar atmospheric conditions of the mountainous desert; setting up standard and makeshift antennas; and the procedure for calling in artillery fire and air strikes, which would be their main task when in their OPs in the Radfan.

Most of the men were already rigid with exhaustion, dehydration and mild sunstroke when Jimbo took another thirty minutes to show them how to make an improvised compass by variously stroking a sewing needle in one direction against a piece of silk and suspending it in a loop of thread so that it pointed north; by laying the needle on a piece of paper or bark and floating it on water in a cup or mess tin; or by stropping a razor-blade against the palm of the hand and, as with the sewing needle, suspending it from a piece of thread to point north.

Mercifully, the sun was starting to sink when he showed them various methods of purifying and conserving water; then, finally, how to improvise water-filtering systems and crude cookers out of old oil drums and biscuit tins.

'And that's it,' he said, studying their glazed faces with thinly veiled amusement. 'Your long day in the desert is done. Now it's back to base camp.'

'Which you can only do,' Dead-eye told them, 'if you manage to leg it back to the Bedfords.'

'Aw, Jesus!' Larry said without thinking. 'Can't we all pile into *that* Bedford and let it take us back to the others?'

'That Bedford is for the equipment only,' Dead-eye told him. 'Besides, you men have to get used to the desert, and this last hike is all part of your training. Now get going.'

Relieved, at least, of the heavy support weapons, the men heaved their packed bergens and other kit onto their aching backs, turned to face the sinking sun, and walked in a daze back to the other Bedfords. Two almost collapsed on the way and had to be helped by the others, which slowed them down considerably; but just before last light they all made it and practically fell into the trucks, which bounced and rattled every yard of the half-hour journey back to the camp.

Battered and bruised, covered in insect bites, smeared with sweat-soaked sand and dust, hungry and unbelievably thirsty, they collapsed on their steel beds in the tents and could hardly rouse themselves even to shower, shave and head off to the mess tent. Indeed, most of them were still lying there, almost catatonic, when Jimbo did a round of the tents, bawling repeatedly that those not seen having a decent meal would be RTU'd – returned to their original unit. Though they all cursed the SAS, so great was the shame attaching to this fate that they rolled off their beds, attended to their ablutions, dressed in clean clothes and marched on aching legs to the mess tent to have their scran and hot tea. Somewhat restored, they then made for the NAAFI tent to get drunk on cold beer. Finally, after what seemed like the longest day of their lives, they surrendered to sleep like children.

4

The men began their proving patrol the following evening, loading up the Bedfords just before last light with their individual kit and support weapons. For their personal weapons, old Borneo hands like Ken Brooke and Les Moody still favoured the M16 5.56mm assault rifle, which accepted a bayonet and could fire a variety of grenades although it was not so good in desert conditions because of its poor long-range accuracy and tendency to jam up with sand.

Dead-eye, said to be the best shot in the Regiment, preferred the L42A1 7.62mm bolt-action sniper rifle, which had a telescopic sight, was robust and reliable, and had good stopping power at long range, making it ideal for sniping from high mountain ridges. While some of the other men likewise favoured this weapon, most of them had been issued with the L1A1 SLR, which had a twenty-round box magazine, could be used on single shot or automatic, and was notable for its long-range accuracy.

The support weapons included the 7.62mm GPMG; the L4A4 LMG, which was actually a Bren gun modified to accommodate the 7.62mm round; the 51mm mortar with base plate, its ammunition distributed among the men; and a couple of US M79 grenade-launchers, which could be fired from the shoulder. All of these weapons were hauled up into the back of the Bedfords, then followed in by the men, making for very cramped conditions.

'Here we go again,' Larry said, moving his head to avoid the A41 tactical radio set being swung into a more comfortable position on the shoulders of the operator, Lance-Corporal Derek Dickerson. 'Another luxurious journey on the Orient Express!'

'It's nice to have these paid holidays,' Ben said, twisting sideways to avoid being hit by Larry's shoulder-slung wooden medical box. 'It makes me feel so important.'

As the men tried to find comfortable positions on the benches along the sides of the lorries, the sun was sinking low over the distant mountains, casting a blood-red light through the shadows. At the same time, a Sikorski S-55 Whirlwind was roaring into life on the nearby landing pad, whipping up billowing clouds of dust as it prepared to lift off.

'Where the fuck is *he* going?' Les asked in his usual peevish way as he settled into his bench seat in the back of the Bedford.

'The RAF airstrip at Habilayn,' answered Ken. 'It's only a couple of minutes by chopper from here.'

'If it's so close,' Taff asked, 'why couldn't we be flown to the drop zone instead of going by lorry, which will take a lot longer?'

'And make you throw up,' Larry chuckled.

'Ha, ha,' Taff retorted, now used to their bullshit and also determined never to throw up again.

'Because the DZ overlooks an Arab village,' Ken explained, 'and an insertion by chopper would be seen by every rebel in the area.'

'Besides,' Larry added sardonically, 'an insertion by chopper would be too *easy*. We have to do it the *hard* way.'

Nodding their agreement, united by their pride, the men all glanced out from the uncovered Bedford as the lead Saladin roared into life. Taking this as their cue, as they had done the day before, the RCT drivers revved up with a frightful din. When the last of the Bedfords had done the same, the column moved off.

Even as the first Saladin was starting forward, the Whirlwind which had taken off a few minutes earlier was descending towards the horizon in the opposite direction, clearly heading for Habilayn.

'They have it fucking easy,' Les said, meaning the RAF pilots. 'Sitting on their fat arses on soft seats, well out of range of enemy fire. A cushy life, those bastards have.'

'I wouldn't say that,' Ken replied. 'A hell of a lot of them get shot out of the skies. They certainly lost a good few choppers and their crews in Malaya and Borneo.'

'Yeah,' Les agreed grudgingly. 'I just wish I was up there right now, instead of in this bloody lorry.'

'I'd rather be in a Bedford than in a chopper,' Larry said with conviction. 'They're death-traps. At least we can get out and run, which gives you some kind of chance.'

'A really heartening conversation we're having here,' Ken said with a crooked grin. 'If you can say any more to boost our morale, I'd be delighted to hear it.'

'Our Father, which art in heaven . . .' Les began.

'Go shove it!' Ken said, laughing.

The column followed the same route it had taken the previous day, heading along the Dhala Road, first passing between rows of handsome coconut and doum palms, then past more thinly scattered acacias, ariatas and tamarisks, all of which looked too pretty to be real. After thinning out gradually, the trees eventually disappeared altogether, vapourizing into the starlit dusk over an immense, flat plain in which nothing of interest could be seen, other than the darkening mountains towards which they were heading.

The patrol eventually came to the area bounded by a horseshoe-shaped mountain range where, the previous day, they had suffered so much, but this time they did not stop. Instead they kept going until, a good two hours later, now mercifully in the cool of the moonlit evening, they arrived at the lower slopes of the mountains of the Radfan. There the column of vehicles ground to a halt and formed a defensive laager, with the 76mm QF guns and .30-inch machine-guns of the Saladins covering opposite directions.

The laager completed, the SAS troops disembarked, adjusted their webbing and the shoulder straps of their bergens, then picked up their weapons and fell into a diamond formation that was spread out across the lower slopes of the mountains, away from the laager. Preferred by the SAS in open country and on 'tabs' by night, this marching formation combined the best features of both file and single-file formations, allowing maximum fire-power to be focused on the front. At the same time, as with the other formations, it was designed to give ample protection to the rear and both sides as well.

Dead-eye, nominally the patrol commander, or PC, had chosen to be well out on point, as lead scout, covering the arc of fire immediately in front of the patrol. Jimbo, his fellow sergeant and second in command, or 2IC, was bringing up the rear as Tail-end Charlie, regularly swinging around to face the opposite direction to that in which the men were marching, covering the arc of fire to the rear and ensuring that the patrol had no blind spots. Lance-Corporal Derek Dickerson, humping the all-important A41 tactical radio, was well protected in the middle of the file. The other men, well strung out, were covering firing arcs to the left and right. While Dead-eye and Jimbo had the most demanding jobs, the other men also suffered great stress, because of the need for constant vigilance during the hike.

Dead-eye as PC and Jimbo as 2IC were both compelled to carry items additional to their normal kit, including more detailed maps, navigational equipment, passive night-vision goggles (PNGs), a spare short-range radio, and a SARBE (surface-to-air rescue beacon) for emergency communication with support or extraction aircraft. In addition, Dead-eye, as lead scout, was carrying special equipment for dealing with land-mines and booby-traps; wire-cutters and hessian for clearing barbed-wire entanglements; and an M23 grenade-launcher, which could be fixed to the barrel of his sniper rifle.

The march into the mountains was no less demanding than the rehearsal of the previous day. Even the lower, flatter slopes were filled with wadis, dried-up seasonal watercourses into which the men had to descend before climbing out again. The windswept plains were a treacherous combination of lava remains, soft sand and silt. Eventually leaving the lowlands behind, they were confronted by highlands of limestone, sandstone and igneous rocks.

Though not forced to endure the relentless heat

of day, they suffered its opposite: air so cold that they were breathing steam. Frost doubled the danger normally presented by loose stones and gravel. Dead-eye could see with great clarity through the eerie green glow of his PNGs, but the other men were dependent on the moonlight, which, reflecting off the ice and frost, rendered the darkness around these gleaming patches almost pitch-black. Nevertheless, they gradually adjusted to the darkness, and were soon on the level ground at the summit of the lowest of the series of ridges.

Not wanting the men to be silhouetted against the skyline, Dead-eye led them down the other side of the ridge, towards the deeper darkness far below. They would have to cross four ridges to get to their chosen OP, which was above an Arab village, and had to do it the hard way, by keeping out of sight. This meant marching up and down the sheer slopes instead of taking the path that circled around the ridges and joined them all. It would be a long, arduous march.

For many of the men, this hike from one peak to the other reminded them of 'cross-graining the bukets' in Malaya – marching from one summit to the next. The new men, on the other hand, were reminded of their hellish forced march across the Pen-y-Fan, the highest peak in the Brecon Beacons, at the culmination of Test Week during Selection Training. Known as the 'Fan Dance', it was probably the most demanding of all the tests undergone by SAS recruits – and this trek from one summit to another was certainly no easier.

But they kept at it, leaning forward as they ascended, slipping and sliding as they descended, whipped constantly by an icy wind and marching with great care in the deceptive moonlight. If they were soon feeling physically exhausted, they were also rendered psychologically so by the need for constant alertness as they strained to see by the moonlight, often mistaking shifting shadows and wind-blown foliage for the stealthy movements of enemy snipers. The relief, when they discovered their mistake, was often as brutal on their nervous systems as the fear that they were about to be shot at.

In fact, the only living creatures they saw on the mountains other than themselves were the odd ibex or oryx. Surprisingly, people did live here. In the valleys an occasional stone tower house or mud-brick hovel with stone foundations could be seen, usually standing alone, though some were in walled hamlets on the edge of meagre patches of cultivated land.

When such dwellings were seen, Dead-eye would give the patrol a rest while he entered details of the area in his logbook, including the exact location and size of the houses, hamlets or cultivated lands. Had any enemy troop movements been seen, he would have entered those as well.

Reaching their high ridge location before first light, the patrol divided into two groups, then constructed two temporary OPs spaced well apart and overlooking an Arab hamlet in the valley below. The OPs were of the star formation, with four 'legs' shaped like a cross: one for the sentry, one for the observer, and the other two serving as rest bays in which the men lay on their waterproof ponchos. To prevent the OPs being observed from the air, they were covered with camouflage netting strewn with stones, dust and any scrap of foliage to be found on the surrounding ground. By dawn, when the OPs were finished, the men designated as observers were doing just that with the aid of binoculars, while the others ate a breakfast of biscuits, chocolate and cold water. No fires could be lit because the smoke would have given away their position, so they continued to freeze.

In fact, the climb had taken so long, in such bitterly cold conditions, that the men had forgotten just how hot it could be during the day. They found out within the hour, when the sun melted the frost on the rocks, the flies and mosquitoes returned in force, and a heat haze shimmered up from the ground. By mid-morning the sun was fierce; by noon it was close to unbearable and made worse for the men because of the need to remain cooped up under the low-hanging camouflage netting.

The hamlet they were observing was believed to be a centre for Yemeni guerrillas, though none were seen throughout that long day. A few Arab men went out to till the small, sparse field, veiled women washed clothes around what looked like a desert spring, and children ran about between barking dogs and animals. None of the men looked remotely like guerrillas and no weapons were to be seen anywhere.

By late afternoon, it was clear to Dead-eye that if guerrillas had ever been in the hamlet, they were long gone by now. He entered this observation in his logbook, then turned to Ken and whispered: 'We're only supposed to spend one day here, which is just as well. There's nothing down there. We'll break up the OPs and move out under cover of darkness.'

'I can't wait,' the corporal replied without a trace of irony.

The rest of the day passed slowly, forcing the men to draw on the patience they had learnt back at Hereford. While none of them lost their concentration completely – they had been trained too rigorously for that – each had his own way of distracting himself from the tedium.

Dead-eye and Jimbo, the two most experienced men in the patrol, had the most concentration and needed little distraction other than repeatedly going over in their minds every detail of the patrol: whose turn it was for sentry duty or rest; every detail of the landscape and any sign of movement on it; any visible activity in the settlement below; the position of the sun in its sinking and the exact time of last light. Jimbo watched and listened while Dead-eye scribbled periodically in his logbook.

The young signaller, Derek Dickerson, was kept busy constantly monitoring the various wavebands on his radio and sending encoded messages from Dead-eye back to the base camp. However, while not thus engaged, his mind tended to wander to thoughts of his old mates back in 264 Signals

Squadron, Royal Corps of Signals, as well as to various girlfriends.

Also easily distracted by vivid memories of his love life was the patrol's medical specialist, Lance-Corporal Larry Johnson, formerly of the Royal Army Medical Corps (RAMC) and the same age as Dickerson. Larry was particularly distracted by thoughts of his latest and most serious girlfriend, Cathy Atkinson, a nineteen-year-old bank clerk whom he had met through a group of friends at a pub in his home town of Paignton.

If Larry was lying belly down in the OP's sentry leg he was fully concentrating, but the minute he had nothing to do he would find himself silently singing pop songs while aching with longing for Cathy. He choked up, in particular, at recalling Roy Orbison's *It's Over*, even though his affair with Cathy had hardly begun. Convinced that he was in love with her and could not live without her, Larry was nevertheless angered by the way in which she could repeatedly impinge on his thoughts, even when he was trying so hard to concentrate. It did not seem like a manly affliction and caused him to doubt himself.

Lance-Corporal Les Moody, on the other hand, was experienced enough to let his mind wander when tedium threatened yet regain full concentration when it was called for. Also keen on pop music, his head was presently filled with *A Hard Day's Night*, which had a certain aptness under these conditions. Indeed, as Les well knew, the only reason this war in Aden was not being reported by the British press was that Fleet Street was presently obsessed with the Beatles, virtually to the exclusion of all else.

Though only twenty-five, Les looked a lot older than the other lance-corporals, mainly because of his badly scarred left eye, broken nose and slightly twisted lower lip, all of which had been gained in various fist-fights in the pubs of Southend. Formerly of the 3rd Battalion, Royal Green Jackets, Les had served in Malaya and Borneo. Between those engagements he had married a local girl, Alison, on impulse – she had practically begged him, he liked to think – and fathered two sons. Though he treated his family decently during his few visits home, he had little interest in domesticity and preferred to be doing a man's work with the Regiment. He thought of Alison and the boys occasionally, but mostly dwelt on his occasional flings with other women, his days at the races – he was an inveterate gambler – various riotous evenings with his mates, and the tragedies and triumphs of his two previous campaigns with the SAS.

Les's good friend, Corporal Ken Brooke, when not on sentry duty, observing the Arab hamlet and the surrounding terrain with the keen eye of the thorough professional, would let his thoughts roam over a fairly wide spectrum. His thoughts roamed from his wife, of whom he was very fond, his three children – two girls and a boy – whom he adored, to the many interests he needed to keep himself busy, being a man of rich imagination and too much energy. Born and raised in Minehead, Ken was a keen wildlife photographer who, when on leave, spent many hours in Somerset's Brendon Hills and the Exmoor National Park, photographing ponies, wild red deer, foxes, rabbits and badgers. He also enjoyed fishing, hiking, train-spotting and collecting stamps, all of which he thought about while keeping alert for possible enemy movements on the landscape or unusual activities in the hamlet below. Though less bored than the others, he was nevertheless glad to see the sun go down, signalling as it did that it would soon be time to leave.

When darkness came, bringing with it the cold,

Dead-eye passed the word along to the other men that the OPs were to be carefully dismantled and all traces of them removed. When this had been done, in complete silence, he used hand signals to lead them away from the ridge, back down the way they had come, into a forbidding, rocky valley of moonlit darkness. They were temporarily protected from the wind there, but once they began climbing the opposite slope, it struck them with unexpected force, at once freezing them and almost bowling them over. Some of them were now grateful for the ruthless training they had undergone on the Brecon Beacons, realizing that without it they would not have survived this particular exercise.

Four hours later, when they were nearing the Dhala Road, dizzy with the cold and exhaustion, they were shocked to hear the sound of rifle fire and feel bullets zipping past their heads.

Marching in a diamond formation, they were able to drop to the ground and return the fire with a sustained fusillade from their personal weapons. Up ahead, they could see the spitting flames of the enemy rifles, which fortunately were not supported by machine-guns. Bullets stitched the earth around them and ricocheted off boulders. The shadowy figures of men ran back and forth up at the front, some gesticulating and shouting.

Out ahead, on point, but now belly down on the ground and about to fire his bolt-action sniper rifle, Dead-eye stopped himself just in time when he heard what he thought was English being shouted by the shadowy figures. Startled, he lowered his weapon, listened more carefully, and realized that he and his men were engaged in a fire-fight with soldiers of the British Army.

Raising his right hand, he indicated that the men behind him should stop firing, which they did only gradually, those at the back not being able to see him. When the hostile fire also tapered off tentatively, Dead-eye bawled: 'We're English! Stop firing! SAS!'

'Oh, Christ!' someone called out from the other side.

'D Squadron, 22 SAS!' Dead-eye called out. 'Sergeant Richard Parker!'

'Sergeant Shaun Clarke, Irish Guards. Stop firing, you men!'

As the last of the 'enemy' gunshots tapered off, Sergeant Clarke, his face blackened with 'cam' cream, stood up, shaking his head in disbelief and grinning ruefully. While their respective men also clambered sheepishly to their feet, wiping frost off their uniforms, Dead-eye and Clarke approached one another like guilty schoolboys. Even Dead-eye, normally impassive, was looking very self-conscious.

'Well,' he said, stopping in front of Sergeant Clarke, 'that was a close one.'

'*Very* close!' the other man replied, grinning. 'Sorry about that, but we weren't told there were friendly forces in the hills. We're just out on a proving patrol.'

'So are we – and *we* weren't told there were friendly forces in the area.'

'Lack of communication,' Clarke said. 'A right bloody cock-up. Anyone hurt?'

'No.'

'Good.' Clarke practically sighed with relief, then nodded down the ridge that led into a pool of deeper darkness. 'Are you heading back now?'

'Yes. Our RV's down there.'

'Lucky you. We've just started. But this little confrontation should give my boys something to think about. Keep them on their toes.' He grinned again and held out his hand. 'Well, best wishes, Sergeant.'

Dead-eye grinned as well, shaking Clarke's hand.

'Same to you,' he said, then marched back to his men, most of whom were grinning broadly at him. 'You men find this amusing?' he asked them. When they grinned even more broadly, he said firmly: 'Well, it's not. We almost shot up our own men and that's no laughing matter. We came out on a proving patrol, we're bringing back nothing, and now we've got to report a potentially fatal encounter with our own men. This patrol has been a bloody disaster, so wipe those grins off your faces.'

The men glanced uneasily at one another before adjusting their webbing, checking their weapons, and starting the rest of the march to the rendezvous point, where they found the Saladins and Bedfords still grouped in a laager. Gratefully, the men loaded their weapons and other kit into the lorries, climbed in themselves, and settled down for the two-hour drive back to base. They all felt a bit foolish.

5

'Actually, it wasn't that bad,' Lieutenant-Colonel Callaghan said reassuringly to Dead-eye and Jimbo in the HQ tent at Thumier. 'Apart from almost being shot up by the Irish Guards – and they fired first, after all! – your patrol did all it was asked to do. I blame the shoot-out on a lack of communication between us and the greens. This time it was the fault of we Ruperts, so you've no need to worry.'

By 'greens' he meant the green-uniformed regular Army, while the word 'Ruperts' was normally used mockingly by the other ranks of the SAS to describe their own officers. In this case, the CO was using the terms as a means of light-heartedly taking the blame for the fire-fight with the Irish Guards. Dead-eye, who had always admired Callaghan, respected him even more for this.

They were facing each other across Callaghan's cluttered desk, which was actually a trestle table. The many papers and maps on the table were pinned down with stones to keep them from blowing away in the hot wind that gusted in from outside. At just after noon, the air in the tent was stifling and made all of them sweat.

'So when do we go back to the Radfan for some real work?' Dead-eye asked him.

Callaghan smiled and held his hand up like a traffic cop. 'Hold on there, Dead-eye. It *is* true that we intend mounting a major operation against the rebels in the Radfan, but we can't do it just yet.'

'Why?' Jimbo asked.

'According to the green slime,' Callaghan replied, referring to the Intelligence Corps, 'a couple of Yemeni-trained agents are perverting our intelligence and have to be dealt with before we can move again. Apparently these agents, who we thought were working for British Intelligence in Aden, are actually double agents, alternately giving us false information and passing on to the enemy information about our activities in the area. Either way, their treachery has led to many failed missions and casualties. So before we go back to the Radfan, we have to get rid of those men.'

'Why us?' Dead-eye asked. 'That's the job of the men based in Aden.'

'Normally, yes, but the way these double agents are operating indicates that they have many friends in our intelligence community. Should their activities be terminated by Intelligence hit men, or one of our Keeni-Meeni teams, the identity of those who do the job will almost certainly be revealed, endangering future operations by that unit. It is therefore felt that outsiders not known to that community should do it.'

'So if we're killed,' Jimbo said tartly, 'we can't be identified. If, on the other hand, we're captured and tortured into revealing our identity, the job still can't be traced back to the greens operating daily out of Aden.'

'Precisely,' Callaghan said.

Jimbo and Dead-eye glanced at one another, raising their eyebrows.

'Very nice for the greens,' Jimbo said, turning back to Callaghan. 'Not so nice for us, boss.'

Callaghan simply sighed and spread his hands in the air. 'What can I say? So do you want it or not?'

'What exactly is it?' Dead-eye asked. 'We've heard about the Keeni-Meeni teams in Aden. Is that what we'll be?'

'Temporarily,' the CO said. 'You'll be shown how to dress and act like an Arab, trained in the special 'double tap', then sent into the highly dangerous Crater and Sheikh Othman districts to do the job without backup or identification in the event of failure. Naturally it's a volunteer job.'

'Naturally,' Dead-eye replied sardonically.

'Yes or no?'

'Yes,' Dead-eye and Jimbo replied as one.

Callaghan smiled and placed his hands back on the table. 'Good. I knew you'd say that. Now go pack your kit, then meet me at the landing pad. We'll be lifted out on the Whirlwind and be away for two days.'

'Sounds good,' Dead-eye said. He and Jimbo pushed back their chairs and left the tent, stepping into the furnace of the midday heat. The sunlight temporarily dazzled them, making them blink and squint as they crossed the clearing between the HQ tent and the smaller tents being used as bashas. When they had adjusted to the searing brightness, they saw that the 25-pounders, 3-inch mortars and Browning 0.5-inch machine-guns in the hedgehogs spread out along the camp's perimeter were silhouetted starkly against the white haze of the sky and appeared unreal in the shimmering heat.

As usual, a lot of men, some from A Squadron, some from D, were lining up at the large mess tent, waiting to be served lunch, many of them wearing only shorts, socks and desert boots, all of them holding their tin plate, mug and eating utensils. As Dead-eye and Jimbo reached the tent they shared with Larry, a Wessex Mark 1 was landing beside the parked Whirlwind, covering the latter in a whipping cloud of sand and dust that also temporarily obscured the sun-scorched mountains beyond. That cloud even reached Dead-eye and Jimbo, making them both cough and cover their mouths as they ducked low and entered their tent. Larry was squatting on the rubber poncho stretched out beside his camp-bed, reading a copy of *Playboy*. He lowered it and glanced up when they entered.

'Filth,' Jimbo said with a straight face, keeping his head low to avoid scraping the top of the tent as he moved to his own side of it.

'What's that, Sarge? Filth? A bit of arse and tit never hurt anyone, Sarge. And it *does* give me something to think about.'

'You should be thinking of your nice girlfriend, Cathy,' Jimbo said, 'instead of wanking over that filthy rag.'

'I swear I haven't laid a hand on myself, Sarge,' Larry said, grinning without embarrassment. 'What's more, I only buy this so-called filthy rag for Hugh Hefner's profound articles on the *Playboy* philosophy – about sex, morality, hypocrisy and the need to be free. Really deep stuff, it is.'

'Yeah, so I've heard. He writes it when he's getting inspiration on his big round bed with birds all around him. A deep thinker that one – or deep diver, more like.'

'I'm taking everything,' Dead-eye said to Jimbo as he carefully packed his kit into his bergen. 'I'm leaving nothing behind for this lot of thieves. You should do the same.'

Dead-eye never discussed things like sex. Ever since he and his wife had divorced, he had kept to himself, having the odd affair, but not really becoming involved. Dead-eye did not like revealing his emotions and sex could make you do that. For that reason, it was best to treat it as a purely physical necessity. Life was easier that way.

'I will,' Jimbo replied, also packing his kit

into his bergen carefully so that all of it would fit. 'Lieutenant-Colonel Callaghan must have a trusting nature, but you and I know better.'

'Are you suggesting I'd steal your kit?' Larry asked, looking outraged.

'Not you,' Jimbo said. 'You wouldn't steal it because you're *in* here. But those other bastards' – he nodded towards the tent flaps, indicating the other SAS tents outside – 'would think we're a right pair of ponces if we left any kit behind. Then they'd nick it on principle.'

'You think so?'

Jimbo grinned and shook his head. 'Nah,' he said. 'Not really. It's just bad luck to leave your kit behind. All right, Dead-eye, I'm ready.'

'Where are you off to, then?' Larry asked.

'On a little trip,' Dead-eye replied. 'We'll be away for a couple of days, so you can have all this space to yourself.'

'To study philosophy,' Jimbo added ironically. 'See you soon, kid.'

They ducked even lower to leave the tent. Straightening up outside, they headed across the clearing, passing a sandbagged gun emplacement, to reach the helicopter LZ just beyond the perimeter. The Wessex had landed and was being unloaded by troops stripped to the waist and gleaming with sweat. Callaghan was standing under the slowly revolving props of the smaller Sikorski, holding his beret on his head as he gave covering instructions for his absence to Captain Ellsworth. He finished talking just as Dead-eye and Jimbo reached the chopper.

'Ah, good,' he said. 'You're here already. Clamber aboard, men.' Hauling up their bergens, Dead-eye and Jimbo climbed up into the Sikorski. They were strapping themselves into their seats, placing their bergens between their legs, when Callaghan followed them in and was in turn followed by the RAF crewman. The latter closed the door behind them, then bawled to the pilot that they were ready for take-off. Within seconds, the engines were roaring and the props were rotating at full speed, surrounding the chopper with a whirlwind of sand that it left behind only when it lifted up well above the earth. Glancing down as the chopper ascended, the three SAS men saw the collection of tents and circle of defensive hedgehogs shrinking until they had merged with the surrounding landscape of lava and desert, finally disappearing completely into it.

Only when the Whirlwind had stopped climbing and was flying horizontally above the parched mountain peaks was Callaghan able to make himself heard at all above the now reduced noise of the engines. Even so, he was forced to shout the whole time, and finally he said he would tell them what they needed to know when they were back on the ground.

They landed shortly afterwards at the RAF airfield at Aden. From there they were driven in a British Army 4×4 Willys jeep, which carried them along a dusty road to the military complex at Khormaksar, where the SAS Keeni-Meeni men were located. Sitting in the front of the jeep and now able to speak without shouting, Callaghan twisted around to face his two sergeants and explain what 'Keeni-Meeni' meant.

'The kind of clandestine plain-clothes operations we're mounting here originated with Major Frank Kitson during Kenya's Mau Mau campaign, which the SAS was briefly involved in. This led to the formation of a few so-called 'counter gangs', or anti-terrorist teams, composed of former terrorists and loyal tribesmen led by British officers disguised as natives. The same type of operation was also used in Cyprus as the basis of the undercover "Q" units.

'However, when we first set up a Close Quarters

Battle course here for a carefully selected group of SAS troopers, we knew that there was no hope of 'turning round' Arab terrorists and so decided to function more like the "Q" squads of the Palestine police as started by Roy Farran, a veteran of the wartime SAS who used a lot of his old buddies from that period. In some instances this involves driving around in Q cars, or unmarked cars, searching out possible Yemeni agents. In others, it involves picking up terrorists alive and bringing them in for questioning. But often it simply means shooting them before they manage to shoot you, which is exactly what they'll do if they recognize you. It's a highly dangerous, face-to-face business that requires lots of nerve.'

'So the basic idea,' Dead-eye said, taking lots of nerve for granted, 'is for disguised, plain-clothes SAS men to go into the alleyways and *souks* of Aden for undercover surveillance and the odd assassination.'

'An ugly word, Dead-eye, but I think you've got the message.'

'Keeni-Meeni's not such an ugly word. What does it mean?'

'It comes from a Swahili phrase that describes the movement of a snake in the long grass: sinuous and unseen. The same term later became a synonym in Africa – and with the slave trade in the Arabian Gulf – for undercover work. The British army picked it up during the Mau Mau campaign, and from Kenya it travelled to the SAS, here in Aden. We, however, relate it specifically to operations involving a standard operating procedure known as the double tap, which is what you're going to learn in one day as part of your quick CQB course in Khormaksar . . . Talking of which . . .'

Callaghan indicated straight ahead with a nod of his head as the jeep approached the heavily guarded military complex. After being checked thoroughly by the sentries at the gate, which had heavily armed sangars on either side, they were driven straight to Ballycastle House, a block of flats formerly used as married quarters but now the operational centre for the twenty-odd members of the SAS Keeni-Meeni squad. Once inside, they were introduced to Sergeant-Major Monnery, who was with the Long Range Desert Group during World War Two and was a founder member of the SAS, a 'green slime' SNCO, and now the man in charge of the Keeni-Meeni teams in Aden.

'As time is of the essence I'll now take my leave,' Callaghan said. 'Sergeant-Major Monnery will show you the ropes and return you to me when, and if, you succeed. Good luck, men.'

When the CO had left, Jimbo said: 'Well, well! If it isn't Wild Bill Monnery of the LRDG. And looking twenty years younger instead of twenty years older. Remember me, Sergeant-Major?'

'How could I forget you?' Monnery replied. 'Came crawling out of the African desert on your hands and knees, bloodied, blistered, black and blue, but with a grin on your stupid face.' He was referring to the extraordinary trek across the North African desert which Jimbo had made with other SAS men, including the legendary Captain John 'Jock' Lewes, creator of the Lewes bomb, after the raid against the Axis airfield at Nofilia in December 1941. As the LRDG sergeant in charge of the transport at the RV, 'Wild Bill' Monnery had been there to witness the extraordinary sight of the sun-scorched, tattered SAS men, having lost their transport, walking, stumbling and, as in Jimbo's case, crawling on hands and knees back to the RV after days in the desert. Now he grinned and put out his beefy hand to let Jimbo shake it. 'Nice to see you, Jimbo.'

'Nice to see *you*, Wild Bill.'

'Sergeant-Major Monnery to you,' Wild Bill

replied with mock outrage, withdrawing his hand and wiping it delicately on his shorts. 'Ah, well, here we go again.' He grinned at the impassive Dead-eye. 'And you're . . .?'

'Sergeant Richard Parker.'

'Known as Dead-eye,' Jimbo said.

'Ah, yes!' Wild Bill said softly, in admiration. 'I've heard all about you. The Telok Anson swamp and . . .'

'That's right,' Dead-eye interjected curtly. 'So what happens now?'

Experienced enough to know that there were barriers you did not cross, Wild Bill just nodded, then said, 'All right, men, come with me. I'll explain what we're up to on the way to the indoor firing range. But first you'll have to be kitted out with an Arab *futah*, which is what you'll be wearing when you go out on your mission.' He led them straight to a store room where a British Army private gave each of them an Arab robe, which they were told to put on immediately. This they did with considerable amusement, studying one another with wide grins when they had slipped their *futahs* over their heads and let them hang down around their body.

'We still don't look like Arabs,' Dead-eye said.

'You will when the times comes,' Wild Bill said. 'Now let's get to the firing range.'

'What we're doing here,' he told them as he led them along another corridor past the doors of the former married quarters, 'is exploiting the trick we developed in Palestine: namely, to disguise ourselves as locals, blend in with the local scenery and way of life, and seize on our targets as the opportunity arises. The high-risk areas of Crater and Sheikh Othman are like rabbit warrens, a maze of narrow alleys jam-packed with shops, stalls, Arabs and animals. You move there hemmed in on all sides, close up, practically nose to nose with your targets. For this reason, when we look for suitable SAS candidates for the Keeni-Meeni squads, we pick men who most resemble Arabs, with the hooked nose and prominent cheekbones of the Semite.'

'My nose is classically beautiful,' Jimbo said. 'I'm obviously in the wrong place.'

'We had to make an exception with you two,' Wild Bill said, 'because of the urgency of this situation. You were chosen not for your looks but because you've proven yourselves expert with the handgun and are known to be daring.'

'That's us!' Jimbo chirped.

'However, while you already know how to fire your 9-milli,' Monnery continued, referring to the Browning High Power handgun, 'what we're going to teach you is the double tap, which is the ability to very quickly draw the Browning from the folds of that *futah* you're wearing and fire it with perfect accuracy at close range.'

He led them through another door, into a large gymnasium converted into a combined firing range and CQB training area. It was, they noticed immediately, filled with Fijian SAS men, including a truly enormous soldier, well over six feet tall.

'Our Fijian brothers,' Wild Bill said. 'That black giant you're all staring at is Corporal Labalaba, the best Keeni-Meeni man we've got. Naturally his kind blends in with the scenery like you never could.' Wild Bill grinned broadly. 'You have to be careful of men like Labalaba. Not so long ago the Royal Anglian Regiment's Special Branch made the mistake of putting some men into the Sheikh Othman district without telling us. Armed and dressed as Arabs, they were mistaken for terrorists by Labalaba's plain-clothes patrol and shot to hell in a few seconds. Labalaba doesn't stop to ask questions, so watch out.' Turning towards a dark-haired, grinning SAS corporal who had just approached them, swathed in a *futah*, he said: 'And this is . . .'

'Trooper Terry Malkin!' Dead-eye explained, giving a rare grin. 'I forgot you'd be posted here, Terry.'

'Three months in the rabbit warrens of Aden,' Terry replied. 'It beats rotting at home.'

The two men shook hands.

'In the three months he's been here,' Wild Bill told them, 'Trooper Malkin's become one of our best Keeni-Meeni operators. Unfortunately for us, three months is the limit for anyone engaged in this work, so after he joins you in this operation, he'll be rejoining the Regiment – going back with you, in fact. In the meantime, he'll teach you all you need to know and take you out on that patrol. Since he's not going to be here tomorrow, it won't matter if he's identified in the *souks*.'

'Terry's going to teach *me* to shoot?' Dead-eye asked, already looking offended.

'Not to shoot,' Wild Bill replied. 'To double tap while wearing that Arab gear, which is something quite different. Now you take note, Dead-eye.' Grinning, Wild Bill took a seat in a hard wooden chair nearby and lit up a cigarette, letting Terry take over.

Instead of having them get used to the firing range, Terry first demonstrated the double tap.

'This SOP was devised by Major Roy Farran during World War Two,' he explained, 'but Farran taught his men what was then this rather unorthodox triangular firing posture . . .' – Terry demonstrated the stance – 'known as the "Grant-Taylor Method". He also insisted that his men should be able to put six rounds through a playing-card at 15 yards.'

Suddenly, with startling speed, Terry spun to the side, whipped a Browning 9mm High Power handgun out from under his robes, spread his legs, raised the pistol two-handed in the triangular firing posture and fired off six shots in quick succession at the target at the end of the firing alley. Only when he had finished firing did the half-deafened men see that his target had been an Ace of Hearts suspended where a proper target would normally have been. A large jagged hole indicated that practically all six shots had gone through the centre of the card.

Terry turned back to face them. 'We expect the same of you,' he said, reloading his pistol. 'You have until tomorrow.'

'Christ!' Jimbo whispered, staring in disbelief at the card.

'Let's get started, gentlemen,' Wild Bill said, exhaling a cloud of cigarette smoke. 'We haven't got all day.'

'Yes, we have,' Terry replied.

They did indeed have all day and Terry ensured that it was a long one, taking them repeatedly through the double tap. Both Dead-eye and Jimbo were experts with the handgun, but the trick in this instance was withdrawing it from beneath the long *futah* and bringing it into the firing position quickly enough, and accurately enough, to cut down the enemy before he could react. As this was made no easier by the complicated folds of the robe, they had to rehearse the withdrawal for hours before getting as far as the actual firing range.

While taking their training seriously, both sergeants could not help being amused at the idea of being trained by a trooper who normally took orders from them. This led to many jokes, which Terry took in good part.

Eventually, however, both men had mastered the rapid withdrawal technique and were able to go on to the firing range, where it was combined with shooting. In this part of the training both men came into their own, showing that their extensive experience of armed combat in many previous operations had honed their shooting skills to a fine edge. Before the long day had ended both were withdrawing the handgun, bringing it into the firing position, and firing with absolute accuracy, repeatedly piercing the playing card right through its centre. When they had done this at least a dozen times, with no misses, Terry, having enjoyed his brief moment of authority, called it a day.

'You blokes are as good as me now,' he said, puffed up with pride. 'We'll go into Aden tomorrow. For now, let's have dinner.'

'Yes, boss,' said Dead-eye and Jimbo simultaneously, before both burst out laughing.

6

Awakening at first light the following morning, Dead-eye, Jimbo and Terry had a shower and shave, then dressed in their olive-green gear, or OGs, and went to the NAAFI canteen in Ballycastle House for a breakfast of fried eggs, bacon, sausage, baked beans and toast, washed down with a couple of mugs each of steaming hot tea.

'Better than that noggie food, I can tell you,' Jimbo said with relish, scooping up his fried egg on his fork.

'That's not very nice, Sarge,' Terry said with some feeling. 'They're Arabs, not noggies.'

'They're all brownies to me,' Jimbo said. 'Apart from that, I've nothing against 'em. I just don't like their grub.'

'If you like your scran so much,' Dead-eye said,

'why don't you fill your mouth with it and let us have some peace?'

'Good old Dead-eye,' Jimbo snorted, shoving a piece of sausage into his mouth and winking at Terry. 'Always sticking up for the lower orders. He developed his little fondness for our coloured brothers in Malaya and Borneo.'

'An enemy to respect,' Dead-eye said. 'You had to admire them.'

'I don't respect anyone trying to nail me. I just treat 'em with care. Your respect for blokes trying to kill you has always bleedin' amazed me.'

'If he respects men who are trying to kill him,' Terry said with a cheeky grin, 'he'll be full of respect in the *souks* of Aden. Have my NCOs finished their breakfast? Good! Let's take off.'

'Is that an order or a request?' Jimbo asked, letting the cocky young trooper know who was in charge.

'We're running late.'

'There's your answer,' Dead-eye said.

Jimbo grinned, greatly amused by the confidence Terry had picked up since joining the Keeni-Meeni squads. 'I'm pretty sure we're in good hands,' he said.

'Thanks a lot, Sarge,' said Terry.

They returned to the 'spider', their sleeping quarters, where they set about making themselves look like Arabs by darkening their skin with a mixture of coffee, lamp-black, iodine and potassium permanganate. Some of them, including Dead-eye, had done the same in Malaya when passing themselves off as Malays or Chinese. The basic mixture could be lightened or darkened with ease, which made it highly adaptable for a wide variety of skin tones. In this case, when the three men had created a colouring similar to that of the local Arabs, they applied it carefully to their faces, hands, wrists and all the way up their arms, to ensure that no white skin would be glimpsed should the loose sleeves of the *futah* ride up. As they were wearing Arab sandals, instead of shoes, they also dyed their feet, ankles and legs up to the knees. Finally, even though they would be wearing the Arab *shemagh* on their heads, they dyed their hair black to ensure that their alien hair colour would not be betrayed by loose strands.

'This is the bit I love most of all,' Terry said, examining himself carefully in the full-length mirror. 'Dressing up for the part. It brings out the natural actor in me. Changes my personality completely. Don't you think so, Sarge?'

'You don't have a personality,' Jimbo replied. 'You're just a walking vacuum in a uniform. Without that, you'd be nothing.'

'Not a uniform today, Sarge. I'm an Arab now.'

'Fucking Lawrence of Arabia, more like it,' Jimbo laughed. 'And every bit as barmy.'

'All these Arabs are mad,' Terry said. Now let's go out and prove it.'

The joking, Dead-eye knew, was a means of holding in check the healthy tension that was now taking hold of them as they thought of mingling with the Arabs, practically face to face. For all the bullshit, the three of them knew, as they strapped their holstered Brownings in the cross-draw position under their *futahs*, that what they were about to do was very dangerous indeed and that they could easily end up dead – either shot by the enemy or murdered by an irate mob after being caught attempting the double tap. In particular, irrespective of the reassuring feel of the 9-milli in the holster strapped around his waist, Dead-eye felt unprotected without his L42A1 bolt-action sniper rifle and heavy bandoliers of 7.62mm rounds; in truth, he felt almost naked.

Walking to the motor pool with their faces

darkened and robes flapping in the breeze, they received a lot of derisory remarks from 'greens' and other SAS men. Used to this by now, Terry just grinned and gave the jokers the finger. At the motor pool, they had to sign for a 'Q' car, or unmarked car, this one a particularly battered old Beetle of the kind used by a lot of the local Arab traders. To emphasize its well-worn appearance, it had been packed with cardboard boxes, wrapping paper with Arabic lettering and other junk merchandise, such as cigarettes, cheap binoculars and cameras, and boxes of ballpens, as sold by the traders in the bum boats.

'Christ,' Jimbo said, studying the car. 'I don't mind it looking so bad, but it smells like it's been pissed in.'

'It probably has been, at one time or another,' Terry said. 'The piss of fear, Sergeant.'

Glancing sideways at Terry as they clambered into the messy, foul-smelling car, Dead-eye realized that the young trooper had matured tremendously since his hellish experiences in Borneo, only a year ago. Straight out of Hereford, Terry had been very unsure of himself at first, the constant butt of the other men's jokes, but he had soon proved to be an excellent soldier, particularly at the climax of the campaign when, with Corporals Alf Laughton (now a member of the directing staff at 22 SAS Training Wing, Hereford) and Pete Welsh, they had fought their way back to base through the hellish swamps surrounding the River Koemba. Welsh had died at the climax of that operation – shot off a walkway, to plunge to his death in the roaring torrents of a gorge over a hundred feet below. Terry, however, had not only survived it but, as the team's signaller, protected his all-important radio every inch of the way. Shaped into a toughened, experienced trooper by that frightful experience, he had been a natural choice for the present highly dangerous task. Now, he was more than a little confident, even with his NCOs.

As Terry drove the two sergeants out of the guarded gates of the military complex and along the dusty road to Aden, in the shadow of the volcanic mountains, he told them a little about the city.

'Being located at the southern entrance to the Red Sea,' he began rather pedantically, 'it's mainly been used as a commercial centre and refuelling stop for ships. However, it first really gained importance with the opening of the Suez canal in

1869, then with the development of the oilfields in Arabia and the Persian Gulf.' Jimbo rolled his eyes, but Terry did not notice. 'It has a few small industries, such as light manufacturing, evaporation of sea water to obtain marine salt, and boatbuilding. Naturally, as a free port, it's much loved by tourists and other seaborne travellers, despite the presence of the armed greens in the streets.'

'Nothing like a little duty free,' Jimbo said, grinning at Dead-eye, 'to make the tourists lose their common sense. So give us the *layout*, lad.'

'Ah!' Terry exclaimed, catching the older man's drift. 'It consists of three sections: Crater, the old commercial quarter; at-Tawahi, the business section; and Ma'alah, the native harbour area. We do most of our work in Crater or around the harbour area.'

'With the tourists,' Dead-eye said.

'Right, Sarge. And those tourists are a bit of a problem when it comes to making a hit.'

'Block your line of fire, do they?' Jimbo asked.

'Exactly. Or go into a panic when you're trying to make your getaway. Run right across your path of flight. Either that or the Arabs, when they see the dead man, take it out on the nearest white person. And who's that?'

'Someone off a boat,' Dead-eye said.

'Exactly,' Terry said. 'Tourists!'

Arriving at the harbour area, they drove through narrow, crowded streets, past the many duty-free shops and food stalls, and parked on Tawahi Main Road, close to the fenced-off harbour, but a good distance from the armed British soldiers guarding the gateway to the Aden Port Trust. The P & O liner *Himalaya* was anchored in the bay, looming large beyond the iron railings, concrete municipal buildings and warehouses of the docks, but passengers were coming ashore from the transit craft and emerging from the gateway to stare goggle-eyed, first at the brazenly importuning taxi drivers, then at the packed, dusty streets of the town.

'Ships' passengers are often a bit frightened when they first set eyes on this area,' Terry said, indicating Tawahi Main Road and its many shops, smoking and steaming food stalls, Sunni and Saydi Muslims, Hindus, Yemeni Jews, holy men and traders, beggars and thieves, veiled women and dirty children – all watched by stony-faced armed British troops – the 'greens' – armed with Sten guns and self-loading rifles. 'But the only real danger here is in having your pocket picked or losing your money when you buy a phoney Parker pen or a pair of binoculars without lenses. The real danger is up in Crater, where most of the terrorists hang around.'

'So what are we doing here?' Dead-eye asked him.

'Just filling you in, Sarge.'

Starting the car again, Terry drove at a crawl along the busy road, into the seething heart of Aden, where the Arabs were as dense as flies and every bit as noisy. As the car passed through side streets filled with shops, all run by Arabs though most had British names such as the London Store or the New Era, Dead-eye took note of the shopkeepers sitting outside on wooden chairs, the tourists haggling as they sipped tea, the tense soldiers standing guard at nearly every corner, and realized that this place, no matter what Terry thought, was a powder-keg waiting to be lit.

'Take the 9-milli out here and fire it,' he said, 'and you'd have bloody chaos.'

'Too right,' Terry confirmed. 'The tourists would shit themselves, the Arabs would take it out on the tourists, and the greens would open fire on the Arabs. A right bloody mess, all right.'

'And Crater?'

'No greens. Few tourists. Just the Arab – ours

and theirs. The ones on our side are poor and can't take sides, so we're all on our own up there.'

'You like it, don't you?' Dead-eye said.

'Yes, I do,' Terry confessed.

'Danger can be addictive,' Jimbo said. 'You've got the bug, kid.' He glanced up the lower slopes of the mountain beyond the town and saw a triangular-shaped maze of white, flat-roofed buildings, partly covered by a layer of dense, low cloud. 'Is that Crater up there?'

'Yes. That's where we're going. We'll be there in ten minutes.' Turning another street corner, Terry left the shops behind, then turned again almost immediately, passing a wire fence that ran alongside the road skirting the lower slopes of the mountains. 'Here,' he said, reaching into the glove compartment and withdrawing the photos of two male Arabs. 'These are the two we're after. They live down in Aden but visit Crater every afternoon to collect funds from various shopkeepers for their Yemeni brothers up in the Radfan. We'll just have to trawl the various places we know they go to and hope to catch them before the day's done. If we do, we finish them off with a double tap, then get the hell out of there.'

'Are we going in this car?' Dead-eye asked.

'No. We park in a residential street at the edge of Crater and walk into the commercial centre. When we've completed the job, we'll all make our own way back to the car, then skedaddle out of there.'

'How long does the first man at the car give the others to reach him?'

'He either gives them five minutes or takes off at the first sign of trouble – such as avenging Arabs.'

'But the other two could just be lost or captured,' Dead-eye said. 'Don't we go back to find out?'

'No. And we don't pick up the wounded or go back for anyone who gets lost. That's why we don't carry identification. It's a win-or-lose game.'

'Fucking great,' Jimbo said.

'Sensible,' Dead-eye corrected him.

'I agree,' Terry said. 'The Arabs are too volatile and unpredictable, so there's no turning back.'

While Terry drove towards Crater, Dead-eye and Jimbo studied the photos of the two Arabs more carefully. When they were sure they had taken in every feature of the two men and would recognize them if they saw them, they put a match to the pictures, let them burn up, then threw the blackened remains out of the car window, thus ensuring that no evidence of their intentions would be found on their person if they were caught.

They reached Crater after a ten-minute drive along a road that wound up the lower slopes of the volcanic mountain. Terry's 'commercial centre' was actually a rabbit warren of narrow streets and *souks*, all packed with shops, small, enclosed bazaars, cafés, Arabs and animals. Many of the Arabs were playing draughts or other games at tables outside the cafés. Others were smoking opium pipes. Nearly all were drinking mint tea. The alleys and *souks* were filled with the smoke from burning braziers and steam from pots of cooking food or boiling tea. Men were leading cattle through the narrow, packed *souks*, letting them ease their way, mooing, through the tide of people, which included many children and their veiled mothers. There were few cripples or blind people, for most of them were down in the harbour area, exploiting the tourists. Even without them, there was still a fearful crush.

'You were right,' Dead-eye said, 'there's no room to breathe here.'

'Which means little room to manoeuvre,' Jimbo added. 'No wonder it calls for special training.'

Terry grinned, pleased. 'Yes,' he said. 'The

training isn't just for accuracy with the 9-milli; it's to get up your speed. When you see the target, you don't have too much time to prepare yourself and take aim. You have to make an instant calculation even as you're whipping out the gun. You have to shoot and scoot, so make sure you get it right the first time. There are no second chances.'

After driving around as much of the area as was possible given the narrowness of the *souks*, pointing out as they went the gathering places for enemy agents, Terry parked on the southern edge of the densely populated area, in a street of flat-roofed stone houses that contained few people and ran out to the mountain slopes, thus providing a quick escape route. After automatically checking that their Brownings were in the proper, cross-draw position under their robes and that their make-up was still in good shape, the men got out of the car, surprised by how hot the sun was, even though it was still overcast.

'It's always like this,' Terry explained, glancing at the few Arabs, mostly women and children, wandering about the residential street. 'Bloody muggy. Are you all set?' Dead-eye and Jimbo both nodded. 'All right,' Terry continued. 'From this point on, we don't speak. We keep well apart

– we'll be less noticeable that way – but make sure we're always in sight of each other. If any Arab speaks to you, try to avoid replying, but without actually offending him. I usually just nod and keep walking. If that's not possible, reply in Arabic, but as briefly as possible, as if you're in a hurry. First man who sees the target pots him. If we all see him at once, we all shoot at once. Try to get as close as possible before firing. We run for it the minute we've fired – we can't stop to check that he's dead. Escape under cover of the confusion caused by the shooting. Any questions?'

Dead-eye and Jimbo both shook their heads.

'I'll lead the way, stopping at the various likely meeting places I've already shown you. You keep a good distance behind me. When I stop, you fan out around me, though still well away from me, mingling with the crowd. Let's go.'

By leading them along the relatively quiet residential street, Terry was able to give them time to adjust to the unease they felt when walking past real Arabs. Though their faces were dyed dark and *shemaghs* half-covered their faces, both Dead-eye and Jimbo felt as white as ever and could not accept that their disguise would pass muster this close to the women and children in the street. In the event, though many of the children and a few of the women and older men glanced at them, none of them seemed to notice anything unusual, and they reached the end of the street without incident.

But as they turned into a narrow, thronging *souk*, a veritable river of densely packed Arab traders and their clamouring customers, both men stiffened automatically, expecting to be detected instantly. Dead-eye was not the kind to admit to feeling fear, but even he could not stop a fleeting moment of panic as he followed Terry, a good ten yards ahead. They passed along the crowded *souk*, no more than an alleyway, between open shopfronts piled high with fruit, vegetables, nuts, carpets, pots and pans, and just about every kind of local household implement. Here, Dead-eye soon noticed, there was little sign of the cameras, binoculars, transistor radios, leather goods and pens that were so popular with the tourists down in the harbour area. Clearly this was a genuine Arab quarter, serving only local people.

Those Arabs were around him now, pressing in on all sides, practically breathing in his face, letting him smell their sweat. He lowered his head as much as possible while still glancing about him, taking in every detail of the narrow *souk*, which, he now noticed, had still narrower, starkly shadowed, but less crowded alleyways leading off it.

Even as Dead-eye was considering the side alleyways as possible escape routes, the *souk* opened out into a small, busy plaza full of cafés and food stalls. Now at the other side of the plaza, Terry stopped and indicated, with an almost imperceptible nod of his head, a café directly opposite where he was standing. There were tables and chairs outside, most of them occupied by Arabs reading newspapers, sipping mint tea or playing dominoes or chess.

Recalling that this was one of the meeting places of the guerrilla agents, Dead-eye also stopped walking and leaned against the nearest wall, as if watching the world go by. Glancing sideways, he saw Jimbo doing the same and was relieved that, at least from this distance, he really did blend in with the crowd.

After signalling, with another prearranged, subtle hand movement, that Dead-eye and Jimbo were to remain where they were, Terry approached the café, wove his way between the tables and disappeared inside. Watching the doorway, Dead-eye tensed himself for the sound of gunfire, but none came. Eventually Terry reappeared. He turned along the side of the café and entered another *souk*.

Dead-eye and Jimbo followed, still keeping well apart. This *souk* was just as narrow as the first one had been, but Dead-eye and Jimbo were starting to slip more naturally into their roles, gaining confidence from not being detected; now they found the experience less hair-raising and, in Jimbo's case, even fun. Dead-eye, as always, took a more pragmatic view, treating it purely as a job of work and determined to do it right.

Though frequently having to stop and press themselves against the wall to let Arab traders pass with heavily laden wheeled barrows, or to avoid cows being herded to market through the narrow *souk*, they eventually reached another busy square, its four sides packed with shops and cafés. Here, again, they kept well apart, each taking a separate side of the square, though all three of them faced the café which Terry had indicated with a barely perceptible nod of his head.

Clearly Terry had learned something about his quarry when he had entered the previous establishment, because this time he took a seat at one of the tables and ordered mint tea. While Terry had been specially trained in Arabic at the Hereford and Army School of Languages and was, reportedly, fairly fluent, Dead-eye felt that he was taking a greater chance than was necessary by sitting at a table and ordering mint tea from an Arab waiter. In any case, another Arab could strike up a conversation, which would make things very tricky.

Dead-eye was even more convinced that Terry was getting too cocky when, half an hour later, he ordered food from what looked like a roadside trader serving a cheap couscous from an unhygienic charcoal stove on wheels. Surprisingly, he got away with it, but watching him tuck into it, expertly scooping the steamed wheat grain up into his mouth like the other Arabs, Dead-eye felt a combination of admiration for Terry's new confidence and concern that it was becoming a dangerous display of bravado.

Glancing sideways, he saw that Jimbo was also intently watching Terry at his table, either simply envying him for having the opportunity to eat or, like Dead-eye, worried that he was playing with fire.

Another fifteen minutes passed. Terry finished his meal, crumpled the heavy paper it had been served in, threw it to the ground at his feet, as others had done, and sat back again, watching the world go by. Dead-eye and Jimbo, meanwhile, meandered around the square, not wanting to remain too long in one place in case an Arab spoke to them, but always needing to be close to the café that Terry was watching.

Dead-eye was only about five yards from the door when he saw Terry move. It happened so fast that even Dead-eye was almost taken by surprise. As a well-built Arab wearing a well-cut suit with a shirt and tie stepped out of the café, Terry pushed his chair back, stood up and walked forward as if about to enter. The Arab did not even bother to look up when Terry, still advancing, reached under the flowing *futah*. Only when Terry had whipped out his pistol, spread his legs and was taking aim, about to fire two-handed, did the man realize what was happening and try to duck sideways. He was too late.

Locking his arms and bending his legs slightly as he had been taught in the 'Killing House' in Hereford, aiming square at his target from a distance of less than five yards, holding the pistol firmly and applying pressure equally between the thumb and fingers of the firing hand, Terry fired two rounds in quick succession.

Dead-eye and Jimbo were still reaching for their weapons when the double roar of Terry's Browning deafened them and the quarry was violently punched back, blood spurting from his chest, to crash over the table directly behind him. The customers cried out and scattered as the table collapsed beneath the shot man and he hit the ground in a welter of smashing bottles and glasses that were spattered with his spurting blood.

Even as the Arab was flopping over onto his side, one bloody hand clawing feebly at the ground, another, also in European dress, emerged from the café, firing a pistol at Terry. The bullets missed and were whining into the scattering, bawling crowd as Dead-eye and Jimbo raised their own weapons in the two-handed firing position and simultaneously discharged two rounds at the man. Their combined double tap, plus Terry's, made the man drop his pistol, convulse wildly, slam back into the door frame and slide to the ground even as his assailants were turning away to flee.

Glancing back, Dead-eye saw a third man emerge from the café, turn in the opposite direction and race around the far corner of the building. Terry saw him too. Without a word, he turned back, vaulting over a table, above the panic-stricken

Arab customers lying on the ground, to run after the man who had fled. Realizing that the third man must be the second target, and that the second man killed was probably only a bodyguard, Dead-eye instantly followed Terry and was in turn followed by Jimbo, who bowled over a few of the Arabs in his haste to catch up with the other two.

As Dead-eye turned the corner of the café, an irate Arab bawled abuse and rushed at him, wielding a knife. Dead-eye ducked. The knife slashed through the air where his head had been. Dead-eye kneed the man in the groin, then clubbed him with the butt of his pistol as he doubled up, gasping.

Dead-eye raced ahead as the Arab was falling. He followed Terry along another narrow alleyway, hearing Jimbo's rapid footsteps echoing behind him. Luckily, this *souk* did not contain shops or stalls, which made progress easier, though the three of them bowled over strolling Arabs as they ran, causing startled or angry shouts to erupt in their wake.

The chase led them eventually to the other, even poorer side of Crater, to a rubbish-strewn square wreathed in smoke from the many open fires and food stalls scattered between the tables and chairs of the shabby cafés.

Clearly knowing where his quarry was heading, Terry had replaced his pistol under his *futah* and stopped running before reaching the square. Instead of entering the square, he took a seat on a wooden bench along the wall of the street leading into it. He then indicated with a nod of his head that Dead-eye and Jimbo should join him, which they did, one sitting either side of him, the three of them together taking up the whole of the bench to ensure that no real Arabs could join them. As no one was near them, they could talk in low voices.

'Our man's in a house between two smaller houses, just about visible from where I'm sitting,' Terry informed them. 'He can't see us from there, though I can see the house, and if we're patient and don't enter the square, he'll finally decide that we didn't follow him and come out again. If he does, I'll see him before he sees us. When I make my move, you back me up, keeping your eye out for anyone who makes a move towards me. If they do, finish them off.'

Terry glanced along the alleyway to check that no one was coming, then studied the busy square again. 'In the meantime,' he said with great authority, forgetting that he was with two NCOs, 'let's pretend we're three old friends, just sitting and talking. We can speak in English as long as no one is around. If Arabs pass, you stop speaking and I'll do all the talking in Arabic, keeping my voice low. That should do the trick.'

'I can't bloody believe this,' Jimbo whispered at the other side of Terry. 'We're both taking orders from this trooper. We're hanging on his every word.'

'He's done all this before,' Dead-eye replied, talking across Terry as if he was not there, though in a soft voice, 'and knows what he's doing. So let's give him his due.'

'Bloody amazing, is all I can say. Would you credit it?'

'Thanks, Sarge,' Terry said. 'I take that as a compliment.'

They talked softly for the next fifty minutes, sometimes trading the traditional SAS bullshit but just as often passing comments on the movements of the many Arabs in the narrow alleyway and the busier square. The fifty minutes became an hour, then two, and when another half-hour had passed without sight of their quarry, even Dead-eye, whose patience was legendary, was starting to feel restless. Suddenly, however, he felt Terry stiffening beside him and Jimbo, at the other side of Terry, asked: 'Is that him?'

Terry nodded and stood as casually as possible, slipping his hand under his *futah* as he did so. Dead-eye and Jimbo followed him as he walked into the square, picking up speed with each step, then suddenly breaking into a run. His quarry, another well-fed Arab in an expensive suit, saw him coming and actually straightened up, shocked.

Dead-eye and Jimbo were fanning out on either side of Terry, both withdrawing their pistols, when an unwitting taxi-driver braked to a halt just ahead of Terry.

The rear passenger door opened.

Terry was just coming abreast of the taxi when an Englishman started to get out. Without breaking his pace, Terry reached out with his left hand to push the Englishman back into the vehicle. The Englishman was straightening up and about to step out again when Terry reached under his *futah* and withdrew his Browning with a quick, smooth sweep of his right hand. Spreading his legs to steady himself, he aimed the pistol at the Arab who had just emerged from the mud-brick house straight ahead and was about to duck down between the pavement tables of the cafés on either side.

Terry fired six shots in rapid succession, punching the Arab backwards, almost lifting him off the ground and then bowling him into the dirt.

As the Arab fell, a woman screamed hysterically from inside the taxi, many Arabs in the square bawled warnings or shouted out in fear, and Terry turned back to be faced with the shocked tourist, half in and half out of the taxi.

'Sorry about that,' Terry said to the Englishman, then pushed him back into the taxi, slammed the door shut, and was disappearing into the crowd as the Muslim taxi-driver, more familiar with the area than his passenger, noisily ground his gears, made a sharp U-turn, and roared off the way he had come, the dust churned up by his spinning wheels settling over the dead Arab on the ground.

Not having fired a shot, but now holding their pistols, Dead-eye and Jimbo raced after the fleeing Terry, giving him cover until he had disappeared into the nearest *souk*. One foolhardy Arab grabbed at Jimbo and was slugged for his troubles. Another dived at Dead-eye and landed on his shoulders, but was spun off and crashed down onto a table under which some other Arabs were hiding. They all yelled and scattered around the falling man as he thudded into the ground.

As Dead-eye straightened up, having thrown off the Arab, he saw two others in suits standing near the dead man, spreading their legs to take aim with their pistols. Calling a warning to Jimbo as he prepared to shoot two-handed, Dead-eye fired at one of the two Arabs before either had managed a shot. His victim was jerking backwards, his pistol flying through the air, as Jimbo's Browning roared beside Dead-eye and the second Arab was also bowled over.

Still not recognized as British, they did not say a word, but turned away and ran as fast as they could along the narrow *souk*, following Terry. It was not a trading area, so they were relatively unhindered, and eventually, when they were sure that they were not being followed, they slowed down to a walk, gradually caught up with one another and walked together, like three Arab friends, to the car parked on the other side of Crater. Only when they were driving away did they let themselves relax, Terry and Jimbo whooping with pleasure while Dead-eye gazed out of the window, impassive and watchful.

'You should have seen the look on the face of that tourist,' Terry said, 'when I spoke to him in English. He couldn't believe it!'

'Must have nearly shit himself,' Jimbo laughed. 'I wish I'd seen his expression.'

'You're becoming too cocky for your own good,' Dead-eye said brusquely, 'and it's making you stupid. First you sit at a table where any Arab could have joined you; then you eat Arab food from a dirty portable stove; then, worst of all, you speak English in the vicinity of the Arabs. How fucking daft can you get? You forgot yourself, kid. Never do that again.'

Realizing that Dead-eye was right, Terry and Jimbo remained silent until the Q car was back in the safety of the military compound at Khormaksar. Terry spoke only when they had signed the car back in and were walking to the HQ tent to make their report.

'I'm sorry, Sarge,' he said to Dead-eye, looking suitably contrite. 'You were absolutely right.'

'No sweat, son,' Dead-eye said quietly.

Even before making their report to Lieutenant-Colonel Callaghan, Dead-eye and Jimbo were told by the RSM that they were being sent back to the squadron at Thumier for a major operation in the Radfan. Terry was going with them.

'Back where I belong,' Terry said. 'I'll be a good boy now.'

'I hope so,' Dead-eye said with the hint of a smile.

7

'Welcome back, gentlemen,' Callaghan said in his HQ tent in the base camp, shaking the three men's hands and indicating that they should take one of the hard wooden chairs facing his cluttered trestle table. 'I believe the Keeni-Meeni operation was a success.'

'Yes, boss,' Dead-eye said as he and Jimbo pulled up chairs and sat facing him. 'The two agents and a bodyguard were topped.'

'How was Trooper Malkin?'

'A bit on the cocky side, but he certainly knew what he was doing and did it precisely.'

Callaghan grinned at his squadron commander, Captain Ellsworth, sitting beside him. 'A bit full of himself, was he? Not grandstanding, I trust!'

'Not grandstanding, boss,' Dead-eye reassured him. 'Just thrilled to be showing two NCOs what to do. A little bit careless here and there from overconfidence, but he certainly proved that he'd learnt a lot during his couple of months with the Keeni-Meeni squads. He didn't let us down that way.'

'Maybe you should have left him in Aden,' Ellsworth said. 'Sounds like he belongs there.'

'It's too free and easy there, sir,' Jimbo explained. 'Terry works unsupervised. The work's dangerous, but being on his own – or with just a friend or two – makes it seem like a game. He's good, but he's still immature and needs to be brought back down to earth. So he's better off back here as part of the squadron. Besides, he's one hell of a signaller – practically psychic – so we wanted him back.'

Callaghan grinned again. 'Irish background, yes?'

'Right, boss. A bit of a Paddy. He doesn't like to be reminded of it, but that's what he is and the Paddy in him gives him great intuition when it comes to using the radio.'

'I don't believe what I'm hearing,' Captain Ellsworth said, shaking his head. 'You're saying that he has psychic abilities that help when it comes to communications?'

Jimbo was grinning now. 'I'm not saying it's

true, boss, but I *am* saying that a lot of the men believe that. They think Terry is an exceptional signaller because he's Irish and has psychic intuition. So they have confidence in him.'

Callaghan chuckled. 'Far be it from me to disillusion them. Fine. He's all yours.' He glanced up automatically when a great roaring passed overhead, indicating that a Wessex was coming in to land. He waited until the chopper had passed on and was descending on the nearby landing pad, then lowered his gaze again. 'So, gentlemen, let's get down to business. Now that those communist double agents have been removed, we can mount our operation in the Radfan without fearing that our every move is going to be telegraphed in advance to the enemy. In other words, you've just won yourselves some work.'

'Christ, boss, what's the second prize?' Jimbo said.

'It's mainly because of the machinations of those agents you terminated,' Callaghan continued in a serious vein, 'that our intelligence concerning the strength and whereabouts of the enemy in the Radfan is negligible. We don't know anything we need to know. We don't even know where there's water. We know precious little about the tribesmen. For this reason we want an improvised group to go back into the mountains and try to pick up as much information as it can, possibly even some prisoners. In fact, Captain Ellsworth has already done that once with a much smaller group.'

Both NCOs stared quizzically at the new, relatively inexperienced captain, who looked slightly embarrassed.

'It was in your absence,' Ellsworth said quietly. 'I took a small patrol up into the Radfan, set up a nocturnal ambush and opened fire on a camel train that refused to halt. A couple of Arabs were killed, but a third was taken prisoner. My initial anxiety was that I might have made a mistake – that the Arabs were legitimate traders. Luckily, when we brought our prisoners back down, a local military intelligence officer identified him as a known guerrilla leader.'

'Congratulations,' Dead-eye said.

'Well deserved, certainly,' Callaghan said. 'However, Captain Ellsworth's initial concern that he might have shot up a perfectly innocent camel train highlights one of the problems we have up there in the Radfan: it's swarming not only with the enemy, but with local traders going about their business – and if we shoot them by mistake it could lead to riots in Aden.'

'In other words,' Ellsworth said, 'we're going to have to be very careful before making any kind of move.'

'Dead right,' Jimbo said.

For a moment there was silence as Captain Ellsworth glanced thoughtfully at the map of the Radfan, spread out before him on the desk, and Callaghan gazed distractedly outside the tent, where the sun was sinking over the base camp, lengthening the shadows of the protective hedgehogs and their armaments. The Wessex pilot had finally switched off his engines and the only sound now heard from the landing pad was the shouting of the ground crew and the lesser roar of a jeep starting up. The mountains of the Radfan, also visible through the opening in the tent, looked distant and mysterious in the dimming light.

'What kind of group are we taking up there?' Dead-eye asked.

'Two battalions of FRA infantry; 45 Royal Marine Commando with B Company; the Parachute Regiment; a troop of Royal Engineers; a battery of the Royal Horse Artillery armed with

105mm howitzers; and a Royal Tank Regiment equipped with Saladins.'

'That's not a small group,' Jimbo noted.

'No, Sergeant Ashman, it's not. But we don't know what we're up against, so we can't chance our arm.'

'What's the objective?' Dead-eye asked.

'Two hills, codenamed Rice Bowl and Cap Badge. Both are of vital importance because they dominate the camel routes from the Yemen and the only two fertile areas in the region. We intend to seize them from the rebels on 1 May.'

'Day or night?' Dead-eye asked tersely.

'To be caught in the valley in the daylight would be suicidal, so both of the assault forces will move out at night. The Royal Marines will march seven miles from the Dhala Road, in Thumier, into hostile territory, to climb and hold the most northerly objective – Rice Bowl. Simultaneously, the Para Company will be dropped by parachute near the foot of Cap Badge.'

Callaghan nodded at Ellsworth, who leant forward to say: 'This is where we come in. To land the Paras on an unmarked, undefended DZ would be just as suicidal as asking the Marines to march in broad daylight. Our task, then, is to establish, mark and protect a suitable DZ for the Paras.'

'What would they do without us?' Jimbo asked.

'How many men do we take, boss?' Dead-eye asked.

'Nine. You move out at dusk on 29 April, under the command of Captain Ellsworth and travelling in Saladins. You'll head due north along the Dhala Road, then leave the road at the Wadi Rabwa and climb up the sides of the wadi into the mountains. You'll have to cover approximately eight miles to reach your objective and you only have twenty-four hours to do so.'

'The opposition?' Jimbo asked.

'Intelligence reports suggest that it won't be serious if you move discreetly.'

'But, sir, you've just said,' Dead-eye reminded him, 'that intelligence about the Radfan is pretty thin – which means unreliable.'

The CO grinned and shrugged. 'What can I say, Dead-eye, other than what I've told you? Intelligence thinks you might get off lightly, but it could be the opposite.'

'Who dares wins,' Dead-eye said, staring out of the tent.

8

Late in the afternoon of the following day, the nine men selected for the patrol prepared to move out by camouflaging themselves and their weapons. Given the cramped size of the tents, most of them did this sitting outside in the mercifully falling temperature, with their weapons and kit spread around them. As usual, they first cleaned their weapons and checked the ammunition, which in this instance included four magazines for the SLRs, a total of eighty rounds, plus a bandolier of the same ammunition and 200 rounds of .303-inch bullets for the patrol's Bren gun. They were, in fact, more lightly armed than usual.

'Why?' Lance-Corporal Larry Johnson asked.

'Because Lieutenant-Colonel Callaghan prefers mobility to fire-power for this kind of operation,' Dead-eye informed him. 'That's why he also stressed that our ammunition's to be conserved as much as possible, even during contact with the enemy. In other words, fire only when strictly necessary.'

'Like when I've got someone's bayonet up my arse?'

'That about sums it up,' Jimbo said.

When the weapons and ammunition checks had been made, they went off to collect their water ration: a one-gallon container and four water bottles per head. Now back doing what he was best at, Terry also collected his A41 tactical radio, which added another 44lb to his heavy load.

Finally, they darkened the exposed parts of the body – in particular the face, neck and hands – with stick camouflage. They also applied 'cam' to the shinier parts of the weapons to prevent them from reflecting the moonlight. Meanwhile the sun was setting beyond the mountains, and the hedgehogs around the perimeter of the camp, bristling with big weapons and howitzers, were receding into the gathering gloom.

'So what were you two doing when you were away?' Lance-Corporal Les Moody asked Dead-eye and Jimbo.

'Not much,' Dead-eye replied.

'That isn't an answer, Sarge.'

'It was confidential,' Jimbo told him.

'But you were with little Terry here?' Les said, indicating the younger soldier with a nod of his head.

'That's right.'

'Which means you were in Aden.'

'You're so bright,' Jimbo said.

'I've heard that we have some special hit squads in Aden: blokes who dress up as Arabs and go into the *souks* for some close-action work with their 9-millis?'

'You've seen too many war films,' Jimbo said.

'I didn't pick it up there. That's the word going round.'

'Bloody rubbish,' Dead-eye told him.

'Is that right, Trooper?' Les asked Terry. 'Bloody rubbish?'

'You had it straight from the horse's mouth,' said Terry rather too curtly.

'Isn't it true that when you disappeared from the Sports and Social Club in Hereford it was to do a quick course in Arabic, then be flown to Aden for a couple of months with one of them Keeni-Meeni squads?'

'Keeni-Meeni?' Terry asked deadpan. 'What's that?'

'You don't know?'

Terry shook his head.

'That's bullshit, Terry. You know exactly what it means and it's what you were doing in Aden.'

'I was acting as a signaller in Aden and that's *all* I was doing. Isn't that right, Dead-eye?'

'That's right,' Dead-eye said.

'I can't get a straight answer to a simple question,' Les complained.

'Ask no questions and we'll tell you no lies,' replied Jimbo.

'My lips are sealed from this moment on,' Les said with a sigh.

They completed their preparations just as the sun was sinking. After heaving their bergens onto their backs, they strapped on their webbing and bandoliers of ammunition, then picked up their personal weapons and marched to the waiting Saladins. Apart from being equipped with 76mm QF guns and Browning .30-inch machine-guns, the armoured cars had been fitted in the manner of the World War Two LRDG Chevrolets, which were specifically equipped for the desert. Among the refinements were reinforced sand tyres, special filters, outsize fans and radiators, wireless sets, sun compasses, sextants, sand shovels, jerry cans, water condensers, woven sand mats and steel sand channels, the latter two to be used when the vehicle became trapped in sand or potholes. The sun had actually sunk when the armoured cars moved out of the camp one after the other.

As the convoy moved along the Dhala Road, into a deepening darkness relieved by moonlight and a sky perforated with stars, Terry glanced at the mountainous desert outside and thought how different it was from the terrain he had first fought in: the dense jungle and steaming swamps of Borneo. Though he had fought well there, earning his winged-dagger badge in no uncertain terms, he was still haunted by nightmares about how he and the rest of his squadron had waded through snake and insect-infested swamps, fighting Indonesian troops all the way.

While Terry's dreams were filled with vivid recollections of the snakes, bloodsucking leeches and countless insects of the stinking swamps, now they were even more frequently haunted by his vivid recollection of how he and a few of the others, including Dead-eye and Jimbo, had eventually been forced to cross an aerial walkway that swayed high above a roaring gorge and was being fired at by vengeful Indonesians. Even fully awake, Terry had only to close his eyes to see his friend, Trooper Pete Welsh, peppered by enemy bullets and pouring blood from his many wounds, slide off the bridge and fall screaming to the bottom of the gorge, where he splashed into the raging rapids, was smashed against the rocks and then swept away out of sight for ever. That sight, Terry was sure, would haunt him for the rest of his life.

The present terrain, though also mountainous, was very different from that of Borneo, being parched by the sun and filled with wide, open spaces instead of dense jungle. Yet it was just as dangerous, with its own brand of the unknown, and Terry was glad to be in the company of Dead-eye, who had successfully led him and the other survivors out of the swamps and mountains of Borneo.

Dead-eye was presently in one of the other Saladins, but Terry thought of him now because he was not feeling too good and thought he knew why. It was because, while in Aden with Dead-eye and Jimbo, he had being doing what both men detested: 'grandstanding'. This term, as

Terry knew only too well, was applied by the SAS to any soldier who forgot that he was part of a team and instead put on a show to earn credit or glory for himself.

Having been a newcomer in Borneo, constantly awed by the coolness and courage of the old hands, particularly Dead-eye, in Aden Terry had been unable to resist showing off to him and that other old-timer, Jimbo. He had sat at that café table in Crater and, even worse, eaten food from one of the notoriously unhygienic food stalls, purely as an act of bravado. It had also been an act of gross stupidity – for which he was now paying the price with an upset stomach.

Compounding his stupidity, he had not confessed before leaving the base camp that he had an upset stomach. Now that the convoy was in the middle of the desert, heading for Wadi Rabwa and the mountains beyond, Terry knew that he could not be taken back or casualty-evacuated. Unless he suffered in silence, he could become a serious burden to the whole patrol.

Unfortunately, his stomach, which at first had only been slightly upset with what seemed like mild indigestion, was now twitching constantly with sharp, darting pains and making him feel nauseous.

'How long's the drive?' Terry asked, glancing out of the Saladin at the vast flat plain running out to the distant mountains.

'We should be at Wadi Rabwa in less than an hour,' answered Jimbo. 'From there it's about eight miles to our objective, but we've got about twenty-four hours to get there. The wadi's pretty steep and the march will be rough. Why do you ask?'

Terry looked uneasy. 'My stomach's playing up,' he mumbled.

'What?'

'I feel queasy,' Terry confessed. 'But don't let on to anyone else. I don't want to be taken off the patrol.'

'How bad is it?'

'It hurts a bit and I feel sick.'

'You must have picked up a bug when you had that Arab food in Crater. That was daft, Trooper.'

'Yes, it was.'

'This is no time to be feeling sick.'

'I know. I'm really sorry, Sarge. I should have told you, but I thought it would go off soon.'

'But it hasn't?'

'No, Sarge.'

Jimbo sighed. 'You think you can stick with it throughout the hike?'

'I'll be OK. I promise.'

Jimbo shook his head in disbelief, then turned away. Squirming with guilt, Terry glanced at the other men in the armoured car – the recently badged troopers, Ben Riley and Taff Thomas – and was relieved that they appeared not to have heard the conversation.

'Are you two all right?' Jimbo asked them.

'Yes, Sarge,' Ben replied while Taff just nodded.

'You weren't the last time,' Jimbo reminded them.

'No, not the last time,' Ben replied in his cocky manner. 'We were only sick on the first trip, Sarge. That was in the middle of the day when the sun was as hot as hell. The last time, when we went out at night, like this, you had no problems with us.'

'I stand corrected,' Jimbo said, then yawned into his clenched fist.

Glancing at Ben and Taff, Terry remembered being told just how ill they had been shortly after arriving at Aden, on the drive from the RAF base in Khormaksar to the SAS camp in Thumier. Hearing about that journey had made Terry feel superior to the newcomers; and that sense of superiority, which he could now see as a weakness, is what had made him behave so badly in Crater, trying to impress his two more experienced sergeants. Now ill himself, he did not feel so superior to the two newcomers, and even felt ashamed.

Even more disconcerting was the knowledge that, while the journey so far had been along the Dhala Road, which was smooth enough, soon they would be leaving the road to ascend into, then climb out of, the steep rocky sides of Wadi Rabwa. After that, the going would be even rougher.

In fact, their descent into the eerily moonlit wadi began five minutes later when the Saladins turned off the road, bounced across very rough terrain, which jolted the vehicles relentlessly, then started inching down into the wadi with gears grinding and powerful engines screaming in protest.

At first the slope of the wadi could be seen in the moonlight, which streaked the loose grey gravel and parched, lunar rocks, but when they finally reached the dried-up watercourse, which ran for miles east and west, the moonlight was almost completely cut off by the opposite slopes and the column moved for a time through almost total darkness.

Time after time, the armoured cars ran into boulders too large to bounce over or became stuck in potholes too deep to traverse. When this happened, the men, guided by Jimbo, who had learned his desert skills with the LRDG in North Africa, had to climb out and either remove the boulders by hand or get the vehicle out of the large potholes with the aid of the woven sand mats or five-feet-long steel sand channels.

This latter operation involved pushing the sand mats or metal channels as far as possible under the wheels that had become stuck in the soft sand. The armoured car could then be either reversed or advanced slowly over them until it was free. A simpler variation on the original LRDG method of rescuing their Chevrolets from sand traps, it was effective but laborious and time-consuming.

Nevertheless, even in the pitch darkness, the men took the opportunity to check the tyres, usually letting some air out lest they burst on the sharper stones. They also checked that there was no sand in the carburettors. These tasks were managed by the light of hand-held torches.

This was a mistake. They realized so when, during an attempt to move another trapped vehicle, gunfire erupted from the hills beyond the wadi and a hail of bullets danced off the rocks nearby, causing pieces of stones to fly off in clouds of dust and showers of sparks.

'Shit!' Jimbo growled, dropping automatically to his knees and raising his SLR into the firing position. 'The bastards saw the torches.'

'Our own fault,' Dead-eye replied, dropping low beside him as the rest of the men scattered to take up firing positions from behind the armoured cars or higher rocks. He turned aside briefly to bawl at the men: 'Don't fire back! You'll be wasting your time. You'll only pinpoint our position. Just lie low and wait for further orders!' He was cut off when another burst of tracer made sand spit up in a jagged line that whipped and coiled nearby, causing more fragments of rock to fly up through clouds of dust and silver sparks that looked like fireflies.

Captain Ellsworth ran back from the first Saladin, crouched low, holding his SLR across his chest, as more green tracer from the enemy machine-guns looped languidly down from the distant hill, appeared to gain speed as it approached, then raced at him in a phosphorescent stream that made the soil explode in a jagged line behind him.

Falling to one knee beside Dead-eye, he stared at the lines of tracer and spitting sand. 'I thought the opposition wasn't going to be serious if we moved discreetly,' he said sarcastically.

'Shining torches at night isn't discreet,' Dead-eye replied.

'The enemy wasn't supposed to be here,' Jimbo reminded him. 'They're supposed to be in the Radfan.'

'That lot have come down from the Radfan,' Dead-eye said, 'and caught us all napping.'

'Caught us working our arses off,' Jimbo corrected him.

The combined firing of rifles and machine-guns on the distant hills was not all that loud from where they were, but once the bullets and tracers reached the area it became a clamorous combination of spitting, hissing, thudding and cracking, with the rocks making a sharp exploding sound when they were split by the bullets.

'I think we should keep moving,' Ellsworth said. 'It's pitch-dark in the bottom of this wadi and as long as we don't climb back up into the moonlight, they won't be able to see us.'

Given Ellsworth's relative inexperience, Dead-eye and Jimbo were both impressed and nodded in agreement. Then Dead-eye raised and lowered his right hand, indicating that the men should get back into their respective armoured cars. As they were hurrying to do so, a mortar shell exploded about

50 yards away, tearing the soil up in a mushroom of smoke and flying foliage, large stones, dust and loose gravel. The debris, when it rained back down, made an eerie hissing sound which grew louder as the roaring of the explosion faded away.

That first mortar explosion was followed by others as the last of the men were practically dragged into the Saladins and the column continued its tentative advance along the wadi without the benefit of lights. As the convoy left its original position, the enemy tracer and mortars spread out in a wider arc, moving away from the column in one direction, advancing towards it in another, indicating that the guerrillas were now firing blind, not knowing in which direction the column was moving and hoping to hit at least part of it by accident.

Luckily, the next time the lead vehicle, Ellsworth's, hit a larger boulder, the column was out of range of the enemy fire. But the tracer and mortar explosions continued to come nearer the column as the men in the captain's vehicle clambered out to roll the stone away. Even as he was directing two of his troopers in this difficult task, the darkness was brilliantly illuminated by the jagged flash of another exploding mortar, which showered the men in stones, gravel and swirling, choking sand.

Dead-eye materialized out of the settling cloud of sand, wiping some of it from his flat, grey eyes. He glanced back over his shoulder as more explosions erupted between the armoured cars and a hail of bullets ricocheted noisily off them. Turning back to Ellsworth, he said: 'I don't think we can make it any further in the Saladins. Those guerrillas will keep firing blindly down here until they hit one of us. When they do, the flames from the burning vehicle will light up the rest of us. I think we should make the rest of the journey by foot.'

'That's one hell of a hike, Sergeant.'

'Better than sitting here and being shot to pieces.'

More mortar shells exploded, one showering Ellsworth and Dead-eye with soil, sand and gravel. The captain glanced up at the dark hills, where he could see the minute flashes of the enemy rifles and machine-guns, then turned back to Dead-eye. 'I think you're right. We can move a boulder in the darkness, but we can't get an armoured car out of a pothole without using the torches, and that would be the end of us.' He nodded, covered his ears to shut out the roaring of another mortar explosion and clapped his hand over his face until the stinging, swirling sand and gravel had settled down, then said: 'Right. We'll hike out of here under covering fire from the Saladins' guns.'

While Ellsworth was telling the two troopers trying to move the boulder to forget it and get their weapons out of the armoured car, Dead-eye was making his way back down the line to tell the other men to do the same. Even before the first of them had climbed down, the 76mm QF guns and Browning .30-inch machine-guns of the armoured cars were roaring into life to rake the distant hills in the general direction of the flickering enemy guns.

Terry was one of the first out, jumping to the ground with his bergen on his back and his SLR in his right hand. Almost bowled over by the explosion from a mortar shell mere yards away, he staggered, steadied himself, ran through the hissing gravel and sand, then doubled up and vomited uncontrollably.

Gasping for breath, he glanced around to see if anyone had noticed. Relieved to see that the other men were too concerned with making their way between the explosions of the mortar shells and spitting lines of machine-gun fire, he knelt down, quickly wiped his boots clean with a paper handkerchief, then straightened up enough to run at the crouch towards the opposite side of the wadi.

Once there, Terry knelt beside Jimbo, Ben and Taff, all of whom were looking up to where the moon was lighting up parts of the steep, rocky slope. Feeling faint, but trying to hide it, he said: 'Well, are we going up or not?'

'Not much fucking choice,' Jimbo replied gruffly. 'Yes, Trooper, we're going up. Ready, lads?' They all nodded. 'Move out!'

With the Saladins' guns roaring in their ears, the men hurried up the lower slopes of the hill, soon leaving the explosions of the mortar shells and rebounding bullets behind them and melting into the moon-streaked darkness.

When the last of the men on foot had left the bed of the wadi, the Saladins turned around and went back the way they had come, keeping up a hail of fire in order to draw the attention of the guerrillas away from the troops scaling the rocky slopes. By the time the enemy guns had finally stopped firing – the guerrillas obviously convinced that they had forced a retreat – the SAS men had melted into the moonlit darkness above the wadi.

Silence enfolded them.

9

Halfway up the hill, the patrol turned east and headed away from where they had seen the guerrilla guns flickering. Adopting the diamond formation more suitable to open country, with Dead-eye out front on point and Jimbo acting as Tail-end Charlie, they marched through the moonlit darkness in silence. Even at night, the heat was stifling, making all of them sweat, but luckily this gave way to a comforting breeze as they climbed ever higher up out of the wadi.

It was not an easy march. Each man was still burdened down with his 60lb bergen, SLR and four magazines, plus a bandolier of the same ammunition and 200 rounds of .303-inch for the patrol's Bren gun, the latter weapon being carried between the even more heavily laden Ben and Taff. Each man also carried his full ration of water –

a one-gallon container and four water bottles per head. As for Terry, he was growing increasingly worried about having vomited, was not feeling any better for it, and soon began feeling exhausted from having to hump the additional weight of his A41 tactical radio.

By contrast, the other members of the patrol were in good spirits as they tramped between rocks and over the dunes of Wadi Rabwa. The higher they climbed, the more they were exposed to moonlight and the less dangerous the march became, given increased visibility. Nearing the top of the hill, they saw the mountains of the Radfan clearly, with the dark mass of the 3900-foot Jebel Ashqab soaring up to their right. Their objective lay on the other side.

The very thought of the climb was enough to fill Terry with fear. When he first saw the mountain, his stomach twitched involuntarily with nerves. This was followed by a spasm of darting pains that almost made him cry out, but he bit his lower lip and continued climbing in silence. His breathing was becoming more difficult and soon he was stopping frequently to fill his lungs.

By the time the patrol had climbed out of the wadi and was crossing open ground to the lower slopes of the Jebel Ashqab, Terry could hardly control the spasms in his guts and knew that he would have to throw up again. This he did after deliberately falling back to the rear of the column, forgetting that Jimbo was bringing up the rear a good distance behind the main formation. Terry was wiping his lips dry when Jimbo caught up with him.

'What are you doing here?' he asked, before seeing the mess around Terry's boots. 'Oh, Christ!' he said softly.

'Sorry, Sarge.'

'Too late for that, Trooper. You don't seem to be improving.'

'I'll probably be all right after this.'

'Let's hope so.' Still holding his SLR at the ready, Jimbo was glancing left, right and back over his shoulder as he talked, not forgetting the possible presence of the enemy and the constant need for alertness. 'All right,' he said, turning back to Terry, 'get back up there with the column. If you don't think you can cope, let me know. Meanwhile, I'll be watching you.'

'Yes, Sarge. Thanks.' Thoroughly ashamed of himself, Terry grabbed his SLR and hurried to catch up with the others and take his position at the rear of the diamond-shaped formation. He managed to keep up for another hour or so, but gradually fell behind again.

This time some of the other men saw him and automatically slowed down to let him catch up. At the head of the column, but well behind Dead-eye, who was still the scout, Captain Ellsworth saw something was happening and was about to make enquiries when Jimbo caught up with Terry and spoke quietly to him. Looking troubled even from where Ellsworth was standing, Terry wiped sweat from his face, adjusted the straps of his radio distractedly, then hurried to catch up with the rest of the men. When they saw him coming, they started off again and Ellsworth, deciding that, whatever was wrong, Jimbo must know what he was doing, marched on with them.

By now they were embarked on the even more arduous climb up the steep, rocky slopes of the mountain itself, where the loose gravel slid underfoot and patches of smooth lava gave way abruptly to sinking sand that could scarcely be seen in the darkness. More than one of the men tripped and fell, rolling downhill in a noisy tide of gravel until he was stopped by a boulder or the hand of a comrade. Others were visibly struggling for breath, owing to a combination of exertion and the night's stifling heat.

Given the problems faced by the healthier men, it came as no surprise to Jimbo when Terry vomited again, fell back again to catch his breath and caused the men nearest to him to stop and wait for him to catch up. This time, Jimbo called the patrol's medic, Lance-Corporal Larry Johnson, down the hill and told him to give the ailing trooper something for his stomach.

'What do you think caused it?' Larry asked, letting down from his shoulder his well-stocked medicine box.

'I don't know,' Terry said.

'Don't bullshit me, Trooper. I can't decide what to give you until I have a rough idea of what's wrong. Was it something you ate?'

'How would I know?' Terry responded, glancing anxiously at Jimbo.

The sergeant shook his head wearily. 'He had something from a food stall in Aden and I'm willing to lay odds that's what did it. Those carts aren't hygienic and he's not used to the food either. He's fucking well poisoned himself.'

Larry nodded. 'Bloody stupid thing to do,' he said, searching through the wooden box.

'I knew you'd say that,' Terry said.

'Not much else to say, is there, Trooper? Any stomach pains?'

'Yes.'

'Nausea?'

'Yes.'

'Fever?'

'I think so. We're all sweating so much climbing this mountain, I'm not sure.'

'Sweat's one thing; heat is another.' Larry placed his hand on Terry's forehead and cheeks. 'Fever. Diarrhoea or constipation?'

'I had pretty severe runs before leaving camp.' Larry glanced automatically at Jimbo. Terry, seeing the glance, hastened to explain: 'But it passed away the night before and I seemed to be all right the next day, which is why I didn't report it.'

'And now?'

'It seems to be constipation.'

'Which won't help your breathing.'

'I'm having trouble with that, too.'

Larry nodded. 'Food poisoning. I can't say how severe. I'll make you a little brew of tea, powdered charcoal and milk of magnesia.' Terry grimaced, but Larry, now grinning, continued: 'It tastes rotten, but it might absorb the poison in your stomach. I'll also give you some aspirin to bring down your fever. If neither remedy works, then the poisoning is severe and we've got problems.'

With the forward half of the patrol continuing to climb the mountain, unaware of what was happening behind them, the other troopers in the rear, not sure what to do, waited for Larry and Terry to finish what they were doing and catch up. Aware of this, Terry felt distinctly uncomfortable, but could only wait until Larry had mixed his potion in a metal cup and handed it to him. It tasted awful.

When Terry handed the cup back, Larry gave him two aspirins, poured some water into the same cup, handed it to him and told him to wash the tablets down. This was marginally easier than swallowing the first potion, but Terry literally took his medicine as punishment.

'If it gets worse, tell me,' said Larry, before packing his medicine box and hurrying back up the steep hill. Chastened, Terry glanced at Jimbo, who just nodded, grim-faced, indicating that he should follow Larry. When Terry had done so, the rest of the men began the climb again, now separated from the others by a large gap.

A cardinal mistake, Jimbo thought. *The guerrillas*

could use that gap to divide us and then we'd be finished. We can't continue like this.

Luckily, they were nearing the summit and the steep slope was gradually levelling out. Though it was still warm, a strong wind was blowing, moaning mournfully across the rolling hills and around the jagged peaks. Below, where the Wadi Rabwa cut through the flat desert, was almost total darkness, illuminated here and there by moonlight catching high rocks. It looked like a black sea of unknown depth.

Terry fell back again – and once more the men nearest to him waited for him to catch up while those in front kept marching, unaware that half of the column had stopped behind them. With another dangerous gap in the column having been created, Captain Ellsworth hurried back down the line to check what was happening.

'Trooper Malkin has an upset stomach,' Jimbo informed him, not mentioning the real reason. 'He must have picked up a bug and not known about it until we were well under way. He told me about it, boss, but by then it was too late to turn back the convoy. Lance-Corporal Johnson's already given him some medicine, but it doesn't appear to be working.'

Ellsworth studied the sweating, white-faced trooper. 'Is it bad?'

'Pretty bad, boss,' Terry readily confessed, grateful that Jimbo had saved his skin.

Ellsworth was about to say something else when Larry came back to join them.

'Still bad?' he asked, placing his hand on Terry's forehead to discover that it was still burning.

'Yes,' Terry said.

'Still feeling nauseous?'

'My stomach's settled down a bit, but I'm still having the pains.'

'Breathing problems?'

'Yes.'

Larry turned to the captain. 'He's suffering from food poisoning, boss. I was hoping it was mild, but I think we're out of luck. Not much I can do for him at the moment, except give him more of the same in the hope that it'll drain out some of the poison.'

'Assuming the second dose works,' Ellsworth asked, 'how long will it be before it takes effect?'

'A couple of hours.'

'So what do we do?' Ellsworth asked of Jimbo as Larry prepared another potion. 'We can't call in a CasEvac chopper and we can't leave him here.'

'Now that we're on the mountain and back in file formation, I suggest we put him in the middle of the file and redistribute the loads, with someone else carrying the radio. Lance-Corporal Moody's pretty good with it, so put him in charge of it.'

'Right, let's do that. Trooper, the radio.'

'But, boss . . .'

'Hand it over!'

Sighing deeply, Terry unstrapped the A41.

'I'll take that,' Ellsworth said. 'Signal when you're ready to move out. This delay has left a breach in the column and that could be dangerous.'

'Right, boss,' Jimbo said.

The captain marched back to the middle of the formation, as far as the gap, to give the radio to Les.

'Bloody typical!' Les complained quietly to his mate, Ken, when the captain had moved on to take up his position at the head of the second group. 'Malkin farts about in Aden, playing cowboys and Indians, then comes down with some bug that I'd bet he picked up from some filthy A-rab grub. They ought to RTU the little prick.'

'Difficult to RTU him from here,' Ken replied, grinning as Les strapped the radio onto his packed bergen. 'Anyway, that extra weight should do you good – keep the fat off you, mate.'

'Fuck you an' all, mate!'

When Larry had given Terry another dose of his potion, both men hiked back up to join the others. There, Terry was placed safely in the middle, so that he could be helped by the others should he falter. The patrol moved off again, the second half hurrying to catch up with the first.

Within half an hour it became clear that Terry was having even more difficulty breathing and was struggling even harder to keep up. At 0200 hours an exasperated Captain Ellsworth, increasingly worried about the gap being caused by Terry's erratic pace, called for a break and huddled down to confer with Dead-eye and Jimbo.

Though short of the precipice rising to the summit, they were now almost at the top of the highest ridge on Jebel Ashqab and, even better, sheltered from the wind by two ancient stone sangars that could only have been constructed as firing positions by local tribesmen.

'According to our original plan,' Ellsworth said, 'we were supposed to be in hiding on the objective before dawn, which is approximately 0530 hours. We'd then lie concealed until dusk, when we'd secure the DZ perimeter and identify it with torches and an Aldis lamp for the Paras' descent later that night. Unfortunately, Trooper Malkin's become a bit of a liability, dividing the patrol too often for my liking and also slowing us down considerably. At our present rate of progress, given the number of times we're having to stop, we won't reach the DZ on time. Any proposals, gentlemen?'

Dead-eye checked his logbook, then looked up again. 'According to my dead reckoning, we're still about three miles from the objective.'

'With this kind of climb, that's a long way. Now too long for us to get there by first light.'

'Right,' Jimbo said. 'And to be caught in the open after sunrise would make us soft targets for the guerrilla snipers hiding on the hilltops.'

'Which would compromise the entire operation,' Ellsworth said grimly.

They were silent for a moment. The captain stared moodily at the wall of the sangar, Jimbo peered over it at the hills silhouetted in the distance against the starry sky, and Dead-eye calmly studied his notes.

'It's not that bad,' he said eventually, raising his steady grey eyes to look directly at them. 'From here, it's all downhill to the DZ, which means we'll move quicker than we've been doing so far – even if we're held up again by Trooper Malkin. I estimate that we can cover the remaining ground at dusk tomorrow and still get to the DZ in time for the Paras' drop.'

Ellsworth nodded his agreement, then glanced around the sangar. 'Well,' he said, 'why not? If these sangars were built by tribesmen, the locals won't be suspicious if they see movement up here – they'll think we're Yemeni guerrillas. So, yes, Sergeant, let's basha down here until tomorrow night. That might also buy enough time for Trooper Malkin to recover.'

'This sangar's bigger than the other one,' Dead-eye observed, glancing over the wall at the sangar opposite, 'so we'll divide into two groups, one of four men, the other of five, and put the largest group in here.'

'That sounds sensible,' Ellsworth said. 'I'll stay here with the radio operator. You divide the rest up as you think best.'

'Corporal Brooke and Lance-Corporal Moody work well together, and since Moody's now got the radio, we'll put Brooke in here with you. As your second in command, I'll stay here as well. I don't think the smaller group should include someone as sick as Trooper Malkin, so we'll have him in here as our fifth man. Sergeant Ashman here . . .' – Dead-eye nodded at Jimbo – 'will be in charge of the other sangar, with Lance-Corporal Johnson and Troopers Riley and Thomas. The latter two will man the Bren gun.'

'Don't you think Johnson should be in with Trooper Malkin, to look after him?'

'No, boss. Johnson's already given Malkin his medicine and says it'll be a couple of hours before it takes effect – if it does. If it doesn't, on the other hand, the sangars are only a few feet apart, so we can get Johnson in here in seconds if the need arises. I think it's more important that the smaller group, being in charge of our sole machine-gun, is composed of healthy, alert men. So Malkin should stay here with us.'

'Fine,' Ellsworth said. 'Please attend to it, Sergeant.'

Dead-eye and Jimbo sorted the men into their two separate groups, each of which took over its own sangar: Captain Ellsworth, Dead-eye, Ken, Les and Terry in the larger one; Jimbo, Larry, Ben and Taff in the smaller.

'We always get the second-rate accommodation,' Ben groaned. 'That's 'cause we're the virgins.'

'They don't respect our finer qualities,' Taff agreed. 'They think we're second-class citizens.'

'You have a complaint, Troopers?' Jimbo asked, appearing out of nowhere and glaring at them.

'What's that, Sarge?' Ben asked, startled.

'Are you complaining about the sangar you've been placed in?'

'No, Sarge!'

'Absolutely not, Sarge!' Taff Thomas added.

'Good. I wouldn't like to think you were unhappy. I like to feel that my men are well pleased with the decisions I make. Otherwise, I'd be forced to put my boot halfway up your arseholes.'

'We're both fine,' Taff said quickly.

'Then get your lucky arseholes into that sangar and start setting things up.'

Once in their respective sangars, the men set them up like regular OPs, with rubber groundsheets rolled out for sleeping on, ponchos raised over the sangars and covered with loose gravel and vegetation, and a well for weapons dug out in the middle between the groundsheets. The men then tossed for who took the first watch and who the first nap. When this was decided, most of them settled in for the night, either sleeping or on sentry duty.

However, just before he lay down for his own three hours of sleep, Captain Ellsworth asked Les to contact Lieutenant-Colonel Callaghan in the Thumier HQ. When Les had done so, Ellsworth explained what had happened and what they planned to do. Callaghan, who had been in worse situations, swept Ellsworth's apologies aside and agreed that there was no alternative. He then told him to have a good sleep and wished him luck for the morrow.

The communication over, a more relaxed Captain Ellsworth sighed and settled down for the night. Though the air beneath the camouflaged ponchos was hot and stifling, he, like most of the men, slept well.

10

The sun rose at 0530 hours as an immense fiery ball that poured what looked like lava along the mountain peaks, increasing the temperature and bringing with it the tormenting flies and mosquitoes. In the morning's crimson-hued light, the men awoke, yawned, rubbed their eyes and joined the sentries at the wall, looking down the hill to see an Arab hamlet a mere 1000 yards below them. The hamlet was little more than a random collection of mud-and-stone houses, with goats tethered to posts, chickens cooped up in wire-mesh cages, mangy, scavenging dogs, and Arab men and women going about their morning chores.

'No guerrillas down there,' Captain Ellsworth said.

'Yes, there are,' Dead-eye corrected him, pointing to the ridge directly above the hamlet, about

50 yards from the sangars, where armed men were tramping uphill to begin what would be a long day's watch.

'Damn!' Ellsworth whispered, as much embarrassed as surprised.

Annoyed to find that they were so close to a village held by the guerrillas, Dead-eye checked his map, then said: 'That must be Shi'b Taym.' Even as he looked up from the map, more guerrillas emerged from some of the primitive houses to eat breakfast around a communal table in the middle of the settlement, near what looked like a well. 'They're holding the village, all right.'

'Damn!' Ellsworth repeated, this time louder.

'Well,' Dead-eye said. 'Not much we can do except take notes, enjoy the scenery and wait for darkness to come. When it does, we can move out unseen.'

Ellsworth sighed. 'I suppose so.' Turning away from the wall to look at the other three men in the sangar, he saw that Terry still looked white and drawn. Ken and Les were making a brew-up with a hexamine stove and unwrapping their cold rations of dried biscuits and cheese. Terry was staring at the ground and licking his dry lips. 'How do you feel, Trooper?' Ellsworth asked.

'Not too good, boss.'

'Should we call Lance-Corporal Johnson over again?'

'I don't think he can do anything, boss. I haven't got diarrhoea and I'm not throwing up any more. It's these pains in my stomach, and I still feel pretty weak.'

Ellsworth glanced at the impassive Dead-eye, then turned back to Terry. 'Have you tried eating?'

The trooper nodded. 'I've tried, but I just can't stomach it. I'm all right until I think about food, then I feel nauseous.'

'He might be better off not eating,' Dead-eye said. 'Eating might start the runs or even make his pains worse. Whatever's wrong with him, no matter how bad it is, he'll just have to bear it until this is over and we're back at base camp. We can't call in a CasEvac.'

'No, I'm afraid not.' Ellsworth turned to Terry. 'But I think you should lie down, Trooper. Rest as much as possible.'

'Right, boss,' Terry replied, obviously relieved, before stretching out on the groundsheet in his shallow 'scrape' and rolling onto his side. He was still breathing harshly.

Turning away from Terry, Ellsworth and Dead-eye looked over the sangar wall. The guerrillas had taken up their lookout positions on the hills above the village and almost certainly could see the SAS men's sangars from where they were. Luckily, though, they were looking at their own rebel army's sangars and would not give them much thought so long as the SAS patrol stayed out of sight.

'Nice touch,' Ken said. 'We could stay here until the Millennium and they wouldn't know we were here. Perhaps we should pay them rent!'

The morning passed uneventfully. Down in the hamlet, the Arabs got on with their business, which consisted largely of feeding their goats and chickens, tending a small area of cultivated land, drawing water from the well and, judging from the smoke coming from various chimneys, lighting fires and cooking. Later some of the veiled women emerged to wash clothes in tubs placed in the middle of the village. The older men sat outside their houses, talking to each other, smoking from hookahs or surveying the empty desert and mountains.

'It's almost biblical,' Les said, taking a break from his radio to glance down over the wall.

'You'll see the parting of the waters any minute. Moses clutching the tablets.'

'I can't believe you've read the Bible,' Ken replied.

'I didn't,' Les replied. 'I saw the film. Cecil B. de Mille's *The Ten Commandments*. Fucking great, it was.'

'All that took place in Egypt,' Ken informed him. 'Not in this hell-hole.'

'Stick a pyramid down there and you'd swear it was Egypt,' Les said. 'Either that or a film set.'

'Get back to your radio,' Dead-eye barked, 'and stop distracting Corporal Brooke with your chit-chat. Corporal Brooke, you're supposed to be the sentry, so keep your eyes on that hamlet.'

'Yes, Sarge!'

'Daft fuckers,' Dead-eye muttered to himself.

In the early hours of the morning, the Arab children ran amok, playing in the dirt or chasing the dogs and goats; but later armed guerrillas emerged from one of the houses, organized them into a small group of three short lines, then marched them around the village clearing. Marching, the children chanted in unison: '*Allah yansir Nasir!*' ('God makes Nasser victorious!'), their voices shrill and pure, rising up clearly to the men hiding in the sangars. Dead-eye suddenly noticed that even the village elders had rifles beside them.

'That's a guerrilla village,' he said. 'They won't be on our side.'

'Let's remember that,' Ellsworth said.

Nevertheless, undetected as they were, they were able to relax, though Les explored the frequencies on his radio, trying to pick up enemy communications, Ken kept his eyes on the guerrillas on the hill opposite, and Dead-eye carefully entered in his logbook everything that was taking place down in the village. He even noted the exact time when the marching, chanting children were disbanded by their guerrilla trainers and allowed to return to their playing. When they did so, the silence returned, broken only by the odd shout of a guerrilla, a burst of laughter from one of the women around the wash tubs, or the barking of the dogs.

The morning passed slowly. By 1100 hours the sun was high in the sky, making the air beneath the camouflaged ponchos hot and stifling. Sweating profusely, the men were attacked by increasing numbers of buzzing, blue-bodied flies and whining mosquitoes. Drifting in and out of sleep, Terry dripped sweat and often groaned and slapped weakly at the insects. The other men cursed and swatted repeatedly at the same, though this merely agitated the insects and made them attack all the more frantically.

By noon the men could smell themselves and the air was even hotter and claustrophobic. Half an hour later the silence below the sangar was broken by the tinkling of small bells. Glancing down, Captain Ellsworth, Dead-eye and Ken, who were peering through the space between the ponchos and the top of the sangar wall, saw a herd of goats approaching along a small wadi only a few feet from the two sangars. The animals were being guided by a herdsman who shouted to a woman coming up the hill, telling her to watch out for the strays. The herdsman, however, apart from his walking stick, also had a .303 Lee-Enfield bolt-action sniper rifle slung over his shoulder.

'Not just your average villager,' Ken whispered as he studied the herdsman. 'That bastard's a Yemeni guerrilla.'

'Correct,' Dead-eye said.

They were joined at the wall by Les. As if communicating telepathically, the four of them cocked and raised their SLRs at the same time, covering the herdsman as he continued advancing up the hill. Thankfully, the woman to whom he was calling out was a good distance behind him, still practically at the bottom of the hill, at the hamlet's unfenced edge.

'He's getting close,' Ellsworth whispered to Dead-eye.

'Yes, boss.'

'We could do with a prisoner for interrogation. Could we grab him without causing a fuss?'

'Hardly, boss. His girlfriend down below would see everything.'

Ellsworth sighed. He then signalled by hand for the others to be silent, as the herdsman was now very close to the other sangar. Though he saw no movement from there, he knew that Jimbo would be on the alert and that Ben and Taff were probably already keeping the man covered with the Bren gun.

There was nothing for it but to wait and pray that the herdsman would not come close enough to spot them.

'If that bastard ...' Ken was saying when suddenly the herdsman stopped, studied the two sangars, then bawled a warning to the woman below. Even as he turned to run back down the hill, unslinging his Lee Enfield on the move, the woman let out a demented falsetto wail that cut the silence like a knife and was clearly a warning to the guerrillas down in the village.

'Fuck!' Dead-eye whispered. 'The game's up.'

Foolishly, the running herdsman stopped briefly to turn back and take aim with his rifle. A single, high-velocity shot exploded in Ellsworth's right ear. Startled, he glanced sideways and saw Dead-eye squinting along the sight of his SLR, which now had smoke drifting out of its barrel. Ellsworth glanced down again as the herdsman, slammed backwards by Dead-eye's bullet, dropped his rifle and then fell and rolled further down the hill in a shower of gravel and sand.

As the woman continued her eerie, high-pitched wailing, meanwhile running back towards the hamlet, armed guerrillas burst from some of the hovels, fanning out as they ran, and started up the lower slopes, firing their rifles as they advanced. The woman threw herself to the ground as her comrades' bullets whistled over her head and bounced off the two sangars.

The Bren gun in the smaller sangar roared into action, tearing up sand and soil in a jagged, dancing line that first cut across, then through, the ranks of advancing guerrillas, making some of them shudder violently and fall over. The roar of the combined fire of the SAS small arms was added to that of the light machine-gun, creating even more havoc among the advancing guerrillas. More died, and others were wounded. The screams of the latter cut through the gunfire. The other guerrillas spread out over a wider arc and advanced uphill by darting from one rock to another under the covering fire of their comrades. Eventually, however, pinned down by the fusillade from the SAS guns, they had to content themselves with taking pot-shots from behind the boulders. Though they did not hit any of the patrol, they came close many times.

'We can keep them pinned down from here,' Ken said. 'No problem at all. The minute they stick their turbaned heads up, we can take their heads off, turbans and all. They can't do too much down there.'

At that moment, however, the guerrillas watching from the opposite ridge also opened fire with their rifles. Given that the ridge was only 50 yards away from the sangars and 20 feet higher, they could survey the whole sweep of the ground and aim with great accuracy. Their bullets ricocheted off the walls of both sangars, fragmenting the rocks and filling the space inside with boiling dust and flying pieces of sharp stone that cut like razors.

'Damn!' Ellsworth exploded, twisting away from the wall and covering his face with his hands until the first burst of enemy gunfire had subsided. Removing his hands and wiping dust from around his eyes, he said to Les: 'Get in touch with Thumier and arrange for some air support to deal with that ridge. Once that's done, we can tackle the men below.'

'Right, boss.'

'Jimbo!' Dead-eye bawled at the second sangar during a brief lull in the firing.

'Yes, Dead-eye!' the cry came back.

'You all right over there?'

'No problem. We're all hale and hearty. Ready, willing and able.'

'Good. We're calling up air support.'

'Bloody right!' Jimbo shouted. 'That fucking ridge is going to do us all in.'

'In the meantime, I want you to keep that ridge covered with the Bren and everything else you've got. We'll concentrate on the ones below.'

'Hear you loud and clear, Dead-eye. Over and out!'

No sooner had Jimbo gone silent than the Bren

gun, manned by Ben and Taff, roared into life again, turning the higher slope of the opposite ridge into a convulsion of spitting soil and spiralling dust that obscured the enemy and temporarily made them keep their heads down. While the two troopers kept up a constant fusillade, Jimbo and Larry gave them support with their SLRs, adding to the hellish destruction on the ridge facing them.

'Here they come!' Dead-eye bawled, lowering the barrel of his SLR and squinting down the Trilux sight and foresight at the Arabs below him. With the Bren gun now concentrating on the ridge, the guerrillas on the slopes below had decided to tackle the hill again and were advancing, as before, by flitting expertly from one rock to another, firing only when safely shielded.

'Conserve your ammo,' Dead-eye reminded the others. 'Fire only when you've got a specific target. We don't know how long we're going to be trapped here, so every bullet counts.'

A fluttering *shemagh* was just about all Dead-eye saw of an Arab who suddenly jumped up from behind a rock and dashed in a cloud of dust towards another. But that was enough. With the speed and accuracy he had perfected in South-east Asia, Dead-eye switched to single shot, squeezed the trigger once, and put a bullet into his target's head. The guerrilla spun away from him, his head jerking violently sideways, his rifle spinning to the ground as his hands clawed at the air, trying desperately to grasp something as the real world dissolved. He fell twisting like a corkscrew, already dead meat and bone, and had barely thudded into the ground when another Arab jumped up and ran.

Dead-eye and Ken fired at the same time, both on single shot. The guerrilla's head jerked to the left, his body twisted to the right, and he dropped his rifle to claw frantically, disbelievingly at his wounds – one hand on his bloody chest, the other covering his shattered head – and then went into a St Vitus's dance and fell face first in the dust.

Some of the Arabs behind the rocks, incensed by the deaths of their comrades, leant out recklessly and fired a few shots. The bullets zipped off the sangar walls, splitting chips off the stones and filling the air with choking dust; but even before the dust cleared Dead-eye and Ken were firing again, keeping the Arabs pinned down. While the two were thus engaged, Captain Ellsworth was kneeling on the ground beside Les, who, having made radio contact with Thumier, was looking enquiringly at his CO.

'You have a link-up?' Ellsworth asked, shouting above the roaring of the guns from both sangars.

'Yes, boss. I've got Major Williamson on the line.'

Relieved, Ellsworth relayed his request for air support to the SAS second in command at HQ. He then turned back to look over the sangar wall at the lower slopes of the hill, where bullets from the SLRs of Dead-eye and Ken were making soil and sand spit heavenwards between the rocks shielding the guerrillas.

'You got through?' Dead-eye asked.

'Yes.'

'How long will they take to get here?'

'Half an hour, I should think,' Ellsworth replied sardonically. 'Apart from the time required for the flight, communication won't be that immediate. First, my message to the SIC at Thumier will have to be amplified by a civilian radio transmitter. It'll then be relayed by field telephone to the RAF Brigade Air Support Officer in another tent. With a telephone in one hand and a microphone in the other, the Air Support Officer will then repeat my request, with specific fire orders, to the Hawker

Hunters at RAF Khormaksar. Add fifteen minutes for take-off and the flight and you have a fair estimate.'

'I'm encouraged,' Dead-eye said.

Ellsworth's estimate was fairly accurate. The first pair of RAF Hawker Hunter F Mark 6 single-seat fighters appeared over the southern horizon about thirty minutes after contact had been made. As more enemy rifle fire struck the sangars from the top of the ridge and the lower slopes below them, the Hunters roared down with guns chattering savagely, wreaking devastation on their positions on the opposite ridge.

The ridge exploded in geysering soil and boiling dust, with foliage, gravel and splintered stones hailing all around the men trying desperately to make their escape. The ground erupted between them, one explosion following another, and soon the summit of the ridge was obscured completely in a dark pall of smoke, falling debris and drifting dust.

The screaming of the wounded reverberated around the hills. Arab voices were shouting frantically, calling to one another to verify who was still alive, who was wounded and how many were dead. When the dust settled down, the surviving guerrillas had fled back down the hill to the comparative safety of the rocks on the lower slopes surrounding the hamlet.

Unable to attack the other guerrillas on the slope directly below Ellsworth's position, the Hunters flew in low over the sangars, saluting the SAS, then turned back and headed for home.

'Jesus!' Ken whispered, taken aback by what he had just seen. Returned to consciousness by the noise, Terry merely looked around him, bewildered, then groaned and closed his eyes again. Ellsworth and Dead-eye, elbow to elbow, stared down the hill.

So violent had been the attack that the dust and smoke over the ridge began drifting down over the hamlet, where the women and children were emerging from their huts to gaze up in fear and awe. At the bottom of the slope, where the other guerrillas were still in hiding, one of them, enraged by the fighter attack, stood up in full view, roared a stream of abuse in Arabic, then raised his rifle to fire.

Dead-eye's SLR spoke first. The guerrilla was thrown back into the dirt as if floored by an invisible fist. Within seconds a fusillade of rifle fire aimed at the sangars tore the silence apart.

Ellsworth and Dead-eye lowered themselves behind the wall as bullets whistled over their heads and ricocheted off the rocks of the sangar wall, filling the stifling space with flying fragments of rock and choking dust.

'At least they'll stay off that ridge,' Ellsworth said, wiping dust from his eyes and lips, 'which means they won't be overlooking us. If they want us, they'll have to come up the hill, and that won't be that easy.'

'It won't be that hard, either,' Dead-eye said in his icily realistic way. 'The survivors from the ridge are joining the others at the bottom of the hill. I think we're in for a tough fight.'

When a low, choked, moaning sound filled the gloom of the sangar, they all looked down at the single shallow scrape near their feet. Terry was tossing and turning on his groundsheet, deathly white, pouring sweat.

'This is bad,' Ken whispered.

11

As the guerrillas flushed out from the devastated ridge moved east to join those hiding on the slopes of the southern hill, it became obvious to Ellsworth and Dead-eye that this conflict was not over by a long shot. In fact, as the first two Hunters disappeared over the horizon, heading back to Khormaksar, the growing numbers of guerrillas behind the rocks below began to spring up and fire rapid single shots, targeting anything they could see moving between the camouflaged poncho sheets and the top of the sangar walls.

The Arabs were good, and though they scored no direct hits, they repeatedly sent fragments of shattered stone into the faces of the SAS men whenever one of them attempted to peer over the sangar wall. After half an hour, both sangars were filled with choking dust and no man had escaped being bruised or cut. Their situation was made all the worse by the growing heat and the buzzing, whining insects, oblivious to the exploding rocks and thickening dust.

Each time a fresh round hit their position, the men in the two sangars would call out to one another, checking that everyone was all right. They also joked to keep up their sinking spirits. But, try as they might, they found it hard to see just where the shots were coming from, as by now the Arabs, more numerous every minute, were running to and fro, changing positions, and only popping up long enough to get off another round. The SAS men were encouraged when a second pair of Hunters appeared overhead. Guided down by the identification panels originally intended for the DZ and now spread out on the ground between the sangars, they wheeled and dived repeatedly on strafing runs that raised a maelstrom of dust, sand and debris around the Arabs, yet, amazingly, failed to dislodge them from their hiding places, from where they continued to fire single shots up the hill.

'Tenacious bastards,' Ken murmured, then raised himself slightly, squinted down through his Trilux sight, and fired off a couple of bursts of his SLR. He had the satisfaction of seeing an Arab throw up his arms in a convulsion of dust raised by the bullets, then drop his rifle and fall back behind the rock.

While the sniping match continued, with Dead-eye and Ken doing the shooting from the larger sangar, Terry continued to writhe in fever, unconscious but groaning. Captain Ellsworth, through Les, concentrated on getting messages to the Hunters, correcting their course during the run-ins to strafe the guerrillas.

'You're doing a good job there, boss,' Ken said.

The captain nodded his gratitude as he squinted intently at the strip of silvery-blue sky visible through the gap between the poncho and the top of the wall. Yet even as the RAF fighters were pounding the guerrillas below, Dead-eye saw more of the enemy coming over the ridge and making their way down through the smoke-filled hamlet, where the women and children were still outdoors, watching the fight as if at a fair. Once through the hamlet, the guerrillas made their way up the southern slope to join the others behind the rocks.

The rifle fire from below was becoming more intense, though Ben and Taff, in the smaller sangar, were keeping most of the Arabs pinned down with a ceaseless fusillade from the Bren gun, supported by Jimbo and Larry's SLRs.

'It's not enough,' Dead-eye observed. 'Those Arabs below are too close to us to be bombed, but we must stop any more guerrillas coming over that ridge. There must be a camp on the other side.'

'Artillery support?' Ellsworth asked.

'I think so,' Dead-eye said. 'I'd also ask for some more Hunters to locate the enemy camp on the other side of that ridge and give it a pounding.'

'Will do,' Ellsworth said.

The artillery strike was called up in the early afternoon and the explosions soon turned the sunlit ridge and the area beyond it into a hell of boiling smoke streaked with crimson and yellow flames. Even as a great mushroom of smoke was forming over the ridge, another couple of Hunters were flying above it to wheel and dive repeatedly on the camp they had obviously found at the other side. The noise of the explosions, combined with the savage chatter of the guns of the fighters, was deafening and nerve-racking, making the guerrillas further down the slope stop firing to look up in fearful awe at the ridge.

The SAS men cheered. Enraged by this, the

guerrillas behind the rocks opened fire once more with their rifles, now determined more than ever to get the accursed Englishmen off the hill. But though the Hunters continued to fly in on strafing runs against the snipers, they were becoming less effective as the sun set and the guerrillas were gradually coming closer, making their way, rock by rock, up the hill. As the sun sank low in the sky, the shadow of the east side of Jebel Ashqab crept over the sangars, then over the boulders below, where the guerrillas were sheltering. It would soon be dark.

'We'll lose our air support completely at last light,' Dead-eye reminded Captain Ellsworth. 'Those guerrillas haven't given up on us; they're just biding their time. Given the bashing they've taken and the destruction of their camp, they'll have a few debts to collect. They don't intend letting us escape. They're just waiting for darkness.'

But they did not wait. About half an hour later, clearly still angry at the bombing and frustrated that they could not dislodge the English soldiers, a group of guerrillas sprang out from behind their shelters and began a serious attempt to climb the hill, sprinting from one rock to the other, firing on the move, and covered by a murderous hail of fire from those still in hiding. So intense was the covering fusillade that both sangars became alive with exploding pieces of rock and dust, the men inside scarcely able to pop up long enough to return a single shot. All of them, including the delirious Terry, were cut by pieces of stone and choked by the dust. But Ken was the first to be actually wounded by a bullet, instinctively letting loose a cry of pain and clutching at his left leg.

'Shit!' he muttered, swiftly regaining control of himself and gritting his teeth. He examined his leg, saw his trouser leg soaked in blood, explored tentatively with his fingers, winced twice, then said: 'Fuck it. I've got two bullets in my left thigh. What a bloody mess!'

The Bren gun roared from the smaller sangar, cutting a swath through the advancing guerrillas, bowling quite a few over, and eventually forced the others to go to ground once more. Just as it stopped roaring, however, to enable Taff to put in another belt, Ben called out to Captain Ellsworth: 'I've been hit, boss!'

'Ben's been hit as well!' Ken echoed mockingly, despite his own pain.

'Shit!' Ben cried out in fear and shock through a

lull in the firing, ignoring Ken's remark. 'My back stings like hell!'

'The round crossed his back,' Larry explained encouragingly to Captain Ellsworth, also shouting between the two sangars, 'leaving a wound like a whiplash. It'll hurt, but he's OK. What about you, Corp'?'

'Two bullets in the fleshy part of the left thigh,' Ken bellowed above the renewed noise. 'It's bleeding a lot.'

It was also hurting badly, but he did not mention that fact. He examined the wounds carefully, his fingers soaked in blood and torn pieces of flesh, pressing here, pinching there, grimacing with pain, but still trying to discover just how bad the wound was.

'I think I've been lucky,' he said to the concerned Captain Ellsworth while Dead-eye jumped up to fire at a running Arab. 'The bullets are .303-inchers, but they're actually refills.'

'Pardon?' Ellsworth asked as Dead-eye's single shot made the running Arab stop, jerk upright, drop his weapon and fall back heavily into the dust.

'Refills,' Ken repeated, removing his dripping fingers from the sticky mess visible through his torn OGs. 'Old shell cases filled with a home-made charge. The velocity isn't great enough to penetrate bone. These wounds are pretty bad, but at least they're only flesh wounds. I'm not finished yet, boss.'

'Good man.' Ellsworth patted Ken on the shoulder, then glanced down the hill where another Arab was at that moment jerked off his feet by another single shot from Dead-eye's SLR. The guerrillas had settled down again and their covering fire had tapered off temporarily.

'Corporal Brooke!' Larry called out from the smaller sangar.

'Yes?'

'I'm going to throw over some extra field dressing weighted with a stone. Make sure someone catches it. Can you bandage yourself?'

'Yes.'

'Here it comes.'

As the extra dressing sailed through the air, from one sangar to the other, Les jumped up and grabbed it, and dropped down again beside Ken.

'Nice catch,' Ken said. He took the bandage from Les, examined it, then shouted over the sangar wall: 'Is this the best you can do after that expensive stint at the US Army Training School in Houston?'

'Any more remarks like that and I'll come over there and cut off that leg.'

'Sincere apologies, Lance-Corporal.' Tearing away the blood-soaked, torn cloth from the two bullet wounds, Ken studied the blood-filled holes with a cool eye. 'Not nice,' he murmured.

Sliding down beside him to examine the wound, Dead-eye said: 'You'll need a tourniquet as well as a bandage. Those wounds are bleeding too much.'

'I reckoned that,' Ken replied.

Dead-eye offered a rare, fleeting grin. 'Can you do it yourself?'

'Yes, Sarge. No sweat.'

'They're coming up the hill again!' Jimbo bawled from the other sangar.

The Bren gun roared into life again as Captain Ellsworth and Dead-eye glanced down through the slit between the poncho above them and the top of the wall. Again, the guerrillas at the front – at least a dozen of them – were making their way up the hill by darting from rock to rock under the covering fire of their comrades lower down, now lost in the gathering dusk. As Ellsworth glanced automatically at Les's radio, instinctively thinking of air support, Dead-eye poked the barrel of his SLR through the slit and began picking the guerrillas off one by one.

'Damn!' Ellsworth said, glancing back down the slope to confirm that darkness was falling rapidly. 'It's too late for air support.'

'Correct,' Dead-eye replied, still squinting through the sight of his SLR and felling the running guerrillas with unerring accuracy.

With no immediate need for the radio, Les picked up his SLR and started rising to his knees to join Ellsworth and Dead-eye at the firing slit. At that moment, the rifles giving covering fire to the guerrillas roared in a sustained burst. A couple of bullets penetrated the sangar and ricocheted from one side of it to another. Les yelped and collapsed, clutching at his right leg. Twisting around, he saw that he had been hit in the thigh, like Ken, but with only one bullet. Although the pain gave way to numbness almost immediately, blood spurted from the wound with the force of water from a burst pipe. Les quickly covered it with his hand, while reaching into the survival belt with the other for a bandage.

'Bloody 'ell!' he exclaimed softly, tentatively

touching the red-fringed hole with his fingers and feeling nothing at all. 'Welcome to the club.' Ken, propped up against the sangar wall beside Ellsworth and Dead-eye, covered in dust and pieces of gravel and stone, with his wounded leg stretched out in front of him, grinned at the remark. Grinning back, trying to make light of their common situation, Les expertly bandaged his own wound, then tried moving his leg. 'Can't feel it, can't move it,' he said. 'No use at all.'

Dead-eye stopped firing at the guerrillas long enough to glance back over his shoulder at Les, who was tentatively pressing the foot of his wounded leg against the wall.

'I can't support myself on this,' Les said.

'That could be fatal,' Dead-eye replied in his pragmatic way. 'If you can't make that leg function by dusk, you'll stay here as dead meat.'

'Thanks a lot, Sarge!'

'Get it working, Lance-Corporal. Keep exercising it. Don't stop until you get feeling and strength back into it. If feeling comes back into it, it'll hurt, but you'll just have to ignore that. Either you march out of here or you stay here and die. So get exercising.

Desperate to have the leg working before the

patrol moved on, Les lay there and started pressing his foot against the wall, over and over, while bullets flew off the sangar wall and filled the air inside with a fog of dust.

Within minutes another bullet whizzed from one side of the sangar interior to the other and grazed the inside of Les's good leg, making him yelp with pain again.

'Christ!' he burst out, examining the slight graze. 'Nearly lost my balls that time!'

Ken chuckled as he sat upright against the wall, testing his own wounded leg and becoming confident that he could walk on it, no matter how painful.

'Your voice went up a few octaves there,' he said. I thought you *had* lost your balls.'

'That's just jealousy and wishful thinking, mate. It's just a graze. I'm all right. At least *this* leg is. It's the right one that bothers me.'

As the battle raged, Les kept testing his leg against the sangar wall. Gradually, feeling returned, bringing excruciating pain with it.

'Christ, it hurts!' he muttered.

'At least now you know you've got it,' Ken replied. 'Thank the Lord for small mercies.'

Wincing with pain, Les picked up his SLR and

turned to the front. At that moment the guerrillas attempted to rush the sangar. In the half light of dusk, partially obscured by the dust kicked up by their running feet, and with their *futahs* and *shemaghs* flapping, they looked like ghosts. They were real enough, though, as was proven when they screamed, quivered and fell, cut down by the Bren gun and sustained small-arms fire of the SAS.

The enemy were now very close and two of them had actually reached the wall of the larger sangar and attempted valiantly to push it over. This was brave, but unwise. Dead-eye and Les stood up simultaneously, the latter ignoring the pain in his wounded leg, and fired short, lethal bursts into the guerrillas, who quivered epileptically, their robes torn to shreds and soaked with blood, then fell back into the billowing dust.

Two more short bursts tore through the other guerrillas, killing some, wounding others, and the remainder fled back down the hill, leaving their dead, but dragging the screaming wounded with them. Before they could be shot at, Dead-eye and Les dropped back into the sangar, leaning against the wall and squinting through the deepening, dust-filled darkness at their ghost-like comrades.

Captain Ellsworth was squatting beside the groaning, restless Terry while Ken, his eyes gleaming sardonically out of circles of dust, methodically exercised his wounded leg.

Sighing, Ellsworth left Terry and returned to the firing slit of the sangar to look down over the wall. The guerrillas had fled back down the hill and could not be seen in the darkness. They had dragged away their wounded, but the dead still littered the moonlit slopes, some so dusty that they resembled the rocks about them. The dust, which was still blowing over them, took the shape of spectral figures and moaned softly, eerily. There was no other sound.

'It's time to leave,' Dead-eye said, brutally breaking the silence.

12

'That was Lieutenant-Colonel Callaghan,' Captain Ellsworth said, handing the microphone of the A41 back to the wounded Les Moody. 'He's just confirmed what we already knew: air cover has been called off for the night. We're all on our own now.'

He glanced down over the wall of the sangar, but saw only moonlight gleaming on the smooth volcanic rock between patches of sand on the slope that ran down to the hamlet. Though seeing nothing else, he knew, as did the others, that the guerrillas were still down there, preparing to move against the sangars. Indeed, they were probably advancing right now by moving stealthily from rock to rock under cover of darkness.

Turning back to his men, he said: 'Might as well admit it. Our original plan to mark the Paras' DZ has gone for a burton. All we can do now is attempt to break out and make our way back to Thumier. There's not going to be a rendezvous, so we might as well get on with it.' Then, as if unable to hold in his frustration, he added explosively: 'What a bloody disaster!'

'Like this whole bloody war,' Ken said, forlornly studying his wounded leg. 'A complete waste of time from start to finish. Lost before it began. Bloody politicians!'

No one said anything, but they all agreed with him. This was one of the few engagements they had been in that had given them no sense of pride or achievement. As their squadron commander had told them, this war was a lost cause created by politicians intent on getting Britain out of the colony while leaving a British presence there at the same time. That remaining presence, of which the SAS was a small part, had the least enviable job of all: defending a people who did not want to be defended and increasingly supported the so-called enemy. Most of the men felt bitter about this and, rather than taking pride in what they were doing, just wanted to do their best while stuck there and get the hell back home as soon as possible. It was not a good way to fight.

'Anyway, Callaghan agrees that we should try to break out and he's arranged to send in another troop by helicopter, to lend us support. That chopper is already on its way and should be here soon. Meanwhile, we wait. Sergeant Parker?'

'Yes, boss,' Dead-eye said from his position at the sangar wall, where he was keeping his eye on the moonlit slope with the aid of his night-vision goggles.

'Any sign of movement down there?'

'Not yet – though I suspect they're on the move. That chopper had better come soon.'

'Indeed it had, Sergeant. Keep your eyes peeled. What about you men? Are you all right?'

'Absolutely fine, boss,' Ken replied laconically, looking down at his bandaged, bloody leg, then glancing across at his similarly wounded friend. 'I've done my left leg, Lance-Corporal Moody's done his right, and Trooper Malkin's practically delirious with an upset stomach and a raging fever. Apart from that, we're fine, boss.'

'Do you think you can make it out of here?'

'Yes, boss. Both of us can just about walk and we'll do anything – and I mean *anything* – to get the hell out of here. As for Trooper Malkin, though, I've got my doubts . . .' He glanced sideways to where Terry was stretched out in his shallow scrape, no longer tossing and turning on his rubber groundsheet because he was now too weak for even that. 'What the hell do we do? The kid's out like a light. Les and I can just about walk – we can't carry Terry. That leaves you and Dead-eye. But if you carry him, boss, you can't use your weapons.'

'We'll carry him if it kills us,' Dead-eye said.

'It just might,' Ken replied. While they waited for the chopper to arrive with the support team, he checked his wounded leg again, tested it against the wall of the sangar, and thought about how nice it would be to be back in Blighty with the Beatles and the Rolling Stones on the radio and all the girls in their miniskirts. It was a good time to be in England, Ken reckoned. He wanted to sit in front of the television, watching the amazing Cassius Clay bring down the lumbering Sonny Liston or, even better, the sexy Christine Keeler and Mandy Rice-Davis bring down a government or, almost as good, the unfolding tale of the Great Train Robbers, who were fast becoming heroes to the British public. He wanted desperately to visit his local and have a pint of decent bitter, read about the antics of Peter Sellers and Britt Ekland in the

Sunday papers, or the fights between Mods and Rockers. Or simply listen to Radio Caroline.

What he did not want to listen to was a lot of stuck-up, self-serving politicians spouting about Aden, Cyprus, Israel, Rhodesia, South Africa or Uganda; or about the fact that they were planning to waste £160 million of taxpayers' money on building a totally unnecessary Channel Tunnel. Who wanted the Frogs on their doorstep?

Ken glanced at Terry, saw that he was still ivory-white, sweaty and unconscious, though mumbling constantly to himself in his delirium, and wondered how the hell they could get him out. Bad enough that he and Les had leg wounds; Terry just made it worse.

He was distracted by the sound of an approaching helicopter. Glancing up, he saw a Wessex S-58 Mark 1 emerge from the southern darkness, blocking out the stars as it drew near, but mercifully bringing the support team with it.

Having seen the chopper as well, Captain Ellsworth began guiding it in to the DZ with his SARBE surface-to-air rescue beacon. Unfortunately, any hopes he might have been harbouring that the guerrillas had disappeared from the lower slopes were brutally dashed when what sounded like a couple of heavy GPMGs roared into action and two streams of green tracer arced up into the sky towards the Wessex. The chopper kept coming, flying between the lines of tracer, but just as it was approaching the hill, some of the tracer hit it, causing showers of sparks to burst from it and making it shudder and list dangerously.

Immediately, the captain and Dead-eye fired savage bursts from their SLRs, hoping to silence the GPMGs down the hill. They were supported by the roaring of Taff's Bren gun and the SLRs of Jimbo and the wounded Ben – but to no avail. The guerrillas returned the fire with a small-arms fusillade, causing bullets to dance off the sangar wall in showers of sparks that acted as beacons to the enemy marksmen.

Simultaneously, the lines of green tracer from the guerrillas' GPMGs converged on the helicopter, turning it into a giant sparkler, making it shudder again and list more heavily, now pouring smoke. Even as the chopper turned away, the pilot was informing Captain Ellsworth over the radio that it was badly damaged and had to return to base while it could still fly. There was no chance of landing the replacements. Over and out.

Though exasperated and disappointed, the SAS

men in both sangars gave the Wessex covering fire until it had limped out of sight, leaving a trail of smoke behind it. When it had disappeared in the dark sky, the men stopped firing, conserving the last of their precious ammunition, and Captain Ellsworth contacted Lieutenant-Colonel Callaghan at Thumier on the encoded A41.

'I'm afraid the Wessex didn't make it through,' he explained. 'It's damaged but luckily still flying, and limping back to base right now.'

'Yes,' Callaghan replied. 'We've been informed. What options are left to you?'

'None,' Ellsworth said bluntly. 'We'll have to make a run for it under cover of darkness.'

'Within range of the enemy?'

'Yes, boss.'

'Any other problems?'

'Two men wounded in the leg; one with a serious stomach complaint and fever – now unconscious.'

'Christ,' Callaghan said softly. After a brief pause, he asked: 'Can the wounded men walk?'

'Not too well, but they can manage.'

'They'll slow you down.'

'We all know that.'

'And the unconscious man?'

'We'll have to carry him on a makeshift stretcher.'

'That means your hands are full.'

Ellsworth actually chuckled. 'Yes, boss.'

'Two leg wounds and an unconscious body. It sounds suicidal.'

'We don't have any option.'

There was a moment's uneasy silence, broken only by the static coming over the radio. The guerrillas, too, were silent, though probably still inching up the dark hill, determined to annihilate the Englishmen.

'What's the time of departure?' Callaghan asked eventually.

'Approximately 1930 hours.'

'Can you make that precisely?'

'Yes.'

'Good. We'll lay down an artillery barrage on the southern hill at 1932 sharp, covering the area between the sangars and the hamlet below it. When you exit the sangars at 1930, take the northern slope. You should be out of the sangars by the time the first shells of the barrage strike the southern hill. With luck, we can keep them engaged long enough for you to get out of range. They'll follow you, but at least you'll have a head start and a fighting chance.'

'We'll be out and gone, boss.'

'Right,' Callaghan replied. 'Good luck to all of you.'

Handing the radio back to Les, Captain Ellsworth said, 'That's it, men. We move out at 1930 sharp. That gives us approximately thirty minutes to pack up our kit.'

'We'll have to travel light,' Dead-eye said, 'so I recommend we leave anything we don't really need or can't reasonably carry.'

'Agreed. But don't leave it for the guerrillas. Destroy anything that might be of use to them.'

'Will do.'

'Right, lads, let's get to it. Dead-eye, can you crawl over to the other sangar and tell them what's happening?'

'Yes, boss.'

Dead-eye left the sangar and did the leopard crawl to the other sangar: wriggling forward on his belly, using his elbows for leverage, with his SLR cradled in both hands. While he was gone, the men he had left behind began to remove what kit they needed from their bergens, strap on their webbing and destroy any equipment they did not intend carrying. Even the A41 was smashed to pieces. The separate Morse set was rendered unusable by extracting the crystals that controlled its operating frequencies; then the men smashed what they could of the set itself. Even before Dead-eye had returned, the sounds of similar destruction could be heard coming from the smaller sangar. By the time he had crawled back into the larger sangar, all the work had been completed and the men, each carrying only his SLR, water bottle, ammunition pouches and emergency rations, were ready to move. All except the still-unconscious Terry.

'We'll have to make a stretcher,' Captain Ellsworth said.

'Right,' Dead-eye agreed. 'By hook or by crook, we've got to carry him out of here. For that reason, the men in the other sangar have agreed to give us covering fire for two minutes, only moving out when the artillery barrage begins.'

'Dangerous,' Ken murmured.

'Good of them to do it,' the captain said. 'Damned decent of them.'

Dead-eye checked his wristwatch. 'Our time's nearly up, boss. Let's get that stretcher made for Terry.'

Before anyone could move, however, the guerrillas, now much higher up the hill and inevitably hearing the noise from the smaller sangar, aimed a sustained fusillade of rifle and machine-gun fire at it. The men in the sangar immediately replied in kind and soon the green tracer of the guerrillas and the blue of the SAS were criss-crossing. Bullets bounced off the sangar and the rocks well below it, sending up showers of sparks.

'Fucking Guy Fawkes Night,' Ken murmured, rising painfully to the crouching position, head bowed to avoid the overhanging ponchos, his SLR in his hand.

Without a word, Dead-eye reached up and tore off the poncho, letting air rush in and revealing the stars directly above. He then removed some of the thicker branches holding the poncho up, checked their strength, then lay them parallel along both ends of the poncho and folded its ends over each stick. With his Sykes-Fairburn commando dagger, he stabbed holes in the turned-over ends and through the poncho below, along the whole length of both covered sticks. Removing a coil of heavy-duty string from his bergen, he cut it into two equal lengths and used the separate pieces to 'stitch' the folded-over ends of the poncho around the thick branches, thus completing a crude but effective stretcher.

He did all of this in about five minutes while Ken and Les, both kneeling by the wall and obviously in agony from their wounded legs, added their SLR fire to the combined Bren-gun and SLR fire from the smaller sangar.

'All right, boss,' Dead-eye said to Captain Ellsworth, 'let's put him onto this stretcher.'

Still kneeling and keeping their heads under the top of the sangar wall, they lifted the shivering, moaning trooper and deposited him awkwardly onto the makeshift stretcher. Dead-eye picked up Terry's SLR and slung it over his own shoulder.

'No point leaving it for the guerrillas,' he explained. 'And it might come in handy.'

Ellsworth checked his wristwatch, then raised his eyes again. 'One minute to go.' He turned to Ken and Les, who had both stopped firing to reload. 'Do you think you can make it on those legs?'

'I've been legless before,' Les said with a grin, 'and I always got home.'

'Same here,' Ken said.

Ellsworth grinned. 'Right. Here's the drill.' He glanced at his wristwatch again. 'When Dead-eye and I hump out with the stretcher, you two exit with us, one at the front, one behind. You give covering fire as all of us move down the northern slope. As we make our escape, we'll also be given covering fire by the other sangar. When we're 100 yards or so down the hill, we'll hit the ground and give covering fire to the men in the other sangar. When they reach us, we all take off together. By that time Callaghan's artillery barrage will have started. That'll put a wall of fire between us and the guerrillas, and give us a fighting chance. Any last-minute questions?'

Ken and Les shook their heads simultaneously.

'Good. Let's get ready.'

The stretcher lay parallel to the front of the sangar, one end pointing towards the gap in the side. Dead-eye knelt in front of the stretcher, between it and the exit, with his back turned to it. He had Terry's SLR slung over one shoulder, his own over the other. His hands were angled backwards to take hold of the ends of the two branches, acting as handles. Ellsworth did the same at the other end, but facing the stretcher. Ken and Les were crouching low, one on each side of the exit, both tormented by the pains shooting through their wounded legs, but both prepared to move out with Dead-eye and Ellsworth. The latter checked his wristwatch. One minute to go. He raised his right hand, preparing to give the signal for 'Go!'.

Suddenly, unexpectedly, a machine-gun roared from lower down the slope. Even before Ellsworth could drop his hand, a great chunk of stone was punched out of the lower part of the sangar's front wall and phosphorescent-green tracer shot through the space like a laser beam, before smashing through the back wall.

The stretcher appeared to explode beneath Terry, with pieces of branch and tattered strips of poncho flying everywhere as he was chopped to pieces by the vicious stream of tracer.

The sick trooper started screaming. He was jerking epileptically as the tracer bullets tore through both him and the stretcher, then passed above them and through the stones in the opposite wall. Some of the bullets flew around the sangar, expiring with a harsh, metallic clatter that only added to the deafening noise.

As abruptly as it had started firing, the machine-gun fell silent. Terry stopped screaming and his spasms subsided into the frozen, anguished posture of violent death. Looking down through the dust settling eerily over him, the shocked survivors in the sangar saw that he had been cut to pieces and now lay, lifeless and soaked in blood, on the smashed, tattered remains of the improvised stretcher.

'Not much we can do for him now,' Dead-eye said eventually, tonelessly. 'I think it's time we left, boss.'

Ellsworth glanced at Terry, then at his own wristwatch. He then raised and lowered his right hand.

'Go!' he screamed.

With a last look at the dead trooper, the four men ran at the crouch from the sangar. Outside, all hell broke loose.

13

As the four men burst out of the sangar to clatter noisily towards the northern slope, two of them wobbling uncertainly on wounded legs, the guerrillas either heard them or saw them silhouetted against the skyline and responded with a clamorous barrage of small-arms fire, most of it coming from behind a couple of large boulders surprisingly close to the two sangars.

Les, in the lead, fired back with his SLR as enemy bullets whistled past his head. Coming up right behind him, Dead-eye was also blasting away at the hostile rocks with the SLR at his hip. Captain Ellsworth was between the two, while Ken, unsteady on his wounded leg, was acting as back marker and managed to get off a burst or two.

'Keep going!' Ellsworth bawled. 'Don't stop! Head for the slope!'

More enemy bullets whipped and hissed about them as, up at the front, Les lurched forward as fast as his injured leg permitted, gritting his teeth against the pains that were stabbing up it with each step. Bringing up the rear, and firing his SLR on the move, Ken was suffering similar agony.

'Stop firing and move faster!' Dead-eye bawled.

'I can't!' Les protested.

In fact, he paused and turned to see if the others were still with him. As he did so, a machine-gun roared into action, adding its noise to the one giving cover from the smaller sangar, and green tracer arced out of the guerrilla positions, zipped between the running men, then moved left to cut across Captain Ellsworth, who shuddered violently, as if being electrocuted. Punched sideways, he was then spun around and hurled violently to the ground, hitting a small rock with a sickening thud and flopping onto his spine.

'Shit!' Dead-eye turned back while waving the other two onward, but they ignored him and stood their ground, giving him covering fire, as he ran up to Ellsworth and knelt beside him to examine him. He was badly mangled and clearly dead.

After stripping Ellsworth of his weapon and ammunition, Dead-eye ran back to the others at the crouch. Even as they were making their escape over the rim of the northern hill, the enemy machine-gunner and others using small arms were concentrating on Ellsworth. The combined force of their bullets jerked his body sideways across the slope until it was stopped by a rock. There it quivered constantly under the impact of more bullets and gradually turned into what looked like a tattered pile of rags.

That, at least, is all Dead-eye and the others saw the guerrillas picking up and carrying triumphantly off as their comrades spread out and advanced on the two sangars.

Deeply shocked by the loss of Captain Ellsworth, the other three men slipped over the rim of the southern hill, some 15 yards from the sangars, then lay belly down on the ground to give covering fire to Jimbo and his men.

Dead-eye groaned softly. 'Those guerrillas are practically on top of the sangar. Jimbo and the others haven't got a chance. They'll never get out of there.'

At that moment a deep thunder swelled up from far behind him and lightning illuminated the distant horizon. Within seconds the first shells from the 25-pounders in Thumier were ploughing into the southern hill, erupting in a series of fearsome explosions that tore up the soil, sand, gravel and rocks around and between the screaming guerrillas. Many Arabs were picked up and smashed back down in this lethal maelstrom.

Les whooped with joy. Ken just grinned at him. Even the inscrutable Dead-eye gave a slight grin; he had forgotten the promised barrage and was relieved to see it.

While the barrage was devastating the hill running down to the hamlet, turning it into a gigantic convulsion of swirling soil and gravel, and mushrooming smoke that obscured the screaming, spinning Arabs, the four survivors from the sangar – the original covering party of Jimbo, Larry, Ben and Taff – burst out into the night and headed rapidly down the north hill to join Dead-eye, Ken and Les.

In the event, they did not need covering fire as the guerrillas were so devastated by the barrage from the distant 25-pounders that they failed to notice the departure of the men from the smaller sangar.

'Where's the Bren?' Dead-eye asked.

'Shot to pieces,' Jimbo replied tersely. 'Not worth bringing out.'

Approaching that sangar in the darkness, out of the hell of explosions erupting further down the hill, the guerrillas opened fire with everything they had. When their bullets struck showers of silver sparks from the sangar walls, the guerrillas mistook them for the return fire of the SAS and decided to charge the position from both directions.

As the SAS men hurried away at the crouch, disappearing into the darkness, the guerrillas broke into two groups, encircled the smaller sangar, and fired on it from both directions. With neither group knowing which way the other had gone, each mistook the other's fire for the return fire of the SAS. They were mowing each other down in a bloody fire-fight.

'Beautiful!' Dead-eye murmured with satisfaction.

Using a pair of binoculars and his PNGs, he observed the activity of the Arabs. The artillery barrage on the lower slope had temporarily stopped when the guerrillas entered the smaller sangar and emerged empty-handed, barking angrily at one another. They then went into the larger sangar and emerged with Terry's lacerated body. As a couple of them carried him clumsily down the hill, another couple picked up the dead Captain Ellsworth and then followed them.

No sooner had they disappeared into the darkness of the southern slope than more shells from the big guns fell on the hill, but this time higher up, blowing the sangars to smithereens and gradually rearranging the topography of the hill with awesome efficiency.

When the barrage had ceased and the smoke had cleared away, no trace of the sangars was left and the top of the hill was pock-marked with enormous shell holes and covered with huge mounds of upturned, smouldering sand and soil.

'The bastards got the bodies of Captain Ellsworth and Terry,' Dead-eye said, lowering his binoculars and removing the PNGs to look steadily and unemotionally at the others. Then, before they could give in to shock, he said: 'Come on, let's get moving.'

Turning away from that still smoking scene of terrible devastation, they hurried all the way down the north hill, then out across the dried-up Wadi Rabwa, heading back towards the Dhala Road and Thumier. But they still had a long way to go.

14

Deeply shocked by their losses – the more so because the bodies had been carried off by the enemy – and suffering from psychological and physical fatigue, the men marched through what seemed like a nightmarish lunar landscape in a gloom that could not be relieved by humour. Dead-eye and Jimbo led the way, with Larry right behind them, still carrying his medical box on his shoulder. Taff and Ben followed Larry, while Ken and Les hobbled along painfully in the rear.

Ben's tunic had been slashed open by the bullet that had scorched across his back, and a bloody bandage showed through the tattered, flapping cloth. Les was limping very badly on his wounded leg, though losing no blood and clearly determined to make it back. But Ken was suffering much more, gradually slowing down, and stopping frequently to adjust the bandage around his thigh, from which blood was still seeping at a dangerous rate.

They were marching along the crest of the hill, heading south-west, parallel to the wadi far below, whose darkness was broken by striations of silver moonlight. Even at night it was warm, with a clammy breeze, and all of them were soon pouring sweat and feeling parched.

After Ken had stopped for the third or fourth time to adjust his bandage, Larry glanced back, saw the seeping blood and hurried to him.

'Jesus,' Larry said, 'why didn't you tell me?'

'I didn't want to hold us up.'

'You'll hold us up more if I don't treat that. Take a seat, soldier.'

With one hand, Larry indicated to Dead-eye and Jimbo that they had to stop for a while; with the other he gently pushed the wincing corporal down onto the stony earth. Kneeling beside him, he removed the original, blood-soaked bandage, cleaned the two bullet holes with antiseptic and applied fresh dressings.

'I wish I could take those bullets out,' he said, 'but I can't risk it here. I've already lost one man; I don't want to lose you.'

'You didn't lose Terry,' Ken told him. 'He was shot to pieces.'

'Which he might not have been had I treated him and kept him off that stretcher. I should have done more for him.'

'You're a medic, not a doctor, for Christ's sake. You did all you could for him.'

'I still feel bad.'

'We all do – for him and for Ellsworth.'

'Yes, a good officer.'

'One of the best.'

Completing the dressing of the wound, Larry patted Ken on the shoulder, then moved across to Les, who was gingerly examining the bloody bandage around his own wounded leg. The bandages were soaked in caked blood to which dust and sand had stuck.

'At least the bleeding's stopped,' Larry said as he cut away the four old dressings that Les had applied himself and which were now flapping loose.

'Yeah,' Les replied with a tight grin. 'That's a blessing, I suppose.'

'Does it hurt?'

'Only when I put my foot on the ground.'

'Which you'll have to do a lot,' Larry said.

'Don't remind me, Sawbones.'

Smiling reassuringly, Larry removed the last of the old bandages, cleaned and checked the wound – it was not too bad, though not helpful for marching – then applied antiseptic and redressed it. He then went over to have a look at Ben, who was at that very moment wincing and arching his wounded back.

'Does it hurt?' Larry asked, kneeling beside Ben, close to Taff.

'What the fuck do *you* think?' Ben replied in his pugnacious manner.

'It's only a scratch,' Taff said with a sly grin. 'Anyone'd think he'd been hurt really badly!'

'Fuck you, Taff,' Ben shot back. 'That bullet gouged out a length of skin and bloody near killed me to boot. I don't see *you* being so brave about it.'

Taff pointed to Ken and Les. 'Those two have *real* wounds,' he said, trying to keep his spirits up by taking a rise out of Ben. 'Not a poxy little scratch across the back.' He turned to Larry. 'His wound doesn't hurt,' he explained. 'It just stings a bit.'

'Go fuck yourself,' Ben said.

When Larry parted the torn tunic, he saw that

there was indeed a combination of gouged skin and a burn mark running in a diagonal line across Ben's back. After getting the trooper to remove the tunic, he examined the wound more thoroughly and saw that the gouge was deep, almost cutting through to the bone, and that the burning effects of the hot bullet had actually congealed the blood, thus doing some good.

Ben, he realized, was not exaggerating when he said that the bullet had nearly killed him. In fact, if he had moved just a fraction backwards, the bullet would have entered through his waist and shot up through his chest at the same angle, shredding everything in its path, before possibly emerging from just under his armpit and then ploughing through his shoulder, which it would have smashed to pieces on its way out. In the event, it had merely left a deep, burnt furrow in the skin, running obliquely across Ben's back from the left side of his spine to the right shoulder. Almost certainly it did more than merely sting; it probably hurt like hell.

'Very nice,' Larry said. 'Really quite artistic. I'm going to apply some cream which will hurt at first, but then gradually act as an anaesthetic. The wound won't sting after the cream takes effect.'

'It's more than a *sting*!' Ben insisted.

'Ha, ha,' Taff cackled.

Ben winced as Larry applied the cream. But he relaxed completely when the wound was covered in cream and already starting to hurt less. Larry then wrapped a lengthy bandage repeatedly around Ben's torso, until most of his back had been covered. When he had finished tying the knot, he stood up and told Ben to put his tunic back on.

'You can close that long tear with safety pins,' he advised him. 'That'll keep the breeze off it.'

'The breeze is warm,' Ben said.

'It'll blow sand over the dressing and some of it could work its way under it and into the wound. Close up that tear, Trooper.'

'Yes, Sawbones,' Ben said, removing some small safety pins from his escape and survival belt and proceeding to pin up the tear in his tunic.

'Feeling better, then?' Taff asked innocently.

'Yeah,' Ben said, speaking with the safety pins in his mouth and clipping one over the tear in his tunic.

'You just needed a little attention,' Taff said. 'All mummy's boys do.'

'Up yours,' Ben grunted.

Returning to the front of the file, Larry was approached by Dead-eye and Jimbo.

'How are they?' the latter asked.

'Trooper Riley's all right – his wound's only superficial. Lance-Corporal Moody's gonna have a painful march, but I think he can make it.'

'And Corporal Brooke?' Dead-eye asked.

'His leg wound's pretty bad. I can't stop the bleeding. He needs a proper surgical operation and I can't give him that. The more he marches, the more he's going to bleed. I don't know how long he can go like that, but the sooner we get back the better.'

'But he *can* march?' Jimbo asked anxiously.

'He'll be slow, but he can march.'

'OK,' Dead-eye said, 'let's march.' He raised his right hand, then let it drop, indicating 'Forward march'.

The men climbed laboriously to their feet and began their long trek south-west, struggling up and down the steep, irregular walls of parched water channels that had once fed the wadi below. The network of gullies criss-crossing the rocky slope did not make the going any easier – and in fact made it hell for the two men with leg wounds – while the walls, even steeper than the hill, were encrusted with sharp stones.

As the march continued and the moon rose

higher, spilling more light on the wadi and the desert plain beyond it, Les limped gamely on, muttering curses each time his leg hurt. Ken, however, was suffering even more, for both his wounds were being opened by the constant strain of the climbs and bleeding even worse than before. Forced to stop twice to let Larry attend to him, he was noticeably white and strained-looking, breathing heavily and undoubtedly weakening. Nevertheless, when his wounds had been attended to, the march had to go on.

'We should have made a stretcher for Corporal Brooke,' Jimbo whispered to Dead-eye when both of them were marching up at the front, on point. 'We need one right now.'

'There was only enough wood for one stretcher,' Dead-eye informed him, 'and the one we got out of it was shot to hell.'

Jimbo glanced left and right at the barren, moonlit hill and the flat desert plain beyond it. 'Nothing here, I suppose.'

'No, Jimbo, nothing. No wood. No poncho sheets.'

Jimbo glanced back over his shoulder at the limping Les and then at Ken, desperately struggling along. 'He's not going to make it,' he said quietly.

'He's got to. Those guerrillas will be on our tail, so we have to keep moving.'

They marched for another hour – until clouds passed over the moon and blocked out most of the light. Then the march became even more difficult because they had to climb in and out of the pitch-black gullies without the benefit of light. At the same time an insidious combination of shock and exhaustion was attacking their nervous systems and making them tense, irritable and – even more dangerous – highly imaginative. They heard the enemy in every unfamiliar sound, and saw him in the shifting of the sands, the rustling of clumps of aloe and euphorbia, the shivering of jujube trees.

They marched over high sand dunes, back down into dark gullies, across stretches of dangerously smooth volcanic rock, staying parallel to the wadi, which would lead them eventually to the Dhala Road. At one point the moon passed between two banks of clouds, briefly shedding its light across the level strip ahead, before plunging it back into near total darkness.

In that brief illumination Jimbo thought he saw a group of Arab tents. He and Dead-eye dropped immediately to the ground, with the men behind them following suit. By the time they were belly down in the sand, the clouds had covered the moon again and the remaining light was of little use. When Jimbo's eyes got used to the darkness, he saw the tents again.

'Arab tents,' he whispered to Dead-eye.

'You think so?'

'For sure.'

'They're certainly shaped like tents,' Dead-eye said, 'but they're very still.'

'Naturally,' Jimbo said. 'Most of the bastards are asleep. The camp will be guarded, though. What should we do? Fight it out, sneak around them, or what?'

Dead-eye tried using his binoculars and PNGs, but even in the green glow of the night vision goggles the tents were relatively indistinct and could not be seen clearly. He did, however, see to the left of the tents what could either have been shivering trees or restless camels. Though doubting his own senses, not sure that what he was looking at was actually an Arab camp, he said: 'With Brooke and Moody in the shape they're in, we can't take any chances. So let's climb higher, circle above them, and maybe we'll see more clearly as we pass over them.'

'Right,' Jimbo said.

Giving the 'Follow me' hand signal, Dead-eye and Jimbo led the others further up the hill in a circular direction that gradually brought them directly above the problem. Looking down, they realized that the tents had been pitched directly above the main wadi and the track they had been looking for themselves.

Cursing under his breath, Dead-eye indicated that the others should lie belly down behind him. He did the same, then studied the tents through his binoculars and his PNGs.

'Rocks,' he said, passing the binoculars and PNGs to Jimbo. 'Rocks and shivering doum palms.' When the latter had also studied the 'tents', he handed back the binoculars and PNGs with a rueful grin. 'You win,' he said.

'Still,' Dead-eye replied, 'we found the track we've been looking for, so let's get ourselves down there.'

To descend they had to march farther around the hill, almost completing their broad arc, until they came to a goat track that wound down in the right direction. It was very steep, and sliding gravel and sand made it difficult for most of the men to keep their balance. If it was hard for them, it was close to hell for the wounded Ken and Les, both of whom were visibly twitching from the pains shooting through their legs and lagging behind with increasing frequency.

Finally, when Dead-eye saw that Ken had fallen behind and this time was making no attempt to catch up, he started back down the line. Ken saw him coming, waved frantically, silently, for him to stay out of sight, then lowered himself to the ground, gingerly holding his leg.

Dead-eye and the others instantly hit the ground, then Dead-eye advanced by the leopard crawl until he reached Ken. The corporal pointed back the way they had come.

'Someone's following us,' he mouthed as if speaking to a deaf person, not wanting to be heard by the guerrillas.

When Dead-eye wrinkled his forehead in a questioning manner, Ken nodded and again pointed back along the track, to where it curved around some rocks and disappeared in the darkness.

Raising his left hand – the other was gripping his SLR – Dead-eye spread his fingers, then dropped them one by one, asking silently how many guerrillas Ken thought he had seen. Ken raised a single finger of his left hand, then three of his right, indicating that one man was in the lead, followed by three others.

Dead-eye glanced at the corporal's leg and saw that again blood was seeping through the soaked bandages and dripping to the ground. Raising his eyes, he carefully studied Ken's face and saw that it was deathly white, the skin drawn taut on the cheekbones, betraying great physical and mental stress. The corporal was clearly in considerable pain and losing strength through loss of blood. Was he hallucinating?

Dead-eye was just about to don his PNGs and unclip his binoculars when he heard a noise from along the trail and looked back to where it curved out of sight around the tall rocks. An Arab in an off-white jellaba appeared around the rock, treading carefully and carrying a .303 Lee-Enfield. His fluttering *shemagh* was covering his mouth and nose, making him look like a bandit.

Dead-eye rolled instantly to one side of the track, indicating that Ken should go to the opposite side. Unable to move so quickly and not willing to roll on his wounded leg, Ken gritted his teeth, then forced himself up into a crouching position and made his way to the other side of the track. Once there, he lay down on his belly behind some thorn bushes, taking aim along the Trilux sight of his SLR. On his own side of the track, Dead-eye did the same.

Glancing back where he had come from, he was relieved to see that the rest of the patrol had disappeared from the track and had doubtless divided up to hide at both sides of it. Glancing to the front, he saw that the Arab scout was drawing ever closer and that three others were just appearing around the tall boulder.

Looking across the track, he saw Ken staring at him, waiting for some kind of instruction. Using his index finger, Dead-eye pointed first to Ken, then to the Arab in the lead, indicating that the corporal was to concentrate on him. When Ken nodded that he understood, Dead-eye pointed to the three men behind, jabbing his finger three times, indicating that he was going to deal with them while Ken was to shoot the scout. Again Ken nodded.

Still belly down on the ground, Dead-eye released the safety-catch on his SLR and carefully took aim. Only the quiet tread of the Arabs' slippers broke what seemed like a very lengthy silence but was in fact no more than a few seconds.

Dead-eye waited until the scout was only ten yards away, then fired the first shot at one of the three men behind him. Even before the guerrilla had staggered back from the impact of the bullet, Ken was firing his own first shot, which punched the scout backwards, then made him twist to the side, dropping his weapon and falling face down. He had yet to hit the ground when Dead-eye fired at the second of the three men behind him.

The sound of his shot was followed almost instantly by Ken's second, both bullets hitting the same man. As this unfortunate was jerking convulsively from the double impact and dropping his weapon, before falling himself, the final man dived desperately for the shelter of the tall rock just behind him.

Dead-eye and Ken fired at the same instant. The latter missed his moving target, but the former put a bullet into the Arab's side, spinning him over and throwing him to the ground with his rifle clattering noisily away from him. Surprisingly, he clambered to his knees, clutching his blood-soaked jellaba, then scrambled forward to get at his weapon.

Again, Dead-eye and Ken fired simultaneously, this time both hitting the target. The Arab was punched left, then right; then he slammed backwards into the rock, his skull cracking as he did so. Sliding slowly along it, he dropped to his knees, then flopped forward into the dust, where he quivered like a bowstring for a few seconds, then collapsed and was still.

None of the guerrillas made a sound. That meant there were no wounded. Even so, Dead-eye climbed carefully to his feet and walked over to the scout. Kicking him gently and receiving no response, he moved on to the other three men and confirmed that all of them were dead.

Relieved, but still wary, he walked to the bend in the track, switched the SLR to automatic, and fired a lengthy burst into the darkness, thereby hoping to dissuade any other guerrillas lurking there from following immediately. When he heard nothing and saw nothing, he turned back the way he had come.

Ken was staring enquiringly at him, his face gleaming with sweat, the skin taut with strain. Dead-eye nodded, indicating that the job was done. He walked up to the corporal and said: 'You didn't do badly for a wounded man. How's the leg?'

'Terrible.' Ken sat down gently in the dirt, his legs stretched out in front of him. He wiped sweat from his face and tentatively exercised his wounded leg. 'Christ!' he said softly.

One by one the rest of the SAS patrol emerged from behind bushes at both sides of the track and walked up to find out what had happened. When Jimbo saw the four dead Arabs on the track, he gave a low whistle and said: 'Not a trick of the moonlight this time!'

'No,' Dead-eye replied. 'They were following us . . . and they certainly wouldn't have come alone. The others can't be far behind.'

'You fired a burst along the track?'

'Yes.'

'No response?'

'No.'

'Still,' Jimbo said, 'I recommend we do a double check by setting up here in ambush positions for another ten minutes. If no one appears by then, we'll know they're a good way behind and we can move off again.'

'You men agree with that?' Dead-eye asked, as if conducting a 'Chinese parliament', taking in the opinions of the others, including the troopers. All of them nodded silently. 'All right, let's spread out.'

They divided intc two groups and assumed ambush positions behind the thorn bushes at both sides of the track. They waited for another ten minutes, but there was no sound except the moaning of the warm wind blowing over the dead men. The dust covered them gradually.

15

Eventually, satisfied that the guerrillas were not close behind them, the SAS men moved off again. This time, however, they marched even more cautiously than before, each man glancing back from time to time, checking that no Arabs were in sight. For the first hour, at least, they saw no one and could march on in peace.

Out in front on point, Dead-eye trudged in grim silence along the track that would lead to the Dhala Road, across a flat stretch of desert, closely bordered on both sides by high ridges. Keeping his eyes peeled and never forgetting what he was doing, he was nevertheless dwelling bitterly on the deaths of Captain Ellsworth and Trooper Malkin.

Impelled by his life-long ambition to be a good soldier, and forged like steel in the hell of the

Telok Anson swamp in Malaya and the jungles of Borneo, Dead-eye usually accepted the death of comrades with equanimity, studiously avoiding any kind of sentimentality. This time, however, while not giving in to sentiment, he was burning up with bitterness, not just because of the loss of two good men but because their deaths had been unnecessary.

Proud to be in the SAS, Dead-eye normally believed in what he was fighting for, but such was not the case here in the Radfan. This was a politicians' war, a public relations campaign, and Dead-eye resented the fact that two worthy men had died for no good reason. He also felt humiliated because, as Callaghan had said, this was not a war that could be won and what had happened to this patrol was proof of that. They were retreating with their tails between their legs and, even more shameful, had left two dead SAS men in the hands of the enemy.

Marching behind Dead-eye, Jimbo was less bitter, though not exactly happy with his lot. Glancing across the flat, dark desert, then left and right at the high, potentially treacherous ridges, he was reminded of his earliest days with the SAS, in the North African desert. That had been a real war, an honourable war, vastly different to this mean little action in a place that few people back home knew existed. Even now, Jimbo could recall his adventures in North Africa only with pride and exhilaration: racing in on the enemy positions in the Chevrolet lorries of the Long Range Desert Group, the wind in your face, machine-guns roaring from the back of the open vehicles, then speeding out again before the enemy knew what had hit them. It had been a war fought by men who believed in what they were doing and were proud to be doing it.

Jimbo was particularly proud of having fought with the original founder of the Regiment, Captain David Stirling, as well as Lieutenant-Colonel Callaghan, his present CO at HQ Thumier and a bit of a regimental legend in his own right. He remembered with fondness, too, the other ranks he had known and respected, many since dead in Malaya or Borneo. That pride in those he had fought with, the fights he had fought and the Regiment in general was something he did not feel now as the patrol made its way along the wind-blown desert track towards the Dhala Road. This was virtually a 'secret' war, unknown to most people. It was secret because it was dirty and fought for no good reason against an enemy that did not respect you and for whom you had no respect. Jimbo could not stomach that.

Marching between Jimbo and Larry, Ben and Taff had no feelings about this war one way or the other, having nothing to compare it with. Being new to the Regiment and on their first mission with it, both of them were in a state of shock over the deaths of Captain Ellsworth and Terry, which, in some unvoiced way, they had not quite expected. They were further depressed by the fact that Ken and Les, the two soldiers from whom they had hoped to learn the most, as they were their direct superiors, were in fact badly wounded and, in Ken's case, starting to show distinct signs of stress.

When they glanced back over their shoulders, as they felt compelled to do often, they saw, well behind Larry, the two back markers, Ken and Les, hobbling along side by side, the latter desperately coaxing his mate onward. Ken was in a bad way, bleeding profusely, and his consequent loss of strength was making him lose control and behave like a crazy man. Les was in better shape, though clearly suffering. Neither man was any longer in a position to help the two troopers.

Ben and Taff felt isolated, more dependent upon one another. They respected Jimbo and were in awe of Dead-eye, but neither NCO was as approachable as Ken or Les had been before they were wounded. Everything had changed, and the two troopers were now besieged by doubts.

Their uncertainty was exaggerated by their mounting physical and mental exhaustion, but they were not experienced enough to know that. Having been badged together, flown to Aden together, thrown up in the trucks together and shared their baptism of fire together, they felt very close, almost like brothers, taking strength from one another in order to combat the rigours of this hellish hike through the dangerous night.

Larry was fighting his fatigue and delayed shock by thinking of his girlfriend, Cathy, and wondering what she was doing right now, back in Devon. Formerly of the Royal Army Medical Corps (RAMC) and having previously served with the SAS in Borneo, Larry was a good, experienced soldier who had witnessed violent death before and suffered the horrors of swamp and jungle. This had not hardened his heart to such a degree that he could, like Dead-eye, bury his feelings about lost comrades. Nor could it make him view romance as something trivial when compared with war's brutal realities. So, while Larry suffered silently like the others, shocked by the two deaths, disturbed by the wounding of the other men, and increasingly twitchy from lack of sleep and exhaustion, he was able to endure it by conjuring up visions of the girl he loved.

He did this, however, while maintaining a good degree of vigilance: on the one hand constantly checking for any sign of enemy movement behind the rocks on the ridges on both sides of the desert track; on the other, occasionally letting himself fall back to where Ken and Les were acting as back markers more by will-power than anything else.

No matter how many times Larry came back down the line to bandage Ken's bloody left thigh, the two bullet holes kept bleeding, relentlessly draining Ken of physical strength and, inevitably, weakening him mentally as well. It was now clear to Larry, as it was to the others, that not only was Ken in serious danger from loss of blood, but he was starting to ramble in thought and action. He jumped at every unfamiliar sound, saw the enemy in every shadow, and had started mumbling constantly to himself in his growing delirium.

Designated as back markers because they were

the slowest and always falling behind anyway, the two wounded men were as mutually supportive as they could be in the circumstances. Les had taken it upon himself to be Ken's crutch. Ken was his friend and a hell of a good soldier, but he was now in a terrible mess.

Hardened by his experiences with the 3rd Battalion, Royal Green Jackets, in Malaya and Borneo, Les was willing and able to endure the screaming agony in his own wounded leg each time he placed his right foot on the ground, which was every second or so for the past two hellish hours. But even he was finding it difficult to endure his own pain while attending to his friend, who kept stopping and starting, and seemed anxious to wander out of the file and head for one or other of the ridges on either side of the desert track. While trying to maintain his own equilibrium by visualizing a foaming pint in his local in Southend, or placing a winning bet, or making love either to his wife or some bint he had picked up in a pub, Les attempted to keep his friend occupied by talking constantly to him about his wife and three children back home in Somerset, the joys of wildlife photography in the Brendon Hills, which Ken had done so often, and the prospect of once again fishing and hiking on

Exmoor. Ken responded coherently at times, but mostly with incomprehension, mumbling about being too warm and having a dry throat.

Unfortunately, the minute Les stopped talking to him, Ken would focus his increasingly unhinged mind on the ridges to left and right, often starting at some imagined sound or movement, raising his weapon, intending to fire it, but always prevented from doing so by Les. He stopped, he started, he slumped down again, severely hampering the progress of the patrol.

Given Ken's penchant for seeing enemies in every shifting shadow and unfamiliar sound, it came as a surprise to Les when he himself thought he had heard movement behind him and turned around to check if someone was following. He did this more than once and never saw anyone, but each time he heard the sound it seemed closer, until eventually it sounded like the rustle of slippered feet.

As the track curved back around the eastern ridge, where it disappeared into darkness, Les could not see very far. Yet when again he stopped and strained to hear, he was convinced he was listening to the sound of more than one man advancing and hurrying to catch up. He was not mistaken.

Ken was just about to wander off the track yet again when Les grabbed him by the shoulder and pulled him down with him to the ground. Turning onto his side, he then used a hand signal to indicate to Larry that someone was following them. The same hand signal then went from man to man along the line until it reached Dead-eye, still out on point. At another hand signal from Dead-eye, the men gathered together, then split into two firing groups, one to each side of the track, as before. Hidden behind parched jujube and doum palms, the men adopted kneeling positions, then cocked their SLRs and aimed them at the trail on a point of impact some 15 yards away.

Ken, Les noticed, was alert enough to have done the same, though his wounded leg, propping him up in the kneeling position, was visibly shaking and seeping blood.

Though the wait seemed interminable, it was less than two minutes. Eventually, the men on their trail emerged stealthily from the darkness, both wearing jellabas and *shemaghs*, and carrying .303 Lee-Enfields. One was looking down to check the footprints on the trail, the other carefully scanning the track ahead. The latter was obviously also scanning both sides of the road, but could not see the SAS men in the distance. Satisfied that they were still well ahead, he nodded to his companion and both men advanced along the track.

The SAS men aimed along their Trilux sights. The signal to fire would be the sound of Dead-eye's first shot. He waited until the guerrillas were at the estimated point of impact for most of the weapons, then he fired at the man nearest to him.

The other SLRs roared simultaneously in a short, shocking fusillade that peppered the two Arabs with 7.62mm bullets, making them convulse wildly, drop their weapons, stagger first left, then right, and finally fling themselves to opposite sides of the track as more bullets spat off rocks and stones, creating billowing, swirling clouds of dust around them. In fact, they were already dead, torn to shreds by the fusillade, but one man, at least, kept firing at them as if he could not stop.

Having switched to automatic and aiming from right to left, from one dead Arab to the other, Ken was continuing to fire as he clambered to his feet, wobbling on his wounded leg, muttering to himself and pumping one burst after another into the dead men. His bullets kicked up a hail of sand, soil, gravel and broken stones over the tattered bodies of the Arabs, jolting them first this way, then that, in an insane dance of death.

Ken kept firing until he ran out of ammunition. Then, in a demented fury, he once again began talking unintelligibly to himself as he frantically changed the twenty-round box magazine, wiped sweat from his white, drawn face, raised the weapon and took aim again.

Les ran up to him, slapped his hand over the plastic foregrip of the SLR, pushed the barrel down, then gently removed the weapon from his friend's hands. Ken stared at him, bewildered, then staggered to the side of the track to sit down and weep.

At a nod from Dead-eye, Larry hurried up to the grieving corporal, knelt beside him, whispered to him and gave him some tablets. Ken swallowed them without protest, then stretched out on his back and closed his wet eyes. He covered his face with his hands and took deep, even breaths.

There was an uneasy silence for what seemed like an eternity. Eventually rejoining the men after checking that the Arabs were dead, Jimbo glanced at Ken, then said to his fellow sergeant: 'It's two in the morning. We've been awake for 30 hours. We've been under pressure for most of that time and I think it's enough. We need a break, Dead-eye.'

'A break won't help Brooke.'

'It won't do him any harm. And the fitter we are tomorrow, the more chance we have of getting back. He can't be helped properly until we get back, so that's our priority.'

'What's your suggestion?'

'We're now far enough away from Shi'b Taym to drop back down towards the main Wadi Rabwa. From there to the camp is only a mile or so.'

'I don't think those guerrillas are from Shi'b Taym. I think they came from the ridge above.'

'So?'

'It doesn't matter that it's only a mile or so to the camp. If the guerrillas have moved along that ridge above us, we're gonna have a rough ride. They'll keep sending men down throughout the night and, if that fails, they'll start sniping at us in the morning as we make our way back.'

Jimbo shrugged. 'What the fuck? We've no choice. Assuming you're wrong and those guerrillas were from Shi'b Taym, I suggest that we march on for another hour, but set an ambush every fifteen minutes to see if anyone catches up. If, after an hour, it's clear that I'm wrong and you're right – that the guerrillas are up on the ridge – then we simply basha down for the night, get the rest we badly need, and take our chances on making it through at first light. At least then we'll feel a lot less tired and be more in control. What do you think?'

'Chinese parliament,' Dead-eye said. Turning to the others, he asked: 'So, what do *you* think? Those of you who agree, put up your hands.'

With the exception of Ken, still covering his face with his hands where he lay on his back, they all raised a hand.

Dead-eye nodded. 'All right, let's do it.' He glanced down at Ken. 'Corporal Brooke?' Ken removed his hands from his face and looked up with wet, red-rimmed eyes. 'Feel better now?' Ken just nodded. 'Can you march for another hour?' Ken nodded again. 'OK,' Dead-eye said, trying to sound as normal as possible. 'Climb to your feet and take your SLR off Moody.'

'Yes, Sarge,' Ken said. He pushed himself to his feet, dusted himself down, glanced uneasily at the two dead Arabs on the track, then took his SLR from Les. 'Thanks, mate,' he said.

'No problem,' Les replied.

'For everything,' Ken emphasized.

'*Still* no problem,' said Les.

Seeing that Ken, though obviously in a dreadful physical condition, had been pacified by the drugs given to him by Larry and was now more in control of himself, Dead-eye nodded at Jimbo, then, without a word, raised his right hand and waved the patrol forward. Falling instinctively into the same file formation as before – Dead-eye and Jimbo sharing point out front, followed by Ben and Taff, with Larry between them, and the two wounded men bringing up the rear as back markers – the men set off again, marching along the desert track that ran parallel to the main Wadi Rabwa.

Every fifteen minutes they stopped and divided into two firing groups, one to each side of the track. There they waited for ten minutes, listening for the sound of approaching footsteps. In the end, after half a dozen such stops in two and a half hours, during which time they covered no more than a mile, no guerrillas materialized and Dead-eye accepted that if they were still in danger, it would not come from the road behind them, but from the ridges above.

'So let's keep going,' he said, 'and get this over and done with.'

'No,' Jimbo said firmly. 'I don't think that's wise.

Apart from the fact that we still need to get some rest, regaining our alertness, we have to consider the possibility that if we approach the base camp in darkness we'll be fired upon by the FRA sentries at Thumier before we get the chance to identify ourselves. On both counts, then, I'd recommend bedding down now and moving on in daylight.'

Aware that Jimbo was a veteran of the SAS's earliest days with the LRDG in North Africa, and therefore bowing down respectfully to his greater experience, Dead-eye asked of the rest of the men: 'Is that all right with you?'

They all nodded.

'All right,' Dead-eye continued. 'Given what Jimbo's just said, I think the best way to avoid the FRA sentries tomorrow is to approach the camp by way of the wadi. The wadi will also offer us some protection from any guerrillas lurking up there on the ridges. So although I know you're exhausted, I'm asking you to take a deep breath and force yourselves to make that final hike back down into the wadi. Once there, we'll basha down for the night, then move out at first light. All agreed?'

There was no opposition to the plan. Dead-eye led the patrol in the same formation off the track, across a short stretch of desert, and back down the steep, rocky slope to the wide, dried-up wadi at the bottom. The descent was, as usual, hazardous, the men repeatedly slipping and sliding on loose gravel, tripping over stones, and becoming entangled in parched thorn bushes. But eventually, dazed with fatigue, they all made it down. Miraculously, they found a thin, babbling stream at the bottom of the hill.

'I don't believe it,' Dead-eye said.

'Wonders never cease,' Jimbo added.

Larry dipped his hand in the stream, then held it up high, letting the water drip off his fingers. 'It's real enough,' he announced.

'We were told not to drink from unpurified water,' Taff said, though he was licking his lips.

'He's right,' Ben said, wiping his lips with his hand.

Larry held his water bottle up high, shaking it to show that it was empty. Then he rapped his medical box with the knuckles of his free hand, saying, with a broad grin: 'I've got a bag full of sterilization tablets if there are any takers.'

'I'm in,' Jimbo said, and the rest all signalled their agreement with nods or raised hands.

'That's it, then,' Dead-eye said. 'We basha down

here for the night and move out in the morning. Let's get organized, men.'

As they were all close to dehydration, the first thing the men did was accept their quota of sterilization tablets from Larry. They dropped them into their empty water bottles, which they filled with water from the river, and then, when the tablets had dissolved, quenched their raging thirst. Slightly rejuvenated, they ate the last of the high-calorie rations from their escape and survival belts – chocolate, dry biscuits and cheese – then made themselves as comfortable as possible on the rough, sandy ground near the tinkling stream, in the shelter of overhanging rocks.

Seriously weakened by loss of blood, Ken sank into unconsciousness. The rest of the men, having slaked their thirst and filled their bellies, soon sank into a desperately needed sleep. Only Les, tormented by his inflamed leg, had trouble dropping off to sleep; though eventually he, too, received this simplest of blessings.

So exhausted were they that all of them slept through first light. Their communal peace was shattered soon after by gunfire.

16

Dead-eye was the first to get back on his feet, in the kneeling position behind his rock, as .303 bullets thudded into the ground between the other men, covering it with spouting, hissing sand. Looking up, he saw that they were being fired at by snipers who had taken up positions high on the eastern ridge and were silhouetted by the rising sun.

'Shit!' Dead-eye muttered, looking sideways to see that the other men were now taking up firing positions behind the rocks they had slept against. The guerrillas' bullets were still kicking up choking dust, dancing noisily off the rocks and hurling jagged pieces of stone at the SAS men. More bullets were hitting the tiny stream, creating small, crazily swirling fountains of water.

'Don't fire back!' Dead-eye bawled, aware that they would now need every last bullet.

Hiding behind a rock about ten feet away, Jimbo suddenly burst out from behind it and ran at the zigzag to Dead-eye, where he threw himself down, then scrambled into the kneeling position. After wiping sand from his face and glancing up at the ridge, where about forty silhouetted figures, all still firing, could clearly be seen, Jimbo spat at the ground.

'Fuck! We can't move!' he hissed.

'We've got to,' Dead-eye said.

'They'll chop us to pieces if we try. There's a lot of them up there.'

Dead-eye glanced at the other men and saw that they were all crouched behind separate rocks: Ben and Taff, both alert; Larry on his own, also alert; and Les whispering something to Ken, who, having regained consciousness during the night, was now squatting on the ground, looking dazed.

'Right,' Jimbo said, following Dead-eye's gaze, 'I can see what you see. Corporal Brooke's going to make the problem worse. We can't move fast with him.'

'Moody's looking after him.'

'Then Moody's going to get shot to pieces. It's goodbye and Amen.'

The shooting suddenly stopped, letting silence descend. Looking up at the ridge, Dead-eye saw that the guerrillas were moving back and forth, taking up better firing positions, now given the benefit of daylight. Most of them were spreading farther along the summit of the ridge, which offered them a broader arc of fire along the wadi, but some were slithering down the slope to get closer to their quarry.

'Hey, Sarge!' Ben called out as he watched the Arabs slithering downhill. 'Those bastards are sitting ducks up there. Let's pick a few off!'

'No!' Dead-eye shouted back. 'We're running short of ammo. We must save what we have until we really need it.'

'When's that?'

'I'll let you know, Trooper.'

The silence was eerie, broken only by the sound of running water and the occasional shout of one Arab calling out to the other.

'They're waiting for us to move out from behind these rocks,' Jimbo said. 'That's why they've stopped firing. The second we step out from cover, they'll start up again.'

Dead-eye studied the wadi that ran towards the Dhala Road and then on to Thumier. It was very wide, perhaps half a mile, and littered with boulders. Checking his map, he estimated that the Dhala Road was less than two miles away. The guerrillas would either have to come off the ridge and then engage in Close Quarters Battle or go back the way they had come.

'The question,' he said to Jimbo, 'is how far can we get in one piece if we move carefully from one rock to another. Can we get clear of the wadi?'

Jimbo checked the terrain, then scratched his nose and pursed his naturally twisted lips. 'It's possible,' he said. 'Not guaranteed, but possible. Given Corporal Brooke's condition, we're going to have to move anyway, so taking our time going from one rock to another won't make that much difference.'

They both studied the wadi again, mentally mapping out the best route to take.

'So what if we reach the end of the wadi?' Jimbo asked. 'Even if they retreat, we might still have the problem of being shot at by our own troops in Thumier.'

'I don't think so,' Dead-eye said. 'In fact, if the guerrillas follow us that far they might do us a favour. At the end of the wadi, we'll be close enough to Thumier for the FRA sentries to hear the sounds of battle. When they do, they'll know it's a fire-fight between us and the guerrillas and come out to support us. I think it's worth trying.'

'You've won my heart, darlin'.'

Dead-eye relayed the plan to the others by shouting at the top of his lungs. Everyone but Ken roared their agreement. Glancing across to where Ken was still squatting on the ground, he saw that he was slipping away, his head bowed, his chin resting on his chest.

'Is he unconscious?' Dead-eye shouted at Les.

When Les deliberately took hold of Ken's shoulder and shook him, the latter raised his head and glanced dazedly around him, blinking wildly.

'Can you get him along the wadi?' Jimbo asked.

'I can try,' Les shouted back. 'At least I'll stick with him all the way.'

'Good.' Dead-eye turned slightly aside to give instructions to the others. 'All right,' he bawled. 'Boulder to boulder, rock to rock. At the crouch, zigzagging. Don't try to get too far on any single run; make each run as short and as quick as possible. Conserve your ammunition. Only fire when giving cover to the men running ahead or when otherwise absolutely necessary – which means if a guerrilla comes down the hill. Any questions before we start?'

'Yes,' Taff called out. 'What happens if one of us is wounded and can't move on?'

'He stays where he lies. We can't afford to go back for him.'

'Charming!' Ben exclaimed.

'The priority is for some of us to get out and, if necessary, bring back support to get the guerrillas off the ridge and rescue those left behind.'

'Nice one,' Taff said sceptically.

'We don't have a choice,' Jimbo said. 'We have to keep going. If you fall, you remain where you are and that's all there is to it. Any *more* questions?'

The silence signified that there were no further questions, so Dead-eye said: 'All right. We leave in strict file formation. First me and Jimbo. Then Ben and Taff. Then Larry. Les and Ken leave last. Everyone agree?'

Again, everyone except Ken called out that they agreed.

'So let's do it,' Dead-eye whispered to Jimbo.

Both of them raised themselves slightly from the crouch, preparing to make the first run. Glancing up at the ridge, they saw that the guerrillas had spread out right along it, for what looked like at least half a mile, and were pointing their rifles at the wadi basin.

Aware that they were about to run a potentially lethal gauntlet, Dead-eye and Jimbo glanced at one another, held their breath, nodded and burst out from behind their cover, bolting for the nearest large rock.

Instantly, a storm of gunfire shattered the silence and filled the wadi around the running men with ricocheting bullets and geysering sand and dust. As Dead-eye and Jimbo ran forward, crouched low, zigzagging, the men behind them fired their SLRs at the guerrillas up on the ridge, not expecting to hit many but hoping to keep as many as possible pinned down. Dead-eye and Jimbo practically hurled themselves the last few feet, falling belly down, supporting themselves on one hand, then rolling over into shelter as bullets thudded into the ground just behind them and zipped off the rock at all angles.

'Made it!' Jimbo said breathlessly.

When both of them had scrambled up into the kneeling position, Dead-eye saw that some of the guerrillas, frustrated at hitting no one, were making their way down the hill. Taking aim, he waited until Ben and Taff had started on their own run before squeezing the trigger on single shot. The two troopers were halfway across when one of the Arabs on the hill threw his arms up, dropped his weapon, flopped backwards, then tumbled noisily in a slide of stones and gravel down the steep, rocky hill. By the time he had crashed lifeless into a boulder, the pair had made it behind their own rock and were preparing to give covering fire to those behind them.

'Next!' Jimbo bawled.

Larry was up and running like a bolt of lightning, zigzagging through spitting sand and small explosions of dust until he could fling himself behind another rock. The moment he was safe, he prepared to give covering fire to Ken and Les. The latter tugged his mate to his feet, said something to him, firmly took hold of his elbow, then shouted: 'Run!' Surprisingly, Ken obeyed, crouched low and zigzagging, missed by whistling bullets and flying stones, until they were practically at their chosen refuge.

It was then that Ken's leg gave out and he fell to his knees, cursed loudly, jerked free of Les, and turned around to aim his SLR at the ridge and fire a short burst on automatic. Two guerrillas who had been darting nimbly down the hill were hurled back by the rapid burst, dropped their weapons, then rolled a good way until they, too, were stopped by boulders.

Les darted back, grabbed his dazed comrade by the arm, and jerked him down behind a rock just as the ground where he had been kneeling was turned into a storm of spewing sand and boiling dust.

'Christ!' Jimbo muttered.

They started again, first Dead-eye and Jimbo, then the others, the running men covered by the others until it was their turn. On the second run, Ken was completely in control, albeit tugged along by Les, but on the third he jerked free again to fire another burst up the hill, this time hitting no one, but again continuing to fire in a crazed frenzy until dragged on by his friend.

Miraculously, neither was hit, though Les, whose own leg was still inflamed, practically collapsed behind the rock, almost sobbing with pain.

'They won't make it,' Jimbo said to Dead-eye.

'Then we leave them,' Dead-eye said.

They jumped up and ran again, weaving through the hail of bullets and making it to the safety of another rock. The three behind them did the same, all reaching safety, but Ken's leg gave way again, causing him to fall and curse in frustration. As Les dropped to his knees beside him, giving him covering fire and yelling at him to get up and run, the ground just in front of them erupted in spitting sand and boiling dust from a fresh hail of .303 bullets.

Ken stood up in full view, aimed his SLR at the guerrillas trying to drop down to the lower slopes, and fired a lengthy burst at those nearest him. Once more, he hit a couple, who fell, tumbling down the slope like rag dolls.

A bullet smashed into Ken's shoulder, making him spin to the side, drop his rifle and fall to his knees, crying out with the pain of this fresh wound. Les also dived sideways as a line of spitting sand snaked towards him, then between him and Ken. The latter hurled himself towards Les and they crashed together in a cloud of boiling sand behind another rock.

Breaking Dead-eye's ruling that no one should turn back, Larry backtracked, dodging lines of spitting sand and ricocheting bullets, until he was with Les and Ken. While the others waited for him, he roughly dressed Ken's bloody shoulder, at least stopping the flow of blood. He then jumped up and dashed back to his original position, narrowly escaping death a second time.

When Dead-eye and Jimbo jumped up and ran forward it all started again.

So they made their way along the wadi, alternately running erratically through a murderous hail of bullets and providing covering fire for the others.

Surprisingly, the wound in Ken's right shoulder, which prevented him from firing his SLR, seemed to have startled him back to some semblance of awareness and now he was no longer stopping during the dangerous runs. As his weapon had, anyway, been left behind in the wadi where he was wounded, he was able to use his arms for better balance when he made the dangerous runs on his wounded leg, hopping along in an ungainly manner.

As for the others, miraculously no one was hurt, and two hours later – the time it took to travel less than two miles – they were approaching the end of the wadi.

The guerrillas, who had followed them all the way, were now perched on the western end of the ridge, parallel to where the wadi opened out into flat, featureless desert. This was where the SAS men would make their escape and it was, ironically, where they would be most exposed.

Safely sheltered behind a group of large boulders at the very end of the wadi, Dead-eye looked up at the Arabs massed on the ridge, then across the featureless desert plain that ran for less than a mile to the Dhala Road and, not too far along it, the Thumier base.

'It's only a quarter of a mile,' Jimbo said hopefully.

'We'll never make it,' Dead-eye said.

They were silent for a long time, both deep in thought, until eventually Jimbo looked up and said: 'We can't stay here for ever.'

'I know,' Dead-eye replied. He glanced up to the ridge and saw that an increasing number of guerrillas were making their way down to the lower slopes, having surmised that the SAS were running out of ammunition and would, if they were forced to fight back, run out completely.

'Smart bastards,' Dead-eye said. 'And absolutely dedicated. They're willing to die charging us to make us run out of ammunition. When we do, the survivors will just march down and cut us to pieces. You've got to admire them.'

'I do,' Jimbo replied. 'I'm forming a fan club

for them. In the meantime, while I print up the letterhead, how do we keep my heroes at bay and still save our ammo?'

'We can't,' Dead-eye confessed.

'So?'

'I say we take a gamble. We gamble that if we start a fire-fight, the sentries at Thumier will hear us and come to the rescue.'

'The gamble being whether the cavalry get here before we run out of ammo or after we've been overrun.'

'I knew you'd understand, Jimbo.'

An urgent Chinese parliament produced agreement from the rest of the men, including Ken, who, though twice wounded and clearly on the brink of collapse, had at least regained his presence of mind.

'We better start soon,' he said, pointing up at the ridge. 'They're coming down to get us.'

Glancing up, they saw that the Arab guerrillas were indeed starting to swarm down the hill like ants, making their way from one rock to another with the skill of mountain goats. Some of them were already halfway down. They all had curved swords on their hips, supplementing their rifles.

'Spread out among these rocks,' said Dead-eye.

'Fix bayonets. Start firing at my signal. We have to make the fire-fight last as long as possible, so only fire on single shot. Any questions?'

'Yes,' Ken said from where he was leaning against a rock, one arm in a sling, his bloody wounded leg stretched out before him, 'what about me?'

'What about you?'

'I don't have an SLR.'

'Then you wait until they get within range and use your 9-milli to pick them off.' Dead-eye unholstered his own Browning, then gave it and his ammunition to Ken. 'Take this as a spare. Try not to use it until they get really close. You can protect yourself, and give us backup if we get involved in a CQB situation. That's it, men, let's shake out.'

The instant they broke apart and ran at the crouch to their respective rocks, the guerrillas on the hills let rip with a hail of rifle fire. The SAS men all managed to find shelter just as the enemy bullets tore up the sand between them and bounced noisily off the rocks, spraying them with flying fragments. As soon as he saw that his men were ready, Dead-eye gave the signal to fire.

'Fire at will!' he bawled, raising and lowering his right fist.

The SLRs roared in unison, picking off the Arabs who were now scrambling down the lower half of the slope. Instantly, the area being covered by the guerrillas turned into a maelstrom of spitting sand, swirling dust and shattered rock as the SLRs' bullets tore the ground up and wounded or dead Arabs rolled down the hill, their jellabas flapping wildly about them. Immediately, the guerrillas higher up the ridge unleashed another fusillade on the SAS positions, turning them into a similar hell of sand, dust and rebounding bullets.

Kneeling beside his friend, Les narrowly missed losing an eye when a bullet blew chunks off the rock and a sharp stone slashed across his left cheekbone. Temporarily blinded by his own blood, he cursed, checked the wound with his fingers and realized that the skin was hanging loose. Seeing Les's predicament, and not yet in a position to take part in the fire-fight, Ken removed a surgical dressing from his belt, and with trembling hands pressed the flapping, bloody skin back into position and applied the dressing. Meanwhile the other men around them kept firing at the advancing guerrillas. When Ken had finished dressing the wound and crawled back to cover, Les gamely picked up his SLR and began firing again.

The clouds of sand and dust created on the lower slopes by the combination of bullets and rolling bodies formed a screen that partially obscured the other guerrillas and allowed many of them to slip down unscathed. The first of them were now bursting through the suspended sand and dust and racing across the bed of the wadi, some firing from the hip, others swinging their curved swords above their heads. Most of them were cut down in a hail of SAS bullets, but the rest kept coming and those cut down were followed by others.

Lying belly down behind his rock, in great pain but more aware of feeling useless and frustrated, Ken smiled when he saw the guerrillas advancing. 'That's it,' he whispered, unholstering his Browning and lying it on the ground by his wounded leg. 'Keep coming, you bastards.' Still holding Dead-eye's 9-milli in his good hand, he released the safety-catch, rested his wrist on the rock, and took aim. 'Just keep coming,' he whispered.

Dead-eye had deliberately taken shelter behind a rock situated well in front of the others, from where he was methodically, unerringly picking off one guerrilla after another, particularly those racing up on either flank. But now, as the surviving Arabs raced straight across the wadi towards him, he saw that those massed on the summit of the ridge had begun to swarm down it as well, eager to hasten the massacre of the SAS troops. Realizing that time was running out and that he would soon be engaged in hand-to-hand fighting, he switched to automatic and started firing in a series of short, savage, lethal bursts that made the advancing guerrillas shudder, jerk, twist sideways and finally collapse amid clouds of exploding sand and billowing dust.

'Grenade!' Jimbo bawled.

Dead-eye saw the hand-grenade sail languidly over his head and fall behind him. He glanced back over his shoulder as it exploded near Ben and Taff, picking up the latter in a fountain of spewing soil and boiling smoke, spinning him over and slamming him back down a few feet away. Without thinking, Ben scrambled out from behind the rock, firing his SLR on the move, to kneel beside the dazed Taff, grab him by the shoulder and shake him back to awareness even as rebel bullets stitched the ground on all sides of them. 'Christ, Taff, get up! Move it!' With his face and body grazed by shrapnel and blistered by the blast,

Taff was not a pretty sight. Nevertheless, he sat up, shook his head from side to side, saw the lines of spitting sand moving in on all sides and, suddenly galvanized back to his senses, grabbed his SLR and scrambled back behind the rock with his friend. They both recommenced firing immediately.

As the lead guerrillas raced up to Dead-eye's position, where he was rising to his feet and firing from the hip, Jimbo, right behind him, realized that the need to save ammunition was past, and switched to automatic as well. The nearest Arab was swinging his sword at Dead-eye's head when Jimbo fired his first short burst, catching the enemy across the stomach, practically cutting him in two, and making him collapse like a blood-soaked banner. Dead-eye, meanwhile, had fired his last shots and was thrusting upwards at another guerrilla with his bayonet. Jimbo therefore made it his business to give Dead-eye cover, cutting down the Arabs nearest to him while Dead-eye expertly stabbed one, cracked the skull of another with the plastic stock, ducked to avoid a second swinging sword and, before coming up, stabbed his bayonet through the man's foot, pinning him to the ground and making him scream terribly, before removing the bayonet and plunging it through his heart.

Even before the Arab had fallen, Dead-eye had heaved the bloody bayonet out again and was turning to face another assault, moving coolly and murderously.

While Dead-eye was thus engaged, other Arabs rushed around him on both sides and came straight at Jimbo, who fired the last of his ammunition, then prepared to defend himself with his bayonet.

Meanwhile Ken was helping the lethal pair by carefully picking off any Arabs coming up on one of their blind sides. Lying belly down on the ground, his bloody, wounded leg stretched out behind him, he was propping himself up on his wounded arm and methodically firing one shot after another from Dead-eye's Browning. When he had emptied this, he picked up his own and began the same methodical procedure with it. Each time he fired, an agonizing pain shot through his wounded shoulder, yet it failed to stop him. He saved Dead-eye and Jimbo from death many times, though neither was aware of it.

Suddenly, the combined roaring of 76mm QF and .30-inch machine-guns resounded over the general din of the battle. Almost simultaneously, a murderous rain of bullets tore through the guerrillas behind those already at the SAS positions and made the area all around them explode in a convulsion of sand, soil, dust and pulverized rock. As the guerrillas to the immediate front were screaming and dying, a hail of bullets from another set of 76mm QF and .30-inch machine-guns started inflicting the same fate on the guerrillas swarming down from the summit of the ridge, cutting bloody swathes through them and making most of them retreat back the way they had come.

Glancing left at the same time, Dead-eye and Jimbo, both still engaged in furious hand-to-hand fighting, saw two 6×6 Saladins, machine-guns blazing, trundling across the plain from the direction of the Dhala Road. While the two armoured cars were heading straight for the besieged SAS troop, another two had broken away towards the lower slopes of the ridge, cutting off the line of retreat of the guerrillas engaged with the SAS and concentrating their fire on the Arabs now attempting to escape back up the ridge. The guerrillas not slaughtered in the vicious inferno of machine-gun fire were heading back the way they had come, along the summit of the ridge, in frantic disorder.

Exhilarated, Jimbo turned back to the fray just as the Arabs in front of Dead-eye were either being cut down by the Saladins or trying to make their escape across the wadi. Behind him, however, Larry had just fired his final bullets at two guerrillas, killing one and making the other turn around and flee. Swinging his sword automatically at Jimbo as he passed, the Arab caught his arm, opening it from shoulder to elbow and exposing the bone beneath the skin.

Screaming, Jimbo dropped his SLR, slapped his left hand over his arm where the blood was pouring out of it, and fell to his knees. The guerrilla, rushing away, was shot in the back of the head with the last bullet from Ben's SLR and lunged forward, his arms flung above his bloody, smashed skull, to fall face first to the ground – as did Jimbo, from shock and loss of blood.

The few guerrillas still remaining at the SAS positions now turned and fled back towards the wadi, but found their retreat blocked by the two Saladins crossing the lower slopes to fire at the guerrillas retreating along the top of the ridge. The other two Saladins kept raining fire on the guerrillas in the wadi, even when they had reached the SAS positions. There, while the two gunners continued firing, the third crew member climbed down to hand out more SLR ammunition to the SAS men still standing.

Dead-eye, Larry, Ben and the bloody, blistered Taff therefore had the pleasure of helping to rout the last of the fleeing guerrillas. Even Ken had crawled through the sand to pick up the unconscious Jimbo's SLR, load it with ammo given to him by the British Army corporal, and make amends for his moments of shock-induced madness by expertly dispatching the last two fleeing guerrillas, firing from the belly-down position, using one arm. He passed out within seconds of having done so.

When the other two Saladins had chased the surviving guerrillas far enough along the wadi to know that they would not come back, they radioed the Habilayn airstrip, asking for air support to clear the last of the guerrillas off the summit of the ridge. They were returning to help the other two Saladins pick up the SAS men when two Hawker Hunters roared low over the ridge and poured a devastating hail of gunfire into the fleeing guerrillas. By the time the two Saladins had reached the SAS men, the summit of the ridge was obscured by an immense cloud of dust and smoke which mercifully concealed the many dead below.

The few survivors crawled out of that pall of smoke and limped back to the Radfan.

While the Hawker Hunters flew back to Habilayn, the four Saladins shared the SAS troop between them. Jimbo's badly sliced right arm was given interim treatment by Larry, who closed it with emergency sutures and stopped the bleeding with a tourniquet and bandages; then the still unconscious sergeant was hoisted up into one of the Saladins.

He was followed in by Les and Larry, the latter intending to replace the blood-soaked emergency bandage on Les's cheek as the Saladin carried them back to the base.

In the second Saladin, Ben and Taff were not in much better shape. The lengthy, scorched gouge across Riley's back had been reopened during the hand-to-hand fighting and was now bleeding profusely, soaking through his tattered shirt and dripping on the steel floor. As for Taff, though the scars of his shrapnel-shredded face would heal eventually, right now, in combination with the blisters caused by the heat of the grenade explosion, they made for a stomach-churning sight.

With his wounded shoulder and twice-wounded left leg, Ken had to be helped into the third

Saladin by the third crew member, Corporal Phil Rossiter. Ken had regained consciousness and was surprisingly alert. After making him comfortable, the Regular Army man turned to Dead-eye, still standing beside the Saladin, and said: 'You men did a hell of a job out there, Sarge. You should be proud of yourselves.'

'We did nothing,' Dead-eye said to Rossiter with icy rage. 'The Saladins did the job. The Hawker Hunters did the job. *You* did it. We didn't do a damned thing! This war stinks to high heaven.' Then, having vented his spleen, he stomped off angrily to take his place in the fourth armoured car.

Corporal Rossiter turned in amazement to Ken. 'What the hell's the matter with him?' he asked. 'Is it because you lost two of your men?'

'Not because we lost them,' Ken replied. 'It's because the Arabs captured the bodies. That's what's eating Dead-eye . . . It could have repercussions.'

'It surely could,' Corporal Rossiter replied dryly, before climbing into the Saladin.

Growling aggressively, the four armoured cars trundled away from the wadi, back across the flat, dusty desert plain, to the tarmacked Dhala Road and, farther along it, the SAS base at Thumier, leaving a pile of dead bodies in the sand as food for the vultures.

It was that kind of war.

17

The operation begun by the SAS in the mountains of the Radfan was continued by the Paras and 45 Royal Marine Commando, who climbed and fought their way up the 3700-foot Al Hajaf hills, where most of the guerrillas were based. The same operation was completed by six major units which, between them, managed to subdue the area five weeks later. The inhabitants were then banished from the region.

A few days after the SAS had returned to Thumier, a macabre intelligence report regarding the fate of the bodies of Captain Ellsworth and Trooper Malkin reached Major-General John Gibbon, the General Officer Commanding in Aden. According to a Radio Taiz Yemeni propaganda broadcast, the heads of the two dead soldiers had been put on public display in the Yemen.

Asked to verify this at a press conference held on 3 May 1964, the GOC confirmed that he had received 'reliable information of their decapitation and the exhibition of their heads on stakes in Yemen'.

This response was to lead to singular embarrassment for the security forces, as the next of kin had been unaware of the deaths and, even worse, had been informed that the men were on a routine exercise on Salisbury Plain.

Following hot on the heels of Major-General Gibbon's press conference, the republican government in Yemen, denying its own propaganda broadcast, denounced the decapitation story as a 'British lie'.

In Taiz, the US Embassy, which was handling British interests in the absence of UK diplomatic recognition of the republicans, investigated the matter and concluded that there was no truth in the rumours that the heads of two British soldiers had been exhibited in the Yemen or anywhere else.

However, ten days after the press conference, confirmation was received that a patrol of the Federal Regular Army had found two headless bodies buried in a shallow grave in the area of the SAS battle. There was no sign of the heads.

For a brief period after their return to Britain, D Squadron SAS became the subject of intense interest to the press. But once this had faded and the squadron had returned to its former anonymity, it went back to serving periodically in Aden during retraining periods between each stint in the jungles of Borneo.

Dead-eye, Jimbo and the other survivors of the first campaign were back in the Radfan when the British withdrew in 1967. Once again, they divided their time between desert and mountain and the lethal Keeni-Meeni actions in Aden. No longer interested in this pointless war, the SAS men in the mountains tried to kill their boredom by endlessly speculating on the good time their mates, the 'urbanites', were having in the flesh-pots of Aden. When in the city, the same men vented their frustration by complaining about the overcrowded *souks*, the treachery of the Arabs and the ineptitude of the 'greens' guarding the streets.

'They stand there at each street corner like limp dicks at a wedding,' Jimbo complained. 'The Arabs should be blowing them kisses, not trying to kill 'em. The British Army! God help us!'

'What we're doing is just as worthless,' Dead-eye

replied in his quiet, bitter way. 'We're just passing time.'

Nevertheless, the nearer the projected withdrawal date came, the more essential were the SAS recce patrols, to give early warning of guerrilla attacks. The guerrillas, in turn, were now receiving early warnings of SAS movements from Arab officers of the FRA who knew that when the British left, their own lives would depend on how helpful they had been to the rebel forces.

The Radfan was handed over to the Federal Regular Army – now the South Arabian Army – on 26 June 1967, at the end of the Six Day War between Israel and Egypt, which led to the singular humiliation of Arab Nationalists and riots in the streets of many Muslim cities.

'This fight's long been a dying cause,' a disillusioned Lieutenant-Colonel Callaghan told his men just before they boarded the Hercules C-130 on the runway at RAF Khormaksar. 'Now, at last, it's been lost.'

No one disagreed as the heavy transport plane lifted off the ground, ascending through the shimmering heat, to deliver them back to RAF Lyneham. From there they would be transported in a convoy of Bedfords to their camp at Bradbury Lines,

Hereford, where, on their bashas, in the chilly darkness of the spider, they would finally rest, trying to forget the nightmares of the Radfan and looking forward to better days.

'Bloody right!' Jimbo exclaimed as the Hercules climbed into the radiant sky. 'Better days always come.'

'There speaks the optimist,' Dead-eye replied, then smiled sadly before closing his weary eyes.

It would be a long flight.